Rise and Fall

Book One of the Blood and Tears Trilogy

Joshua P. Simon

Rise and Fall: Book One of the Blood and Tears Trilogy

An ill-prepared queen, a soft-hearted mercenary, and a crippled warrior struggle as a kingdom falls and an empire rises.

For years the High Mages of Cadonia have maintained an uneasy peace among the nobles disgruntled with the rule of the king. In the aftermath of a tragic event, Elyse, the king's daughter, is thrust into a role she is not ready for. As queen, she must now determine who to trust while struggling to keep the kingdom from collapsing around her.

The Hell Patrol, a legendary mercenary outfit commanded by Jonrell, finds itself disenfranchised with their current employer. Recalling a promise he made over a decade ago, Jonrell breaks his contract in order to right the wrongs of his past.

On the continent of Hesh, the Blue Island Clan has long been ignored by its neighbors. Tobin, a warrior and son of the Clan's ruler, struggles as an outcast as he watches his brother Kaz lead his father's army to glory. Emboldened by a new friendship with a mysterious shaman, Tobin finds himself gaining the respect he always wanted.

ISBN-978-0-9846988-2-0

Visit the author at www.joshuapsimon.blogspot.com

Contact joshuapsimon.author@gmail.com with any comments.

Cover Design by Brooke White with Sprout Studios (Houston, TX)
brooke@sproutstudio.us

Editing by Joshua Essoe (www.joshuaessoe.com)

WORKS IN THE
BLOOD AND TEARS WORLD

Warleader: A Blood and Tears Prequel Short Story

Rise and Fall: Book One of the Blood and Tears Trilogy

Walk Through Fire: A Blood and Tears Prequel Novella

Steel and Sorrow: Book Two of the Blood and Tears Trilogy

Hero of Slaves: A Blood and Tears Novella

Trail and Glory: Book Three of the Blood and Tears Trilogy *Forthcoming*

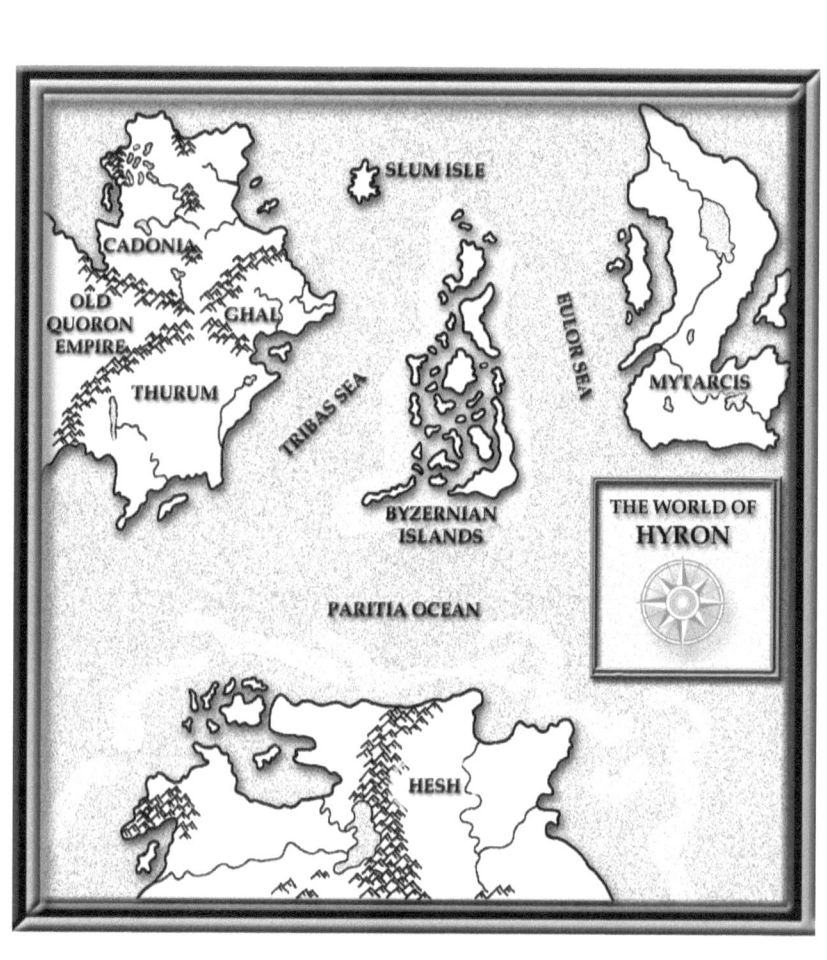

THE KINGDOM
OF
CADONIA

1. ITHANTHUL
2. LYROSENE
3. FLOROSON
4. NAMARIS
5. CATHYRIUM
6. NOROCOVA
7. ASATRYA
8. BOLYSIUS
9. LUCARTIAS
10. SEGAVONA
11. ARCAS ISLAND
12. ESTUL ISLAND
13. TRIBAS SEA
14. ASYCIUM RIVER
15. TYRESEOS RIVER
16. THE HIGH PASS
17. CATARIC RANGE

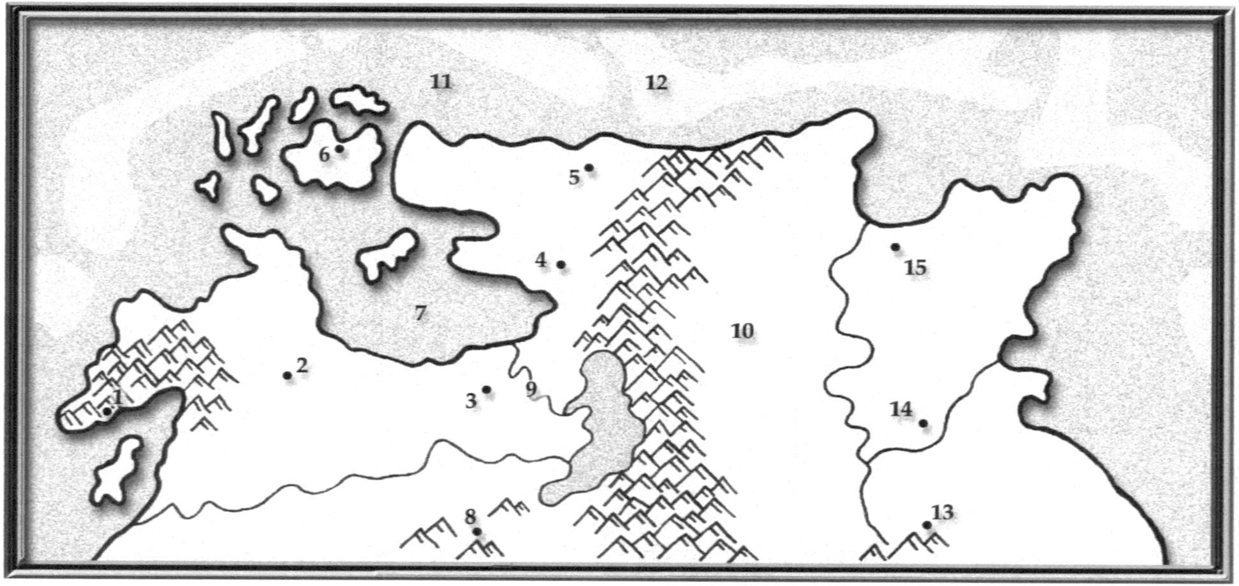

THE
CONTINENT OF
HESH

1. GUARONOPE
2. FERUSE
3. CYPRONYA
4. ACTUR
5. NUBINYA
6. JUANOQ
7. GULF OF EURINUL
8. ERUNDIS
9. DYLIS RIVER
10. THE GREAT DIVIDE
11. PARITIA OCEAN
12. NATURAL REEF
13. QUARNOQ
14. MOLACAT
15. POLIKTAS

DEDICATION

    I would like to thank all of those who helped me make this book what it is today; my parents, my sister, my betareaders, and my editor.

    However, I especially want to thank my wife Leah for her continued support as I chase my dream. It has meant everything to me. Thank you for putting up with all my mindless ramblings, odd hours and quirky behavior, acting as my alpha reader, my IT support, marketing coordinator and personal assistant. I can't imagine how difficult this would have been without you. I love you!

CHAPTER 1

A deafening silence filled the inner courtyard. Massacred bodies with faces frozen in fear and despair covered the space once home to beautiful gardens. Nothing stirred except for the five High Mages fanning out amongst the motionless forms, each searching for a sign of life. The smell of burnt flesh enveloped Amcaro and worked its way into his nostrils and robes. More than two dozen royal guards lay dead, joined by half as many servants—charred husks against the white stone floor.

Standing amid the devastation, Amcaro's mouth hung open in disbelief. "One Above, how did this happen?" he whispered.

After feeling the immense wave of sorcery, he and the only other mages powerful enough to teleport had arrived from afar. He wanted to help search for survivors but he couldn't turn his attention away from the woman before him. Her beautiful face unrecognizable, her body blackened, there was no denying that the dark red remnants of her robes belonged to one of their order, a High Mage. She was one of only seven in Cadonia. Amcaro felt his gut tighten at the realization that his former pupil, Fei, was dead.

His thoughts wandered back to the time she first approached him at the age of eight, wanting to be his apprentice. *Many thought I was wasting my time when I accepted a student so young. But they didn't see the passion in her eyes, the eagerness, and the yearning to make something of her life. Now those eyes that were once so full of life are empty. Would she still be alive if I denied her request all those years ago?*

"Master!" Acus shouted from across the courtyard. "Come quick."

Amcaro jumped at the voice, and like the other High Mages interspersed throughout the open area, scrambled toward Acus who held a body in his arms. Closing in, he saw the figure was that of a boy, no more than fourteen. The boy grasped at Acus's robe, pulling the High Mage down to his face. His body convulsed between whispers and then relaxed. His hands fell away. Acus's paled face told Amcaro that whatever he had learned, it was not good.

Edali, the most gifted healer among them, fell to his knees and checked the boy over but Amcaro knew the effort would be wasted. The boy was dead. Edali confirmed Amcaro's thoughts with a slight nod, eyes sullen, distant.

"Well? Spit it out, Acus. Did you get anything?" asked an impatient voice.

1

Amcaro turned to his left and scowled. Rhindora was tall, homely, and stout. By appearance alone, she was the most intimidating mage of the group. She did little to intimidate Amcaro who gritted his teeth. "Show a little compassion."

"We'll have plenty of time for compassion after we learn what happened here, Master. We have yet to move past the inner courtyard," said Rhindora.

"Although I don't agree with her tone, she's right. One Above knows what awaits us within the castle itself." Essan ran fingers through his thick blond hair as he looked over the lifeless form that Acus still cradled.

Amcaro opened his mouth to respond but was cut off.

"It was Nareash," said Acus.

"I knew it!" said Rhindora pacing about. "I never did trust that snake."

Amcaro looked down to Acus, whose bald head was still bowed over the boy's body. "Is that what the boy told you?"

Acus finally set the boy down and slowly rose to his feet. "Yes."

"Well, there were rumors among the peasants about the King being manipulated," said Edali, standing in turn and wiping the dirt from the bottom of his robes.

"And do we just take the gossip of peasants as fact now?" asked Essan, throwing his short pudgy arms into the air.

"The boy saw Nareash," said Acus.

"Was he sure? How do we know it wasn't someone or something else he mistook for Nareash?" said Essan.

"Look at this place," said Rhindora, picking up speed as she paced. "Look at Fei. Who else but Nareash could do this? Don't let your friendship with the man cloud your vision."

"My friendship with Nareash has nothing to do with it. I just find it hard to believe that the man we grew up with could do all of this." Essan spread his hands wide. "He's never shown this kind of power before. It doesn't make sense."

"The boy told me a few things before he died. Together with other bits and pieces we've pulled together I think I have an idea of what happened," said Acus. "Over the last couple of days, several suspicious deaths among the staff left many uneasy in the castle. Those who died were all near an open flame that seemed to take on a life of its own. They were all vehemently outspoken against Nareash, spreading discord among the rest of the staff. After their deaths, most others who were dissatisfied with Nareash stayed silent except the mother of Captain Marc of the Royal Guard. When she died under similar circumstances, the captain went to the king who acted as if nothing was the matter. In secret, Marc convinced many of the guards and staff to work with him to overtake Nareash."

"And there it is," said Essan. "Nareash was falsely accused and then attacked. He acted in self-defense."

Edali shook his head. "Wake up, Essan. Look at the path of each sorcerous attack. Most of these people, especially the servants, were running away."

Amcaro rested a hand on Essan's shoulder. "This is not easy on any of us but I know you see the truth here."

Essan started to argue again but shook his head. Shoulders coming forward, he seemed to lose any desire to put up a fight. "No sense in putting it off then. We must rein in Nareash. Rhindora..." His voice trailed off as he faced where the woman was pacing only moments ago. Seething and red-faced, he added, "That brainless woman."

Amcaro turned to the sound of great double doors closing on the opposite end of the square. Essan was stalking toward the doors when Amcaro called out, "Essan, wait!"

Essan halted. "Wait for what, Master?" He pointed toward the doors. "You know those two have always hated each other. This is exactly the justification she needs for settling her own vendetta. We need to catch her before she does something stupid."

"She's already accomplished that. We will not make the same mistake as her or Fei by doing this alone. We will stay together and go after Nareash with caution. He knows we're here and he will be ready for us. Let's not give him another advantage by having our emotions get the best of us."

"But Master, Nareash is not a match for you. Together, we have nothing to worry about." said Edali.

"Think, Edali. Look at this devastation. Nareash fought and killed dozens of armed guardsmen while also battling Fei. She may have been the least experienced among us, but she was still a High Mage." He paused. "And we still have yet to see the rest of the castle. Something is not right."

"All the more reason to hurry after Rhindora," said Essan.

"No. I will not risk our lives and the safety of the kingdom to run off recklessly after one so careless. She is on her own. Now isn't the time for emotion to get in the way of judgment."

Amcaro noticed a few looks of displeasure from the others but none said a word. The mages readied themselves, preparing sorcery that could be unleashed at a moment's notice. Once finished, Amcaro led the way to the massive oak doors. Although grand in dimension, the craftsmanship was more impressive. On the face of each, carvings showed key events from Aurnon the First's conquering of Thurum, and the settling of Cadonia. *And there at Aurnon's side throughout all his accomplishments stood Sacrynon. Not just allies, but friends as well. A great king and a great high mage stood side by side, working together, earning the adoration of the people.* Amcaro shook his head as he compared the carvings to the present day. *Nareash, what happened between you and Aurnon the Eighth?*

Amcaro and the others entered the vast common hall of the castle. Large wooden rafters supported the ceiling and from them hung dozens of singed banners. Five banners dominated the ceiling, greater than all others, emblazoned with the seals of Cadonia's dukes. Smaller hangings surrounded each of the five with their own unique seals representing the lords within each Duke's province. Aurnon the First had designed the ceiling himself, believing that a king should always be mindful of those who serve him. *"The needs of the people should be above the wants of the king," he often said. A great man. Too bad the meaning of your design was lost on many of your namesakes.*

Amcaro's eyes drifted past the bare walls, focusing instead on the four long tables at the room's center where servants of the castle would have their meals. Benches were overturned. To the left and right were the round tables used for members of the Royal Guard or the rare guest. Wisps of smoke drifted up from the broken and splintered remains of the chairs that would normally encircle them.

Just as before, smoldering bodies covered the scene. Contorted into misshapen forms, their number more than tripled those littering the courtyard. If not for the armor or the blackened swords in their hands, it would be impossible to discern that the figures were once members of the Royal Guard. As it was, many of the bodies were barely recognizable as human. One body in particular caught Amcaro's eye. Belonging to a servant, the lifeless form crouched, frozen, under one of the center tables. *There was no mercy for even one as defenseless as you. Nareash what has happened to you?*

Essan took a step forward, eyes still taking in the carnage. He spoke so quietly, Amcaro had to listen hard to catch his words. "There must be over a hundred guardsmen in this room." Turning to Amcaro with a look of disbelief he continued, his voice rising. "Just between here and the courtyard alone, half of the royal guard is dead. Nareash has lost his mind. There is no other explanation. Has anyone been left alive?"

Somber, Amcaro answered, "We should assume the worst."

Both mages turned as Edali dashed through the hall. Edali maneuvered toward the table on the far end of the room, opposite the doors. Unless the king extended a special invitation, only the royal family and its closest advisors gathered in the back of the hall. Acus was a step behind, weaving in and out of the wreckage.

"What do you see?" Amcaro called out.

"It's the king! He's somehow unscathed by the devastation around him," said Edali as he reached the opposite side of the room.

Essan and Amcaro made their way toward Edali and Acus. Amcaro, last in line, saw what the others had noticed; a plump man lay on his side in light blue robes. His back was to the advancing mage, but there was no mistaking the round shape and the salt-and-pepper hair visible through the top of the man's clothing. A gaudy crown still sat crooked on his head. Amcaro came to a sudden halt. *This isn't right.*

Edali bent down to examine the king. Acus kneeled on the ruler's other side.

One Above!

"Don't touch him!" Amcaro called out, realizing the danger. His words echoed throughout the hall but were a moment too late.

As Edali turned the king over to check his condition and perform the healing arts, a ball of fire engulfed the mage. He flew back, landing on the remains of a guardsman. The fire burned with such ferocity, the air in the room thinned.

Amcaro watched Acus repel the exploding fire. However, the sorcerous attack distracted him from noticing the jeweled dagger in the king's pale right hand. The king's chubby arm arced across his bulky frame with surprising speed and the dagger opened Acus's throat. Blood pulsed onto the floor.

Amcaro reached out with an invisible hand, and pinned the king's arms at his sides. The overweight ruler struggled to break free, but the king was no match for the mage's power. After a moment he relaxed in the unseen bindings, an emotionless expression on his face.

Essan rushed over to Acus's side to assess the damage caused by the king's attack. There was no sense in checking on Edali. As the fire slowly subsided, Amcaro could see the mage was no more. The crackle of burnt flesh made Amcaro flinch. "Is Acus alive?"

Essan closed his eyes and his hand clutched Acus's throat. Blood oozed from between his fingers. "No."

That one word expressed so many meanings. Sorrow for losing a friend, frustration for not acting sooner, desire to change places, emptiness that will never be filled—but of all things it spoke of hate.

Amcaro took a deep breath, steadying himself. "I know what you're thinking. But now isn't the time to allow our feelings to cloud our judgment. Edali and Acus did just that and so did Rhindora by running on ahead of us. One Above knows what has happened to her as it seems she continued without even checking the hall. Such carelessness will lead to our death too, Essan."

"I am well aware of the situation," said Essan in a tight voice, his chin resting on his chest.

Amcaro sighed and shook his head. "I'm sorry. You're right."

Essan looked up and turned to the king. "Is this truly the king?"

Amcaro stared at Cadonia's ruler, sorrowful. "It is his body, but his mind is no longer his own."

"How is that possible? I thought mind control was just a myth from old."

"No, it's possible. It is a dark path with many dangers—which is why I never taught it to you or anyone else. Mind control carries many risks since each person's mind is unique. Over time it will turn the victim into what you see before you."

"Then who would have taught Nareash?"

"I don't know." Amcaro paused, studying the blank face of the king. "This man will never be more than a risk to everyone he comes in contact with."

"Then we have no choice."

Amcaro looked over to Essan and nodded. His eyes returned to the king and then a moment later the man collapsed to the ground next to Acus, as lifeless as the bloody High Mage.

Amcaro stood for a moment, thinking. *I was here only a couple of months ago when the castle was bustling with life. Now only an eerie stillness remains. How could I have missed the signs? How could Nareash come into such power and keep it hidden from me?* Amcaro straightened, mouth tightening as he composed himself. "Come, we mustn't tarry here any longer."

Amcaro headed toward a lone staircase in the hall, near the arched doorway to the kitchen. Essan followed close behind, matching his master's stride.

* * *

Nothing passed between the High Mages as they ascended the stairs to Nareash's personal quarters. They climbed slowly, pausing at the top of each flight to step over another group of felled guardsmen; many still held unfired crossbows in their hands. Neither of the High Mages bothered checking the rooms on each floor. Amcaro knew they would be filled with more horror, but empty of the man they sought.

During the last two flights of stairs, Amcaro checked over several spells he prepared after leaving the common hall. He felt Essan do the same as they approached an open doorway. Amcaro glanced back at his friend and saw worry and dread beneath his seething anger. *We share the same thoughts, don't we? I feel the power emanating from the room and I've not felt its like for some time.*

They exchanged nods. Amcaro was ready to climb the last step before the doorway when a voice came from inside.

"Can we get on with this already? I swear you two move as slow as a couple of old crones."

The two mages leaped through the door. Bursts of light shot from their hands toward their target, but the attacks seemed to have no effect as Nareash stood opposite them wearing a smug grin. When they realized Nareash had no intention of attacking them, they ceased their attacks, remaining wary of their situation.

"Come now, I hope that wasn't the best you two had," said Nareash. "Even Rhindora made a stronger show." He nodded to the floor.

Amcaro's gut tightened again at the loss of another of his former students.

Essan bent over to examine the woman's body after an approving nod from Amcaro. No longer intimidating, she looked small and fragile. "She's dead," stated Essan in an emotionless tone.

"Of course," said Nareash. "She tried to kill me."

"Then why not attack us?" asked Essan.

As Essan probed Nareash, Amcaro took in his surroundings. Nareash stood at the room's center, tall and slim with dark hair, his skin tanned bronze. His stance was one of confidence, hands tucked into the sleeves of his robe. The princess stood several steps behind Nareash. Elyse's wavy auburn hair framed the fair skin of her face. Hands clasped at her waist, she wore a simple emerald dress that accentuated her light green eyes. *I can feel your bonds, my dear. Nareash, is this your true advantage?*

The room was deep but otherwise empty with very little in the way of furniture. Other than a small bed and a simple desk near the window, there was nothing. Various books and papers lay scattered over the floor in uneven stacks and piles.

Nareash shook his head. "Our relationship is far different than the one I shared with that foul woman. I hoped we could come to an understanding." Nareash flicked his eyes toward Amcaro. "And, Master, without you all of this wouldn't be possible. The last thing I want is to continue this senseless killing." His eyes turned dark for a moment. "However, I will do what I must."

Nareash's grin broadened. "You have yet to speak, Master."

"Let the princess go so we can speak in private."

"Elyse will stay."

"Is she what all this is about?" asked Amcaro.

Nareash chuckled. "What do you take me for, some teenage boy with a crush? She is easy on the eyes, but the only thing I care about is the power she'll bring. Besides, you and I both know there is not enough sorcery in the world that can make a woman love." He sighed. "Women are just too stubborn." Nareash turned to the princess. "Isn't that right?"

Elyse stood motionless as if unaware what had been said. *But her eyes… she is still cognizant of her surroundings*, thought Amcaro.

Turning back to the two mages, Nareash continued. "No, as you can see I have to settle for what she is. A beautiful woman trapped in her own mind, unable to let her mouth ruin her appeal." He paused before chuckling again. "Some would say the perfect woman, no?"

"I don't know what you've become Nareash but you are not the friend I knew," said Essan.

"Please, self righteousness doesn't suit you. I would have tried to work something out with *you* at the very least, but like the others it seems your lips are too firmly pressed against our Master's rear to do anything other than what *he* defines as moral." Nareash then turned to Amcaro. "Isn't that right, Master?"

Amcaro didn't answer, too busy searching for a solution to the situation.

"One Above, I will not be ignored by you." The sleeves of Nareash's robes separated revealing his long spindly fingers. In his right hand, he held a short ivory colored scepter.

In a soft whisper, Amcaro spoke, "Sacrynon's Scepter."

"They called Sacrynon the Mad Mage in his later years, right?" Nareash's eyes drifted down absently at the hollow cylinder in his hand.

While Nareash was distracted by the scepter, Amcaro quickly looked to Elyse. *If I could just get some sort of recognition from her that she understands. There. Was that it? Yes dear, you do understand, unfortunately all too well. I hope that you'll know what to do when the time comes.*

Amcaro's eyes returned to Nareash just as the mage looked up. "You don't sound surprised that I have it, Master."

"I had my suspicions after witnessing the destruction you caused. Still, I never imagined you would be such a fool! Don't you understand that the implement turned Sacrynon into a lunatic?" He paused. "It affects you already, doesn't it? Where did you find it? Aurnon the First took the scepter to Quoron four hundred years ago, never to return. He was to destroy the abomination."

"It affects only my power. And obviously, Aurnon the First failed. Imagine my surprise when I discovered one of the most powerful weapons in the world used as a candle holder by a naïve king." Nareash grinned. "I laughed for days. To have something so powerful and not know it, *that* is truly madness. Who cares how it got there? I have it now."

Without warning, Essan lashed out at Nareash with blue tendrils of sorcery flowing from his hands. At such close range, the power would send most to the ground in agony. However, Nareash used the scepter to absorb and nullify Essan's attack. Amcaro joined in and together they sought to overwhelm the deranged man they had once called a friend.

* * *

Elyse's world was void of sound. In the small room with her were three others and yet she felt completely alone. Since discovering her father's manipulation weeks ago, Nareash had kept her in a state where she was unable to communicate with anyone. She could not move, speak, nor even hear unless he chose to allow it. Mostly, the High Mage gave her only sight, generous he had he said in giving her anything at all. *The only proof I have of existence is watching life go by around me.*

Today she realized that the shred of mercy Nareash had granted her was the cruelest thing of all. She had watched the High Mage burn and murder all she held dear. Anyone and everyone fell under his wrath and she was the sole living witness to it. At first, she was thankful she could not hear the cries of despair, but without that distraction she was more attuned to the expressed anguish in each victim's face as it twisted in pain.

And she was unable to look away.

The silent screams still echoed in her deaf ears, the images forever etched into her memories. During the ordeal she prayed ceaselessly to the One Above. She prayed for just one moment free of constraint to help them. *Maybe I could have used that moment to shout a word of warning or even whisper one of comfort. No doubt I would be dead as well, but isn't death better than this?*

Now the same scene repeated itself before her eyes, only the actors were different. Elyse watched in bitter anguish, helpless again as the last two people able to stop her nightmare lived their last moments. She knew they would die just as all the others had today. Even Amcaro, a man she thought of as more of a father than her own looked doubtful about the task before him. *If the resolve of one as powerful as he falters, then what hope do I have?*

Elyse watched the interaction between the High Mages with fascination. Nareash opened his sleeves, revealing the hollow cylinder in his hand. Essan's reaction was one of confusion, coupled with fright. *But Amcaro seems as if he expected it.* Whatever it was, she understood its importance to Nareash. *I haven't seen it out of his hand since he first started carrying it, back when the whisperings of my father's manipulation started.*

Elyse focused on Essan who seemed to regain his nerve. She watched the High Mage's face tighten. *He is ready to attack. One Above, help them please.* She looked back to Amcaro. *He's looking at me! He must know that I can't respond.* Elyse's eyes locked on Amcaro's for a moment, his eyes flicked to the white object in Nareash's hand and then a moment later met her eyes once again. *I...I know what you want.* The High Mage's jaw clenched for a second, nodding his head ever so slightly, the movement so small anyone other than the intended person would miss it. *He knows...that I know. He wants me to help, but I can't do anything like this...*

Essan lashed out at Nareash, the power vibrating through Elyse's body. But Nareash didn't even flinch. The wand glowed and the flames hoping to engulf the mage dissipated without any ill effect. Undeterred, Essan attacked again and again, now alternating with Amcaro. From what Elyse could tell, their attempts were little more than a bother to Nareash. With the slightest of gestures, Nareash struck both High Mages at once, knocking them off of their feet. The deranged mage threw his head back and although she was deaf, Elyse knew he was laughing as he approached the fallen men. *Not again. One Above, please don't leave me so helpless.*

Nareash lifted the wand and pointed it at Essan who began to writhe in pain. Amcaro attempted to stop the attack, but a wave of Nareash's other hand blocked the effort. Amcaro tried once again, but this time Elyse saw that his eyes looked at her and not at Nareash. Elyse's body tingled, starting in her limbs and then moving to her torso and head. To her surprise, she felt the weight of her body after being unable to do so for weeks. She heard Nareash laugh. Amcaro's eyes returned to Nareash and Elyse understood what happened.

"Master, I never expected it to be this easy," said Nareash. "I didn't even feel your last pathetic attempt to stop me. And to think I once admired you." He paused. "Master." He said disgusted. "I have no Master." The scepter hovered over Amcaro now that Essan's body lay still.

Elyse's eyes darted about the space looking for something that she could use to stop the mad man. Her gaze finally rested on the simple desk in the room where a thin knife lay. *I'm to attack a High Mage with a weapon more suited to clean one's nails. No matter, I'd rather die than live as before.* She reached, her body almost forgetting how to respond.

Elyse crept across the room, moving as fast as she dared. Her body screamed with every step and her heart pounded in her chest as she moved her stiff limbs. She was certain he would hear her clumsy movements, and any second Nareash would turn to her, trapping her once again in an invisible cell, this time not even with sight to keep her company. Amcaro feebly attacked in two consecutive bursts of fire but Nareash brushed them off as if they were no more than dust on his robes.

"You are done," said Nareash in a solemn tone.

The scepter began to shimmer and the air thinned. Recognizing the urgency, Elyse leaped and sank the thin blade deep into Nareash's shoulder. The High Mage screamed as the wand flew from his hand, just as Amcaro released a concussive blast of his own, filling the room with blue light. Nareash tumbled backward, sent sprawling across the room and Elyse was thrown into a corner.

After a moment she slowly opened her eyes, realizing as she sat up, groggy, that she was the only person moving. She scurried over to Amcaro who was face down on the floor. She turned him over. "Master Amcaro, please. You must wake up! Master?"

"I'm here, dear," said Amcaro through shallowed breaths.

"Oh, thank the One Above, you're alright."

A thin smile formed on his face as he tried to speak, interrupted by a coughing fit, blood spraying from his mouth. "Hardly. I'm dying."

"No, you can't. You saved me. You stopped Nareash. My father's dead. Everyone is dead. I need you. I don't know what to do."

"What do you mean? You will rule your kingdom."

"But I can't. I…"

"You needn't worry," said Nareash.

Elyse whipped her head around. On the far side of the room, Nareash staggered to his feet.

"I am more than capable of ruling without you." He turned his eyes to Amcaro. "And Master, I spoke too hastily of you. Even now you teach me a valuable lesson in acting. Quite convincing. Still, you left yourself in a less than ideal position in doing so." The High Mage limped across the room, arm hanging at his side.

Watching his crooked path, Elyse realized that he was not walking toward her and Amcaro but instead to a stack of fallen papers. Barely visible underneath laid an ivory scepter.

Elyse dove across the floor an instant before the hobbled mage had time to react. She crawled back as Nareash came forward and slapped the cylinder into Amcaro's outstretched arm.

Elyse saw Nareash begin to glow as he readied an attack. He screamed. "No!"

A burst of self contained energy shot from the Scepter and struck Nareash. When the energy dissipated, Elyse's mouth dropped open, eyes welling in relief. Nareash, her tormentor, was gone. *Obliterated.*

Elyse returned to Amcaro's side. He gasped for air.

"Rest, Master. You'll be alright."

With a worried look and eyes wide, he tried to speak, "He...He..." and another coughing fit seized him, taking control of his body.

"Please, rest. He's gone, but you've weakened yourself further, you need to stay calm."

Amcaro tried to speak again, this time between breaths, his chest rising with each word. "No...too weak...listen...to me...the Scepter...tell no one...show no one...Nareash..." A sharp intake of breath and then his chest relaxed.

"No. I need you. Please." Elyse's words trailed off. She knew her pleas were worthless. *One Above, help me.* She sat on the floor, head in her hands as tears held in for weeks flowed. She wept for everyone, the servants, the guardsmen, the High Mages, Amcaro, and even her father. But most of all she wept for herself. She was alone again.

CHAPTER 2

Waves crashed against a weathered shore and masked the sounds of Kifzo warriors slipping into the water. Tobin cringed as the cold water lapped against the exposed black skin of his torso. He tensed his muscles, shook off a chill, and breathed in a chest full of the cool night air to still his racing heart. He ignored another shiver as he guided his craft inland behind the warriors preceding him.

The full moon provided enough light for him to make out the lead warrior edging his boat onto land. Their warleader crouched low and, gesturing, sent scouts off in several directions. Tobin was last out of the water and sand crunched softly beneath his feet as he made his way up shore.

The voyage from Juanoq had gone better than he had anticipated. Only one Kifzo died during the long trip that began weeks ago, a freak accident that ended with a broken neck. Although one man, the loss was great as even the lowliest Kifzo was equal to three ordinary warriors. However, they could not be delayed with a proper burial, for the man had not fallen in combat. Their warleader chose to push on instead, so the fallen warrior lay rotting where he fell. "We have no time for the dead," was the only explanation given for the decision. More than Tobin had expected.

"I'm surprised to see you so far behind, *Brother*," said Kaz, his mocking voice cutting through the night.

Tobin paused and glanced to either side. He saw that the first of the scouts had returned and reported. Coupled with his brother's raised voice, Tobin concluded there was no immediate threat nearby. "First or last makes no difference to me." He came up to Kaz.

"I'm glad that you feel so comfortable in the rear, *Brother*." The word *brother* rolled off Kaz's tongue as if a foul curse. It was no secret that Kaz hated Tobin. Yet the warleader was always quick to remind him.

"Where would you have me next, Warleader?" asked Tobin, ignoring the jibe.

"Go to Walor," Kaz growled, "Stay with him until the last of his scouts have returned. Come back when you have all the details. We move within the hour."

"Such a short rest?"

"Nubinya's capture is dependent upon our success. That means for tonight we must push on." He spat. "Besides, you remember what Uncle Cef taught us about rest?"

Tobin made a face. *How could I forget?* "Aye, rest is for women and the weak."

Kaz looked down at Tobin's left ankle. "So, do you need rest?"

You wonder if the ankle bothers me. The ankle you broke ten years ago. Of course it does, but I dare not admit it. "No. I was only thinking of the others after the long journey."

"It isn't your place to think on such things, *Brother*, not unless I tell you to do so," said Kaz, taking a step forward, closing the distance between them. Tobin could see the hate in his brother's eyes, their whites a contrast to his black skin.

Tobin never knew when Kaz's temper would get the best of him nor the reason for it. *No doubt deciding whether or not it would be worth it to kill me. But you still need me, don't you?*

Only inches apart, he could feel the heated breath from Kaz's flared nostrils. *So much anger and yet I don't even know why you hate me.*

The two men were near matches in size and physical appearance, hardened from years of training under their father's watchful eyes, pushed to their physical limits by their uncle. At one time a fight between the two would have been too close to call, but now, with a poorly mended ankle, Tobin knew he could not match his brother physically. Certainly not his ruthlessness.

Despite these things, Tobin did not fear Kaz, nor did he fear death. Shame deterred him from engaging his brother. The shame he knew he would bring to their father by dying at his own brother's hands calmed his temper. *Besides, I put my ambitions aside long ago. I won't walk down Kaz's path to have a better life.*

Tobin conceded and turned his eyes away. "As you say, Warleader."

As he walked away, Tobin noticed several of the Kifzo readying their weapons for the work ahead of them. Many regarded him, hate in their eyes, having witnessed what passed between him and Kaz.

Just like Kaz, they tolerate me because they must.

* * *

Tobin found Walor further up shore, atop a sandbank covered in loose gravel, near an outcropping of windswept rocks with edges smoothed away. Walor's odd stance and short stature singled him out from the others. The Kifzo had a leg propped up on one of the battered rocks and his body leaned forward while he listened intently to a steady stream of reports from returning scouts. Tobin stood off to the side and waited until the last warrior left.

"What's the word?" asked Tobin.

"Sore from the trip. Thankful to be on land for awhile," said Walor, dropping his leg down and stretching. "Itching to do something other than wait." Then with a sharp twist and jerk to the side, there was a pop. "Ah, there it is." Flashing a grin, he continued, "I'm guessing that isn't what you wanted to know though, is it?"

Tobin had always enjoyed talking to Walor. A lighthearted man was a rare thing among the Kifzo, and the head scout was one of the few men to engage Tobin in real conversation. "Kaz is looking for a layout of the villages in the area."

Walor gestured with his head in Kaz's direction. "I figured as much when I saw the show between you two had ended. It amazes me you put up with so much, even from him."

Tobin started to respond but thought better of it, choosing to ignore the remark. "The layout?"

Walor let out a heavy sigh and shook his head. Pulling a dagger from his belt, he squatted down, and began to draw in the sand. A crude map took shape. "Based on the reports, we are close to where we wanted to be, only a few miles east of the trail used by those along the coast to bring their catches into Nubinya. If we keep heading east, we should run into small villages every couple of miles before reaching some of the larger settlements. I'm guessing we'll use one of those villages to draw Nubinya's forces away from the city."

"That's up to Kaz. Is there anything to the west, near the trail?"

"You would think so, but no. From what I can tell, the resources near there aren't as plentiful. The trail is simply used because the terrain is more favorable for travel even if it is out of their way. It appears the more direct route is a harder journey."

"And how far is the first village to the east?"

Walor stood up and stretched again. "A little over a mile."

Tobin nodded. "I'll let Kaz know."

* * *

Propped up on his elbows, Tobin lay face down atop a small sand dune. As always, he had taken point after the initial scouting, a role he enjoyed. All Kifzo endured years of training to hone their bodies, but no other warrior boasted senses as heightened as his.

Not even Kaz, and he knows it.

Below, three huts of poor condition sat in a small circle. Their walls of uneven stone looked ready to topple over with the next gust of wind. Dried grass served as their roofs. *Barely enough to keep out the elements.*

Behind the three huts, two llamas and a goat slept. *Is this truly a village? It's almost laughable.*

Tobin's eyes moved to his left, unsurprised to see a makeshift landing near the water's edge in similar condition to the dwellings. Five small fishing boats floated nearby, tied to the dilapidated structure. To his surprise, the vessels were unspoiled and well cared for. *One would assume this place abandoned if not for the animals and boats. At least they show some pride in their trade.*

Tobin slid down the slope to where the Kifzo waited a hundred feet or so behind the sand dune. Barely audible, he whispered to Kaz, "All are asleep. Two llamas and a goat on the far side."

Kaz nodded and signaled assignments to the others with stabbing hand gestures. It seemed unfair for a dozen or so sleeping fishermen to face ninety-nine of the best Kifzo warriors the Blue Island Clan had to offer. Tobin shook his head. *If I've learned nothing else about life, it is that death comes to everyone, and rarely do we decide when.*

The Kifzo approached the small camp downwind so as not to alarm the animals. In silence, thirty of the warriors surrounded the huts. Twenty more went to the boats, while another silenced the animals. The remaining warriors stayed hidden, forming a wide circle, outlining the small area, ready for any that might escape. Despite the precaution, Tobin knew that none would break through the battle hardened men.

Tobin was assigned to the remaining group held back. He did not mind the task, even if others considered it a slight to be away from the assault. He had no taste for killing men in their sleep. It was one thing to kill a man in battle, but another to simply butcher men as defenseless as these, and even another to kill a woman or child. Of course, that line of thinking did not echo the Kifzo mentality. The trouble his feelings had caused him in the past taught him to be discrete about such things.

"Any idiot with a weapon can kill, but few can do so without making a sound," as Uncle used to say. Less than a second after the last animal went down, the others made their move, creeping inside each hut and searching the boats.

No sooner had it started than it was over. Several Kifzo left the huts, cleaning the blood off their daggers and swords before carefully placing them back into their wooden scabbards.

The last of the warriors exited moments later, severed heads in hand. They skewered the trophies on the poles once used by the fishermen to dry their catch.

Now the poles are used to dry ours. He sucked in a mouthful of the cool air and let it out slowly. *Kaz, it's just like you to go to the extreme to send a message to anyone later stumbling across the area. Are the bodies not enough?*

The warriors gathered in the center of the huts, near a dung filled fire pit. Upon approaching, Tobin saw that the heads of men adorned the poles, not those of women or children. *I guess I can find some consolation in that.*

Then Kaz spoke. "Tonight was easy, as it should have been. But this is only the beginning, for we still have much to do if we are to draw the Orange

Desert Clan's main army away from Nubinya." He paused for a second, his rigid face meeting the eyes of each warrior. "However, we'll make camp here for the rest of the night and into tomorrow." The surprise was evident among the Kifzo and each nodded their heads in agreement.

Perhaps he heeded my advice after all?

"Now," said Kaz turning toward the dead animals, "let's get this meat ready. I'd rather not have another meal of stale bread and dried fish." The warriors grunted in agreement, eager to have a warm meal after traveling for weeks on the same bland diet.

Willing to do his part, Tobin set off toward the closest llama, when a hand clasped his shoulder. "Organize the watch, *Brother*. There are more important things to do than fill your belly."

Tobin bit his tongue. "As you say, Warleader."

* * *

Life had become a blur of monotony. The welcome rest of each day was interrupted by merciless killing that filled the night. The gloom provided a natural cover to the dark skinned warriors as well as relief from the arid daytime climate. If there was perfect weather for killing, Tobin was sure the desert nights provided it.

Since coming upon those first three huts four days ago, a dozen more fishing villages suffered similar fates. No two villages they came upon were the same, each varying in size and setup. Only one common element stood out to Tobin as the Kifzo moved between settlements—they found only men. Although he had no appetite for it, killing men in their sleep at least made sense. *Fewer to face in battle. Kill them now or kill them later.* Still, he found it odd there were no signs of women or children. *Maybe the families reside in Nubinya while the men work along the coast? I hope that continues to hold true.*

Tobin's hope ended when one of Walor's scouts returned with new information on their next target. An estimated five hundred inhabitants, including families—the largest settlement by far and only a short distance away.

The scout described the village in great detail and included the surrounding terrain and landmarks. Standing with his brow furrowed, Kaz said not a word the entire time Walor spoke. His right hand stroked the neatly trimmed goatee that wrapped his chin, a habit picked up as a teenager when his beard began to grow in.

Walor finished, took a step back, and waited with the rest of the Kifzo for his orders. The moments began to pass by, yet Kaz stood motionless. Tobin glanced around and saw agitation on the faces of others.

Finally, Kaz spoke. "Your scout missed something."

A confused look. "Missed something? He gave us a detailed layout of the entire settlement."

"And that's the problem. Your report didn't mention anything about the people living there. It's still early enough that they wouldn't all be sleeping. Who is still awake? Why? What were they doing? What was their behavior like?"

Walor turned to his scout for an answer but the blank look on the man's face said enough. Obviously embarrassed, he had no answers to Kaz's questions.

A voice to the right cut in, saving the head scout from any further humiliation. "What nonsense is this? What the people are cooking makes little difference. Does fear cause you to hesitate, Warleader? Surely you aren't afraid of a village filled with fishermen and their families." The warrior chuckled and several others joined in.

Tobin's gaze went to the large Kifzo as he spoke. Durahn stood a head above even the tallest of men. In size, the behemoth dwarfed even he and Kaz who were both well over six feet in height. Like many of the other Kifzo, Durahn chose to wear his long black hair in thick braids down to his shoulders. His long beard came to a braided point. Hair and beard framed a massive head with a flat nose and wide-set eyes.

As the deep but quiet laughter faded from the large warrior, Kaz swung his broad shoulders around to face him. Tobin watched as Durahn readied himself. Like everyone else, Durahn expected a confrontation and it looked like he wanted it. Kaz tilted his head up, eyeing the man with an inquisitive expression. "Do you wish to carelessly throw away the lives of your clan tonight?"

The response was not what Durahn expected and it took him a moment to collect himself. "Any Kifzo who dies by the hand of a weak fisherman is better off dead to me," he said at last, satisfied with himself.

Disgusted, Kaz spat to the side. "And yet you desire to lead in my place, don't you? Let's hope your brethren show more regard for your life than you do for theirs." Not allowing Durahn to respond, Kaz turned his back on the large man, showing his contempt. He looked at Tobin. "*Brother*, take Walor with you and do not return until you discover what was missed."

* * *

They made their way toward the settlement, meandering between several rock-covered hills. Tobin surveyed the terrain upon their approach, searching for the ideal vantage point. His eyes swung to the left where a rock formation protruded from the top of the nearest rise. Tobin gestured toward the stone configuration, and the two men climbed to the selected spot. Walor was the first to crest the hill. Tobin trailed several steps behind, his ankle slowing him.

Several hours past dusk, the two men finally settled. The location allowed for an unobstructed view of the village. Tobin took a moment to confirm the scout's information before looking more closely at his surroundings.

Just as reported, the town consisted of five clusters of huts. In the center of each tight cluster sat a shared fire pit. The five groups surrounded a small oasis which included several date trees and other simple vegetation.

Tobin turned his attention back to the fire pits. Tobin saw what he dreaded, what he hoped to avoid. Entire families sat around doing what looked to be nothing more than trying to stay warm on the cool night.

He turned his attention to an animal pen outside the clusters, to the left. The pen consisted of several small sections, each one housing a different breed of animal. Goats and llamas dominated the population, but for the first time since arriving along the coast, Tobin also saw half a dozen camels, and almost double that number of horses.

A perk of having fresh water nearby.

A glint caught his eye. Tobin leaned in to Walor and whispered, "I need to get closer."

"There isn't enough cover to get any closer."

Tobin inclined his head to the right toward the village. "There. That boulder should be fine."

"That's over fifty yards away and I'd hardly call that a boulder. I've skipped rocks bigger than that."

"From this angle there isn't anything else between here and the village I can use."

"What are you hoping to get a better look at?"

"Call it a hunch."

"A hunch, huh?" Walor paused. "Well, I'm faster and smaller. Tell me what your hunch is and I'll go."

"No. I can see better at night. It might not be anything, but I need to be certain. Besides, standing that close to the flames, the villagers aren't likely to see me anyway."

Not waiting for Walor to argue, Tobin set off down the opposite side of the hill, staying low to the ground. He paused once near the bottom then darted to the cover he had pointed out, ducking behind the boulder. Grimacing, Tobin took his time to position himself before peering out.

I hate to admit it, but Walor was right about the stone's size.

Tobin stared into the night, eyes flickering between the huts and animal pens, confirming his suspicions. Rather than returning to Walor immediately, he lay motionless for another half hour until the last fire died out and the villagers returned to their huts for the night.

Finally satisfied, Tobin made his way back to Walor, careful not to pry loose any gravel. He rested a hand on Walor's shoulder at the top of the rise, signaling it was time to leave.

When they rejoined their fellow Kifzo, Kaz stood waiting, arms crossed. Tobin noted the restlessness in the others as he approached.

"We expected you back some time ago. I trust you have some news, *Brother*?"

"Yes. They know we're coming and they're ready for us." Tobin paused. "As ready as they can be anyway."

"What?" said Walor.

"I told you I followed a hunch. Structurally, the village is exactly as reported. The huts, the oasis, the animal pen, the fire pits are all laid out as described. But if you look closer, there's more. They wanted us to see families around the fire pits oblivious to what was going on, an easy prey. However, those families are incomplete. There weren't any men around the fires."

Walor interjected, "Are you telling me you saw the faces of those people from that distance?"

"Of course not. I didn't need to see their faces. I watched them move. It was a clever thing to disguise their women in men's clothing but they couldn't disguise their mannerisms or their gait. I can't be sure, but I think only two pits were lit simply because there weren't enough women to light all the pits and still convince us of the deception. So instead, they hoped we would reason the other pits were out because those clusters were already asleep."

"Do you know where the men are?" asked Kaz.

"Hiding. Waiting for us to take the bait. I'm sure that many of them are dispersed throughout the village, but from what I could tell, the animal pen is the primary location. They probably hope to take advantage of the few mounts they have."

"How can you be so sure?"

"They made the mistake of lighting the fires nearest the pen. After watching the horses long enough I saw several glints near their heads from the flames bouncing off the bridles still in their mouths. There were also several shadows moving about nearby that did not belong to any animal."

"And the oasis?"

"I would guess several stationed there as well, given the location. However, the huts were blocking my line of sight."

Kaz grunted, a disgusted look on his face. He turned his back on Tobin. "We leave in ten minutes and will make do with the incomplete information."

Never enough is it, Kaz? Without my warning it is likely we'd lose more men. My report also made your point against Durahn as well. Yet, you give me nothing. Tobin sighed and looked over to Walor who gave a small shrug.

* * *

A short while later the Kifzo split into three groups. The first group would approach the settlement along the coast. They would search the fishing vessels docked ashore before making their way up the beach.

The second group waited near the rock formation Tobin and Walor used earlier for scouting. When the time came, they would veer to the right of the village, capturing the hut clusters presumed to be least occupied. Afterward, they would push forward toward the oasis, gaining control of the village's central position. Once the first group charged, the second group would attack and signal the third group into action.

The third group sat above the village on a series of ragged hills, overlooking the animal pens. Jutting rocks and dark shadows provided more than adequate cover for the group. Their task was to release a volley of arrows at the animal pen where Tobin suspected many of the male villagers hid. After the initial volley, most of the warriors from the third position would charge down the rock-strewn terrain toward the pens while the villagers were distracted. Tobin and several other handpicked warriors of his choosing would continue the arrow fire until the second and third groups engaged. Only then would they move down into the fray. If all went as planned, the three groups would strike as one in three different areas of the settlement, causing confusion and chaos.

Tobin directed the third company into position, not satisfied until he found the optimal formation for the warriors. He ignored the aggravated looks on their faces as he shuffled them about. He was used to such disdain after all these years. *But they have no choice but to take orders from me on this matter.*

Even Kaz, who rarely relinquished command, especially to him, deferred to Tobin when it came to the bow. Since injuring his ankle, the long range weapons of the Kifzo had become the focus of his training. Tobin could still fight hand to hand better than most but with unsure footing it only made sense to cater to his strengths.

Tonight Kaz opted to lead the second group from the coast. With little cover, they easily faced the highest risk. Tobin caught the significance of Kaz's choice for his group; taking Durahn as well as several others caught chuckling earlier at his brother's expense.

Always thinking, eh Kaz? Punish the ones confident enough to challenge you by giving them the most dangerous position. And if they should fall tonight, you've cleansed the infection before it spreads.

Tobin took a moment to review the positioning of his warriors one last time. Including himself, the most skilled archers waited in back and occupied the best vantage point. They would hold their position the longest. In front of the lead archers, Tobin organized the Kifzo according to experience.

Satisfied with the formation, he made one final check over his equipment, examining his bow for any cracks, though he already knew none existed. He notched an arrow, crept into position, and locked his sight on the animal pen. Walor came up behind him. The two exchanged a nod.

Tobin waited for what seemed like hours when, in fact, he knew only minutes had passed. Anticipation had always been his least favorite part of an attack. During the time when all one could do was wait, his mind drifted off to images that so often haunted his dreams. Corpses of all ages, shapes, and sizes—men, women and children alike. Each of them stabbed, slashed, gored, or mutilated. Their eyes seemed to hold just enough life to pierce his soul deeper than any sword thrust could.

The images didn't frighten him like they once had though. He had grown accustomed to their company years ago. Yet it never made his nights any more restful, or the moments before a battle any less unnerving.

His head turned at a sudden movement and he saw the second group far closer than he would have expected them to be, still unnoticed. *Their lookouts are useless. We'll be lucky to get more than a couple shots off before they're engaged at this rate.*

A war cry filled the night and Tobin concluded that Kaz had reached a similar decision as the once creeping warriors rushed the village at a full sprint. Loud clanging erupted from the animal pens and Tobin saw villagers scrambling to ready themselves. He aimed his bow, shouting "Now!" without looking back. A hail of arrows rained down, striking man and animal alike. Screams echoed across the landscape. The archers fired their second volley as men charged down the uneven slope, crying out in unison. Between the second and third flight of arrows, Tobin spared a glance and saw the first group of Kifzo fast approaching the hut clusters on the opposite side of the village.

The remainder of Tobin's group released four rounds of arrows before the charging Kifzo engaged the villagers. Tobin signaled his men to fan out as they made their way down to the action, pausing here and there to pick off anyone escaping. Despite their numbers, the outmatched villagers died in droves. Tobin found little joy in slaughtering fishermen, but it was his task, and a life of blood was all Tobin knew.

Moving in close, he saw Kifzo already searching huts, a sign that the worst was over. *As if the bloodied bodies were not evidence enough. So many dead in so little time.*

Soon after entering the clusters, piercing screams reverberated in his ears, women and children crying out, some for help, others for mercy. Tobin knew neither would come.

Unable to turn away from the scenes of entire families being murdered, raped, or both, his stomach lurched and he swallowed back bile. Devilish grins filled the faces of those warriors already satiating their lusts, men he'd known and trained with most of his life.

How can you allow such brutality, Kaz? What would Lucia say if she knew such things existed?

A flash of light filled the night sky. Tobin stepped back and shielded his eyes from the sudden glare. Blinking, he set off toward the village center near the oasis.

Has to be sorcery. But here?

He arrived a few moments later with other Kifzo close behind. The ground around the oasis resembled the rest of the village. Dead littered the orange sand, oozing dark fluids from fresh wounds. Tobin's eyes widened in shock. As many Kifzo warriors lay dead and dying as villagers.

Looking up from the bloody mess, several Kifzo caught his eye. Struggling to stand, they fought to defend themselves, pressed and battered by fishermen carrying little else but crude weapons more suited to their trade than for battle.

Tobin called out to those who had followed him, "Quick, help them."

The warriors ran off to join the fray, putting the fishermen on the defensive. Tobin scanned the area, crouched at the ready. Sudden movement drew his attention to the shadows of a date tree. His hand snatched the throwing ax at his belt and whipped it toward the lurking figure hiding in the gloom. Tobin watched his throw sail through the air, confident he'd found his mark. However the ax came to a halt mid-air, hovering for a moment before falling to the ground. The figure stepped forward and another wave of light assaulted his senses. He found himself beset with sudden weakness, unable to focus. Stumbling to one knee, he saw Kifzo staggering and falling all around him, straining to keep their weapons up as the villagers surged forward.

The figure by the trees approached Tobin. He saw bones of both animal and human hanging from the shaman's robes. Raising a hand, the shaman extended his index finger at Tobin as he tried to rise from his knees.

Tobin inhaled a deep breath, ready for whatever fate brought him. But the shaman burst into flames and convulsed to the ground. Tobin shook his head in denial as he watched the shaman's body grow still, the remains of his clothing crackling under the intense heat.

How did that happen? But he had no time to consider such things. With the grogginess clearing and strength returning to his limbs, he picked up his bow and began firing shots at villagers eager to escape now that the Kifzo were unhindered by sorcery. His eyes widened as a fleeing villager burst into flames only a moment before his arrow caught the man.

Tobin twisted to his right where a tall man dressed in tattered red garb stood bent and out of breath. Tobin's hand immediately went for his other throwing ax but the man stood up first, one arm raised in submission, the other hung at his side. "Wait. Please."

Ax in hand, Tobin closed in on the man. "Did you kill the shaman? And that man?" he asked gesturing with the weapon.

Still panting, the man responded. "Yes. I'm sorry I couldn't do more but I am still weak from my journey."

"Journey? What are you doing here?"

Breathing heavy, the man shook his head. "Too much to explain. For now, just know that your enemy is mine." Swallowing hard, he gestured toward several wounded Kifzo. "I've never been a strong healer but I have enough strength that if you'll allow me, I may be able to help the worst of your men now that the battle appears over."

Tobin saw it was true. The last few villagers fell under Kifzo blades. "Who are you? And why would you help us?"

"My name is Nachun. And as I said, your enemy is mine." Nachun inclined his head in the direction of a fallen Kifzo whose hand staunched the flow of blood at his side. "May I?"

Reluctant at first, Tobin lowered his weapon and nodded.

Nachun moved with caution toward the fallen Kifzo. Tobin followed, scanning the area and taking in the damages. Close to twenty Kifzo lay dead, mostly those tasked to gain control of the oasis. An additional half dozen teetered on the edge of death themselves. The losses were much greater than expected.

Tobin looked down thoughtfully at Nachun. *Our losses would have been much worse without this stranger.* Nachun bent over the fallen Kifzo, hand resting over the large gash in his side.

"Will he live?" asked Tobin.

"For now. Unfortunately, all I can do at the moment is slow the bleeding. If he survives the night, I should be able to help more, once I've rested and regained some strength."

"Very well. Do what you can and, if you're able, treat any others in similar shape."

Nachun nodded.

"What's going on here?" said Kaz, anger in his voice.

Tobin looked up and met his brother's glare as he and several other warriors approached. "This man saved many lives. The villagers had a shaman," he said, gesturing to the smoldering remains. "He cast a spell that made us unable to fight the fishermen." Tobin looked down "Nachun came to our aid and killed him."

Kaz spat. "And you trust *this* shaman?"

"Yes. Even while weak he tries to help our fallen." Tobin paused and looked at the other wounded warriors near the oasis who, without Nachun's help, would have died. "Do I speak false? Do we not owe this man?"

Hesitant at first, several of the men nodded and mumbled in agreement.

Kaz grunted. "He'll live. For now. When he's done here, make sure he's put in one of the huts under guard."

"This man..." Tobin began to argue.

"This man is still a stranger, *Brother*." Kaz cut in. "I will speak no more on the matter until we know his story."

The two men shared an intense stare before Tobin once again broke the gaze. "Where would you have me then?" he asked.

"The village is ours and the huts are being searched. Go help the others with the search."

Tobin pushed his way past Kaz, feeling helpless and frustrated by his brother's reaction. *No doubt Kaz will kill the man.* He spared a glance back and saw Nachun working on another wounded Kifzo under his brother's watchful eye. Tobin shook his head. *Too bad.*

* * *

In the battle's aftermath, Tobin maneuvered through the twisted carnage that littered the ground. He noted that the huts were better constructed here, the stone walls carefully formed and secured with mortar. Roofs even held a basic framework on which the dried grass could rest. Unlike the squalor he'd seen before, this place actually resembled a real village, where one could settle down and raise a family. *But not anymore*, he thought, as he stepped over a corpse with its mouth hanging open and eyes wide with terror.

The first several huts he came upon stood empty, already ransacked of valuables. The next was a wreck and smeared with blood. Draped over a small table lay a man with his throat slashed, his lifeless hand gripping a knife more suited for filleting fish than fighting. Against the back wall, a dog lapped up the blood of another victim as it oozed onto the gritty floor. Tobin walked away as the dog tugged at the wound in an effort to pull loose the man's entrails.

The next hut was worse still. Tobin walked in on a Kifzo raping a gray haired woman who thrashed under the grunting warrior until a fist came down to silence her. Shamed, Tobin left the hut in a hurry before the image could etch itself into his mind. But he knew it was too late.

Another one I'll never be rid of.

Tobin reached the last hut in the cluster. He peered inside as light crept in from the relit fire pits. A small sound, barely above a whisper, caught his attention and he unsheathed the dagger at his thigh. Scanning the dim room, he spotted the tiniest movement in the back, near broken pottery and overturned linen. Stepping further inside, his eyes focused. A little girl, no more than four sat huddled into a ball, gently rocking back and forth, mumbling to herself. *Maybe there is a chance to do some good.* He looked over his shoulder then back. He crouched down and whispered. "Do you think you can stay quiet and remain hidden here?"

The girl looked up, eyes filled only with tears.

"I know you are frightened but I can help you. You must promise not to let anyone else see you. Alright?"

The child just stared at him—through him—scared and unable to move. *Why would she trust me after what she's seen and heard?* "Please, I…"

A booming voice came from the doorway, cutting him off. "Who is that I hear talking?"

On instinct, Tobin whipped around at the sound and faced the man in the entranceway, exposing the child.

"Well, what do we have here?" A wide grin broke out across the warrior's face as he leaned to look at the young girl still trembling in terror. "Hmmm, and young too. I was just looking for someone to warm my bed tonight," said Durahn.

The massive warrior ducked low as he stepped into the hut. In response, Tobin's fingers tightened around the grip of the dagger, more out of reflex than courage. He looked back at the girl, meeting those hollow eyes.

Already dead.

Durahn stopped cold and leaned back, noticing the dagger in Tobin's hand. "Ah, now I see." His thick hands opened and closed as if inviting a fight. "Don't worry, cripple, you can have her when I'm done." The demon of a man turned to the girl and smiled wider. "Well, whatever's left of her."

Tobin crouched. *Cripple. A reminder. What can I expect to do against him?* His hand lashed out, drawing a line across the child's throat. He stood there watching as her body went limp and fell. Blood poured out from the young girl. "Looks like there's already nothing left."

Tobin stared back at Durahn, unsure what to expect. The Kifzo smiled, and then laughed. It was a sadistic cackle. "After all these years, cripple, you never fail to surprise me." He turned and walked back to the doorway, swinging around at the last moment. "Killing puts me in a good mood, so I'll give you that one. Stop me again though, and next time it'll be you I use for my pleasure." Durahn snorted in mirth, leaving Tobin alone once again.

Hanging his head, Tobin watched the lifeless girl, a pool of crimson enveloping her tiny frame. *I really meant to help you. But this was all I could offer.* He clenched the dagger in his hand even harder in frustration. *This is your fault, Kaz. You don't participate and think that makes you different than the others, but you still let it happen. You're no better than they are.* He looked down at the blade in his hand, covered in the innocent blood of a child and sighed.

CHAPTER 3

"…This is the one that will break their back for sure, Commander. We'll smash them to pieces. They will be talking about tomorrow for years to come…"

Aye, for years to come they'll talk about tomorrow as one of the worst bloodbaths this continent has ever seen.

Jonrell stared across the open landscape below. The cliff gave him a full view of an expansive plain, littered with rows upon rows of tents from the opposing army's encampment, more than double the size of their own forces. *Two years after taking this job and I've regretted every minute of it. Shorting us on pay, ignoring advice, putting us in dangerous positions…why am I here again?*

"…I won't be able to sleep tonight in anticipation…"

Anticipation of what? Stuffing your face while others fix your mess? I haven't seen you do anything besides that since I've known you. "I think the men are a little too eager," said Jonrell.

Melchizan continued. "…Oh, yes. Naturally. They feel the significance of tomorrow as well…"

Jonrell cleared his throat and cut in, "I think we should withdraw to more favorable ground."

"…yes, we will slaughter them, we will…" The would-be conqueror almost choked on his last words as he turned in the saddle of his mount. The short man's demeanor suddenly turned from one of excitement to confusion, and then anger. "What do you mean withdraw? We have them right where we want them. This is what we've been waiting for…"

The setting sun bled across the land, reflecting dark purples and reds off the white canvases of the enemy's camp. *Reminiscent of a bruise. A bleak reminder of what awaits us tomorrow. No Melchizan, I haven't waited for that.*

"Commander! I'm speaking to you," said Melchizan, his great jowls swaying.

"I hear you. And unlike you, I actually listen to the person I'm talking to."

Melchizan's face reddened. "It's bad enough you and the rest of your tattered outfit of mercenaries fail to address me as your lord, but I will not be spoken to like some common soldier. Is that understood?"

"No. You are not our lord and definitely not a soldier, just an employer. The Hell Patrol will not bend a knee to you. If you want someone to kiss your rear, you'll have to look to the rest of that motley army of yours."

"Have you forgotten that motley army has conquered over a dozen cities and hundreds of miles of land? An army *you* command?"

Jonrell snorted a laugh. "Cities? Most of that land was filled with nothing more than small tribes and villages. Your army is not ready for this," said Jonrell, pointing toward the encampment. "The men are going to face more than two to one odds against a better armed and better trained force."

"If *they* fail, then *you* have failed as a commander."

"No. I've told you we needed to spend money on better weapons, rather than your lavish indulgences. We need to push the men to work on actual skill sets rather than allow them to function as a badly organized mob. But you're too greedy to see that, so you keep pushing for more and undermining what I'm trying to do. Then you decide to engage an opposing army on a wide open plain without cavalry to match theirs."

Melchizan ignored Jonrell's remarks, his voice low and even. "I've waited too long for a kingdom to call my own. We will attack tomorrow and we will win. Otherwise, you and your outfit won't see the rest of your contract."

Jonrell stared at Melchizan, ready to reply, when the sound of approaching hooves and a shout from behind caught his attention. He held his employer's glare for a moment longer, then turned toward the approaching rider. He refused to continue the conversation and instead kicked his mount forward.

"I'm glad you've seen it my way, Commander," Melchizan called out.

Jonrell heard the amusement in his employer's voice as if the man had won some victory over him. *Idiot. There will be no victory tomorrow. I hope you slice your own throat when you try to draw your sword in terror.*

The advancing rider bobbed in his saddle as he pulled beside Jonrell. The two mercenaries descended the rocky trail in silence, interrupted by Jonrell's heavy sigh and the grinding of teeth.

"Keep it up and you're liable to crack another tooth."

Jonrell turned to the man in faded black robes. "Are you my mother now?"

"That's right, take it out on me," the mage muttered.

"That man is an absolute imbecile and he's going to get us all killed," said Jonrell.

"Probably," said Krytien. "But let me remind you who signed the contract..."

"I know who signed the contract. If I wanted to take this abuse, I would have stayed with... what does Raker call him? Lord Roundness?" said Jonrell coming to a halt. He drew a breath and calmed himself. "Now what do you want?"

"Well, remember that item I bought off a trader last time we were in Slum Isle? You know, to keep track of that particular situation of interest to you?" whispered Krytien.

Jonrell straightened in his saddle. "Yes?"

"Well, it worked. I mean, the king," he paused, "passed away." Krytien ran his fingers over his head, wiping the sweat from his brow and pushed back his thin white hair.

"How?"

"I don't know. The device wasn't designed to tell us how, just when."

"You sound surprised." said Jonrell.

"Well, there was always some question on whether it would work or not. The workings of such magical tools are not my expertise, you know."

"Don't give me that. That's not what you told me before. If I recall, you assured me that the moment something happened, the device would brighten and you'd be made aware of it. That was years ago." Jonrell scowled, growing agitated. "Now, you're saying this was all in question?"

Krytien cleared his throat. "The uncertainty came when trying to confirm the tool's effectiveness at the time of purchase. Only the one who created the item could figure that out. However, I do know the device worked as intended."

"Would you swear on it?"

"I'd swear on my honor as a mage."

Jonrell snorted. "Honor? Isn't that the same pledge you make when Raker accuses you of cheating at dice?"

"Well, that's different," he smirked. "My fingers are crossed then." The mage raised his hands and wiggled his fingers as the smile vanished. "It's true. I'm sorry for your loss."

A breeze from the north blew Jonrell's long auburn hair into his face. "You have nothing to be sorry for, I'm not." He turned and kicked his horse into a quick trot and the mage did the same. "When we get to camp, gather the crew together and bring them back to my tent. Hell Patrol only."

"I brought the device with me in case you wanted to see it for yourself." Krytien reached into his robes and pulled out a round stone similar in appearance to a pearl, only larger.

Jonrell reached out and grabbed the device without examining it, sticking it in his pocket.

"I'll ride ahead then." The short mage gave his horse a kick and galloped toward camp, bobbing in his saddle.

* * *

When Jonrell entered camp, the sun had dropped below the horizon. A clear sky allowed the moon and stars to cast an eerie light on their sorry excuse for a camp, illuminating the soldiers' questionable activities. Jonrell didn't like what he saw. Men joked, drank, and did just about everything but ready themselves for the next day. *The fools have grown just as overconfident as Melchizan.*

Jonrell shook his head in disgust as he harkened back to the days when he and Cassus had first left home and joined the Hell Patrol. They were led then by a man named Ronav, a hard but fair man who had taught Jonrell what it meant to truly lead an army. Jonrell was forced into command after Ronav died and kept the group's survivors together while rebuilding what Ronav had started.

But now? He would bash my teeth in if he saw us working for Melchizan. What was I thinking these past couple of years? I should have cut our losses long ago.

As he made his way through camp, Jonrell stopped to speak with a few of the men at several fires. The soldiers had the sense to appear as if they cared about his advice regarding the impending battle, but Jonrell saw the truth of things behind their eyes. *Melchizan called this my army? It doesn't matter what I say or do because he will come in behind me and undermine my authority. This has never been my army.*

A man with short black hair waited outside the command tent. "I take it you tried to talk some sense into them again?" asked Cassus.

Jonrell gave the man a frustrated look but ignored the comment. "Is everyone here?"

"Almost. What's going on?"

Jonrell clasped Cassus on the shoulder. "You'll have to wait like everyone else. Who are we missing?"

"Just Hag. She said not to wait for her. She…uh…well, let's just say she and one of the Byzernians are a little busy right now." Cassus let out a shudder after finishing the comment.

"You're joking. I didn't think there was anyone here old enough or desperate enough?"

"Apparently, she was quite convincing."

The remainder of Jonrell's scowl vanished, replaced by a grin. "Well, maybe it will improve her disposition."

"Ha. It couldn't hurt it," said Cassus as he opened the tent flap. Jonrell entered first and Cassus followed after, securing the flap behind him.

The command tent was packed. Never meant to comfortably hold more than twenty men, fifty soldiers now filled the space. Jonrell made his way through the press, heading toward the back of the noisy tent, interrupting conversations along the way. He did no more to greet those he passed than offer a nod or a quick clasp of the arm. He wasted no time with small talk. Cassus remained by the tent entrance, ensuring no one uninvited snuck in.

At the back of the tent, Krytien waited next to a stool. "I figured you might want to use this."

Jonrell took a step up and looked down at Krytien. "Are we good?"

"Yeah. People outside the tent can still hear our voices but no longer clear enough to understand what's being said."

Jonrell raised his hands to get everyone's attention. "Alright, that's enough." He paused until everyone settled. "We're moving out tonight. We'll leave after everyone is passed out or asleep. There's a more pressing job ahead for us."

Conversations erupted amidst a press of questions. Jonrell raised his hands again for silence, "I know you have questions so let's make this quick and I'll answer what I can for now. The rest will have to wait."

A man leaning against one of the tent poles was the first to speak. He held a small dagger in one hand, cleaning his fingernails. The man didn't look up when he spoke but his words were clear and to the point. "I know things are looking pretty bleak out there but it's not like us to renege on a contract, Boss. Doesn't help our rep, you know," said Kroke.

"Aye and some contract it is. We've been moving around this continent for over two years now with Melchizan and haven't been paid half what he owes us. The way I look at it, he broke our contract a long time ago. I take the blame for letting things get this bad. But trust me, thanks to his spending habits the man is penniless. He's counting on tomorrow's battle to bring in the cash he sorely needs. That's not a situation I want to be a part of. As far as our rep goes, I think staying and getting crushed along with him would do more harm than leaving now, don't you?" He paused and then glared at everyone around the tent.

"It's about time you came around, Boss," said Kroke, cold eyes flashing. "We were starting to wonder about you. Its one thing to die if you're leading us, but another thing entirely to fight under Melchizan. I'd rather cut my own throat and be done with it."

Jonrell looked around the room. "Does he speak for everyone?" Heads nodded and a few grunted in agreement. "Good. What else?"

Usually too shy to speak up in front of others, the young woman surprised Jonrell. "I know that army out there isn't much, Commander, but there are a few we could use that'd be willing to come with us. Some might even be Hell Patrol material after a couple of real battles." The deep color of her tight red ponytail contrasted against pale skin and blue eyes.

"Is there something specific you're asking?" said Jonrell.

Yanasi shifted the black long bow from her right hand to her left, whispering. "Can we take those who are interested in coming with us, Sir?"

"If you're looking for someone to warm your bed at night, I'd be more than happy to oblige. We don't need to bring another squad aboard for that, do we?" said the man next to her as he flashed a dirty grin.

Yanasi turned and jabbed him in the groin with her bow. The ragged man fell to the ground, hands between his legs, groaning in pain. "Raker, if you open your mouth one more time, I'll cut off what little you got, do you hear me!"

The commander had witnessed the scene far too many times. The comments toward Yanasi used to bother him since he took her in as a young girl, treating her like the sister he left behind. But over the years, she had proven more than once that when pushed, she could take care of herself. So he learned to let those comments go, knowing no ill was meant by them.

Just the way Raker is anyway, always knowing how to get under people's skin.

Her voice quieted again as she turned back to Jonrell. "It's not like that, Sir. Rygar is one of them and he's one of the best scouts we've ever had. I just think it'd be a waste to leave anyone behind if they could help us on the next job is all."

Ah, now I see. I'll have to talk to her in private then, and perhaps Rygar for that matter. Jonrell answered her question by addressing everyone. "If you can actually find someone out there that is worth taking along then so be it. I'll trust your judgment. But don't bring it up until we are about to leave. I don't want our plans to reach Melchizan. If anyone looks like they'll be trouble, end it quick. I don't want someone flapping off the second we turn our backs." He paused. "Anything else? We need to wrap this up before the camp starts to get suspicious."

"One more," said Cassus, still standing in the back of the tent. "What's the job?"

Jonrell smiled, eyeing the man who had been his best friend since they were both boys. "We're going home, Cassus." There were several questioning looks and grunts at that. Jonrell paused to let them die down before continuing. "We're going to Cadonia. The princess, soon to be queen, is hiring us, only she doesn't know it yet," said Jonrell, watching as his friend's face went white.

* * *

"Where are Cassus and Krytien? They should be here by now."

"You got me, Boss," said Kroke, again cleaning his nails.

"We'll give them ten more minutes and then we head out. They can catch up later."

"Whatever you say."

"Is that really necessary?"

"Is what necessary?"

"That," said Jonrell pointing at the dagger. "How can they be dirty if you're constantly cleaning them?"

"They aren't. Just habit I guess. Like the way a blade feels in my hand is all." Kroke sheathed the knife and looked up. "Don't sweat it, Boss. They'll be here."

Jonrell sighed. *They better.*

"See, that's them coming out the camp now," said Kroke with a nod. He pulled out a different knife, picking at the nails on his other hand.

Jonrell shook his head and turned toward the encampment. He squinted and saw some movement but couldn't make out more than a few shapes in the night. The distance was too great. "How can you tell it's them?"

"I can't." Kroke shrugged his shoulders. "Just trying to be positive is all."

"You're unbelievable, you know that."

"Thanks."

"It wasn't a compliment."

Kroke sheathed his blade and pulled out another that he started spinning in his hand, a small grin crawled across his face and he watched the blade dance in the moonlight.

"How about you do something useful and grab Yanasi? Something's up and I need her eyes. That's definitely Cassus in front but there is no way that many soldiers were worth bringing with us."

"Sure thing, Boss."

Jonrell watched the line continue to creep along, ending with several wagons in tow. *One Above, there must be over two hundred horses in that group. That's near half the cavalry.* Jonrell twisted his head around as he heard a soft voice. "Kroke said you needed me, Sir?"

"I thought you said only a few men were worth bringing along?"

"Well Sir, the number was probably closer to fifteen."

"Then I need you to get up that hill and tell me what's going on because there are a lot more than fifteen soldiers coming this way."

"Yes, sir," said Yanasi.

Jonrell watched her scamper up the hill. She took a moment to position herself.

Jonrell gave her a few moments then asked, "Well, do we have trouble?"

"I don't think so."

"I need something more than that."

"Well, that's definitely Cassus in front and you can tell that's Krytien way in back by the way he can barely stay on his horse. So if it was a trap, I don't understand why Melchizan would let them ride unguarded. The real issue is what's going on with everyone else."

"What do you mean?"

"Well, they look more uncomfortable than Krytien on those horses, almost like they never rode one before. They're all pretty small too and don't carry themselves like a bunch of soldiers."

Jonrell squinted into the night, thankful for the clear sky. His eyes weren't nearly as good as Yanasi's but now he knew what to look for and what she said made sense. He realized what was going on.

"Sir, is everything all right? Do I need to ready the rest of the men?"

"No, everything isn't all right. But we aren't in any trouble just yet," snapped Jonrell. He sighed as Yanasi flinched from his tone and he realized he was taking his anger out on the wrong person. "Good job."

Even in the dark, he saw the young woman blush. "Thank you, Sir. But I don't understand what's wrong."

He muttered a curse. "Those aren't soldiers in that train. Those are Melchizan's slaves."

Jonrell waited at the bottom of the small rise, watching in silence. With each step the horses took, he saw how awkward the riders were. Cassus came up to Jonrell. Neither said a word.

The commander watched each brown-skinned slave make their way past, noticing not only men, but women and children, tucked away in the covered wagons. Jonrell waited until Krytien neared before speaking. "You two. Come with me."

The three men rode off and stopped just out of earshot of the others. Jonrell's eyes went back to the slaves trying to keep control of their animals. His men were in the midst of the chaos, doing their best to manage the situation. The commotion could wake the dead. Jonrell's face hardened. He spoke, ice lining his voice. "Start explaining."

The plump mage cleared his throat and started to reply, "Well, you see..."

But Jonrell cut him off, scowling at the two men. "I wasn't asking you." He glared at Cassus. "I know this was your idea."

"Well, you said we could take anyone who was interested in coming with us," said Cassus.

Jonrell cut in again. "Don't give me that. These people aren't soldiers. What were you thinking? They belong to Melchizan and so do the horses and wagons."

"Well, I figured he still owes us quite a bit on our contract. We could sell the horses and wagons when we make it to port. That should cover most of it."

"And leave the cavalry even weaker than before? Very compassionate. What about the slaves?" said Jonrell.

Cassus spat, growing agitated. "That's what I think about Melchizan, his cavalry, and his army. He was going to send the Byzernians to their deaths tomorrow."

"What do you mean?"

"I overheard him talking to one of his captains. They were planning to have the slaves in front of the infantry. They were going to give them some crude weapons, and use them as human shields. He said it was becoming too costly to keep them alive."

"And so you thought to take them with us?"

"Seemed like the right thing to do."

"Maybe. But it definitely wasn't the smartest. This continent has kept Byzernians as slaves for decades. No one would find fault with Melchizan for doing what he liked with his property."

"That doesn't make it right, Jonrell."

Jonrell shook his head. "He may have overlooked the Hell Patrol and a few deserters leaving, but almost three hundred slaves besides? Not likely."

"I wasn't going to leave them to their deaths," said Cassus.

Jonrell sighed. He looked up into the night sky, speaking to no one in particular. "Why do you keep testing me?" He met Cassus's eyes. "Then they're your responsibility. You're in charge of their organization, their needs, and their final destination because they aren't coming with us to Cadonia and I won't have them place us in any unnecessary danger."

Cassus nodded. "I expected as much."

Jonrell turned to Krytien, jabbing a finger at him. "You're going to help him the entire way to port."

"What? I just happened to be leaving camp at the same time as they did," said Krytien.

"Don't take me for a fool. You did something to the camp; otherwise they'd already be after us."

"Well, I may have added some of my own special brew to their mugs. It's designed to ensure a man sleeps soundly the night before a big day, you know. But I really don't see what that has to do with anything." The mage ran his fingers through the few wisps of long hair remaining on his head, trying to repress a grin.

"Of course you don't. But they are just as much your responsibility as Cassus's." Jonrell glared at both men waiting for an argument, surprised there was none. He added, "When will your *special brew* wear off?"

"In a few hours, not long after dawn," said Krytien with a sullen huff.

"Plenty enough time to prepare for their deaths then? You're getting soft from hanging around Cassus so much."

The sound of hooves approaching caught their attention and the three men looked back toward the disorder. Sitting astride a white mount rode one of the slaves. Like most slaves from the Byzernian Islands, the man was very thin, and average in height. As the rider pulled up, Jonrell could make out his age by the bright moonlight, late fifties by his estimate. The man had a spryness about him though, evident by the confident way he sat upon the horse.

The slave gave a bow, showing far more control at the reins then the others of his race. "Wiqua, good to see you," said Cassus with a smile. "Your skills with a horse are impressive."

"My previous master had me care for his animals. I am a bit more familiar with the beasts than most of my people." He bowed again, addressing Jonrell.

"Commander, I came to thank you on behalf of my people. Your kindness is unmatched for a man in your profession."

"Keep your thanks, Wiqua, and give it to Cassus. This was his idea, not mine."

"Even so, the final decision is yours as commander." The old man's eyes glanced to each of the three mercenaries. "And pardon my assumption, but it appears you will allow us to travel with you and for that I am grateful. We promise not to be too much of a burden on you or your men during our journey."

A loud crash ripped through the night and they looked up to the shuffling mounts of the Byzernians. The mercenaries pointed and cursed at an overturned wagon, Glacar the most vocal of all. The bear of a man threw people around left and right for not moving quickly to rectify the situation. Jonrell snorted, "Well Wiqua, here is your chance to keep your promise."

"Yes, Commander. I must return to my people. Very few speak anything other than their native tongue." He bowed again before riding away.

"That bowing is going to get annoying," said Jonrell.

"Well be prepared to see a lot of him. That's uh, the one Hag latched onto," said Cassus.

"What?" said Krytien, gagging.

Jonrell decided against saying anything as he watched the commotion of slaves fumbling with righting the overturned wagon. He nodded at the two men. "Your responsibility, remember?"

The two men looked at each other and mumbled something as they rode. Jonrell shook his head. *One Above, what did I get myself into?*

* * *

For two weeks, the Hell Patrol struggled across broken terrain that hindered them at every move, and the coast still lay another week ahead. The journey should have taken ten days at most but with so many slaves and their families, they struggled each day just breaking camp, let alone traversing through the expansive plain and now into the rocky hills. Cassus had sworn to Jonrell that the slaves would not hinder his progress when they left Melchizan's army, but that is exactly what happened. *I should leave them behind. Each day here is one less in Cadonia and one I can't afford to lose.* Jonrell glanced back to Cassus who talked with Wiqua as they rode. *He knows I won't leave them behind now.*

Orange and red lines seeped across the horizon as the sun fell behind low lying clouds that lay over distant hills. Jonrell halted, and ran fingers through his long hair before scratching the stubble at his neck. His hand went to his breast pocket, feeling for the stone Krytien had given him.

Another day gone and yet I feel no closer.

Kroke came up beside him, spinning a knife in his hand, the eagle shaped hilt shimmering in the fading sunlight. He looked up, blade turning as he spoke. "I think those slaves are done for the day, Boss."

"It seems we're stopping earlier each day." He sighed. "Make camp and have Yanasi set up the watch."

Kroke shifted the knife from one hand to the other.

Jonrell looked over at him, his gray eyes weary. "Why don't you grab a dozen men to go hunting. I'm getting sick of salted beef."

Kroke nodded and rode off.

* * *

Night came quick and they finished camp by firelight.

Kroke had come across a small herd of wild buffalo, almost getting himself killed while taking one down with only a pair of throwing knives he had sunk into each of the charging beast's eye sockets. The men who accompanied Kroke told the tale to all who would listen, saying it was one of the most amazing things they'd ever seen.

Stupidity can often be confused for amazing.

Larger pieces of the massive beast roasted over spits while cooks sawed off smaller chunks to throw into soup pots. Soon after, Jonrell sat near one of the cook fires, spooning the rich stew from a trencher. Staring into the flames, his hand subconsciously reached for his breast pocket again.

"Good stew," said Krytien, sitting down beside him.

Jonrell blinked away the glaze from his eyes, scratching his chest with the hand he had reached with. He took another bite and nodded. "A perk of dragging this group around with us. I'm surprised Hag has stayed out of the Byzernian women's way. She can ruin a dish just by looking at it."

The mage chuckled and set a pair of cups down on the ground between them. "Oh, she's tried a few times but with only a half-hearted effort. Too anxious to do some cooking of her own under the sheets with that old-timer."

"Old-timer? Last I checked Wiqua wasn't much older than you."

"That's uncalled for. I may be old but I've got enough of my wits not to go messing around with her."

"I'll give you that." Jonrell looked down at the tin cups. He picked one up and held it to his nose, smelling the contents. "I hope it isn't your special brew?"

"Insults and now, accusations." The mage shook his head and clutched his faded cloak. "I am truly hurt."

"I'm waiting."

"Don't worry. It's some tea that Wiqua made. I know better than to give you anything with alcohol in it."

36

Jonrell inhaled the contents again before taking a sip. He nodded in satisfaction. "I like it. Thanks."

The two men grew silent, watching the flames dance around a roasting leg, crackling as fat dripped into them. Men sat in smaller groups around the various campfires, some playing dice, others checking their weapons. The smartest slept while time permitted.

"You need to talk to him, you know," said Krytien.

Jonrell inclined his head. "Talk to who?"

"Cassus. The man has been a wreck ever since you mentioned Cadonia."

Jonrell snorted. "And that's my fault? I've tried to approach him several times. I've known the man since we were boys. He'll talk to me when he's ready."

"He's scared. Mentioned something about his father," said Krytien.

"The man has fought in more battles than I can remember and he fears seeing disappointment in the face of a feeble old man?" Jonrell shook his head. "Cassus has to face his fears one day."

"And this return home doesn't bother you?"

Jonrell opened his mouth, but a shout from behind cut him off. "Commander!"

He stood up, seeing the young man running toward him. The youth was tall and lean with blond hair and blue eyes, face without even a day's worth of growth. The boy looked more like some dashing knight or fabled prince than a scout for a group of mercenaries. Still, Rygar's skills as a scout exceeded anything Jonrell had seen in years.

"Three hundred and twenty horses are camped just a couple leagues away. Melchizan is leading them."

"The fool survived?"

"Yes, sir. He's looking pretty beat up, right arm in a sling, but it's him alright."

"What about the rest? What shape are they in?"

"They've been pushed hard. Most of their horses are ready to drop and some of the soldiers aren't far behind. Still, they're well armed and from the looks of it pretty determined."

"Looking to take their failings out on us it would seem," said Jonrell.

"Well, we did skip out on them," said Krytien.

"Take half a dozen men. Find a place we can make our stand." Jonrell jerked his head back to his left. "Those hills we spotted earlier could be a likely spot. Start there and be quick about it." Then he turned to Krytien. "Pass the word to break camp. We leave in half an hour. No exceptions. You and Yanasi have rear guard. Tell Cassus to arm as many of those slaves as he can. Melchizan has more than four times our number so we'll need all the help we can get come tomorrow." The men nodded and set off to their tasks,

Rygar sprinting with all the vigor of youth and Krytien plodding along as fast as his frame would allow.

* * *

Jonrell overlooked a deep valley as the first light crept in from the eastern sky. The floor of the valley descended in a gradual slope, covered in rocks. From his vantage point, he could see the rocks rested in a dry riverbed, likely to flood again with the next hard rain. Other hills overlooked similar views but no other valley was quite so deep or filled with such hazardous terrain. From the floor, the landscape did not seem as treacherous with small outcroppings of vegetation covering holes and rocks half-hidden beneath the plant life. Such terrain would twist a leg at best, cripple or kill at worst.

Last night men, women, and children alike worked in the dusky gloom, first traversing the harsh valley, pushing and prodding animals and wagons. All got by with only minor injuries. The focus then turned to preparing for Melchizan. Jonrell assumed his former employer had no clue how close his outfit camped to them. *If he had, last night would have been the time for an attack while we were scrambling around in the dark, hindered by the Byzernians.* But Jonrell knew he could rely on Melchizan's lack of experience.

Sunlight crawled across the hilly land and spread into the valley just as the last of Jonrell's men moved into position. The sound of soft footsteps approached from behind, but Jonrell kept his gaze set on the western entrance to the basin. If all went well, Melchizan's outfit would enter there, riding into the sunlight. "Are we ready?" he asked.

"Yep," said Cassus.

Jonrell turned to face his friend. "I wasn't expecting to see you here."

"I thought it best to bring you the news."

Jonrell grunted as he caught friend's meaning. "They haven't changed their minds then?"

"No. Wiqua said that his people will not fight. They can help in other ways but it is against their beliefs to physically harm another."

"And they wonder why they were slaves," Jonrell muttered under his breath.

"I'm just the messenger. You do have to admire their resolve though."

"The One Above can have their resolve. I'd rather have fighters. Will their men still participate as decoys at least?"

"Yes."

Jonrell shook his head. "Hypocrites. I ought to leave them here for Melchizan. That would buy us enough time to get ahead of his company."

"Many in your position would," said Cassus. "But you won't."

The commander paused, breaking his stare with Cassus. "No. I won't. But that doesn't mean I haven't given it thought."

"Of course you gave it thought."

"What is that supposed to mean?"

"It means you always consider every scenario. But in the end, your decision tends to be the right one."

Jonrell considered his friend's words, thoughts drifting back to a time in their youth. "Twelve years ago, Cassus. Did I make the right decision then?"

Cassus frowned. "I...I don't know." He paused. "But I know you're making the right one now by going back home." He bit his lip. "I just hope that when the time comes, I make the right decision as well."

Jonrell opened his mouth, wanting to ask what he meant but couldn't find the words in time. An arrow struck the ground no more than two feet from him, shaft vibrating to and fro. Red fletching told him the arrow belonged to one of his men. He looked up and spotted the archer waving from a nearby hill. He waved back and the archer let fly two more arrows. One landed near a group of men stationed around wagons on the eastern side of the valley. The second struck near a group of archers stationed on Jonrell's hill, just below his position. In both cases men jumped, nearly falling over as the shaft struck within a hair's length of them. The archer waved again before ducking out of sight.

"Yanasi sure is getting bold, showing off like that."

Cassus grunted. "Bold as long as she has a bow in her hand, without it she's still as shy as ever and will barely meet your eyes."

"I wish I knew why."

"You can't be serious, Jonrell. As much as you notice everything else in this group, it seems you'd realize she wants your approval and can't stand to let you down. Why else do you think she is so obsessive about that bow? She wants to be the best—probably for your sake more than her own."

Jonrell shook his head. "She knows how I feel."

"I don't think she..." started Cassus.

"Melchizan's earlier than I thought he would be," cut in Jonrell. *Now isn't the time for this, Cassus.* "He isn't known as an early riser."

Cassus let it drop. "Well, you always found a way to get him up before. Why should that change now?"

At the base of the hill, men positioned behind wagons waited for the enemy to appear, staring into the dawn. The archers on the ridges stood in orderly ranks, waiting for the command to fire. Jonrell felt the tension rising from his men.

"C'mon, we need to get ready ourselves."

* * *

The sound of pounding hooves reached Jonrell's ears as Melchizan's men entered the mouth of the valley. The ground near the western entrance did little to reveal the treacherous slope that followed deeper after a small bend in the path. Jonrell suspected Melchizan would ignore the glaring sun and push on over the rough terrain, bent on reclaiming his slaves. Still, to encourage the poor decision from his former employer, Jonrell sent many of the Byzernians to fill in holes and clear away stone near the entrance of the gorge during the night before.

Byzernians moved about on the opposite side of the valley, acting as if caught unaware by the sight of Melchizan rounding the turn on the other end. Some of the former slaves even fled and Jonrell saw Melchizan shout back orders to his men, signaling a charge and spurring his horse forward.

Jonrell chuckled to himself as the plump man took the bait, nearly falling from his saddle at the sudden increase in speed. His men poured ahead of their would-be lord, impatient to wait for their leader to regain his seat. The wave of cavalry advanced, seeing what they wanted to see, easy prey fleeing on foot, a chance to seek retribution.

But no sooner did the charge seem to come together, than it fell apart. Camouflaged holes snapped horses' legs from the cavalry traps set the night before by Hell Patrol members while the Byzernians worked on clearing the valley entrance.

Jonrell stood up, waving both hands above his head, signaling men on another ridge. Krytien stood, lifting one palm to the sky and aiming the other at what remained of Melchizan's army. A flash of light shot from his outstretched hand, blinding man and beast alike. Then with a shout, the Hell Patrol loosed their arrows.

Those still saddled wheeled their mounts and those unhorsed still able to walk, fled on foot. Among the later group Melchizan hobbled along, using his sword to support himself. Jonrell allowed himself a smile as he watched the man raise a fist in anger at every rider who passed him.

Arrows continued to drop during the retreat as men perched on either side of the valley descended the slopes. A quick thrust from sword or knife silenced screams of agony from the dozens of riders. Man and beast alike had shattered their bones on the stone covered ground, nearly a third of those who entered the valley.

Raker was among those on the ground, grinning ear to ear. He looked up as Jonrell neared, his left cheek puffed out with a mouth full of chew. "Woo, we got'em good," he said, running another man through. "I can't wait to find Lord Roundness down here. Think I'll give him a stab whether he needs one or not for ol' time's sake." He laughed.

"Sorry but I saw him stumbling away with the others."

The mercenary's eyes widened as he let out a string of curses. "We gotta get after him then."

Jonrell just shook his head. "He's done. No sense in wasting more time. Those on horse that got away still outnumber us and we already know we can't rely on the Byzernians to fight. We need to get moving in case they decide to attack again once we're on open land."

Raker spat. "Ain't that more of a reason to go after'em?"

"No. Those who came into the valley looked pretty beat up from the battle we skipped out on, but we don't know if others still loyal to Melchizan survived the fight."

Slaves hurried about near the wagons, getting ready to move when the order came.

Raker shook his head in disgust and stabbed another groaning soldier in the gut, twisting the blade until the man heaved his last breath. The mercenary spat on the man's face when he was done.

"Is that really necessary?"

"Is what?"

Jonrell gestured toward the body.

"Oh that? That was personal. I remember this one calling me a cheater when we were playing cards once."

"Were you cheating?"

"Of course. But that don't give him the right to call me one," said Raker.

Jonrell shook his head.

"Commander! Commander, wait. Please," said Wiqua, sprinting across the valley with the grace of a man half his age. *However old that is.* Jonrell barely noticed the desperation in his voice, too busy watching the man negotiate the rough ground far better than he could.

"What is it Wiqua?"

"Commander, please. I beg you to stop these men from what they are doing." He held a look of horror as Raker slit a man's throat. "I can help those who have fallen as well as the horses."

"Why? Are you some kind of healer? We don't have time for that," said Jonrell agitated at the thought.

"Yes. Many of my people are. It is our way to heal, not harm. I promise you it will not take long."

Jonrell considered what he said for a moment. "Then work on the horses, but leave the men."

"But, Commander, these men…"

Jonrell cut in, his voice turning to ice in the warm morning air. "These men tried to kill you, your people, and mine. Before that, they treated you like scum. If we allow them to live, expect more of the same. Now, if you want to do something to feel better about yourself, heal the horses. We could use them."

Wiqua bowed his head, but the expression on his face said he was not pleased with the answer. "Very well. You have kept my people safe again and I am grateful. I will do as you command."

* * *

The Hell Patrol made camp a day and half's ride from Pontysor, the largest port on the continent, Mytarcis. The extra half day in distance pushed everyone far from the busy road to avoid undue attention. A mercenary group coupled with several hundred Byzernians would raise questions.

Digging trenches and setting up palisades with the midday sun high overhead, men and women worked in a silent rhythm. The silence did not last long.

"I'm too old for this, you know. Liable to catch a stroke or something," mumbled Hag in a raspy voice. The squat woman paused for a moment, waiting for acknowledgement. With no response, she spoke again, this time louder. "I said I'm liable to catch a stroke with all this work." The old woman threw a spade of dirt on Jonrell's leg, punctuating the remark.

The commander stopped and knocked the soil away, though he didn't know why. *I haven't seen a bath in weeks.* He met her eye. "Funny how you've got the energy for that *young* stud of yours, but when it comes to actually doing your job you start to gripe about being old." He motioned to Wiqua, a man young enough to be Hag's son, but old enough to be Jonrell's father. The Byzernian was busy sharpening stakes. "You don't hear him complaining."

"Yeah well, that's why I like him. He doesn't say much. If I wanted a bunch of useless conversation, I'd come looking for you."

"You ever thought he doesn't say much because he can't get a word in edgewise?" Jonrell looked to Wiqua and swore he saw the smallest of grins creep across his face.

The short woman threw another spade of dirt on Jonrell's leg. "Keep it up. I've never seen such ungratefulness after all I've done, taking care of them animals for all these years now."

"Aye, you know your way around a mule when the urge strikes you. Speaking of that, you've been growing lax on those duties as well."

"I'm doing nothing of the sort. Just doesn't make sense to waste my time on all the ones we picked up from Melchizan if we're going to turn around and sell them. I still mind your mount and the others I know that'll be coming with us."

"Good. Since you are up on your other duties, then you have plenty enough time to help here like everyone else."

The old woman just grunted and grumbled again, flicking one last spade of dirt before returning to her task. Jonrell knew digging a third trench was over-doing it, but he wasn't taking any chances as he expected Cassus back some time yesterday. *Besides, it always helps to keep a soldier busy.*

Upon arrival, he sent Cassus and a small group of men into the city. They were to secure passage across the ocean based on what Melchizan's goods fetched on the open market. Jonrell sent Krytien with the group for added protection, but he was also glad to have him out of his hair. The old mage had been acting strange since finding out Cadonia's king had died, and stranger still since the skirmish in the valley. Krytien had said that he had never seen anyone heal with greater ease or knowledge as Wiqua had.

Impressed over a bunch of horses. He shook his head.

Hag remained quiet far longer than Jonrell would have thought possible before she started back up again. This time she directed her wrath elsewhere, taking her aggression out on the Byzernian women who cooked. She didn't seem to care that most of them couldn't understand a word she said. It only enticed her further. Before long, she began flinging dirt into the path of women as they carried firewood for the cook fires. Eventually, even those peaceful women showed irritation and sent icy stares in Hag's direction.

She hasn't lost that magic touch. Jonrell grinned.

A shout from Yanasi, signaling that Cassus and the others were returning, put an end to the strife. *It's about time.* Jonrell jumped at the chance to send Hag to care for their animals and climbed out of the trench. He told Yanasi to have Cassus and Krytien join him in the command tent.

* * *

Glacar had been cursing under his breath for almost an hour. Kroke knew that was a record somewhere. He sure couldn't imagine spending that much time talking, especially repeating the same four or five words. After an hour of hearing Glacar go on and on, he reckoned it was about time he at least asked what bothered him.

Kroke threw his spade into the dirt and pulled out a dirk. He began picking at his nails, noticing a few specks of grime that had accumulated. "You gonna keep that up the whole day, Glacar?"

The wild man from Thurum turned around, sweat soaked his hair and beard. He spat, most of it dribbling down into the thick tangled mess on his chin. "What are you jawing about?"

"You ain't shut up since we moved to this part of camp. What's got you all worked up?"

"Not what. Who."

"Huh?"

"Jonrell's lost it, Kroke. Sticking our necks out for these brown devils ain't what the Hell Patrol's about. And yet, we've been dragging them around for weeks. On top of that we're going to buy them passage home. That's money that could be in our pocket."

"You ain't seemed to mind them Byzernians when they were Melchizan's. I believe you visited a few of their women pretty regularly?"

"Yeah, that's about all they're good for, too. But now, they act like they're suddenly too good for that."

"And there it is," said Kroke, clicking his tongue. "Since they ain't slaves any longer, they won't let you have your fun anymore."

Glacar spat. "Ain't no woman gonna tell me what I can or can't do. Especially not any of them brown-skinned dogs."

"But Jonrell did, didn't he?"

"You know he's always been too soft. That background of his and his high and mighty standards."

"Ain't nothing soft about showing some respect to women."

"That's funny coming from a killer like you."

Kroke shrugged. "Killing and raping ain't really the same thing."

Glacar laughed. "Sure they are. They both get your heart racing and when I'm done, I'm the only one who's happy."

Glacar went back to shoveling. Kroke sheathed the blade and followed suit. *And that's why you ain't the one leading us.*

* * *

Jonrell had just enough time to splash some cool water on his face and neck, washing off the day's grime, when the two men strolled into his tent, looking ragged. Jonrell took a sip of tea and gestured for them to have a seat. "I was beginning to grow worried."

"No doubt," said Krytien easing into a chair. "You've got a stronger camp here than I've seen in some time."

Jonrell shrugged. "Better safe than sorry. Was there any trouble? I expected you a day ago."

"Some, but nothing major. We scared off a few men looking to rob us as we left the city. Cassus thought it best to take a different route back. We covered our tracks in case they returned with more."

"Good. Do we have ships secured?"

"Two. One for us and one for the Byzernians. The ships are owned by the same man. The price is reasonable and best of all he'll organize the sale to pay for the ships after inspecting the goods we hauled with us."

Jonrell looked over at Cassus who had yet to sit down. "What kind of shape are the ships in?"

Krytien answered though Jonrell had directed the question at Cassus. "Although they're traders, both ships are strong and in fair enough shape." The old mage glanced nervously about. "Given that we may have to improvise in open water if pirates attack, we spoke with the captains as well. Both are well-seasoned men."

"Can we trust them?" asked Jonrell, as he watched Cassus pace the room.

The old mage gave a tense chuckle and fidgeted in his seat. "I learned a long time ago not to trust anyone, Jonrell. You know that."

Cassus's face held a far-away stare. The commander set his cup down. "Cassus, you haven't said a word. What's bugging you? Do we need to be wary about the captains?"

"The captains are fine." He looked up and cleared his throat after a long pause. "I've decided to go on with the Byzernians."

Jonrell felt like the chair was taken from under him. He looked to Krytien. "Is he serious?" Silence. Jonrell turned back to Cassus. "I don't believe this."

"They'll need help," said Cassus. "The ships we procured are going in opposite directions. You'll be heading north while the other is entering a southern port near one of their islands. They won't have any protection on their journey home."

"Protection? You're one man," said Jonrell.

"One is better than none."

"This is crazy. Do you have any idea how long it will take you to secure a ship from there back to Cadonia to meet up with us."

"I'm not going to Cadonia."

Jonrell's mouth hung open. *I've lost my mind. That's the only thing that could explain what I'm hearing. I've gone mad.*

Cassus cut in. "Look, I know this is a surprise."

"A surprise?! I'd call it more of a slap in the face. We're going home. I need you with me."

Cassus laughed, shaking his head. "You've never needed me. I was the one who needed you. And you made sure to look out for me. Now I have the chance to do the same thing for these people as well as others."

"What do you mean others?"

"There are slaves all over Mytarcis, most are from the Byzernia Islands. I want to stay and help them."

Jonrell looked up and mumbled to himself. "One Above, what have I done to deserve this?" He snorted. "Cassus, Hero of Slaves. What about your parents?"

"What about them? Don't pretend that they ever cared for me. I doubt they even remember they had a son."

"I can command you to stay," said Jonrell, trying a different approach.

"Not if I quit."

"I can command to have you restrained and loaded on the ship to Cadonia."

Cassus smiled and stepped forward, placing a hand on Jonrell's shoulder. "You can. But you won't."

Jonrell felt the fight leave him. He knew his friend well enough to know there was no changing his mind this time.

CHAPTER 4

Tobin stared across the bleak landscape atop the highest ridge in the hills rimming the settlement. His back was to Munai, the village's name discovered by Kaz's cruel questioning of the prisoners. Even in daylight, the terrain varied little, mostly orange rock, dirt, and sand with the occasional patches of sparse vegetation. Having memorized the land around him, he reflected on the events surrounding the last few days.

Two days after Munai's capture, another eight hundred Kifzo had landed by boat along the weathered coast, adding their number to the surviving warriors occupying the settlement. The reinforcements reported that Tobin's father, Bazraki, was in position to move against Nubinya once the city's forces were drawn away.

With that in mind, Kaz allowed several of the prisoners to flee under the guise that within a week an even larger group of warriors would land at Munai. Kaz led them to believe that the warriors in Munai would then launch an assault against Nubinya. The orchestrated escape forced villagers to pass through every small settlement the Kifzo previously destroyed. Coupled with the destruction those people witnessed firsthand, their tales of horror would force the Orange Desert Clan's warchiefs into swift action, hoping to retake Munai before the Blue Island Clan's army swelled in number.

After weakening Nubinya's defenses, Bazraki and his main army intended to pounce on the desert capital, bringing it under his rule.

Then it will be up to us to defeat whatever armies are sent against us, regardless of the odds. If all went as planned, the surviving Kifzo would then move south and join Bazraki.

Tobin sighed as he scanned the horizon, checking for anything unusual. His eyes moved first to landmarks he had previously scouted as the most probable areas of advance. His vision shifted to the rest of the landscape, making sure he didn't overlook even the least ideal approaches. Satisfied, he removed the large camel skin he used to protect himself against the sun and stood, stretching his legs and shaking the stiffness from his limbs. He removed the top from his water skin and drank deeply.

Weeks had passed since first arriving in the Burnt Sands desert, and still he was not completely acclimated to the high temperatures and scorching heat of the day. The climate was much different than what he was used to in the Blue Islands. At home, a tropical thickness to the air hampered one's breathing, but at least the frequent rains relieved that discomfort. Here the dry warmth could deceive you, slowly sucking the moisture from your skin as it surfaced. Breathing was never a problem, but if not careful, the heat could weaken even the healthiest of men, causing fits of dizziness.

He replaced the top after another long pull from his skin, ready to return to his miserable position. His ears pricked. Footsteps sounded from behind in the loose gravel and sand that lined the hill's side. His hands dropped to the throwing axes at his waist, but then relaxed as he saw the source of the careless footfalls. A tall man made his way up the steep incline. The man reached out with spindly hands sticking out of tattered sleeves. He clutched at protruding rocks as he pulled himself upward. The man looked up with calm eyes and a friendly smile.

"I didn't expect to see you," said Tobin, unaccustomed to the friendly expression.

The shaman took a few more steps and stopped near Tobin. "Your brother gave me leave to move about and Walor pointed me in your direction," said Nachun, breathing deep. He unslung a water skin of his own and took a drink.

"I'm surprised Kaz allowed someone he's unfamiliar with to roam about without restraint."

"I think he's satisfied with my story. But in the end, it was your fellow warriors who fought near the oasis that tipped the scales in my favor." He paused for a moment. "I came to thank you for stepping in that night and encouraging them to speak up. Kindness is something I have seen very little of as of late."

Tobin was taken aback by such candidness. "You've no need to thank me; without your aid I'd be dead."

"I helped you and in return you helped me. It is as it should be," said the shaman with a soft smile.

"Perhaps, but I should warn you about saying such things amongst the others. They are not as..." Tobin shuffled his stance while trying to find the right word, "*understanding*."

"I gathered as much when talking to your brother. However, I thought you might be different than the others," he added, more of a question than statement.

Tobin shrugged. "You're free to speak as you wish. In fact, I'm curious to hear this story you told Kaz."

"And your duty?" said Nachun, shading his eyes with a free hand and scanning the empty horizon.

"Even if Nubinya were to send forces immediately, it would be another two days at the earliest before they would reach us." Tobin gestured to a boulder a few paces down and to the right. With the time of day, it provided a ring of shade from the afternoon sun. "I can spare a few moments."

The two men settled down with their backs against the cool rock face. Nachun unwrapped a small bundle he had hidden beneath his clothing, revealing some fresh dates and dried fish.

"I thought you might be hungry," said the shaman, laying the food between them.

Tobin snatched up a date, not realizing how hungry he had grown. He took a bite and wiped away the juices dribbling down his chin with the back of his hand, grunting in appreciation. "So, tell me how you came to the Burnt Sands? You're not native to these lands."

"Is it that obvious?" Nachun asked, taking a more conscientious bite from a piece of fish.

Tobin nodded. "Very. Your accent is different. And your clothes don't match those of the Desert Clan."

The shaman smiled again. "You are quite observant. And as clever as your brother. He made the same points." He sat thoughtfully for a moment; his cheerful expression fading, and when he spoke again his voice took on a more somber tone. "I was born amongst the Red Mountain Clan."

"The Red Mountains?" Tobin asked, coughing on a date.

Nachun sighed, his shoulders sagging as if under the weight of a great burden. "Yes. Until a year ago, my family lived in Guaronope. A man named Charu became warchief of a powerful tribe within our clan. His power grew very quickly even though he was younger than the other warchiefs that sat upon our council. My family was part of another large, well respected tribe and my father was our warchief. He became outspoken against Charu as he felt the sudden rise was unwarranted, and the ideas he championed not consistent with our people's past. In response, Charu began manipulating the tribes in his favor, turning them against my father in an effort to oust him from the council. My father confronted Charu hoping to come to some agreement that would end their quarrel, but Charu said he would only make peace with our tribe if given my sister's hand in marriage." Nachun paused, taking a swig of water from his skin.

"My father was outraged as my sister was already betrothed to another tribe's son, a weaker tribe according to Charu. When my father refused to nullify her engagement, Charu rallied the warchiefs in his favor and denounced our family as a lesser tribe, taking away our seat from the council. But that wasn't enough for Charu." Nachun's mouth twisted into a frown, then a scowl, unable to hide his contempt for the man.

"He murdered the man my sister was betrothed to and took her as his own, defiling her. My father held back his anger and instead pleaded with the council for retribution but they did nothing. With all others against us, we could not risk retaliation for the odds were too great. So my father did what he felt was best and our tribe left the Red Mountains, the only home we ever knew. But before leaving, we stole my sister from under Charu's nose." Nachun grew quiet, shoveling several bites of fish into his mouth.

"Then why come to the Burnt Sands? Was there no other place between here and the Red Mountains for your family to settle?" asked Tobin.

Nachun chuckled and held up his hands. He gestured at the dusty and withered landscape. "Is this not an ideal place to live?" He laughed. "No. This was not our first choice. We could have become nomadic like many of the small tribes; however, that was never an option after we took my sister. Charu would not forget such a thing nor would he ever let us live in peace. So, we sought to align ourselves with one of the other large clans, to try to gain their protection." Nachun paused again, biting into a date. The faraway look in his eyes told Tobin the shaman was reliving those memories, searching for the right words to describe them.

"We journeyed to the capital city of every major clan's territory. Southeast to Erundis of the White Tundra Clan. Northwest to Feruse of the Dark Forest Clan. East to Cypronya of the Gray Marsh Clan. Then north to Actur of the Yellow Plain Clan. And finally as far north as one could go on this side of the Great Divide. To Nubinya of the Orange Desert Clan. None would take us," said Nachun. A light chuckle touched his voice but Tobin heard little humor. "We were actually on our way west again, to your home of Juanoq. Our last hope was that the Blue Island Clan would have us. Funny, how you came here instead."

"And the rest of your tribe and family?" asked Tobin, though he had already guessed the answer.

"Dead," said Nachun in an icy tone that cut through the bitter heat of the afternoon. "On the run, we were harassed continually by those seeking to gain Charu's favor. Some were of the Red Mountain Clan but many were smaller nomadic tribes. We lost many traveling across Hesh…" Nachun's voice trailed off, face filling with despair. "And then, word of Charu's vendetta must have finally overtaken us for we were denied entrance into Nubinya upon our arrival. But a day later, our clan was approached by a group of riders under a sign of peace. We were led to believe that their warchiefs had a sudden change of mind, though it was all an act of deception. They brought half a dozen shamans with them, recognizing me for what I am. I was taken off guard and thrown from my horse. Knocked unconscious, they assumed I was dead. Regardless, I could not help as they slaughtered my entire tribe. That was two weeks ago."

"The shaman you killed here was one of those who attacked your clan, wasn't he?" asked Tobin.

"Yes. I must admit that my reason for helping the other night was not entirely selfless. I was hesitant about interfering, being so weary from my time alone in this cursed land and with very little sustenance of late. But when I saw the shaman, my decision was made. I wanted him dead. As I said that night to you, your enemy is mine." He met Tobin's eye for the first time since beginning his tale. "And that is my story."

There was a long pause as Tobin contemplated what he had heard. "What will you do now?"

"Your brother has granted me the opportunity to fight with your warriors here, and afterward will allow me to travel with you to Nubinya. From there, he said I must speak with your father who'll have the final say on the matter."

"On what matter?"

"To join your clan. I know I am only one man, but I can prove myself very useful. Besides, I am the last survivor of my tribe and my family. My father would have wanted me to continue on, and here is where I have the best chance to do so."

"So is this something you want only out of memory of your father?"

Nachun shook his head. "No. That is only a small part of why I want to speak with Bazraki." His jaw clenched. "There is a larger part, one my father would disapprove of. I want to seek retribution for those wrongs done against us."

"And how do you plan on accomplishing that as a member of our clan?"

Nachun chuckled. "Ha. Don't think me as naïve. I've seen enough here to know that this attack against the Orange Desert Clan is not the result of some small conflict. No, this is a group of warriors bent on conquest and that means Nubinya is only the beginning. I'd be surprised if your father has not thought about conquering all of Hesh." He paused looking to gauge Tobin's reaction, but the Kifzo did his best to reveal nothing. "It's an ambitious goal but one that, in time, will match my own. So, I seek to help him now, knowing that eventually he must face Charu. And then I shall be ready."

The two men sat there in silence for several minutes as they finished their meal. Tobin was thinking in particular about who this man next to him really was.

A complicated one for sure. In only a few moments, Nachun had revealed himself in many ways to the Kifzo. *Powerful to survive an attack from six shamans. Caring and loyal to follow his father's wishes. Hateful against those who wronged him. Observant to pick up on Father's goals. Intelligent to manipulate Kaz at some level. A complicated man indeed. And dangerous.*

"Does my story trouble you? Your reaction is much different than your brother's."

Tobin shrugged his shoulders and grunted. "You'll find that Kaz and I have little in common outside of appearances."

"I apologize for the comment," said Nachun bowing his head.

Tobin waved him off. "Keep your apologies; you're not the first to make such an assumption." He paused. "Your story isn't what I've been thinking on. It's your reason for wanting to join our clan. You said your goals and my father's are similar, and I wonder where that similarity ends," said Tobin cocking his head.

"Ah. I think I understand. You are wondering what my stance is on raping and killing women and children. What would I do if I found myself facing that massive man as you had the other night? Durahn was it? Don't look surprised. I'm sure you realize most of the others talk about you behind your back," said Nachun. "Well, I can only say that I am not one to participate in such things. But I also understand that I have to choose my battles as you did then."

Tobin felt his anger rising as he remembered the look on Durahn's face and recalled his solution. "Some battle. Killing a defenseless child."

"Call it what you will but you gave her mercy where she would have not found any. There is something that can be said for that. I guess what I am saying is that if choosing sides on such an issue; I would sooner take yours than theirs."

"Thanks," said Tobin, extending his hand to the shaman.

"For what," said Nachun reaching out, confused.

"For your honesty. That is something *I* have seen very little of."

Nachun smiled. "Think nothing of it." Nachun released his grip and rose to his feet. "I won't keep you any longer from your post, and I promised your brother to help where I could. I'll speak to you later, my friend." Nachun headed down the hill, stepping carefully as he traversed the uneven terrain. At the bottom, he turned back and raised a hand in parting before making his way back to Munai.

Tobin sat and watched the shaman for several minutes, finishing the remaining fish and dates. He returned to his spot, hidden away from prying eyes in a jagged crevasse of rock. He repositioned the camel skin overhead to extend the shade underneath. He scanned the landscape, once again checking for any changes. Only after satisfying himself that all was well did he give his conversation with Nachun any more thought. He mulled over the last words the shaman had uttered.

Hmm...my friend?

* * *

An hour past dawn, the sun leaked across the horizon, illuminating a scorched landscape where thick cacti protruded from the ground as fingers would from a hand. There Tobin spotted movement. He was not surprised. The natural makeup of the terrain made it an ideal place for scouting. Rock and bones provided further protection from watchful eyes as they enveloped the cacti. In the dead air, the slightest bit of kicked up dust grabbed his attention. Then all became still. But it was too late, for the scouts' carelessness allowed a brief flash of orange and black, revealing the colors of the Desert Clan warriors in hiding.

Like all major clans, armor and even weapons were dyed to match the colors of their homeland. The Burnt Sands Desert had gotten its name long ago from the black rock, dark as charcoal, scattered across its surface. In combination with the clay and sand, colored with various hues of orange, mixed with hints of yellow and red, the desert itself looked as if engulfed in flames. Such visuals only reminded Tobin of the blistering heat. Despite the early hour, sweat rolled from his brow.

Tobin slithered out of position, hugging the ground like a rattlesnake. He worked his way across the twisting, serrated terrain where he situated himself behind the cacti on the opposite side of a small mound. He removed a dagger from his belt and placed the blue blade between his teeth. With calculated movements, he removed an arrow from his quiver and notched it across his bow, mindful to avoid the scraping of wood.

He peered around a small rock formation. Two lithe scouts lay face down, peering at the hillcrest Tobin watched from earlier. Their armor, mostly boiled leather, was dyed dark orange and beset with elaborate black patterns, signifying things like rank and family. Thin black cloth wrapped their heads. Each carried a scimitar across their back, the preferred weapon of the desert tribes, while short bows lay on the ground next to them. The two men communicated with hand signals.

Arguing? They recognize the rock formation as a likely vantage point, but see and hear nothing so are unsure how to proceed.

With the scouts' attention directed elsewhere Tobin rose to his feet, drew his bow in one fluid motion, and fired a quick shot on the run. Tobin covered half the distance to the two scouts as the arrow pierced the back of his target's neck. The other man turned toward Tobin at the sound of arrow hitting flesh, his hand moving for the sword at his back. He reacted too slowly. Tobin snatched the dagger from his mouth, and hurled the blade toward the second scout. The knife caught the scout in his shoulder, causing the arm he reached with to go limp. The man's eyes widened as his free hand frantically reached for the dagger jutting from his shoulder. Tobin's knee pinned the scout's arm across the man's chest. To his credit, the man continued to struggle. A second dagger flashed into Tobin's hand. The touch of its edge against the scout's throat caused the man to release a small gasp.

The scout opened his mouth to speak when Tobin cut him off. "You will say nothing unless you are answering my questions. Is that understood?"

"Yes."

Tobin growled in a low voice. "Are you the only two scouts?"

"Yes." The man stuttered, "Please don't kill me, I'll…"

Tobin used his free hand to twist the blade in the man's shoulder, stopping just before the man let out a cry. "Silence. What I do with you will depend on your cooperation. You do anything other than answer my questions and I promise, you'll suffer. How far away are the others?"

"Over an hour, maybe two," said the man with a slight whimper.

"How many?"

"Three thousand riders."

"None on foot?"

"No."

The news came at a surprise, but Tobin did not let it show as he continued. "Shamans?"

"Uh…"

Tobin pressed the blade harder into the warrior's throat, slicing through the thin black cloth and exposing the scout's dark skin. "How many shamans?"

"Ten."

Tobin's gut wrenched. "Ten? Why so many?"

"The warchiefs wanted to ensure a swift victory."

"What direction are the riders coming from?"

"North."

"Why not use the trail along the coast?"

"The north is a harder journey but shorter."

"You said that all were riders, where is your horse and his?" said Tobin gesturing toward the dead warrior.

"About one hundred yards east of here, behind a group of boulders at the bottom of two small hills."

Tobin paused. *This seems too easy. Can he be that scared or is he trying to deceive me?* "What are you not telling me?" he asked.

The scout's eyes flickered down to the blade at his throat and managed a swallow between gasping breaths. "That's it. I promise. I've answered all your questions truthfully."

Tobin nodded. "I believe you," he said with a comforting calmness to his voice.

The scout relaxed. "Thank…" Words of gratitude turned into a gag as Tobin's blade slid across the man's throat, soaking the black cloth around it.

Tobin wiped his knives clean and sheathed them. Gathering his bow, he edged to the east. He had no way of knowing whether another scout would be waiting at the next turn.

A hundred yards later, he found two lean horses tied to a cactus, their heads down, nipping on the sparse vegetation. He shook his head in disbelief. *He actually told me the truth…so far anyway.* The muscular animals were hard and beautiful. Their black coats reflected the glare of the sun above. *A far cry from the workhorses in Munai. These are specifically bred for battle.*

He moved to take the two animals when a disturbance coming from the other side of a large hill, some fifty yards away, pricked his ears. The thunderous beating of hooves faded as he listened, replaced by shouting voices. He sat crouched behind a boulder for several minutes waiting for something to come into his line of sight, but nothing happened.

He muttered a curse. He would have to work his way over to that hill and see what was on the other side. The barren land between the two points lacked cover. He'd have to chance a sprint—something he dreaded with his ankle.

No use in thinking about it.

He leaped to his feet and raced across the clearing, hasty in ascending the next hill. He stumbled but once, a third of the way up as his ankle buckled. Recovering quickly, he paid little attention to the noise he created while cresting the hill, confident the commotion near him would drown out any extra sound he made.

He inched along on his stomach, working toward the ridge above, arm over arm, dagger in hand. Stealing a look over the rise's peak, a set of dark eyes encircled in black cloth met his at the same moment, widening, as a howl started from the man's mouth. Tobin's hand snapped forward like a viper. His dagger stabbed into one of the desert warrior's eyes. Pushing hard, until the blade struck bone and jarred his hand to a stop.

The cry, although brief, alerted three others nearby. Each pulled a large scimitar from leather scabbards, dyed orange and striped black. They took up the howl started by the other man as they closed in on Tobin.

They swung their swords down in unison. Tobin half-rolled, half-stumbled to his feet, narrowly avoiding their reach as he unsheathed his short sword. They gave him little time to slide the blade free and he narrowly avoided the flashes of whirling steel around him.

Tobin kicked sand into the face of the man to his right. He continued to move that way and dodged dual strokes attacking from the other two. Loose gravel fell away beneath him. He gasped and tumbled down the hill.

He stood just as the first warrior reached him and Tobin's sword swept out to deflect a slash meant to disembowel him. Tobin stepped back as the other warriors joined the first in forming a circle around him. Their eyes glinted with violence.

In the space between the warriors' attacks, Tobin noticed the furious clamor rising in volume behind the hill.

I need to get to the horses. Tobin sheathed his sword and in its place withdrew his throwing axes, weapons he felt more comfortable with. He rushed the nearest clansmen.

The man let out a yell and raised his scimitar overhead, gripped in both hands. Tobin deflected the man's swing with one axe, stepping into his opponent's exposed side and drove his second weapon into the warrior's skull.

Without pause, Tobin spun and let fly his second axe as the other two warriors charged him. The man deflected the throw with a flick of his sword but unknowingly diverted its path into the trailing warrior's. Embedding itself in the trailing warrior's leg, he crashed face first into the ground. The warrior's scimitar came loose and tangled itself in the feet of the warrior in front. *I couldn't have planned that better if I tried.*

After two quick stabs Tobin hurried away in the direction of the two horses. He ran no more than twenty yards before a wall of orange and black cut off his path. With weapons drawn, several dozen riders approached. Tobin spun around and saw another group coming in from the rear. He instead ran to a small opposing hill where the riders had yet to form. He drew his short sword. He eyed the riders' short bows nervously, eyes darting. Gaining higher ground remained his only option.

One rider separated himself from the others and advanced. The man's dress stood out from the others. More ornate, pieces of fire opal, orange coral, onyx, and obsidian decorated into his armor and scabbard. *A warchief.* "You are alone and far enough away from Munai that no one will come to your aid, warrior."

Tobin said nothing, standing ready in a crouched position. *If I die, I'm taking this one with me.*

Frustrated by the Kifzo's silence, the warchief continued with an edge to his voice. "You must be aware your situation is hopeless." He paused, removing the covering from his face and revealing a beard, formed into a thin line against a hard face. The man removed a water skin from his side and took a drink. He held the skin out to Tobin. "You must be thirsty after such tiring work," he said, trying a different approach as he gestured toward the dead bodies. "You are a talented man. With such skill, you could rise high in Nubinya if you are willing to help us."

Tobin spat, tightening his grip on his sword, turning the blade over in his hand so it caught the sun's rays. "You would kill me the second you got what you wanted from me." He chuckled. "Many in my clan would take a blade to my heart if they could, but at least they would do so while looking me in the eye. You would wait until my back was turned."

The war chief sighed, and moved the water skin back to the place on his saddle. He covered his face again and shook his head. "The choice was yours." He gestured two men forward, one without any visible weapons, bones rattling with each step. *A shaman.* "Make him talk."

The shaman extended a hand and Tobin felt just as he did at the oasis in Munai, body weak and limbs heavy as if the weight of a mountain rested on his shoulders. He struggled to stay upright, but his efforts were in vain. The other man held a rope tight in his hands. Tobin's heart raced. A quick death in battle was one thing but if captured, there would be torture first.

And no one will come for me. Even to Father, I am nothing.

Panicked, Tobin attempted to raise his sword in a defensive position but his body ignored the command. His head slumped on his wide shoulders, unable to even lift his gaze past a few feet in front of him, just far enough to see black leather boots come into view. A hand grabbed his arm. Silent curses screamed in his mind, incapable of voicing his anger.

The sun was bright that morning but not so bright to cause the sudden white glare. At first Tobin thought the effect came from the sorcery working against him, but a chorus of yells erupting from the clansmen around him told him there was something more. With head hung low, Tobin blinked away the cloudiness and saw a man collapse in front of him, clutching at his eyes. The rope fell at the man's feet. Tobin realized that a hand no longer held his arm, and life returned to his deadened limbs. He lunged with his short sword, stabbing the clansmen lying before him through the side. He started for the shaman, but a familiar shout above the confusion halted him.

He spun and saw Nachun astride a black horse, another at his side. Slung on the empty saddle rested the bow and quiver he had left behind.

Tobin covered the distance in haste, flinging himself atop the empty mount. Reaching for his bow, he pulled free an arrow.

"What are you doing? We're running out of time." asked Nachun.

"Then go," said Tobin as he drew back the bow. Nachun stayed at his side. Taking aim, Tobin fired and watched the arrow sail across the disorder of horse and human, piercing the neck of the Warchief, toppling him from his mount.

He kicked the horse forward and Nachun followed close behind. Without a word, they raced across the unforgiving desert as fast as the animals and land would allow before reaching the rim of hills that circled Munai.

Approaching the ridge, Tobin unsheathed his sword once again and holding it aloft, let out a warning to any of Walor's scouts patrolling the area. They descended the last rise. A horn blew somewhere close by, signaling the others of their arrival. *Good.*

Tobin pulled up on his reins.

"What are you stopping for? We must tell your brother!" said Nachun panting, forehead covered in a sheen of sweat.

"No," said Tobin, turning in the saddle. "You go. We stick to the plan. I need to help Walor recall his scouts and organize our archers. Tell Kaz that I questioned one of their scouts. If we believe what he said, they come with three thousand men on horseback and ten shamans."

"So many?" said Nachun surprised. "Then those we saw were not their full strength."

"No, I suspect they were sent ahead to prepare for the main force."

"How much time then?"

"Maybe an hour. Probably sooner."

"Is that all?"

"No. What can we do about the shamans? We were not expecting so many and all of ours are with my father's army."

"I was only in Nubinya for a short period, but I picked up quickly that their offensive skills are effective but limited. Their defense is almost nonexistent. They can deflect an arrow like that shaman near the oasis did with your ax. But he was ready, and I doubt that under a more stressful situation these shamans would be as effective, especially while trying to attack. Expect them to be heavily guarded, shielded perhaps, and stationed in the middle of their columns for added protection. Their armor may be thicker too, but they still have the same weaknesses as any other warrior."

Tobin nodded. "I will spread the word. Make sure you tell Kaz as well. And also tell him where the two scouts we passed are located. It may be of use." Nachun gave him a nod farewell and kicked his horse into a gallop as he headed toward the village.

I didn't tell him thank you. That's twice he's saved my life.

Tobin hoped that when this was all done, he'd be able to rectify the situation and show his gratitude. But he knew nothing was guaranteed. Odd, but the recent events had brightened his mood; in fact he found himself smiling as he turned his horse toward a small camp of Walor's scouts and a group of archers. His smile would be unsettling to most but to him it made sense. The Orange Desert Clan warriors they would face were not women and children, not helpless victims of war. Nor were these fishermen caught unaware as they rested in their beds. No, these were warriors—men he had been trained his entire life to fight. And it felt good knowing the men he would kill today would not add to his haunting dreams.

* * *

Plans changed once Kaz received the news from Nachun. The old plan called for Tobin's group to harass the enemy with a company of longbows, firing when the Desert Clan came within range. Once engaged and distracted with falling arrows, the remaining Kifzo would move in on foot, relying on the Kifzo's skill to overcome any disadvantage in numbers. The tactic was a familiar one, but given the additional shamans and mounted soldiers, Kaz opted for a more deceptive approach—one that required a great deal of work with little time to accomplish it.

As luck would have it, Tobin's earlier encounter with their foe and Nachun's sorcery must have given the Desert Clan something more to consider. Overly cautious, almost two hours passed before their riders were spotted, giving them enough time to accomplish Kaz's plan.

The Desert Clan riders descended the rimmed slope of hills in the distance, pausing at their base to form battle lines. Tobin watched the scene alone, situated once again on the hill across from the village's animal pens.

In the daylight, the mound of scalding sand looked no different than any other he had grown intimate with these last few days. Yet, the broken gravel and jagged black rock that covered its surface seemed a starker contrast under the watchful eye of the sun.

Even from far away, there seemed to be a sense of hesitancy about the desert warriors' movements. With weapons drawn, they stared out across the empty land that separated them from Munai. *They expected us to meet them head on.*

Then, without warning, the riders set off at a gallop, racing across the open land as would the sound of thunder travel across an empty sky. Rising battle cries filled Tobin's ears. Dispersed throughout the mass of some three thousand riders, ten shamans became visible, each surrounded by men with large wooden shields. *Just as Nachun said.*

The riders reached the village at full charge. The first line of warriors passed through the far side of the settlement unopposed. Coming to a halt, they turned, twisting to and fro in their saddle, scanning the land around them. They anticipated the Kifzo to use the cluster of huts as cover but to the naked eye Munai appeared deserted. Weaving around these huts while circling the village's exterior, confused riders searched within the disordered mass of bodies. Shouts of frustration tickled Tobin's ears.

With skill, two Kifzo worked their way into the fold atop stolen black horses. If Tobin hadn't known where Ral and Ufer were coming from, or what to look for, even he would have missed them attired in confiscated garb taken from the two scouts Tobin had killed. Kaz personally selected them to infiltrate the Orange Desert Clan forces based on their ability to blend in. Their unique skills had been key during Bazraki's rise as leader of the Blue Island Clan some years ago.

Tobin peered down on the scene and spotted what looked to be the lead Orange Clan warchief, assailed with questions from his men. At his command, half a dozen riders broke out from the group and galloped off toward the coast between hills narrowing from either side. They rounded a bend and disappeared only to return a short time later while standing in their saddles and pointing off toward the coast. Sword aloft, the warchief barked an order and without reforming lines, the riders began spurring their mounts forward in clumps.

This may work.

Tobin drew his bowstring back. His eyes flickered about, patient, waiting for the two Kifzo below to make their move. *There.*

Tobin had to give the shield bearers protecting the shamans credit. Despite the tangled mess below, their guards never faltered. In the group closest to Tobin, an opening appeared as the shield and rider fell to the ground. Ral slipped quickly away from the group as Tobin released his shot and hit a shaman just under the left armpit. The shaman folded over his mount.

A similar opening appeared soon after and this time Tobin struck his target through the neck. Those around the shaman shouted out at the dead man wavering in the saddle.

Tobin smiled—two arrows and two shamans. The commotion that resulted worked further against the desert riders as they sought an enemy they could not find.

Tobin chanced another shot. The arrow zipped through a small crevasse. A shaman wailed, an arrow protruding from his back. Warriors looked in Tobin's direction, assessing the trajectory of his shots. He was in no situation to confront anyone, so he set off, unwilling to engage the Orange Desert Clan alone.

* * *

Skirting the valley below, Tobin traversed the desolate mounds of sand that led to the coast. Following the contours of those bleak hills, the uneven land provided a dangerous ground for the frantic pace he maintained. As he weaved along, he did his best to leave false trails where possible, hoping to distract anyone who might follow. He stole the occasional glance down to the valley floor, peering through a cloud of dust kicked up by another group of riders.

So focused on what lay behind him and to the sides, he became careless to what was in front, nearly falling victim to an arrow from his own clan. Walor spotted him with longbow drawn. Tobin came to a tense halt. Walor shifted his neck to the side with a loud crack and a smile crawled across his face. He swung his bow down and fired it toward the next group of riders. Tobin relaxed and grinned back.

Fifty other archers joined Walor, raining flight after flight of arrows down on each group of desert warriors that made their way up the dusty trail. An equal number of archers fired on the hill just opposite them, where the valley was at its most narrow. With the desert riders coming in range in such small groups, the land below changed from a drab orange to a bright red, stained with the blood of those who would never reach the shore.

"Looks like its working. Not sure what's going on along the beach though. How long before the last of them make it to us?" asked Walor as he pulled another arrow loose from his quiver.

"Soon. I'd guess another six or seven hundred left." said Tobin.

"Shamans?"

"I think four made it down in the first wave. I shot three. So, that leaves another three left unless Ral and Ufer got anymore."

"Three by yourself? Ral and Ufer will have to get at least one a piece or they'll never forgive you for taking all the fun."

Tobin shrugged. "They gave me a shot on two of them. They can have credit for those. It makes no difference to me." He glanced over and noticed many of the other Kifzo were near the end of their quivers. Tobin grabbed three out of his own before passing the rest down to Walor. "Here. Take what you need and pass these along. We've only got enough for a few volleys." Walor grabbed two arrows for himself, setting each of their blue dyed tips down point first in the loose sand at his feet before tossing the quiver down to the next warrior.

Tobin heard the advance of beating hooves long before he saw the swarm of desert warriors round the bend. Animal and warrior had reorganized, forming a solid sheet of shadow that cascaded down the weathered trail, leaving behind a whirlwind of austere powder in their wake. "No word from the beach, you said?" asked Tobin.

"None," said Walor in a grim tone.

Tobin grunted in response. Walor gave a nod as if reading his thoughts.

The Kifzo drew back bowstrings as the desert warriors howled over even the thunderous hooves of their mounts. Riders crossed an imaginary line in the ground and a hail of arrows filled Tobin's intervening space. Bodies tumbled from their saddles, falling left and right, blue shafts piercing orange and black armor. Two successive flights followed the first.

I'm out.

Tobin dropped his bow and with quivers empty, other Kifzo did the same. The Kifzo shouted war cries down to the riders who now broke off and climbed the smaller hills in an attempt to reach their position. Shamans unleashed three quick bursts of sorcery, hitting the slopes in a blast of heat. The Kifzo scattered to avoid becoming easy targets. Out of habit, Tobin reached for his throwing axes but his belt loops were empty. Cursing, he remembered where he had left them and with a sigh pulled free his sword instead.

Within moments, ringing steel, blood curdling screams, and sliding rock joined the cacophony of sounds. Another flash of sorcery struck the hillside less than twenty feet from where Tobin stood, killing a half dozen men—Kifzo and desert warriors alike. The concussive jolt knocked him from his feet and in his fall, he bruised his head on half-buried rock. He rolled to his knees amidst blurred vision. *Outnumbered, without mounts, and unable to match their sorcery. Curse you Father, for not allowing us the support of even a handful of shaman.* He lifted his clouded gaze and his heart sank. Warriors galloped down from the beachfront, wheeling their weapons in the air. *Dying in battle. Perhaps Father will find some pride in me for that.*

But as his eyes came into focus, Tobin saw that these warriors were not of the Desert Clan. Their armor shone dull blue and murky gray, rather than the orange and black now swarming the hills like ants on an overturned mound. A flash of sorcery reached that approaching group of Kifzo only to dissipate before impact. Tobin grinned. Though he could not see his face among the throng of Kifzo, he knew that Nachun had survived.

Desert riders who had yet to scale the heaps of sand before them, wheeled in an attempt to reform lines to face the oncoming charge. Their efforts were frantic and futile as the Kifzo smashed into them in a blood-frenzied rage.

Still on one knee, a war cry drew his attention away from the excitement and Tobin half-rolled, half-dove in time to avoid an arrow flitting across the air toward him. The rider threw down the short bow he held, and replaced it with a scimitar, as he galloped toward Tobin, high in the saddle.

Overconfident fool.

Crouching, he unsheathed the dagger at his thigh. He flipped the dagger over, catching the blade with his fingers, and whipped it forward. Sinking hilt deep into the horse's unprotected chest, the mount buckled, throwing the rider. The clansmen's scimitar skidded across the sand as he crashed to the ground. Tobin was on him in a few short steps, sword cutting through boiled leather and sliding between ribs. The desert warrior gasped. Tobin twisted his wrist and wrenched the sword free. He watched the man's life drain away and felt nothing.

Expecting another attacker, he spun about, but was surprised, disappointed, to see the battle ending. Though a few small pockets of fighting remained, many desert warriors were being rounded up, and in some cases, dragged to a common area where they could be watched. Somehow in the moments it took him to finish the rider, the Kifzo had overwhelmed the Desert Clan. Many threw their weapons to the ground rather than face death.

What could have caused such a sudden change?

Smoldering figures caught Tobin's eye as he worked his way down the incline. Burned to a shriveled husk, the bodies leaked grayish smoke into the air. Many of those charred figures held the remnants of what appeared to be shields at their side.

Protectors of the shamans. He snorted. *Effective against arrows but useless against other shamans. Useless against Nachun that is. To kill so many by himself!* He shook his head in disbelief.

Tobin looked up at the sound of scraping sand to see Nachun dragging a rattling corpse, the bones strapped to its person no longer a pale white, but black as tar. Nachun dumped the body on top of two others in similar condition. Ashes fluttered up, strengthening the already pungent smell of burnt flesh that hung in the air. "You've done well today."

The shaman turned, his face at first a scowl, until recognition reached his mind and a friendly smile formed in its place. "Yes," he said gesturing to the pile of death he had created. "I heard from Ufer you had a hand in taking out the others,"

"So he made it out then? And Ral? They deserve credit."

"Ral died according to Ufer."

His loss will be felt. He was about to say as much when a deep voice sounded from behind.

"*Brother*, I see you decided to join us." Tobin turned round and saw Kaz. Sweat and blood covered the man, armor torn and gouged. He looked at the graze on Tobin's arm and chuckled. "It looks like you injured yourself. Let us hope it heals better than your ankle." He paused, coming to a halt. "Lucky for us and for *you*," Kaz said, "that Nachun was here to finish the task I gave you."

Nachun cleared his throat. "Tobin, Ral, and Ufer killed many of them. I would think you pleased at their work."

Kaz glared at Nachun through narrowed eyes and then turned to meet Tobin's. "And you would be wrong. Their task was to kill them all, and Tobin was given the lead. The failure is his to bear. And a man like Ral is not easily replaced. Father will be displeased to hear of his death."

And what would it take to please Father? You seem to be the only one with that answer.

"I take it by your silence you have nothing to say, *Brother*? Good. You are in charge of counting our dead. I want to know every man who gave his life today. As will Father."

"As you say," said Tobin.

Kaz turned, barking more orders as he strode through the masses. Tobin watched him for a moment and then started to walk away. Nachun called out to him with a reassuring smile, "You did do well, and we will celebrate our victory tonight, together."

Tobin shook his head as he eyed Kaz. "I will not be part of any celebration tonight. I promise you that."

* * *

He swayed in the saddle of his agitated mount. The animal plodded along, impatient with the slow pace Tobin kept. He was dressed in the same leather armor he had worn since arriving some weeks ago, gray and blue in color, matching the stone that covered the islands of his birth. Daggers were at his thigh and boots, throwing axes once again looped at his sides, sword strapped to his back. A longbow and quiver rested across the back of his mount, atop a small pack. The pack only further annoyed his horse and it snorted in frustration at him. Twice Tobin took out his anger on the animal, each time just after a nip at his leg or hand. Yet, the beast persisted.

Even he shows me no respect.

Within hours after the battle at Munai, the march to Nubinya began. If one was to ride up on the long train shuffling its way across the lifeless landscape, Tobin was sure that person would be astonished. Five hundred surviving Kifzo, remarkable numbers when considering the odds leading into the confrontation, led approximately twelve hundred desert clansmen, tied and bound to each other.

For the most part, submission of so many came easily. Kaz personally eliminated any man who showed even the faintest hint of defiance toward his command. As a result, most others quickly fell in line. But that did not surprise Tobin.

Fear is the backbone of Kaz's rule.

The surprise came when Tobin observed the utter awe in a desert warrior groveling at Nachun's feet, muttering about the unnatural things he had witnessed from him. Such a scene unsettled many of the Kifzo who had already felt uncomfortable around the shaman. Kaz's sword plunging through the man's back was all the warning necessary to make others think twice before doing the same.

You've become another threat to him, Nachun, and Kaz made everyone aware of his feelings toward you then.

Those unnatural things muttered by the now-dead warrior, and the other stories Tobin overheard regarding the battle along the coast, had even raised an alarm in his mind. *And he called me friend. Yet, am I? Can I trust him?* After all, the shaman was said to have performed things that none had ever seen before, nor even heard of, except in the ancient songs and tales of their ancestors, from a time before the crossing of the Great Divide. He wouldn't have believed half of those mutterings had he not ridden down to the coast to look upon the twenty foot gorge in the shore. They said the ground opened up, swallowing man and horse alike.

Nachun later admitted the act nearly finished him, leaving him just enough strength to defeat the last three shamans.

But I saw him dragging the bodies of those shamans. Other than a little sweat and grime, he looked no different than before. And if I know Kaz, that is what he likes least of all. Too many uncertainties, too much misdirection. I wonder how Father will react to such news.

The horse bit his leg, interrupting his thoughts. He jerked the reins and whipped his mount's head forward, cursing it for its stubbornness. Looking up, he gazed upon Nubinya, the heart of an otherwise dead land, the capital of the Orange Desert Clan.

The city had come into view some time ago. Maybe he was used to the grandeur of Juanoq, having watched his home grow in size and majesty with each passing year, but from outside Nubinya's walls, the view disappointed him. Said to be the first city established by settlers after crossing the Great Divide, it was also the oldest known city in all of Hesh.

And it looks that way. Black walls, made from the desert's charcoaled stone, looked gnarled from centuries of windstorms. Piles of sand against the exterior walls, lessened their height to barely six feet, negating the need for siege ladders.

There is no excuse for such laziness. It's as if they never fathomed anyone would assault them here. Tobin looked around at the barren landscape. *But then who but my father would want any of this?*

Following the columns through Nubinya's narrow entrance, Tobin noticed crude towers to either side of the opening and at the corners of each wall. Their size and positioning appeared to offer little defense from would-be invaders. *Considering father's success, they were ineffective.*

The first few buildings, just inside the city's walls, reminded Tobin of a larger version of the huts at Munai. Granted, the quality of their construction was an improvement over the fisherman's dwellings, but something about their simplicity left him unimpressed.

However, his opinion of Nubinya changed as he ventured farther away from the outer walls. Traveling the main thoroughfare, buildings grew in size and craftsmanship improved. Stone walls were etched with designs similar to the markings on the desert clansmen's armor, each building becoming its own unique piece of artwork. In some instances, blocks of orange clay were worked between the black stones, forming intricate patterns within the structure itself. Tobin appreciated such skill. *These structures have stood hundreds of years. Perhaps thousands.* He wondered if someone would be able to make the same observations of his own home. Of his people.

Prisoners shuffled their tired feet down the long road, heads hung low in shame as the columns moved closer to the capital's center.

Assigned rear guard as usual, Tobin remained isolated from many of the other Kifzo during the long journey into the city. As a result, he was the last to witness the majesty that gave Nubinya, *Paradise* in the old tongue, its name. A massive oasis rested at the city's center. A large fountain of clear water flowed from underground, cascading over several levels of rock and rippling down into a large pool. Groves of date, olive, and acacia trees surrounded by various bushes and wildflowers, encircled the water.

Tobin's first reaction to such a sight was an open mouth, surprised to see such beauty and life standing defiant against the Burnt Sands Desert.

His second reaction twisted his mouth and he spat. *With a real wall, these fools could have held out for months. We would have starved or died of thirst while they drank away at their hearts content.*

Blue Island Clan warriors, formidable but less skilled than the Kifzo, corralled the prisoners into smaller groups. The captives joined the sullen faces of others that Bazraki had isolated.

Tobin dismounted and tied his horse to a post nearby. In the process, the animal whipped his head around one last time and nipped at Tobin's leg. He started to raise a hand against the beast but resigned to let the animal get in the last strike.

I'll walk home before I ride that beast again, bad ankle or not.

He moved toward a group of Blue Island Clan soldiers, doing his best to hide the limp in his gait. The men noticed his approach and lowered their eyes. Although warriors themselves, neither were Kifzo, who by Bazraki's law were regarded the highest among the Blue Island Clan army. They acknowledged his position. After a brief exchange with the men, Tobin learned that his father had set up his base in Nubinya's council chambers. One of the warriors pointed Tobin in the direction of a building less than a hundred paces away.

The building, unique in almost every way, stood out from the other structures in the city. Rather than walls of right angles and sharp edges, the cylindrical building appeared seamless, as if made from one solid piece of stone. A dome enclosed the structure. Even the designs decorating the outer walls were far more elaborate than those he had passed earlier. Much more than just a family crest, the carvings displayed the entire Orange Desert Clan's past. These people prided themselves in their history.

And now that history belongs to my father.

As Tobin rounded the building, he came upon several Kifzo guarding a great arched entrance. He nodded to them as he passed through, but each failed to return the gesture.

No surprise there.

He spotted his father standing in the great room, talking amidst his advisors. Kaz had already joined the discussion and stood at their father's right hand.

Despite the gray in his hair, Bazraki dominated the room. He may have lacked the bulk that Tobin and Kaz possessed, but his muscled frame stood out nonetheless. He wore an open leather vest, striped in blue, with lean arms jutting through the sleeveless openings. His trousers were a solid brown as were his boots. The only elaborate item he wore was a large azurite stone, polished smooth, with a hollowed center. The necklace hung from his neck and stood out sharply against the black skin of his barrel chest.

Better to get this over with.

Tobin slipped in amid the group of men as Bazraki issued commands. If his father noticed his son's presence, he made no effort to acknowledge him. Kaz on the other hand offered a brief scowl. Tobin stood in silence, hands clasped behind his back, not daring to interrupt while Bazraki sent each man among them off on some task, one by one.

Only after the last man left, did Bazraki turn to acknowledge Tobin, his voice absent of any warmth. "Have the prisoners been segregated?"

"Yes, Father," said Tobin with a slight bow.

"Good. Then let us get to the heart of things. Your brother has filled me in on the details of Munai." Bazraki paused, looking to gauge Tobin's reaction, but he had learned long ago to keep such things hidden. "There is one area of particular interest that I would discuss with you."

"Yes, Father?"

"Your brother arrived ahead of the train with several men, one of whom was this shaman you ran across at Munai. As I understand it, you and he have spoken at length on several occasions. This is so?" Bazraki asked the question, but his tone hinted that he already knew the answer.

"Yes, Father. His name is Nachun."

"You are aware of his intentions then? To join our clan?"

"I am."

"And what do you think about his…proposal?"

Tobin was taken aback. *What is he doing? Never has he sought my opinion. He must be baiting me. Did Kaz set this up?* He glanced to his brother but saw nothing that would give him insight into his father's questions. *Best to play this safe.*

"It is not my duty to think about such things, Father. The decision is yours and as always, I will support it."

"I did not question your loyalty. I have spoken to the man in private and have done the same with several Kifzo, including your brother. I would listen to your view of the man now as I have theirs. Then I will make my decision," said Bazraki, growing impatient.

Tobin nodded, pausing for a moment to choose his words. *This can be used against me just as easily as it can be used against Nachun.* "Nachun seems sincere and he has been open with his reasons for wishing to join us. He's proven himself in battle. Not only did he save my life on more than one occasion, but also the lives of other Kifzo." A hiss came from Kaz but Tobin ignored it. "He is a clever man, educated, and as a shaman we have no equal among us."

"You sound as if you are ready to embrace him then?" said Bazraki, folding his arms across his chest.

Careful, Tobin. "Not without caution. There is ample reason for doubt. He is more powerful than he lets on which makes me wonder why another clan would not have accepted his family, if not just to make use of his skill. And despite helping our cause, there is still much to learn about him."

"I see." Bazraki paused; weighing Tobin's words as he bobbed his head. "So, you would have him join us if you were in my place. Your brother…" He gestured toward Kaz. "holds a different belief."

"And the other Kifzo?" asked Tobin.

"Mixed overall but the majority seems to reluctantly share your view. Based on what I have heard and my own discussions with the shaman, I am inclined to allow the man to join us as well."

"Father, you must not allow this man to become one of us. He cannot be trusted," said Kaz, voice rising. "Do not listen to my *brother*. He only wishes to have this shaman around to cover his own failings."

Bazraki shook his head. "He will join our clan and from here on be included as an advisor to me. We have already spoken on some of his ideas I would hear more about."

"Father, this is a mistake. The man should be killed now before…." said Kaz, clenching his fists.

"Enough," said Bazraki. "The matter is closed and will not be discussed further. Leave us now."

Before leaving, Kaz turned to face Tobin with eyes burning like two hot coals. Tobin cast his gaze downward in shame though he knew there was little reason to feel such a thing. Kaz grunted in disgust and left, brushing past one of the guards near the doorway.

Now alone, Bazraki spoke to Tobin in a hushed manner. "Although Nachun will join our clan, I do not trust him. You will be his shadow, and you will report to me all his doings. I want to know who he talks with, what is said, where he goes. Everything. No one is to know that you are doing this for me, not even Kaz. Is that understood?"

"Yes, Father."

"You know, he has taken a liking to you. In fact, he spoke quite highly of you. He contradicted Kaz's account of your deeds at Munai. He said that without your bow, he would have been unable to handle so many shamans."

"Ral and Ufer…."

Bazraki cut him off. "I care little about the details and I know well enough what happened from your brother. Nubinya is mine and that is all that matters."

Tobin fell quiet.

"Now, leave me. I have much to do. Go and inform Nachun of the good news."

Tobin bowed. "As you say, Father."

CHAPTER 5

High Priest Burgeone had done his best to honor King Aurnon the Eighth with a funeral unlike any other Elyse had witnessed. The cathedral burst at the seams with lush flowers, dark greens for the floors, light blues hanging across the high ceiling, and in the middle every other color imaginable. The High Priest's sermon referenced the décor, saying it was representative of the beautiful life their King had given the land. Elyse thought she heard a few snickers at that. If the High Priest heard them, he ignored them, delivering a sermon so passionate she thought the man would break into tears. Yet for all his efforts, the service would be remembered for all the wrong reasons. The building sat half empty, and those that had bothered to pay their respects seemed to be present only out of duty rather than desire.

Well over a month had passed since the king's death, enough time for those in the far reaches of Cadonia to make the trip to Lyrosene. Yet for many, duty was not enough to compel them to make the journey.

Nor was it enough for them to show me their support.

Elyse wore black, befitting the occasion. Long hair pulled tight into a bun, a veil matching the pattern of her gown covered her head. Outside of the simple crown she chose to wear, her only spark of color was a silver necklace; hung with a pale green stone, mirroring the color of her eyes. She had never taken off the piece since receiving the gift as a child. It was the sign of a promise made to her long ago, and she had prayed to the One Above each night since her father's passing that the words of that promise would come true.

"Your Grace, the Great Hall is ready for your arrival," said a servant, bowing.

"Thank you, Lobella."

Elyse slowly descended the staircase into the Great Hall. It was much different than she had remembered it, newer in fact. Tables, benches, chairs, and banners—all replaced. Floors, walls, and even ceilings, scrubbed clean. Like many other places in the castle that haunted her nightmares, it was the first time she had set foot in the space since her father's passing. Instead of eating with others, she had grown accustomed to taking meals in her room, doing her best to avoid anything that reminded her of that awful day.

Yet all the new faces are reminder enough. Those slain can never be replaced.

Looking around at the sparkling hall, she imagined that it resembled what it must have looked like when Aurnon the First built the castle after settling Cadonia. Her mood lightened as she thought of such storied times, giving her a respite from the present.

A hush went over the Great Hall at the announcement of her name and all rose from their seats. Elyse felt their eyes turn to her as she walked toward the head table. Her mood changed, growing dimmer, as she passed several guests. Their uncaring faces reminded her that the glorious days of Aurnon the First had ended long ago. Several times she paused to receive condolences, though their words did little to comfort her. She reached the dais where the head table sat. A welcome hand assisted her as she stepped up.

Gauge had been on her father's council for as far back as she could remember, though the king had diminished his role as the years passed, ignoring any council that opposed his own. He was the first person she sought out when her father died, not knowing where else to turn. Without him, she would not have made it through those first few days. Before long, Gauge had become her most trusted advisor.

His thinly cropped hair was offset by a well trimmed beard of black and gray. His eyes were full of care when he smiled. She kissed him lightly on the cheek.

As they parted, she moved to stand by her seat at the table's center. Gauge sat to her right, a place of honor she happily bestowed.

Elyse took a deep breath. "I would like to thank you all for being here today. Your support means a great deal to me after such a tragedy. I would not speak ill of my father on a day like this, but I will freely admit he was a man like any other, with fault. However, like those who reigned before him, he loved his people and would not want us to ruin a wonderful meal in mourning." *One Above, forgive me for the small lie.* "Please enjoy yourselves today and think of him kindly. Pray that the One Above watch over him. Let us celebrate Cadonia's bright future." She finished to a half-hearted round of applause.

They question how bright that future will be. And who can blame them? She motioned to her guests to be seated and within moments, dishes began streaming out of the kitchen.

Gauge leaned in close, "You did well, Your Majesty. But the day is not over I'm afraid, the dukes will want to meet with you after the meal is served. Try to eat. The food will settle any nerves you may have."

Elyse nodded as the first dishes appeared for her approval. There were cold and warm salads, one of fresh greens, the other of beans and peppers. The meal continued with soups and stews, followed by roast fowl, suckling pig, and baked fish. Elyse forced down a bite or two of each dish. The desserts came out next, but she dismissed them before they arrived at her table, allowing others to have first choice. Instead, she nibbled on bites of fresh bread, nervous.

The meal closed with little fanfare and conversations continued over wine and cheese. As Gauge predicted, Elyse noticed that each of the dukes stirred in his seat, wondering whether or not the time was appropriate to speak with her. She had reserved the chair to her left for their discussions as Gauge suggested earlier. Jeldor, who sat farthest from Elyse made a motion to rise and she thought he would be the first to approach. However, Olasi rose just a moment after, and reached the dais before Jeldor could climb around those blocking his path. With a look of agitation, Jeldor returned to his chair and drained his wine.

Duke Olasi lived on the eastern coast of Cadonia in a city named Lucartias. Since Aurnon the First's conquering of Cadonia, his family had a reputation of being as dedicated to the realm as the crown itself. Olasi was no exception. Despite the grumblings of dissatisfaction that plagued her father's reign, little discord from Olasi's province ever reached Lyrosene. He was a much older man, near eighty, which many mistook for a sign of weakness. However, Gauge told her many stories of Olasi putting men in their place thanks to a sharp wit few could match, including High Mage Amcaro himself.

Elyse was glad to see him first. His loving eyes gave her comfort and eased her nerves. A servant helped the duke struggle onto the dais. His voice rasped when he spoke, but she found it full of care, "Your Majesty, the realm weeps not only for your loss, but also for its own. As it did when your father succeeded his father, I offer all I have to you for the sake of Cadonia."

Olasi motioned to take a knee but Elyse quickly reached out and touched his arm, steadying him. "Please my lord, the loyalty and devotion of your family has never been in doubt. I would much rather you sit with me than kneel," she said motioning to the empty chair to her left.

He smiled and sat with a heavy sigh. "Thank you, Your Majesty. You do an old man a great service. Please tell me what I may do for you."

"For now, something simple, something to take my mind away from such a somber occasion. Tell me of your family. I have not seen them in some time. I did not know your children well, but I do remember playing with your granddaughter Arine, as a child."

The old man's eyes lit up and his smile grew wide at the mention of family. "Your Majesty has touched on a spot true and dear to my heart. Thank the One Above, my wife is alive and well, as are my children—though my oldest son, Markus, has become reckless at times I fear. However, I'm sure it is just the case of a father unable to see his son as anything but the boy he raised. My grandchildren are doing equally as well, all twelve of them. It is funny you should mention Arine, she was wed earlier this year to a fine young lord and they are expecting what will be my first great-grandchild." Olasi lit up as he spoke of the news. "I thank the One Above each day for being so blessed."

"That is wonderful news and brings my heart much needed warmth during this troublesome time. Please give your family my regards upon your return," said Elyse with a smile her own.

"If I may ask Your Majesty...how well are you holding up?"

Elyse paused unsure how to answer the question and turned to Gauge for advice. He gave a slight nod, assuring her she could speak freely. "I am better each day, but to be honest, everywhere I look is a reminder of the past. My father alienated many people during the later years of his life—long before the blame could be placed on High Mage Nareash. I feel overwhelmed at times, governing a kingdom and reassuring the people of my ability to rule."

"I understand. I have my own apprehensions, especially without a High Mage on my council any longer. I'm sure you remember your history, Your Majesty. Aurnon the First assigned High Mages to each province not only to advise, but also to deter ambition, something each ruler must be careful of. I lost many things when Rhindora passed away. A friend, an advisor, but most of all a sense of security."

"With no one to watch over the instruction on Estul Island, I'm afraid it will be some time before we see another High Mage, let alone one for each of the six provinces."

"Your Majesty, we need our High Mages now." He paused. "The events that surrounded your father's death have tipped the scales in favor of those with stronger knights and soldiers, I'm afraid. Sure there are still mages of various strengths, but none possess the awe that a red robe inspires." He paused again. "I pray to the One Above each day for the safety of us all."

"Do you really believe such dark times are upon us?" asked Elyse. The way he spoke made her uncomfortable and she shifted in her seat.

"Possibly, but I am not here to add to your worries, only to assure you where my loyalty lies." Then suddenly as if the topic changed back to his family, the bright smile returned to his face. "Now if you would grant me leave, this old man could do with a good night's sleep."

The conversation with Duke Olasi left her unsettled but she nodded his dismissal all the same. *Does he believe there will be a rebellion? In the four hundred years since Aurnon the First conquered Cadonia, no one has made a grab for the crown. Sure, dukes and minor lords have squabbled over land, but even at their worst, things were resolved quickly. Could he mean Thurum? There is always the threat of the High Pass. But those walls have never been scaled since Aurnon the Second built them.*

"Your Majesty? Unfortunately, the night is not finished and there are still others who wish to speak with you," said Gauge, jarring her from her thoughts.

She nodded and took a sip of wine, forcing a smile. Jeldor rose from his seat again, much quicker than before, twisting and turning between guests seated around him. However, he halted when Tomalt stood abruptly, cutting Jeldor off so that he nearly tripped. Rather than acknowledging his error and offering an apology, Tomalt headed straight to the queen as if Jeldor did not exist. Jeldor's face turned red. He returned to his seat again, all the while staring daggers at Tomalt's back.

Duke Tomalt called the city of Bolysius his home, a place second only to Lyrosene in its grandeur. Situated along the eastern half of Cadonia, Tomalt's province sat between the crown's land and Olasi's. Cadonia's largest province benefited from the taxes that came with it. The duke had continued the legacy his father started during his lifetime, rebuilding and renovating the older buildings within Bolysius's large double walls, turning the city into an architectural wonder. The pride Tomalt took in his home was outweighed only by his own self worth.

Tall, lean, and straight as a board, many joked behind Tomalt's back that the duke had sat on an arrow as a boy, causing his unusually stiff stride. His face held sharp features, dominated by a large nose. He wore the finest clothing though none would call it gaudy.

He makes even me feel like a pauper.

He strode to the queen with a confidence one could not help but be intimidated by. He came to an abrupt stop, clicking his heels and bowing in half at the waist. "Your Majesty, I would be most pleased if you would allow me to join you for a few moments." He spoke in a strong monotone, and waited for an answer with his hands at his sides. Head held high, not once did he meet the queen's eyes.

Elyse responded with a kindness the duke lacked. "Duke Tomalt, I would be honored if you would join me," she said gesturing to the now empty seat.

He sat down while straightening the creases in his clothes and, once satisfied with his appearance, began. "Thank you. My condolences for your loss, your father's death was a pity," said Tomalt without emotion.

"It was a pity. Though I think of it more grievous than that," said Elyse, upset by the lack of sincerity.

"Yes, of course. However, with such a sudden shift in rule, I would like to offer you my services, if I may, and assist you during your reign."

"I appreciate your generosity, Duke Tomalt."

"You see, Your Majesty, as a woman, I know that you were not raised with a proper education in military strategy. Therefore, it is very important for you to feel confident in the commander of your forces. I feel that placing a strong presence, such as myself, in the role would add a certain strength and authority that, to be honest, grew lax during your father's reign. I'm sure you would agree."

Elyse was surprised by the suggestion but if it showed on her face, Tomalt ignored the reaction. "Such a thing would be impossible. General Grayer holds the position," she said. "Would you consider…"

"I would not consider anything else, Your Majesty. Moreover I must disagree—the situation is not impossible. Simply excuse the man of his duties. He has served long enough and I believe it is time someone more competent took over the role."

"I'm afraid I will have to decline your offer. As I said, General Grayer is our army's commander."

His brow furrowed and he finally met her eyes, the most emotion he had shown since sitting down. A lump formed in Elyse's throat and her hands began to sweat. *It's like I am nothing to him.*

"And this folly is something I cannot persuade the queen to change her mind on, is it?"

Thankfully, Gauge spoke on her behalf as she struggled to find her voice again. "The queen is most certain of General Grayer's capabilities."

"I see. A mistake you may one day regret." Tomalt rose suddenly, clicking his heels together and bowing again in a quick, fluid motion. "Very well. If it pleases Your Majesty, I have other duties to attend to." He stood motionless, waiting for a response.

Tomalt's abruptness took her off guard once again, but she still managed a nod. Before she could offer a parting word, the duke pivoted on his heels, striding away as rigid as before.

Elyse leaned over. "Why would he ask such a thing? Surely he would know my answer."

"Your Majesty, control of our military, along with his resources, would have made him the most powerful man in the kingdom. I think he assumed you naïve to such a thing. But you proved him wrong."

One Above, I am naïve to such things. My decision had nothing to do with preventing him from coming into such power.

Gauge continued, "Tomalt was never a man who knew the finer points of conversation. If he had more talent with words, maybe he could have enticed you into making a poor decision. Still, you made the right choice." He inclined his head. "I believe Duke Jeldor is about to approach you once again, Your Highness."

True enough, Duke Jeldor of Ithanthul jumped from his seat, moving toward the dais in a rush, pushing and shoving guests and servants alike out of his path. The stout man was passing a table when Duke Bronn pushed his chair out, knocking Jeldor into a servant carrying empty plates. They both tumbled to the floor in a clatter of noise. A sudden, but brief, silence fell over the hall that ended with the sound of Bronn chuckling. Soon others joined in and laughter filled the expansive room. Bronn helped Jeldor to his feet and made a show of dusting him off before Jeldor pushed him away, face contorted in anger. The laughter died as Bronn sat down and took a sip of wine, waving Duke Jeldor ahead of him in a condescending manner. Jeldor was not happy about the gesture but he continued his approach nonetheless, more careful than before.

The redness in his face subsided as he reached the queen, though his displeasure was still obvious. He wore plainer clothes than the other nobles, thick wool in place of silk, and the color mostly brown with touches of gray.

His house was not a rich one, despite having control of the iron mines of Arcas Island. His family rarely attended court as well, choosing to remain isolated in their dreary lands in the northwest portion of Cadonia.

The duke's long beard and bushy brown hair appeared tussled from the fall. Sweat glistened on his forehead. He looked out of place among the other lords and ladies in the hall.

He stopped before the queen with a huff and a slight bow. "Your Majesty."

"Duke Jeldor, are you alright from your spill?" asked Elyse, concern in her voice.

He seemed only to grow more agitated. "I am fine, no thanks to that arrogant twit. Though he wasn't the first, now was he? Each of them made it a point to disrespect me in some manner, only Bronn was the most open about it."

"My lord, I'm sure there is a misunderstanding and no ill was meant."

"Whether intentional or not is beside the point. My family has been looked on as the stepchild of Cadonia ever since Aurnon the First conquered this land. After hundreds of years, that has not changed. I also see that your feelings are no different, having placed my house farthest from your table. Now I remember why I seldom attend such events." He remembered himself for a moment and bowed. "I am sorry for your loss, Your Majesty."

"Thank you, my lord. Won't you please sit for a while? Maybe we can speak on some of your concerns."

"My only concern is whether you will finally reduce the taxes instituted by Aurnon the Third on my lands," said Jeldor, still standing.

Gauge cleared his throat. "My lord, those taxes were put in place as punishment for your family's transgressions."

"Transgressions that occurred hundreds of years ago. Must I suffer for my ancestor's mistake?"

"Aurnon the Third was very specific that the taxes should not be lifted."

Jeldor looked to the queen. "And how does Your Majesty feel about this?"

Elyse swallowed. She had no clue about the transgressions Jeldor and Gauge spoke of.

Jeldor grunted. "I'll take it by your silence that you feel the same then."

Elyse found her voice. "Perhaps we can discuss something else, my lord."

"No. Next time I hope we can discuss matters under better terms. Perhaps even my own." He muttered the last part under his breath, but then remembered himself again. "By your leave, I would return to my holdfast."

"Yes, of course."

Jeldor turned and left the room, exiting the hall through the nearest door, not once looking back. The rest of his house followed him. Elyse turned to Gauge, confused by the show. "What was that about?"

"Your Grace, when Aurnon the First conquered the land known as Cadonia, he gave provinces to each of the five families most responsible for aiding him in his conquest. Jeldor's family received the smallest territory of those families, littered with lakes, mountains, and rough terrain. His family has never forgotten the slight. They once even staged a rebellion during Aurnon the Third's reign. After that, the crown levied the hefty tax on their main source of income, iron ore. By rights, their family should be one of the richest, but with the taxes, they are left the poorest. The other dukes and lords have not forgotten, and constantly ridicule his family. Jeldor's father always talked of a day when his family would gain the respect they deserved. I'm not sure how much of his father's beliefs he shares, but I have to imagine that after today, his opinion is not dissimilar."

"I see." *I'm so unprepared for this. I haven't done anything since my father died to ready myself for this crown.*

Never one to be made to rush, Duke Bronn slid his chair back once more. Young at twenty-two years of age, the duke called Astrya his home, located in the west between Jeldor and Conroy. He became duke after his father's passing the previous summer. As Bronn rose from his chair, the women in the hall lifted their heads with longing in their eyes. He was a handsome man with soft features, eyes as blue as the ocean.

I remember looking that way at him once, but not any longer.

Bronn approached the queen with a smile and a bow. "Your Majesty, you look lovely this evening despite such a somber occasion. May I join you?" he asked pointing to the empty chair. Rather than wait for her response, he seated himself next to her.

"Your Majesty has not granted permission for you to sit, my lord," said Gauge.

Bronn flashed a warm smile. "Right you are. But, please, let us put away such formalities for now. Elyse and I have quite the history together and I only wish to ease her troubles today." He turned to Elyse, face washed with concern. "I am terribly sorry for your father's passing. How are you faring?"

He lies so well, but I know the true Bronn. "I am well enough. Thankfully, I am keeping busy with my responsibilities…"

Bronn cut in. "Oh no, you mustn't. Now is the time to rest after what you have been through. Ruling a country is far too much trouble for someone as lovely as you to worry about. Give someone else leave to perform those tedious tasks."

"And who would you have me give such tedious tasks to? Yourself?"

"A splendid idea." He looked back over to Gauge. "I told you we had a history together. It's as if we finish each other's thoughts."

"My lord, how could you help with such things when your lands are far away from Lyrosene?" said Gauge, obviously trying to hide the agitation in his voice.

"Ah, a sharp man. I see why Elyse has placed you so high at her table. Well, as fate would have it, I have already thought of such things and have the answer. My younger cousin turns eighteen in less than a month. He would make an excellent Duke of Astrya in my stead."

"And what would that make you, my lord?" said Gauge.

"Why, king of course. With His Majesty now laid to rest, Elyse and I could marry at once, the sooner the better, really. Elyse can then focus on her hobbies."

Gauge's jaw dropped.

"You seemed shocked at what I say," said Bronn. "Did you forget that Elyse and I were set to be married once before?"

"You dare to make such an assumption…" Gauge started. *It doesn't take long for Bronn to leave an impression.*

"I have no hobbies," said Elyse, cutting her advisor off.

"Needlework perhaps?" asked Bronn.

"I have no desire for needlework."

"Well, I'm sure we can find something of interest. That's not really the point…."

"I know what your point is, but you fail to see mine. I have no need for hobbies now that my father is dead. It is my responsibility to rule Cadonia."

"A responsibility I only wish to ease…"

"You must not remember that my father dissolved the marriage arrangement between us years ago for good reason. It is not something I wish to renew. In time I will find my own husband."

The arrogant smile vanished from Bronn's face. He replaced it with a look of exaggerated concern. He shook his head and tsked Elyse like a mother scolding her child. "I thought you would have grown wiser. Please, let me make you aware of the truth of things since your advisor has not." His gaze shifted to Gauge for a second before returning to her. He leaned in close. "I want you to look around the hall, my sweet. Go on," he said, gesturing with his head. "Some of the most powerful men in the realm reside here tonight, and those are only the ones who bothered to show up. They all know the fool your father died as, and they know Nareash held control over you. What they don't know is for how long or at what costs. They think as little of you as they did your father. What makes you think that any of them would marry you with such uncertainty unless they were promised the throne?" He paused and his smile returned. "I do not share their concerns. I know the kind of woman you are and I think that between us, we will have a small horde of fine looking children running around the castle." His smile grew wider. "And just think of the fun we'll have making them."

Gauge erupted, face reddening, "You forget yourself."

"You forget as well. As I said earlier, Elyse and I have a history." He turned to Elyse. "I apologize, Your Majesty. But please, think on what I've said."

Elyse wanted to respond with some intimidating bark, authoritative and strong, as any ruler would. But she kept quiet, not even speaking as Bronn left without her approval, moving back to his seat, flashing his smile to the ladies he passed. It made her sick to hear him talk as he had, but she knew he was right, and it scared her.

Each of the dukes gave little reason for Elyse to feel confident as queen, and they were the ones who showed. Duke Conroy had sent word that he could not attend due to his obligations at the High Pass, the passage separating Cadonia's southern border from Thurum.

I had thought his reason admirable but now, I wonder if he is the most dangerous of them all. And if the people truly feel that way about me, what support could I hope to secure from their lords?

Elyse found herself clutching the necklace around her neck, caressing the green stone between her fingers. "Your Majesty." She jumped, startled. "Your Majesty, are you alright?" said Gauge.

"Yes," she said, lowering her hand. "I was only thinking about what Olasi first said regarding the threat of war."

"Such rumors are disheartening." He shook his head. "If only you had access to the power Nareash wielded against the other High Mages. No one would dare threaten your rule."

Elyse paled, her eyes glazing over as she thought about that power, and the devastation such power caused.

Gauge touched her arm and she turned to see a look of concern on his face. "Your Majesty? Oh, I'm so sorry. I should not have mentioned Nareash."

She took a breath and whispered. "That power. No one should ever have access to it again." She shuddered.

"Yes, of course. Well, it's a good thing Amcaro destroyed the scepter with his last breath as you said."

"Yes, it was," said Elyse, visibly shaking.

Gauge coughed and handed her a glass. "Here Your Majesty, please have some wine. I apologize again for bringing the subject up."

Elyse shook her head, finding herself clutching her necklace once again.

Gauge glanced to the necklace and then placed a hand on her arm with a gentle touch. "Your Majesty, I know you treasure the gift for what you told me it means, but you cannot hope to rule on a promise."

Elyse nodded, annoyed. "Are we done here this evening?"

"Yes, but it would be good for appearances if you remained a while…"

"I've been helpful enough today. I'll be in my room."

She stood up and left.

* * *

Elyse's bedroom was spacious with high ceilings and wide windows. Positioned on the wall to the right of the doorway, stood a great canopy bed, covered in fine linen. Two tall dressers stood opposite the bed, each decorated with delicate woodwork. Across from the door sat a simple desk and chair, plain in comparison to the rest of the room, yet this is where Elyse sat.

She gazed out the window overlooking the city and countryside below. *My old instructor, Fredrick, must be laughing from above now. If only I would have paid better attention to my histories. I shouldn't have needed Olasi to tell me of the High Mages' importance, and Tomalt is right that I know nothing of military strategy. How will I know which decision is right if I understand little of what my advisors speak of? If I was more knowledgeable of the past, maybe I could have seated Jeldor closer to me in the Great Hall and soften the insults from others.*

But Bronn's words scared her most of all.

She fiddled with her necklace and thought back to how Bronn talked down to her. *Like I'm still some silly little girl. But he has the right of it doesn't he.* She dropped her hands from her neck.

"Your Majesty, are you alright?" said a voice from behind.

Elyse turned. "Oh, Lobella, I'm sorry. I hadn't realized you were still here. Yes, I'm fine. It's just been a long day."

The woman bowed. She was close in age to Elyse and quite beautiful for a servant, though she never carried herself that way. She spoke in a soft voice. Elyse remembered it took her almost a year to get Lobella to open up. Since then, they had grown close. Elyse liked to think of her as a friend though she didn't know if Lobella felt the same.

"I can imagine, Your Majesty. I've prepared your bed for tonight. Will you need anything else?"

Elyse's thoughts drifted back to the Great Hall and the looks on everyone's faces, the uncertainty in their eyes.

"Your Majesty? Are you sure you are alright?"

"Yes, I'm fine. That will be all for tonight. Please get some rest and tell your mother I said hello."

She smiled. "She will be pleased that you remembered her."

Elyse smiled back and realized her hand had returned to the stone around her neck. "Actually, before you go could you fetch me the jewelry box in the dresser. It is near the top and you are taller than I."

"Of course, Your Majesty." Lobella located a simple white wooden box and opened the top as she neared the queen. Then she stopped in shock, almost dropping the box. "Elyse, your necklace. I'm sorry, I mean Your Majesty. I've never seen you without it."

Elyse smiled and placed the necklace in the box. "You have no need to apologize; I've asked you to call me Elyse in private." She looked at the silver thread and light green stone sitting on padded red silk. "Yes, this gift has been the most precious thing in my life since it was given to me." She paused. "But that was long ago, when I was a girl. If I want my people to see a woman, a queen, I need to put those things away."

Lobella nodded and closed the box, returning it to the dresser. "Is there anything else?"

"Yes. On your way out, please stop by Gillian's quarters. I have need of several books."

"Poetry, Your Majesty?"

Elyse had always been a lover of poetry and in times of distress she would turn either to the One Above in prayer or to the pages of her favorite poets. As of late, she had exhausted both avenues.

"No. Ask Gillian for those volumes that document the histories of Cadonia, from Aurnon the First through my father. Also, tell him to bring me his favorite books on military strategy."

"Your Majesty, that isn't what I would call light reading."

Elyse smiled at the rare joke. "No, but they contain the knowledge to rule a kingdom."

CHAPTER 6

The sails hung limp from lack of wind. Yet the ship still moved across calm waters with a gentle sway in the deep blue ocean. From the railing, Jonrell watched oars dip in and out of the water, matching the pace set by the beating drum. There had not been so much as a breeze in two days and he grew anxious from the delay. After the first day, he had convinced the ship's captain to work the oarsmen in longer shifts. Hoping to make up time, the old seadog was happy to oblige.

The promise of extra gold, didn't hurt either.

The Hell Patrol had been at sea nearly a week, and it seemed only his mood hadn't improved. Many had never been to Cadonia and after suffering through the debacle of their last job, a renewed excitement permeated through the group as they ventured off into the unknown. He would have given anything to share in their optimism but the more he dwelled on what awaited him upon his return home, the more overwhelmed he felt.

He had been gone twelve years and only one thing was certain in his mind. *There will be a rebellion.* The personalities, the politics, old feuds, a restless people, all on top of a king no one loved. *My only hope is that Amcaro and the High Mages can keep the balance in power from shifting.* His hand clutched his breast pocket again, cupping the stone inside as he thought about home. *Home. Can I really call it that after being away for so long? Cassus and I barely even spoke of the place.*

He pulled the stone from his pocket, caressing its smooth features between his finger and thumb, thoughts wandering to his past. Since leaving port, old memories resurfaced. At sea, there seemed little else to do but remember a youth filled with both pain and pleasure.

His men spent most of their days rolling dice, playing cards, and betting on anything and everything, using the money left over after they procured safe passage. They tried to get Jonrell involved in the games but he declined, doing nothing more than watching, away from the action, alone with his thoughts.

What would make Cassus think I had no need of him? Who else am I supposed to confide in, who else understands me as well as he did? He looked up and muttered, "One Above, I hope you at least find this funny."

"The men are right to be worried about you," said a voice from behind.

Jonrell turned.

This is how you answer my prayer? Now I know you're laughing at me. "Go away," he told Krytien.

The mage ignored the comment and leaned on the railing next to him, running his fingers through the pale wisps of long hair on top his head.

"You know, all that rubbing isn't going to make it grow anew," said Jonrell.

Krytien shook his head. "So I come over here out of concern and this is the thanks I get? I could have stayed at the dice game and at least made some money for suffering through the jibes."

Jonrell shrugged his shoulders. "I told you to go away." He turned to the mage. "What is with you anyway? Ever since you brought me news of the king, you've been acting odd. No remarks in retaliation, no mutterings under your breath. Nothing?"

Krytien shook his head. "You need to straighten yourself out because I'm getting sick of covering for you."

"Covering for me?"

"It was one thing with Melchizan. He beat all of us down to a point where few even noticed you weren't acting like yourself. But I did. I've known you since you joined this outfit with Cassus, both green as can be. I watched you grow up quicker than I thought possible and command respect from a bunch of cutthroats without even trying. Before Ronav passed, he had already made up his mind that you'd follow after him. As young as you were, I had some doubts." He paused. "At least until Asantia. It was then that I realized there was no one better to fill Ronav's place."

"Is there a point in all of this?"

A chubby hand shot out and slapped the commander across his cheek. His jaw dropped in surprise.

"You lackwit! The death of the king and the thought of returning home is affecting you in a bad way, far more than you realize." said Krytien. "You've been moping around rather than planning for the future. Our future. If you don't get yourself together, you're liable to get us all killed."

Jonrell rubbed his jaw. *I can't believe he struck me. I've never seen him move so fast.* "The king's death is nothing."

"Don't give me that. He was still your father."

"And?"

"You left home without ever settling your differences and now that chance is gone. Don't tell me you haven't thought of it. I see you worrying that stone in your hand each day."

Jonrell looked down to his hand and sighed, his fingers still working the surface. *He's got me now.* "There may be some truth to that but that's only part of it."

"You regret your decision to leave Cadonia all those years ago."

Jonrell nodded. "I think I always did. I had just made sure to keep myself busy enough not to think about it. But now..." he waved a hand over the ocean "...now what else is there to do but think. What kind of a man leaves a young girl all alone?"

"You mean the princess?"

"My sister." He paused. "Father loved her deeply, more than me at least, for if nothing else she resembled our mother. Still, as fickle as he was after our brother died, who knows if that changed or not?" He paused again, looking out over the open water. "And I left her. I left her because it was easier to run away than to face my problems head on. Who does something like that to someone they love?"

"You're returning now. This is your chance to make things right."

Jonrell sighed. "I hope so. But she is a woman now. I've been away from her longer than I was with her." He started to laugh. "One Above, what right did I have to tell Cassus he was afraid to face his past when I'm just as scared?"

"Still, you are facing it," said Krytien. "You know Cassus didn't leave to spite you."

"I never said he did."

"You didn't have to. I see the look you make when his name comes up."

Jonrell paused, thinking. "I know it's not fair of me. In a way I respect the fact he went out on his own. I guess I just always imagined that we would return together as heroes, and him not being here makes me realize how childish that idea was."

"Can I make a suggestion?"

Jonrell smirked. "When have you ever needed my permission to speak your mind?"

Krytien smiled. "Good point. Don't be afraid of the past. I've done a lot of things I regret. We all have. Instead of hiding it in the corners of your mind and hoping never to hear from it again, embrace it. Make it yours and learn from it. Aren't you always the one who says, 'A little fear makes you feel alive'?"

"Sure. But I was talking more along the lines of facing an enemy in battle."

"Is there an enemy more dangerous to a man than himself?" asked the old mage.

"When did you become so wise? I've never heard you talk like this."

"Well if truth be told, I like to keep some things secret so you don't give me even more work to do."

"But now your secret's out," said Jonrell with a grin.

"Aye, and I'm sure you'll make up for the lost time." The mage looked over his shoulder. "I hear a game of dice calling my name."

"Haven't you lost enough? Raker said you were down five silvers just today."

The old mage winked. "I've got him right where I want him." He walked away leaving Jonrell to his thoughts.

Not exactly the insight I was looking for but it'll do. He looked up and whispered "Thanks." He moved the stone from his fingers to his palm, squeezing it hard one last time before wheeling his arm back and tossing it into the still water. The small splash it made contrasted against the sudden relief he felt. He turned from the rail, and walked toward the game of dice.

"Seven again. Today must be my day," said Krytien.

"You better not be cheating. I'll run you through if I find out you are," said Raker.

"He's got to be cheating," said Hag. "He hadn't won a game in two days and now he can't lose."

"Hag's right," said Raker, working hard on some chew. "That's almost eleven in a row."

Krytien paused, grabbing the dice from the ground. "Whoa. Why is it when I was in a slump and everyone was taking my money, no one said a word. But now that the roles are reversed everyone is upset." He looked to Jonrell. "Commander, help me out. Surely you see what's going on."

Jonrell chuckled, holding his hands up. "Oh, I see what's going on." He leaned down by Hag's ear and whispered, "Check his left sleeve. He's been switching dice the whole game."

The old woman's squinted eyes grew wide and a quiver ran across her shriveled lips. "Raker, hold that fat mage down while I skin him. He's got the dice rigged. Kroke, give me your knife."

Krytien looked shocked. "What? That's ridiculous. I would never do such a thing." He cast a glare at Jonrell.

"Then let's see what's up those sleeves," said Kroke, spinning a dagger.

Other shouts joined in and Krytien backed away until coming against the main mast. He held his hands up in submission and pulled up his sleeves, exposing both arms and his pasty white skin.

"I told you there was nothing."

Half a dozen dice fell from under his robe and clattered across the deck.

Jonrell let out a laugh so loud it caused everyone to turn. "You better give them back their money." He kept laughing. "You had to get greedy. If you would have lost a few here and there, no one would have been wiser."

"Just getting our money back from today isn't enough. Who knows how many other times he's cheated us," said Hag.

"Oh plenty," said Jonrell still chuckling. "But no more than anyone else and that's what's so funny."

"You better not be calling me a cheat," said the old woman.

"Oh I am. I'm calling all of you cheats, just some are better than others. Hag, you've a marked deck you keep in your trousers for whenever you play cards." He turned to Kroke, "Your deck isn't marked, but you sure like to keep a few extra face cards in it." He looked to another. "And Raker, you're the worst of all. You keep trying to cheat with Yanasi, trusting her to tell you her hand and the whole time she's lying while she's got you giving away everything in yours." He started laughing again. "Now you know why I only play chess."

The Hell Patrol stood there looking at Jonrell with an array of emotions. Confusion, shock, frustration, and even amusement in some of the old hands.

One Above, Krytien was right. It feels good to laugh again. It's been too long.

"Commander!" a shout came from above.

Jonrell looked up and saw Rygar scurrying down the main mast, leaving the crow's nest behind. His thick blond hair tossed about as he slid down the ladder.

Less than ten minutes ago, they had unfurled the square sails as a breeze picked up. The oarsmen used the opportunity to take their first break in days.

All eyes went up to the shirtless man, baked by the sun. He landed with a thud, jumping down the last several rungs. "Commander, we've got trouble. There's a ship coming out over the horizon," he said out of breath.

"It's the ocean. We're bound to run into another using it sooner or later."

"It's more than that," said Rygar. "Yanasi and I spotted it in the distance moments ago. We used that spyglass the captain gave us and got a better look. It's a war galley, Sir. And it's heading right for us."

"He's right, Sir. We both saw it," said Yanasi, descending the ladder. Her red hair was pulled back into a tight ponytail as usual; somehow her fair skin remained unscathed by the sun.

One Above, she is so much a woman now. And yet all I think about is the half starved little girl I took in all those years ago.

"It's amazing they saw anything with both of them up there alone," someone muttered.

"I heard that, Raker, and don't think I won't pay you back for it," said Yanasi with an edge to her voice that she seemed to save just for him. Unlike Rygar, she landed on the deck taking each rung down to the bottom. "Go on commander, take a look," she said in a soft voice. She pulled a long cylindrical tube from round her neck and held it out in her hand.

Jonrell took the spyglass and walked to the sterncastle. Yanasi pointed out the speck in the distance they called a ship.

How in the world did they even see that? Squinting, he found his target and scanned the other ship. What he saw troubled him. "Twice our size and with twin decks of oars. Rygar, go wake Captain Sylik and give him the details."

Rygar raced toward Sylik's quarters.

"What are they coming after us for?" asked Raker.

Jonrell handed him the spyglass. "Have a look."

The mercenary took the device. "You've got to be kidding me!"

"Will somebody just spit it out already," said Hag. "I'm liable to die before I ever get an answer."

Raker spat, "Lord Roundness. I knew we should have chased him on Mytarcis." He handed the spyglass back to Jonrell. "If he would have been this determined before, he might've made a better boss."

"Well, he's determined now. Leaving before a major battle and stealing a couple hundred slaves would get under most people's skin," said Jonrell. He turned to Krytien. "He's got two mages with him—one green and one yellow."

"One green, one yellow? I can handle them."

"Both?"

"Are you saying I can't handle a couple of sorry apprentices?"

"You haven't faced very many mages in battle of late. I figured you may be out of practice."

"I won't even work up a sweat. Maybe I should send something out over the ocean now? You know just to give them an idea of what's waiting for them." He took a step forward, pushing the sleeves back up his arms. Another pair of die fell out and hit the deck, rolling just under his foot as he walked. The mage's legs came right out from under him and he fell flat on his back, banging his head with a thud. A loud cackle went up at the sight but only for a moment when they saw he wasn't moving.

Hag leaned over and slapped the mage a couple of times. "He's out cold."

"Not surprised. All that weight coming down on his head," said Raker.

Rygar ran back up, breathing heavy. "Sylik's on his way, Commander." Jonrell nodded.

"Maybe we can outrun them." said Yanasi, looking out over the water.

"We'll never outrun that ship in open waters," said Jonrell. "It's best to just let the oarsmen rest for now so we can use them for maneuvering when the galley approaches." Jonrell handed the spyglass back to Yanasi. "Get back up in that crow's nest and keep an eye on their approach. And make sure you're tied down. The last thing I want is you falling to the deck in the heat of battle."

"Yes, sir," said Yanasi, before scurrying off. Rygar followed on her heels.

Jonrell called out to no one in particular as he bent over the old mage sprawled out at his feet. "Someone go grab Wiqua. Let's see if he's as good with healing humans as he is with horses."

"Brown devil," Glacar muttered, walking away. "I'd rather die than have that dog look at me."

Jonrell shook his head, choosing not to respond to the comment. He was more interested in the condition of his friend. He felt the back of Krytien's head and pulling his hand away saw it was damp with blood. *That's not good.*

* * *

Minutes passed without any change in Krytien's condition. The approaching galley closed the distance between the two ships and Jonrell worried he would enter battle against two mages without the support of his own.

Sylik had his crew running around and prepping the ship for combat. The Hell Patrol dressed for battle.

Jonrell waited near Krytien, watching Wiqua hurry up the stern of the ship. Hag stood at Jonrell's side.

Wiqua bowed. "What can I do to help?"

"We've got trouble coming and I need him ready."

"I'll take a look."

Wiqua bent down over the mage and moved his hand across the plump body, stopping and touching him in various places. With closed eyes, he made it to the mage's head and lingered. He glanced up at Jonrell. "Other than a few minor bumps, he's physically alright."

"Then why isn't he awake?"

"He hit his head pretty hard and knocked himself unconscious"

"I know. Heal him. Krytien himself kept going on about how powerful you were."

Wiqua lowered his head. "You are too kind, Commander, but there have been many others among my people more powerful than I. And yes, I have some talent with healing but when dealing with matters of the mind, there is only so much one can do. I've reduced the swelling around his head but he will have to wake on his own."

"I don't understand. If there isn't anything physically wrong with him, why can't you just wake him? I saw horses that had broken legs walking shortly after they were healed."

"Animals and humans are different. And more importantly, healing the body and healing the mind are leagues apart, especially the human mind. It is too complex, too unique, and too specific to each individual."

"So you're saying you can't get him to wake up."

"No, I can wake him, I choose not to. I never touch another's mind without the consent of the individual. Even the slightest push or prod could affect a person's sanity. Then again, everything could be fine. It is not my place to make such decisions and it is against my belief to take such a risk. I'm sure you would not want your friend to wake and discover he is not the man you knew."

"I say wake him anyway. Any change can only improve him as far as I'm concerned," said Hag.

Jonrell gave the old woman an icy stare, his gray eyes grew cold under the warm sun. "No. I won't risk it. Wiqua, grab some men and take him down below. Stay with him and do all you can." *Great. Now we're outnumbered, facing a better ship, and going against two mages with no one to throw back against them.*

Hag just shook her head, watching Krytien be carried below deck. "There goes our ace in the hole."

"That's alright." Jonrell said with a grin, putting his hand on her shoulder. "I've got the perfect wild card."

* * *

Sails had come in, secured tight with rigging.

No need to give those mages a target.

Oarsmen churned away at the now choppy waves, propelling *Ocean Spirit* forward at cruising speed. The earlier breeze had strengthened. A storm brewed off in the distance. Heralded by flashes of lightning, the ship was on course to meet the leaden sky.

Jonrell pulled open the captain's spyglass as a light spray covered its lens. The approaching galley had exposed its name. *Sea Beast.* In comparison to *Ocean Spirit*, a beast is just what the ship reminded Jonrell of. Weighed down in full armor, men struggled to keep their feet on the swaying deck.

Good old Melchizan. Better protection does little when you're rolling on an unsteady deck or sinking to the ocean floor.

Jonrell smiled when he moved his spyglass to the ship's wheel and saw Melchizan himself bringing the galley in. He wore heavy plate, including a thick helm with the visor down. *This should be interesting.*

A man who looked to be *Sea Beast*'s captain yelled in Melchizan's direction, gesturing wildly with his hands. He made a move toward the wheel, but several of Melchizan's guards shoved him back. The captain fell into one of his own crew's arms, gesturing obscenely as he stormed off.

Hmm, if I can even the odds a bit, the ship's crew might take care of my problems for me. Just got to get rid of those mages.

Sea Beast's sails were taut in the wind. However, the galley's approach slowed. The oarsmen's strokes grew uneven and out of sync, a sign of either a poor rowmaster or fatigue.

They've spent themselves just trying to reach us.

Jonrell closed the spyglass and handed it back to Sylik. The old man carried a face hardened by a life at sea and exposed sun. His beard hung low and so did the opening in his shirt. The captain led a merchant ship now but Sylik had spoken to Jonrell of his time as a smuggler in his younger days. He had given up the life after he lost his entire ship and crew at sea.

Sylik and he had reached an agreement and the old seadog had deferred everything to Jonrell except the wheel and command of his oarsmen.

"It's time. Any questions?" Jonrell asked.

"You do your part, I'll see we do ours." The old man peered across the water at the approaching galley, his mouth parting into a smile filled with rotting teeth. "The way that ship's rolling about, can't say it'll be much of a challenge anyway." The captain took over the ship's wheel from his first mate and started bellowing orders to his crew.

Jonrell looked down to the main deck. He gestured first to a group of thirty men, a third of whom were the ship's deckhands, and the rest his own. They took cover behind barrels stacked in the deck's center, and at his signal notched their arrows.

"Anyone fires a shot before I give command, I'll make sure it's the last one they ever fire. Remember your orders," Jonrell bellowed over the wind. There was an edge to his voice, and men looked more focused than before.

Near the portside railings, most of his remaining men crouched down using shields, crates, and heavy tarps for cover. They waited with a calmness about them, gripping tight the weapons in hand. Jonrell didn't bother with any final words for that group. They were his most trusted and most experienced, chosen because of their resolve.

"She's gaining fast," said Raker, standing a dozen feet behind the commander.

Sea Beast was only a few hundred yards away, oarsmen still out of step, beating the waves with an uneven sense of urgency.

"Aye, just a couple of minutes." He glanced back. "Don't you go off half-cocked either. Wait until Hag has done her part."

"Aw c'mon. I may get antsy but this right here is what I live for," said Raker, patting the tarp.

"I hope that thing works," said Jonrell.

"Trust me," said Raker. He spat a wad of chew on the deck. "Like Hag, she ain't pretty, but she'll get the job done." He looked over to Hag. A rope ran up through a set of pulleys situated high on the main mast. Several sailors held one end while another secured the other end around the woman. She had bottles strapped to her in every which way and another sailor pulled a cloak over her head, covering the bottles beneath. "Why you got her doing this anyway?"

"She's four and a half feet tall and older than dirt. Who would be intimidated by that?" asked Jonrell.

"I would."

Jonrell smiled. "That's because you know her." They shared a laugh and Jonrell looked out across the ship one last time, eyes meeting Kroke who waited at the bow in solitude. He caught Jonrell's eye and nodded. *I swear that man has a death wish to volunteer for what he's attempting.*

A stack of bottles filled with lamp oil lay at Jonrell's feet. Three old timers among the *Ocean Spirit*'s crew stood next to the bottles.

In the last two hundred yards, *Sea Beast* came roaring in, bobbing erratically in the waves as Melchizan kept precariously on course for a boarding action. Their novice mages attacked first, sending small fire balls across the span of the two ships. The mages showed their inexperience, as many sailed over the deck or sizzled into the water between the ships. Sylik's call to soak the tarps and deck itself paid off as the flames failed to catch.

"A hundred yards, captain!" Jonrell shouted.

"Aye!"

Sylik shouted down orders to his first mate who relayed them to the rowmaster below.

Jonrell turned back to *Sea Beast* where men prepared gangplanks and twirled grappling hooks, ready for when the ships met.

Jonrell drew his sword. "Take aim!"

The galley inched closer and Sylik shouted for oars to be pulled in portside.

"Release!" Jonrell called out.

Arrows sailed over *Sea Beast*'s railing, falling in one concentrated spot, where Melchizan stood. Despite his protection, the barrage caught him off guard and he stumbled to the ship's deck.

Grappling hooks sailed above the span and clacked over *Ocean Spirit*'s railing. Jonrell's men hacked away at the ropes until Melchizan's men swung across amid a gust of wind from the mages, helping propel the fully armored men.

Jonrell cursed. *I didn't count on the mages doing that!*

Melchizan's guards held up shields to protect their leader from the continued arrow fire as he struggled to regain control of his ship. Jonrell signaled Sylik and the old captain seized advantage of the moment, separating the two ships with a turn of the wheel and a push from the portside oarsmen.

At least that worked out.

Shouting, chopping of wood, glass breaking, and steel clanging all rang in Jonrell's ears but over the next few moments he saw none of it, as the last several men to chance the leap across *Sea Beast* down to *Ocean Spirit* swung toward him on the sterncastle.

As the first came in, Jonrell sidestepped the man's stroke, and countered with a slash of his own that severed the man's arm at the elbow. Two others followed but the three old timers near the railing dumped each over the side before they gathered themselves.

Another two swung right past Jonrell, high overhead, just as a loud *whoosh* whisked past his ear.

One Above. How many made it across?

Jonrell turned to catch a high blow with his shield. He nearly dropped down to one knee at the impact of the strike, but quickly recovered. Jonrell used his speed against the stronger, more heavily armored foe. He avoided a thrust and swung his sword across the back of the man's neck.

He kicked the lifeless form under the railing and over the side, chain mail scraping wood as the body careened into the ocean. The commander looked up at Raker throwing a mutilated figure over the railing himself. The bloodied mace he used lay on the deck just near the mercenary's ballista, now uncovered and empty.

He got the shot off.

Most of the fighting had ended on the rest of the ship. The last two men to have crossed over to *Ocean Spirit* did their best to defend themselves, but their effort was wasted as two arrows from the crow's nest pierced each man's neck.

The commander scanned the area at his feet quickly and breathed a small sigh of relief. *Good, the bottles are gone.*

Sea Beast came under control, struggling to turn about and pursue the fleeing merchant ship.

"Any damage captain?"

"Nothing major," said Sylik. Two arrows stood near his feet and another embedded in the wheel, neither seemed to cause him concern. Blood covered his sleeve and neck.

"Are you hurt?"

Sylik looked down at his arm. "Not mine."

A ball of magefire hit *Ocean Spirit*'s deck while several others splashed harmlessly into the water. Crew members ran over and beat out the sputtering flames before they caused any damage.

"Good," said Jonrell. "How soon before we can let them catch up?"

"Whenever you're ready. I'm just playing cat and mouse with them now while we make some minor repairs." He laughed. "Most of them fools never made it across the span and are lost in the black below."

Jonrell pulled out his spyglass to get a better look at the galley. A man clung to the side of the hull, a blade in his teeth.

One Above, that man is lucky.

Kroke's ripped shirt exposed sinewy arms flexing as he worked his way across the ship's side. *He doesn't look like much, but I sure wouldn't want to be on his bad side.* "Kroke made it. We'll give him a couple of minutes while we ready ourselves for the next pass."

The old man roared out orders over the wind and his crew ran around desperate to fill them. The sky above darkened with each passing moment.

Jonrell panned his spyglass over the main deck and spotted the green mage. He failed to see the yellow mage. The rest of the deck moved about in a frenzy as many prepared for the next pass as well. Melchizan stood back at the wheel, still in armor and visor down. "Raker, you got the yellow one."

"I told you she would work."

"And I told you to aim for the green one. He's the one I'm concerned with."

"I didn't have a shot. The yellow one was the only one distracted by Hag swinging overhead on the rope and throwing the bottles of oil. The green one knew better."

Jonrell let out a sigh. "Load the ballista again and fire at the green mage this time."

Hag yelled and pitched a fit as Jonrell made his way to the main deck to survey the damage. He yelled to the man set on untangling her from the rigging. "Is she hurt?" he asked, noting several arrows sticking from her chest, the front of her tarp blackened.

"No. Just in a bad mood is all. The padding and armor stopped any arrows and we soaked the tarp well enough where she only got singed."

"Only singed! I swear I'm going kill all of you when I get down from here. You swore to me that I was only to be a distraction and nothing more. I didn't know I'd be target practice for them lackwits."

"Complain to me all you want later. Did you drop the bottles?"

"Aye. I dropped them all. And I'll be doing more to you than complain later, that's for sure."

Jonrell turned to the man still struggling with the rigging as Hag cursed his clumsiness and lack of speed. "Put her off to the side for now. She won't be going up again and I need you with the archers on this pass." The man smiled and Hag swore but Jonrell paid neither any mind.

Jonrell met Glacar at the railing, as he tossed the last dead body overboard and picked his double sided axe back up, grip wrapped in shark skin. The man's beard and hair were so wild and unkept they nearly met in the middle of his face, with just a scarred nose and a hint of dark eyes peeking out. Glacar had turned out to be one of the few positives from their last trip to Thurum so many years ago. The burly man had stayed on with the group after the nightmare surrounding the battle of Asantia.

"How did we fare?" asked Jonrell.

"Well enough." The mercenary looked down at Jonrell's blood sprayed gauntlet.

"Did we lose anyone?"

"Two of the ship's crewman, both burned from the green mage. We've got a couple men of our own bloodied up, but they ain't dead yet."

"Good. See that they last another pass. We'll tend to them afterward."

"Aye." Glacar grabbed a passing soldier by his arm and spun him around, bellowing orders of his own, determined not to let anyone relax.

Next, Jonrell turned to the archers as they restacked and secured the barrels that fell during the first boarding. "Get those braziers lit." He pointed. "Next pass I want you eight to aim for the stern near the captain's wheel." He pointed again. "You ten will concentrate your fire on the center, especially where the green mage is positioned if you can. Everyone else, light up their sails."

"What about us, Sir?" came a voice from above.

Jonrell peered up to the crow's nest where Rygar hung over the side, looking down at him. "Aim for any broken glass near that mage."

"Sir?"

"The lamp oil Hag dropped should be concentrated there and with only a green robe, that mage won't be able to extend his barrier of protection more than a few feet while still mounting an attack."

"Yes, sir."

"She's coming back round, Commander!" Sylik shouted from behind. "You ready to meet her?"

"Aye."

Back at the stern, Jonrell looked through the captain's spyglass once again. The men on *Sea Beast* scrambled to remove their heavy armor before they reengaged.

Sea Beast's second pass seemed about as unsteady as her first as she mauled her way through the choppy water. Her oarsmen looked all but useless, and the ship seemed to be relying instead on her sails.

Lightening illuminated the scene as rain began to fall.

The ships edged closer and the green mage glowered out front, sending several fireballs across the water and onto the main deck. This time, many more hit their mark and water crews struggled to keep the deck from going up.

A massive bolt flew past Jonrell from behind. The mage threw his hands out in a warding gesture, and a wave of force knocked the missile aside where it bit deeply into the decking at his feet.

Great.

The mage countered with a shadowy figure that oozed from his sleeve and then skirted across the water, heading straight for the ship's stern.

The commander yelled out "Archers now! I want that ship burning." Fire arrows filled the space between the two ships, battering the war galley. *Sea Beast* erupted in flames, and with that, the galley lurched off course.

The shadow crossed the span and reached their position. One of the old timers drew a sword from his belt and slashed at the blackness, but his blade passed through with no effect. The shape seized the man by wrapping its form around his, pinning his limbs at the side. The old timer let out a cry as the shape constricted, and Jonrell heard the man's bones snapping from the pressure. The body let out a shudder and fell limp to the deck. The creature uncoiled itself and then feinted toward another of the old men before changing course and coming right for Jonrell.

"One Above," he muttered under his breath.

He slashed out with his sword and edged away from the shadow. The commander twisted and dodged but could not avoid its grasp. His chest compressed as it coiled around him. Jonrell caught the look of panic in Raker's eyes and the mercenary made an effort to help him.

"Stay back," Jonrell managed through gasping breaths.

He felt the air leave his lungs, his arms lose strength. He wanted to fight the creature, but he hadn't the power to do so.

This is it. Dead before I reach Cadonia.

But then the pressure dissipated.

What?

His relief swirled around him in a nauseating tangle of dizziness that dropped him to hands and knees. Someone's hands wrapped around his arms and pulled him up. From the smell he knew right away it was Raker.

"How did you stop it?" asked Jonrell.

"I ain't did nothing. Someone finally woke up from their nap and joined the fun," said Raker, inclining his head behind him.

Krytien held the shadow with some invisible grip. The mage's lips moved, void of sound, and the creature vanished. Sweat covered Krytien's face, his thin hair drenched from the ordeal. "Are you alright?"

"I should be asking you the same," said Jonrell.

"I'm fine. Still weak from my fall. I've never seen a green mage able to conjure up such a creature before."

"Can you take care of him before he sends another?"

"I don't need to." He inclined his head toward the galley. Flames danced across its decks and up its masts, playing in the sails and burning men alive. The green mage staggered with a dagger in his gut, twisting about from arrows fired by *Ocean Spirit*'s crew. Now that the battle seemed lost, the captain had rallied his men to turn on Melchizan's soldiers. Jonrell started to chuckle but caught himself. "Where's Kroke?"

Krytien looked confused.

"He's on *Sea Beast*. You were out and there were two mages to deal with. Where do you think the knife came from?" Jonrell spotted the thin man clinging once again to the side of the galley. Alarmed, he realized that the two ships were drifting apart. "Captain! What are you doing?"

"Getting my ship to safety."

"Turn her back round. We've got a man back there."

"Not my problem. I ain't turning back so the whole ship can catch fire and die to save one man. He knew what he was getting into."

Raker slipped a blade under the captain's throat, raising his chin.

"If you don't turn this ship around now, Raker will open your throat right at the wheel."

"You'll die," said the captain. His eyes drifted off into the distance. "That storm will tear us apart without me at the wheel. We need to get the old girl ready."

"Then we die. Turn this ship around."

Sylik let out a curse and spun the wheel around. Raker moved the blade away from the captain's throat as Sylik shouted out orders.

Sea Beast was adrift, its crew fighting against Melchizan's men.

"Bring her in captain," said Jonrell.

"I can't."

Raker pushed the blade back into his throat. "I don't recall Jonrell asking you a question."

"Slice my throat open then, but if I get too close to that ship, we'll all die for sure. The waves are too rough now and she's moving in such a way that it's impossible to reach her unscathed. If I get too close we won't have to worry about the storm because we'll all drown."

Jonrell looked at the haphazard sway of the ship. *One Above, he's right.* "Raker, load up the ballista one last time and tie some rope up to her shaft. Secure the other end to the main deck."

"What about him?" he said, nodding to the captain.

"Forget him. Do it." He turned to Sylik. "How close can you bring her in and how long can you keep her in line?"

"I know what you're doing. You're crazy."

"Answer my question captain. We are not leaving him to die," said Jonrell.

"A couple hundred feet at best. I can't hold her long though."

"You heard that Raker?"

"I'm working on it."

"Well get it done then," said Jonrell.

Raker finished setting the ballista in record time. Sylik called down to his rowmaster and the oarsmen stopped as the captain glided her in toward the burning pyre, using the current itself to propel the merchant ship.

One Above, he's good. Jonrell stared at the war galley as it burned. Many of the ship's crew not busy fighting against Melchizan's soldiers sought desperately to put out the spreading fire.

How is that thing staying afloat?

"You never told me what I'm aiming for. Both mages are down," said Raker.

"You're going to aim for a spot about two feet to the side of Kroke. Preferably to his left since that is his strong hand."

"And what if I hit him?" asked Raker.

"Then I'll know Kroke was right," said Jonrell.

"Right about what?"

"That your aim turns to mud when you're under pressure."

"He said what?"

The mechanism went off and Jonrell barely had a moment to whip his head around to see the spear slam into the hull, mere inches from Kroke's head.

"Ha. How's that for aim?" said Raker.

Without hesitating, Kroke reached out and grabbed the rope, moving arm over arm across the taught line. An arrow protruded from his shoulder and yet the mercenary's pace remained steady.

Several of Melchizan's soldiers hung crossbows over *Sea Beast's* side, firing at the thin man swinging above the crashing blue waves. His legs swung up and he grabbed the rope with his ankles as well, wrapping both arms and legs around it. "Give him some cover," Jonrell yelled to his bowmen. A blade appeared in Kroke's hands and he began cutting the rope under his feet. A bolt struck him in the side just as the last thread snapped. He and the rope fell into the waves.

Jonrell and several others raced to the other end of the rope, heaving and pulling with all their might. "Get us out of here, captain," Jonrell called out as he watched the mercenary bob along in the rough waves, attempting to stay above water.

The oarsmen put their shoulders into it just as they lifted Kroke from the water, scraping against the side of the ship. Jonrell pushed others aside to pull Kroke onto the deck himself.

The mercenary struggled to breathe, coughing up water and blood. *One Above, that last arrow hit something major.*

"That's one less mage in the world," Kroke said with a grin before passing out.

Jonrell looked up to Krytien. "Do something."

"I can only do so much. Wiqua would be...."

"He isn't a horse. I want someone I can trust."

"Then trust me. Wiqua can save him, I'm not skilled enough."

"Get him, now."

Krytien hurried off, pushing through the crowd that had gathered.

"Everyone get back to work. Follow Sylik's command to get the ship repaired before we all die in the storm ahead," Jonrell snapped.

A moment later Krytien returned with the healer. "Can you help him? You look as though you lack the strength."

"I was helping the others from their wounds. I can help him but only if we hurry, he is fading fast. I need you to do as I say," said Wiqua.

Jonrell and Krytien did as instructed, pushing here, holding there, as the healer removed each arrow. His hands glowed and moved with a skillful grace. When he finished, his head hung low and he breathed heavy. "He will recover, though he will be sore. I'll have someone help me take him below deck to recover." He looked at Jonrell. "I'm sorry that I won't have the strength to help you with your bruises as well. It was poor planning on my part not to tend to you earlier."

Jonrell sat in awe of Wiqua. Kroke's skin had sealed under the healer's touch, stitching itself back together. "I owe you an apology." He turned to Krytien. "And you as well."

"Commander?" asked Wiqua.

"Krytien had been going on about how great of a healer you were and I dismissed it. But I have never seen such talent with the human body in all my life, not even in my years studying on Estul Island." He paused. "Thank you for your help."

Wiqua smiled. "You're welcome but this is what my people do. It is nothing," he said looking weary.

"Nothing? You'll have to tell me how...."

Krytien touched his arm. "How about we give him a chance to rest first?"

Jonrell nodded. "Yes. You're right."

"Commander!" Jonrell looked up at the shout coming from the wheel, recognizing Sylik's voice over the gusting wind. "If you're done down there, I could use all the hands I can get." The captain pointed.

A flash of lightning burst across the blackened sky, illuminating the turbulent dark waters ahead.

The rain came down harder, battering the bright flames on *Sea Beast*'s deck. A smile crawled across Jonrell's face as he saw a lone lifeboat lowered into the tumbling waves. *They'll never make it.*

"Are you smiling?" Krytien asked. He looked closer. "You are smiling. What is wrong with you?"

Jonrell turned to the mage, grinning ear to ear. He knew he should be worried, he should be stressed, concerned even, and he was to an extent. But this was different. His worries didn't control him. *Ocean Spirit* had faced impossible odds and came out with minimal losses, none from his crew.

I forgot what it felt to live in the moment, to trust my instincts.

"Nothing is wrong. Now let's have some fun." He moved away to help the crew, leaving Krytien to reason things out himself.

CHAPTER 7

The streets of the Blue Island Clan capital puddled with water from a passing storm, cooling the hot cobblestones under busy feet. Splitting the city down its center, Juanoq's main road stretched in a straight line from its entrance to the docks. Paved in gray, its width allowed for more than a dozen wagons to travel side by side without any hindrance. Only dirt covered the narrower side streets and alleys.

"Eventually the roads will all be the same, but as of late, priority has shifted," said Tobin.

He and Nachun veered onto a side street to the left.

As usual for this time of year, men and women donned light clothing, all of which seemed to contain at least some accent of blue. Many of the men chose to clothe themselves as Tobin, wearing trousers, moccasins, and a vest to cover their torso in place of a shirt. The women wore long dresses to their ankles. The streets teamed with people as the two men maneuvered their way through the press. Nachun nearly ran into the back of someone as he craned his neck to take in all of the sights.

Lasting weeks, the return trip to the Blue Islands had given the two men a chance to bond. As an advisor to Tobin's father, Nachun spent a great deal of time in Bazraki's company, busy with increasingly important tasks. The shaman turned out to be so efficient in those duties that within a week after taking Nubinya, Bazraki had felt comfortable enough to leave the city in the hands of its new government.

Kaz recognized the growing favor in which Bazraki held Nachun. Rather than punish Nachun for the resentment Kaz felt toward the shaman, he took it out on Tobin. Despite such abuse, Tobin was not bitter about the extra work. Many a night, Nachun would stand watch at his side, keeping silent company with him on an otherwise lonely night as Tobin pulled a double watch. And regardless of what the shaman worked on for his father, he had always found a way to join Tobin for meals so they could pass the time in conversation.

Tobin realized early on that he dominated those discussions. Nachun never seemed to care, always listening and asking more questions about the history of Tobin's clan. Tobin didn't mind Nachun's reluctance to open up further. Given the recent upheaval in his life, it only seemed natural for the shaman to avoid his past. Tobin also didn't want to push him away.

Having come to enjoy Nachun's company, the thought of reporting their discussions back to Bazraki almost felt like betrayal.

But one day Father will ask me what I've learned. He shook his head, determined not to allow such thoughts to ruin his day.

The men rounded another corner and found themselves at the entrance to Juanoq's bustling market district. Tall buildings encircled the large open area located to the west of the city's center. Merchants sold an assortment of goods, both common and exotic. The smell of various delicacies overpowered the senses as the two men moved about the organized chaos.

The occasional moneylender stood between the rows of merchant stands, always wearing a warm smile. *And daggers up their sleeves.*

"Juanoq is so new. Much newer than Nubinya or any of the other cities in Hesh I've visited. It's as if you cut the brick and stone yesterday and laid them overnight," said Nachun, wonder in his voice.

"In some cases that may very well be true." Tobin pointed to the construction of several tall buildings, the most complex of which he singled out. "That one began just before I ventured off along the Burnt Sands coast. Now, look at it. After a couple of months, it is higher than those that surround it." He sighed. "I remember a time when this city lacked even a wall for protection. Once my father came into power, it was the first thing he demanded, a wall stronger than any other in all of Hesh."

"Did your father visit the homes of other clans? There are pieces here that are reminiscent of those other cities." He gestured toward a pattern of blue azurite stones adorning a gray brick wall.

"No, he did not visit those places himself. However, others were sent in his stead." Tobin rested his hand on the wall Nachun singled out. "After seeing Nubinya, I realized that many of his ideas were probably borrowed from other clans." He paused, thinking. "Though at least in Nubinya's case, it seems as though he improved upon their techniques."

Nachun nodded. "I would have to agree."

They continued walking, and Tobin noticed the influx of wares from the plunder of Nubinya. Bazraki had not bled the desert city dry, but he was sure to take enough of their past from them to break their spirit. The most valuable items, Tobin's father kept for himself. His most loyal and trusted allies then chose several items for themselves as a reward for their services. Merchants received the remaining items to sell in the market where Bazraki would tax their profit. Yesterday's cast-offs were now today's fastest selling and most expensive items in the market. People clamored to purchase such goods at nearly ten times their worth.

The trash of a ruler is a prize to the commoner.

Nachun came across an older man selling scrolls, books, and even ancient stone tablets. The shaman's eyes lit up and he eagerly began asking questions about their contents, seeking documents about the most ancient histories of the continent of Hesh.

"I may be here for awhile. Go on. I'll catch up," said Nachun while examining one of the scrolls.

"I can wait," said Tobin shrugging.

Without looking up the shaman answered with a grunt. "I know you have no interest in such things. Please, do not stay for my benefit." Nachun went back to his questions with the merchant, discussing the accuracy of several items, haggling over price.

Tobin decided to wait anyway, leaning against a nearby post. Shaded from the sun by a canopy, his eyes roamed about, taking in the scene. *It seems that every time I return, the city changes. I barely even remember what it looked like when I was a boy.* His eyes stopped on a group of merchants selling fresh fruit, focusing on one stand selling breadfruit.

A petite woman with skin like polished onyx spoke to the merchant. She reached out and touched the man's arm as the two shared a laugh. She did this while loading a basket, one breadfruit after the other into her basket with no help from the merchant. Her beauty distracted the man, and Tobin watched him undress her with his eyes. Tobin walked over to the stand, agitated by the merchant's behavior.

"Are all merchants as poor a salesman as you?" asked Tobin.

The beaded jewelry about the round man's neck jingled as he jumped, looking around nervously.

At least he has the decency to be embarrassed.

The merchant lowered his gaze, ready to offer an apology.

"Tobin?" The woman looked up from the basket, her full lips parting into a wide smile. "I knew that was your voice!" She reached up, almost jumping, wrapping her arms around him and giving a tight squeeze before letting go.

"T-Tobin?" The merchant stuttered. "I beg your forgiveness. I had no idea you knew the woman or ..."

"Or what?" Tobin cut in. He pointed down. "You would have helped her load the basket."

"Y-yes, I'm very sorry. Please, what can I do to make things right?" said the man bowing as low as he dared without falling over.

Tobin folded his arms. "Reducing the cost by one quarter of the total for a start."

"One quarter?" the merchant whispered.

"It is only fair. Also, this is much too heavy for someone so delicate. Wouldn't you agree?"

Defeated, the merchant let out a sigh. "I can have my son deliver the fruit wherever you like."

"The palace."

"Yes, of course." The merchant paused, scratching the top of his hands. "So all is settled then? We won't need to bring this before your father or brother, correct?"

"Both my father and brother have more pressing concerns," said Tobin, more angry than intended. *He knows who and what I am and yet his fear lies with those I know, not me.* "We're settled."

The merchant bowed lower. "Thank you." He pulled a flap to the tent behind his stand, shouting a boy's name as he entered.

When the tent flap closed, a soft voice spoke up. "Why did you do that? He was harmless. Besides, I am more than capable of carrying the basket myself."

"I never said you weren't. But that doesn't mean you should have to carry it either."

Lucia smiled, shaking her head. "You are too good to me."

"I could never be such a thing."

She smiled again, putting her head down in embarrassment. Then as though remembering something, she looked up with concern. "Where were you yesterday? I didn't see you with the rest of the army returning from Nubinya. People were waiting to glimpse Tobin," she said, deepening her voice, "the mighty Kifzo warrior."

Tobin chuckled. "Now who is being too good to whom?" He paused, shaking his head. "No. Juanoq cares little for me." He inclined his head toward the merchant's tent. "This one didn't know who I was until you said my name. And even then, he feared not me, but Bazraki and Kaz."

Lucia frowned, laying a hand on his arm. "You are always so hard on yourself. You're a good man."

Remembering the little girl cowering in the gloom of her hut at Munai, his blade lashing out and striking across her throat, Tobin tensed at Lucia's touch. *I wish I felt the same.*

A clamor of noise rose up behind the two, and Lucia let her hand drop. The people in the market swarmed around a Kifzo moving through the masses, ignoring the cheers and praise directed at him. Kaz walked tall and confident with his head held high and chest puffed out. His eyes flashed about, searching. A rare but genuinely warm smile crept across his face having spotted Lucia. The moment faded, face turning into a scowl, as Kaz's eyes crawled upward and met Tobin's.

Tobin turned to Lucia whose face lit up in a way that made him feel insignificant.

How can she be so happy to see him?

She ran and leaped into Kaz's arms, the couple embracing until the crowd dispersed, having realized their hero would not entertain their conversations or buy their goods. Tobin looked on, gawking in disbelief, as Lucia giggled from an unheard whisper spoken by Kaz.

Even after all these years, I can't forget. Kaz met Tobin's eyes as the couple separated, grinning all the same. *And he knows it. He knows I wanted her first. But just like everything else in my life that he's taken from me, he took her before I even had my chance.*

"*Brother*, I hope you weren't bothering my wife again."

"Kaz, be nice. Tobin could never bother me. We're family." said Lucia.

Kaz said nothing in reply but grunted, the look on his face telling Tobin what he thought of that.

"It was pure coincidence that we ran into each other," said Tobin, trying to smooth things over.

"Yes and Tobin got a better deal on the breadfruit I was buying for the dinner tonight. It was the last thing on my list," said Lucia

Kaz grinned. He took Lucia by the arm, "Good. If you are done, then we have some time for ourselves."

"But Kaz, I haven't paid the merchant yet," said Lucia, protesting.

"Don't worry. I'm sure my *brother* will be more than happy to take care of that for you. Won't you?"

Tobin answered, looking only at Lucia. "Go on."

She smiled. "Thank you. I'll make the breadfruit extra special for you tonight."

Tobin smiled and in return Kaz growled. "C'mon. Leave my *brother* to his errands." Kaz took his wife by the arm and left the market.

Turning back to the merchant's stand, a young, gangly boy, no more than eleven, barreled through the tent's flap in a rush, shouts from his father following him. "And be quick about it, you hear? I've been too easy on you." The boy came around front in a hurry, picking up the basket with a pull and a grunt. Taking a moment to gain his balance, he wobbled down the road in direction of the palace, basket resting on one shoulder.

The merchant stared after him, muttering something under his breath. He waved a dismissive hand and turned back to face Tobin, noticing for the first time that Lucia was no longer there. "Where is the lovely woman?" he said worried.

"Gone. I'll settle the bill. How much?" asked Tobin with a sigh.

"Eight coppers."

"And the reduced price?"

"Oh, of course," said the merchant, bowing low. "Please forgive me. Six coppers then."

"Six coppers for a basket of fruit?"

"I picked these breadfruit this very morning with my own hand! You cannot get any fresher without bringing the tree here itself."

"Fine, I'll pay your price." Though after looking the large man over once more, Tobin knew the likelihood of him picking the fruit himself was slim. He removed a pouch from the inside of his vest and threw six coins on the stand, which the merchant scooped up before they came to a rest.

Tobin left the breadfruit stand and returned to Nachun as the shaman wrapped up his purchase of a large pile of scrolls, maps, books, and tablets.

"When can you have these delivered?" asked Nachun.

"I should have them to you this evening," said the old man.

"So soon?" said the shaman.

The old merchant smiled. "I always take care of my best customers."

Nachun nodded, handing over a stack of coins. "Half now and half again when they reach my door."

The merchant's smile soured some, but he nodded in agreement all the same.

Nachun and Tobin set off down the road, but this time without speaking. Nachun was the first to speak. "Are you well?"

"I'm fine."

After a few more moments the shaman asked, "Was that Kaz's wife? She is quite beautiful."

"Yes." Tobin paused. "Please do not speak of her again to me."

The two continued their walk in silence before they parted ways.

* * *

Construction on Juanoq's walls ended almost ten years ago. Jutting out of an otherwise flat but lush land, the granite and azurite stonework towered one hundred feet and built a third as thick as they were tall. Scholars often remarked that the colossal structure had no equal in the known lands of Hesh, and only those ancient cities across The Great Divide were all that could be compared to it in brilliance. Many, including Tobin, questioned such claims, as little evidence suggested such places existed any longer.

Since Bazraki had come into power, his advisors had pleaded with him to build a palace to match his own might, but it wasn't until those walls were completed that Tobin's father finally allowed construction to begin on a new home. Yet almost a decade later, work on the palace still plodded along. The reason for the delays resulted from Bazraki's continual abandonment of the project in order to further strengthen Juanoq's defenses.

The first interruption of work occurred just a few short months into preparing the palace's foundation when Bazraki reassigned workers from the excavation process, tasking them instead to erect towers along the city's walls, each thirty feet high. Construction of a large moat around the city caused the next work stoppage. Filled by diverting a tributary of the Dahan River, the moat not only provided the city with easy access to the river's resources, but with the Paritia Ocean on one side, water completely surrounded Juanoq.

After the moat's completion, Bazraki allowed work to resume on the palace until once again resources were diverted to bolster the defenses of the city. Workers built a dozen defensive towers, as high as Juanoq's walls, cylindrical in shape, outside of the city on the opposite side of the moat. The positioning of the towers ensured that an invading army would not be able to attack any one tower without also facing fire from at least three others. Such design created a unique killing ground for any group daring enough to challenge the Blue Island Clan's growing power and stability.

Not long after garrisoning the towers, Bazraki set out to conquer the Orange Desert Clan and thus something as trivial as a palace, fell by the wayside. Still, his advisors never stopped their endless squawking, saying that a completed palace would bring Bazraki a greater sense of awe in the minds of his enemies. Bazraki scoffed back saying, "What better way to inspire awe than to give them something to fear?" They had no answer to such a blunt point.

As Tobin made his way through the palace's iron gates, he saw that his father had appeased his advisors once again. Workers expanded the ever growing gardens. Flowers, bushes, shrubs and trees, some even bearing fruit, provided a landscape flourishing with life. Though most of the garden grew plants from the Blue Islands, a separate section housed vegetation not indigenous to the Blue Islands. Here, Tobin saw herbalists studying the plants recently obtained from the Burnt Sands Desert.

No doubt for medicinal purposes.

Tobin walked across a solid path of blue stone that led through the garden and to the palace doors. Ducking the occasional branch, he passed several of his father's guards, each barely acknowledging his presence.

Even in my father's own house it continues.

Inside the building, chaos ruled. Workers moved at a frantic pace, almost stumbling over each other, carrying loads of stone, mortar, tools, and scaffolding; all mingling with servants still tasked with overseeing the day to day duties of the palace. The commotion made his head spin.

So many new walls up, doorways that once were, are no longer there. This place is a maze.

Snaking his way down long twisted corridors, moving from room to room, he eventually reached a winding staircase, absent of railing, which led to a second floor hallway. Reaching the top, Tobin negotiated another labyrinth of scaffolding before he located the dining hall.

Bazraki and his advisors sat around a large wooden table that dominated the space. Nachun, Lucia, and Kaz joined them. Supported by rich, hand-carved legs, the blood red color of the table stood in contrast to the equally elaborate chairs, crafted from a pale wood. Oversized windows covered by slatted shutters lined the outside walls, allowing a breeze to cool the room.

Tobin sidestepped a stack of bricks as he limped over the threshold. He caught the end of a conversation between several of Bazraki's advisors, hearing the words "Gray Marsh Clan" and "Mawkuk," though he was unsure of their context.

Would he attempt to conquer them before the Yellow Plain Clan? Interesting.

"*Brother.* Is your leg so bad that it hinders your ability to arrive on time?" said Kaz, loud enough to cause the room to take note of Tobin's arrival.

Tobin ignored Kaz and turned instead to Bazraki. "I apologize, Father. It seems the route I used to take to the dining hall is no longer available. I was forced to find another."

"Yes, these fools can't seem to make up their minds on what they want to do," said Bazraki, gesturing to a group of advisors.

The advisors his father singled out stirred in their seats at the comment, one chanced to speak. "El Olam, please forgive us if we've been a nuisance to you. We only wish your palace to be perfect and in order to make it that way, changes are sometimes made to the original plans."

Bazraki waved a hand. "Enough. I hear enough of this monstrosity and your countless changes each day. I will not have it at my dinner table."

The man bowed his head.

"El Olam?" asked Tobin, puzzled.

Nachun responded, "It means *Everlasting One* in the old tongue. I thought it only fitting as your father's greatness will not be forgotten."

"Everlasting One?" What is Nachun up to?

"Take your seat, Tobin. We've started without you," said Bazraki, ignoring Nachun's answer.

Tobin bowed his head in respect and sat, taking in the wide array of food adorning the table. He began filling his plate, mouth watering at the smell of spices filling the air. He took a bite of baked fish, feeling it almost melt in his mouth, and relaxed. *I always forget how much I miss Lucia's food until I'm home again.*

Tobin was set to enjoy his meal when one of Bazraki's guests, a merchant jingling gaudy jewelry, and sleeves pushed up so as not to dirty his expensive clothing spoke over the smaller conversations in the room.

"Nachun, there were whispers in the city this morning about the awesome power you displayed in Munai. There is even talk that nature itself obeyed your commands. Surely these things cannot all be true?"

The shaman let out a light chuckle. "I appreciate the flattery but my contribution to the Blue Clan's success that day was dependent on many others."

Tobin grinned. *Clever.*

Nachun continued, gesturing with a hand toward Tobin who had just taken a bite of bread. "For instance, without Tobin's bow taking out three shamans and causing confusion amid our enemy's ranks, the outcome may have turned out much differently."

Tobin's mouth hung open, and he nearly had to force it closed to prevent food from spilling out.

What is he doing? Now is not the place for this.

All eyes looked his way as if expecting him to speak. Kaz glared over at him, starting to simmer.

"Enough, shaman," said Kaz.

Nachun glanced to Lucia and back to Kaz. "But Kaz, it seems your own wife is eager to hear more."

Tobin looked over and saw that what Nachun said was true. Lucia did appear to be hanging on every word. *And looking as beautiful as ever.*

"Perhaps if we shifted our focus, then? We cannot forget our warleader, after all." said Nachun, turning back to Lucia, who seemed to perk up further at Kaz's mention. "Your husband was a ferocious beast on the field, slaying the desert clansmen with such intensity, the likes of which I had never seen before." Nachun picked up a knife near his plate, imitating sword strokes. "Slashing here, stabbing there, gouging, ripping, and tearing, with each and every breath. And that was only the beginning, afterward he…"

"I said enough, shaman! It is not our way to speak about such things." said Kaz, slamming his fist on the table, then rising to his feet as he glared at Nachun through squinted eyes.

Tobin saw Lucia frown in confusion as she looked upon her husband. *Can she really be so naïve to what Kaz is? Does he keep his true self that well hidden from her?*

"Sit down, Kaz," said Bazraki in a calm voice. "Nachun is still new to our clan. He doesn't know that we do not boast so openly about our accomplishments."

Nachun bowed his head. "I apologize, El Olam. I meant no harm. I only wished to honor your sons in front of so many guests."

"Kaz is honored as warleader of the Kifzo. His men obey and his enemies fear. *That* makes me proud."

"And Tobin?" said Nachun, pushing the issue further.

Why is he doing this?

Bazraki shrugged, turning to Tobin. "Do you need accolades from me for performing your duties? A parade perhaps?"

"Of course not, Father," said Tobin, eyes averted. *Not a complete lie. A kind word, even only in private would be enough, just a fraction of what you give Kaz.*

"El Olam," said Bazraki.

"Father?" asked Tobin, looking up, confused.

"You will refer to me as 'El Olam.'"

His eyes widened in surprise, but he did not protest. "As you say…El Olam."

Tobin remained silent throughout the rest of dinner, picking at the pile of food before him. Despite his initial hunger, he could no longer enjoy the meal. On the one occasion he chanced a look from his plate, his gaze met three faces that stung in their own unique ways; Kaz's satisfied grin, Lucia's frown of pity, and Nachun's look of concern.

He was accustomed to the looks from his brother and after years of abuse, he easily ignored Kaz's. Lucia's expression stung harder, but again, he understood it. *Kaz has kept her in the dark after all.*

But to Tobin, Nachun's actions felt like betrayal. *Did he not listen to anything we spoke about returning from Nubinya? Why would he embarrass me in front of everyone, especially my father?* His stomach turned in disgust and immediately he decided he had enough of the evening. He pushed himself away from the table and stood, bowing. "El Olam, may I be excused?"

"Why?"

He lied. "I have some duties that need completing before the morrow."

A chuckle from Kaz.

Bazraki cast a glance at Tobin's food and then at him, raising an eyebrow. "Very well."

Tobin left in a hurry. Catching a glimpse from one of the dining room windows, he saw that the moon rested high in the night sky. The long hallway, absent of workers who had finished their shift for the day, was now filled with an eerie feeling, its walls echoing even the smallest of sounds underneath its vaulted ceilings.

"Tobin, wait a moment."

He stopped but did not turn around. "What do you want, Nachun?"

"I did not have a chance to speak with you in private."

"I think you did enough talking tonight," said Tobin, wheeling about to face the shaman.

"What do you mean? I only…"

"You only embarrassed me. Did you not listen to any of the things we spoke of concerning my relationship with my family?" Tobin paused. "I trusted you."

"I only wished to help, to raise you up in your father's eyes, so that he could better see your value." Nachun put his head down. "I'm sorry."

Tobin sighed, letting a long pause hang in the air. "My mother died when I was five and Kaz was six. I remember almost nothing of her, or what our family was like before her death. But I remember everything since then. From that time on, Kaz was the one my father relied on, the one he trusted, the one he was proud of, and the one he loved." He shook his head. "I used to work so hard to be better than him. At one point, I believe I was. But that ended when Kaz was made warleader. The things he did…," he said trailing off. He gestured toward the ground. "And any hope I had of overtaking him or proving myself better and more capable to lead ended when he broke my ankle."

"But you are still Bazraki's son, his blood."

"Blood is all I am to him. So long as he has Kaz, I am nothing else."

"I think I understand now. I should have handled things differently."

Tobin nodded. "Good. Then return to the meal. There is little point in you leaving with me now."

The shaman apologized again and left. Tobin turned and slowly descended the staircase, eager to put this day behind him.

CHAPTER 8

"Why don't you ever let me win? Everyone else does," she said pouting.

"That's because you're a princess and they think they need to let you win or else they'll fall out of favor with you," he replied.

"Why aren't you worried about falling out of my favor?" Elyse asked, frustrated. She stood with her hands on her hips.

The boy laughed and shook his head. "Because I'm your brother. Besides, someone needs to teach you that to get the things you want out of life, you have to work for them."

"I get almost everything I ask for now. Why should I work?" Elyse asked in a defiant tone.

"Now, yes. But it won't always be that way," said the boy more serious than before.

"Why not? I'll still be a princess."

"Yes. Maybe even a queen one day. And people will still fawn over you, flattering you with words and gifts alike, all the while making it seem as though they are your friends and that they love you."

"What's wrong with that? Isn't that what friends do?" she asked confused.

"What's wrong is that there will be very little truth in their actions. As you grow older, you will only become more important. Dukes, barons, minor lords, and even servants will try to manipulate you to get what they want. The best ones will even make you think that it was all your idea."

"You're lying. Why would people do that?" asked Elyse.

The boy shrugged his shoulders. "Money. Land. Many reasons. But in the end it all comes down to power."

The girl thought about what her brother had said for a moment, biting her bottom lip. "I'm worried. How will I know who to trust?"

He looked at her as he always did when she was troubled, in a way that made her feel safe. "You'll have plenty of time to learn how. And I promise I'll be there to watch out for you when you need it most."

"What about father? Why can't he watch out for me?"

He sighed. "I don't expect you to fully understand until you're older but Father isn't someone you can rely on…at least not anymore…not after Aurnon and mother died." His voice caught for a moment when he mentioned their brother and mother. Elyse never had the chance to know either as Aurnon was much older and died before she was born. Her mother died from the Red Fever when she was only a few months old.

Jonrell stood up straighter after gathering himself. "And I know I'm young but I'm trying to learn all that I can. Master Amcaro said I'm one of his better students, even better than those who are much older."

The time her brother spent studying with Master Amcaro was a sore spot for her, as it would take him away from the castle for weeks at a time. "Is that why you spend so much time on that stupid island with him? Because you can't figure out who your real friends are?"

He sighed again. "It's a little more complex than that. But yes, that is one of the things I've studied." He paused and his tone changed to something sterner. "You should start reading more. When you get older, maybe Master Amcaro will take you to Estul as well and you can study in his great library."

"No way," she blurted. "You look at those boring history books. I like to read about romance and poetry."

"You are young yet, little sister. One day, your interests will change." His tone changed again, more caring than before as he put his arm around her. "Until then I guess I'll just have to keep an extra eye out for you."

* * *

"Your Majesty? Your Majesty, are you awake?" a voice echoed in her subconscious.

Elyse realized she was dreaming, dreaming of a time many years ago. The realization startled her as she jerked her head up from her folded arms. She had fallen asleep at her desk again for the third straight night. It was becoming more of a habit than she would have liked these past few weeks.

Her body ached from the unnatural position.

"I'm sorry to wake you but I know you have much to do today," said Lobella.

Elyse yawned and rubbed the sleep from her eyes. "Am I late?"

"No, Your Majesty. I made sure not to let you sleep in, just as you requested last evening."

"Thank you," said Elyse trying to manage a smile through the grogginess. She stood slowly, stretching out the stiffness. It wouldn't do for her to be seen hobbling around the castle, too tired to keep her eyes open.

"Which book was it this time, Your Majesty?" asked Lobella as she prepared Elyse's clothes for the day.

Elyse glanced back to the desk, noticing the first hints of dawn drifting through the window, and dancing across the worn pages. Having spent so much time looking at the book the previous night, she should have been able to recall its name without thumbing through its pages. It was a boring book, like most of them, but it was also one she should have read years ago.

Is that why I dreamed of you, Jonrell? To let you know you were right? But then, you said you would watch over me. Where have you been all these years?

"The Military Campaigns of Aurnon the First: Settlement of Cadonia," Elyse finally answered.

Trying to be polite, Lobella responded, "It sounds very interesting."

Elyse chuckled as she splashed cool water from the basin near her dresser onto her face. The water gave her goose bumps and she welcomed the sensation as she tried to bring life to her tired eyes. "The book is about as interesting as my undergarments." She sighed. "Still, I must read it."

"As you say."

"Lobella?"

"Yes, Your Majesty."

"For the hundredth time, please call me 'Elyse' in private. It will mean so much to me."

The girl blushed. "I'm sorry. I keep forgetting. I promise I'll do better."

Elyse smiled. "No need to apologize. It is just nice to relax in my chambers, away from everyone else." Light slowly filled the room and Elyse breathed in deeply. "When is Gauge expecting me?"

"In half an hour."

"Very well. Help me get dressed then. As you said earlier, I have much to do today."

* * *

"Ah, Your Majesty. How are you this morning?" said Gauge rising from his seat.

"I'm doing well," said Elyse, forcing a smile, fighting her exhaustion. They chose to meet in a secluded section of the castle's gardens for privacy. The space was beautiful, but the view overlooked the inner courtyard where the marble had not fully come clean from the assault by High Mage Nareash some months ago. She suppressed a shudder. "How are you?"

"I'm afraid I've had better days."

She waved him to a seat after taking hers and gestured for him to continue.

"There is a growing sense of unease, the first rumblings of rebellion."

Elyse inhaled as her stomach knotted. *No. I'm not ready for this.* "Where are these rumblings coming from?" she asked, trying to seem calm.

"Inns and taverns mostly. War is becoming a popular topic of conversation."

"These conversations are amongst the peasants though, correct? They often talk of such things to pass the time."

"True, the common man enjoys gossip as much as the nobility. However, I think there may be some merit in preparation."

"Preparation for war? Because of a few conversations amongst the commoners? That seems drastic. What happens if the nobility discovers us doing so?"

Gauge rubbed the forefinger and thumb of his right hand across his temple as he spoke, obviously stressed. "Actually, Your Majesty, I have reason to believe that the nobility have already started preparations of their own."

"How so?"

"Well, as you know, we have informants throughout the land hidden in each duke's inner circle. Aurnon the Third instituted this after the rebellion led by Jeldor's family some years ago."

Spies? Father kept me in the dark about so much. Elyse nodded.

"Well, we've had reports that Duke Conroy has held more frequent and more private meetings as of late, each with his most loyal lords."

"Can we really make an assumption that Conroy is likely to commit treason based on a few private meetings amongst his own lords? I understand your caution, but it is still his right to do so."

Gauge reached into his breast pocket, pulling out a folded message that he handed over to Elyse. "I received this just half an hour ago."

Elyse carefully read the letter, written by one of the informants. The writing was obviously a woman's, the wife of a lord perhaps, though she gave no name. However, the queen gleaned enough information from the letter to understand that Duke Conroy arrested the woman's husband on false charges, for his part in an elaborate plot to assassinate the duke. The wife suspected that the arrest was meant to draw her out of hiding and force a confession from her. She ended the letter by stating that many other arrests were made under similar circumstances but none of those actions would deter her from doing her duty. Elyse was speechless to hear that someone was so dedicated to the throne, despite never having met the queen in person.

A pang of guilt hit her. Feeling responsible for this woman's distress, her stomach knotted further. "The letter mentions others. How many?"

"We aren't sure, but it seems that nearly all of our contacts in Segavona, have disappeared, been arrested, or, in some instances, killed."

"One Above," she whispered under her breath.

Gauge continued. "We know that Olasi has already taken precautions to strengthen the borders he shares with Conroy and Tomalt. He was the first to return home after your father's funeral. So far he has been able to keep most of the activity hidden, though I'm sure they will find out soon enough. I doubt either will do anything about it for now."

"So Tomalt is gathering his forces as well?" she asked.

"We don't know for sure, Your Majesty. We haven't heard anything from our informants since your father's funeral," said Gauge, shaking his head.

"Maybe there is nothing to report then?"

"There is always something to report, Your Majesty. Even the most mundane messages about the cost of silk in other cities are sent to us. It would be one thing not to receive word on any military activity, but to not receive any messages at all is most troubling."

"What about Jeldor and Bronn? You haven't mentioned them," she said, afraid to hear Gauge's answer.

"We still receive our regular updates on Jeldor, though there is little in them. He is a man content to sulk around his castle and keep to himself."

"And Bronn?"

"He had not reached Astrya, last we heard. In fact, some say he headed further south, though to where, we don't know. Possibly Conroy? But, it could be nothing. Our reports have been steady but also conflicting. There has been a lot of activity around his northern border, near Jeldor, and we haven't been able to discern why."

Elyse's head spun as she tried to process the information. Thankfully, it took her mind off her nervous stomach. "What does all this mean?"

"It's hard to say with certainty. It could mean nothing, but then again it could mean everything."

"So what you're saying is that Conroy seems to be the biggest threat; Olasi is taking matters into his own hands; Tomalt might be a threat too, but no one is sure; Jeldor isn't doing anything of importance; and no one can really figure out what Bronn's doing. Is that it?"

Gauge grunted. "I believe that sums it up nicely, Your Majesty."

"Anything else?" she asked with a heavy intake of breath.

"Not at the moment. I just wanted to make sure you were aware of these reports before meeting with the rest of your advisors. Speaking of your advisors…." Gauge leaned to the side of his chair, looking over the queen's shoulder. Elyse followed his gaze. A young boy waited, bouncing in place and looking anxious. "I do believe the council is awaiting our arrival."

* * *

Gauge opened the heavy oak door to the council chambers and entered to announce her arrival. Although this was not Elyse's first time in council, her palms began to sweat.

Mostly men, few women held a seat on the council. Each person in attendance came from two distinct backgrounds, those whose reputation of hard work earned them their position, and those granted a spot on the council as a result of their wealth and status.

The former group was tough and hardnosed, never willing to give an inch in any discussion, thinking doing so would make them appear weak.

The latter group differed little, never budging from their stance as they felt entitled to be heard above the others. Therefore, it often took weeks for even the simplest of decisions to be reached.

At first glance, the meeting room resembled a holding cell for its lack of comfort. The chamber contained a lone distinguishing feature, a black marbled half wall that shielded a raised dais encircling the room.

The walls were free of any hangings, just as the floor was free of any rugs. Windows surrounded the room, closer to the ceiling than the floor, ensuring that no one would be distracted by the activity on the outside and no assassin could loose an arrow from afar. Aurnon the First had been very specific about the construction and adornment of each room in the castle. He was adamant that any room used to decide the fate of a country should be filled with nothing but the thoughts of those in charge of the task.

A domed ceiling, its center glass, allowed even more sunlight into the room. On days like today, when the sun shined brightly and a breeze blew in from the windows, the room felt less intimidating to Elyse.

All parties managed the appropriate smile and greeting as Elyse walked across the open floor. She crossed the room with grace, stepping lightly up stone steps where she joined the rest of her council seated behind the half wall. Seats faced inward toward the room's center.

Elyse imagined how horrific it must be to be an advisor, standing in the room's center over the great seal, the entire council glaring in disapproval, searching for a weakness in your words and eager to pounce on any mistake. Thankfully, her comments could be made from her seat. Still, she admired those who took the floor with confidence, almost daring someone to challenge their views.

What gives them such strength?

The usual people each took turns discussing the usual topics. Typically, there was plenty to say by all, regardless of how insignificant it all seemed to Elyse with the threat of rebellion fresh on her mind. She had only been queen for a couple of months and yet she felt bored with the same tired routine.

Phasin would often start things off by saying that the crown must build more merchant ships to increase trade with the Byzernian Islands and the great continent of Mytarcis across the sea. He would pound his fist into his hand, accentuating each sentence as sweat glistened off a head quickly baring more skin each day.

Vulira would then take the floor countering every point Phasin made before her. As often the case when discussing trade, Vulira would argue that Cadonia needed to grow more self-sufficient and rely less on foreign trade. She would argue that the only way to do so was to provide better equipment and more land for the farmers, more funds for the researchers and so on.

As rumor had it, the two were ex-lovers and the relationship ended on a sour note. The queen could not confirm whether the whispers were true but it was as good a reason as any for the special hatred the two shared for one another.

Vulira always took a much different approach than her supposed ex-lover. She spoke soft and sweet while nurturing each idea rather than beating the other council members over the head as Phasin did.

In the end, the room would be split, no one would budge on their stance and it would be decided to revisit the topic at another time. And so, the process would repeat itself once again upon their next meeting.

Each topic discussed thereafter often resulted in a similar outcome. Only minor topics seemed to get resolved, as none felt threatened by them.

Elyse could put a stop to the endless back and forth. Her advisors were meant to advise, not rule. But to do that, she would have to take a stance on the matters herself and she knew she lacked the knowledge and confidence to do so. The last thing she wanted was to appear incompetent to others, regardless of the truth of it. She might have had stacks of books in her room on trading routes, farming, and economics but her readings were focused elsewhere as she tried to gain a stronger understanding of her country's history and overall political environment. So, when the council met, she did what anyone else in her position would do. She stalled, pushing topics she felt uncomfortable with to another day. Few seemed to mind her procrastination.

Probably delighting in the opportunity to argue their stance once again while never having to face the possibility they may be on the losing side.

Illyan, a small man, barely five feet in height, had the floor now and despite his stature, his voice held a great deal of power as it boomed against the chamber's walls. His pleas contained a passion that many of the others lacked, though Elyse felt it overdone. Today he argued again the validity of improving the roads leading to and from Lyrosene and those lands directly managed by the crown.

Advisors noticeably yawned as Illyan carried on. Elyse had learned from Lobella, that many felt Illyan pushed his own agenda rather than looking out for Cadonia's best interests.

Isn't everyone pushing their own agenda?

Curly black hair bounced atop Illyan's head as he strode around the room in a tone reminiscent of a father lecturing his child. Frustration crept into his voice and he stopped mid-sentence breathing a sigh. Starting again, he tried a different approach.

"Do my fellow advisors really wish to lose their position of power on this council? Do you wish to lose your lands or possibly even your lives?" Illyan asked.

A voice called out, disgust and anger lined the tone. "Are you threatening us now, Illyan? Is that the only way you hope to pass your ridiculous ideas?" The councilors stirred, muttering curses under their breath, all aimed at the short man.

Illyan chuckled. "No. I would never threaten. However, it is apparent that many of you walk the castle with heads held too high to be bothered with the rumblings muttered by those beneath you." He cleared his throat. "Surely everyone here cannot be so oblivious to the happenings of this country. The possibility of rebellion or even outright war grows each day and yet we do nothing." He said that last statement while looking at Elyse.

He means that I do nothing. I am so overwhelmed that I have chosen not to act at all. And it seems he knows the information I found out only this morning, or at least he suspects it.

Illyan continued. "I understand everyone's hesitancy to do anything that may appear openly aggressive. However, repairing our roads would improve the transport of troops and supplies in a time of war."

"And if there isn't a war?" asked Gauge.

"Well, then we would have improved the infrastructure of our lands which is never a bad thing."

Another round of mutterings and noise rose from amongst the advisors as Illyan stood in the room's center waiting for a response. Above all the clamoring an exaggerated laugh rose up to stifle the whisperings of all others. Adein rose from his seat and continued laughing as he strode to the center of the room to join Illyan. The two were quite the contrast. Where Illyan was short and thin, Adein was tall and round.

Adein slapped his belly one last time to punctuate his amusement before pushing the sweat from his forehead back through his short brown hair. "My lords and ladies, Illyan has cleverly used a real threat to push his own agenda. Ask yourselves, how many battles have been won by the quality of roads? I would venture to guess it had something to do with armor and weapons. Wouldn't you all agree?" He laughed again, patting Illyan on his shoulder as one would a dog. Heads nodded in agreement with Adein's statements.

Illyan shrugged the hand off his shoulder and stepped away from Adein while addressing the council. "So you say armor and weapons win battles? Would you have us send an army against those we feel threatened by? That seems far more likely to cause unease than simply repairing roads."

"Lord Illyan raises a good point," said Gauge.

"He does, doesn't he?" said Adein. "However, as on many other things, Illyan does not understand the big picture. We hear these rumors of Conroy marshaling his forces but then we ignore the possibility that the tribes of Thurum may once again be readying themselves to assault the fortress used to defend the High Pass. Has anyone considered that he simply is doing the duty entrusted to his family centuries ago by Aurnon the First." He paused, scowling at everyone. "Yet, we accuse him of treason. And why? Because he failed to make the king's funeral?" He paused again, but not long enough that Illyan could chime in. "So yes, I do say we send troops out, but only to

Conroy's aid as he defends Cadonia. What better way to show our trust in the man and ease any perceived strain than to help him?"

Illyan opened his mouth to speak when another voice shouted from above. Lord Vicalli made his way to the center of the room as well. The rules of the council stated that only one man, two if in debate, may have the floor at one time. Elyse didn't know how to respond, and it seemed no one else minded, so she let the action go.

"My good Lord Adein, a splendid idea except I have a feeling that you are missing a matter of vital importance." Lord Vicalli joined the others in the middle of the room. He was of medium build and height, though more muscular than either the round Adein or the thin Illyan.

"We are all assuming that Conroy is upset with us but I disagree," continued Lord Vicalli. "He is a hard man and not one to pay attention to gossip. He focuses more on his own duties. I think a simple letter from the queen granting him her confidence would be all that is needed to smooth things over with the good duke. No, I think our real concern is with Duke Bronn."

"Both are cause for concern, my dear Councilors," boomed Illyan, finally able to get a word in, "as well as every other duke, even the loyal Olasi. Every action they partake in can directly affect the future of Cadonia."

"Always the pessimist, Illyan, of which we all grow weary," said Vicalli. "And as I was saying about Duke Bronn, I have heard from several reliable sources that he was most upset by the conversation he had with Her Majesty at the king's funeral." People stirred in their seats at his suggestion and he held up his hands innocently. "Now, it is not my place to speculate on what was said since they are only rumors, but I was thinking that a personal letter from the queen may be helpful to smooth things over, perhaps granting him some sort of gift as a gesture of good faith."

Illyan burst out, "You want to reward a man for participating in suspicious activity?"

"That is ridiculous," said Adein, ignoring Illyan's comment. "How will a letter find him when we do not know his current whereabouts?"

"Several copies of each letter sent to multiple locations would do the trick. A royal escort for each would be appropriate to add to Her Majesty's sincerity, I think. Wouldn't you agree Your Highness?" asked Vicalli, leering at Elyse.

"Yes, would you agree, Your Highness?" asked Adein in a prodding way, obviously not in agreement with Vicalli's question.

Elyse noticed that Illyan stood with his arms folded in front, not even attempting to hide his anger and frustration at the two advisors who took the floor from him. The rest of the room seemed eager for her response as well. She realized then, for the first time, that despite being the most powerful advisors in her council, both Adein and Vicalli had waited to raise their points until the end and only after Illyan readied the audience for their news.

They expect an answer this time. What do I do? I don't know who is right.

"Your Majesty? Do you have an answer?" asked Vicalli.

"Your Majesty, these ideas are unreasonable. Do not entertain either. We should be discussing the roads," said Illyan, pushing Vicalli aside.

Illyan did Elyse a favor as the chambers erupted in argument again. Lords and ladies who, despite their differences, were usually civil to one another now shouted and pointed fingers as the topic of war and rebellion rang out. Many took sides with Adein and Vicalli, others shouted about Tomalt and a few even of Jeldor or Olasi. However, none agreed with Illyan, and his face turned beet red in anger.

With the chambers in such an uproar, Gauge acted, saving Elyse the embarrassment of doing so herself. He stood up, arms raised, and shouted. "My fellow Councilors, we should be ashamed of ourselves to act in such a way. Aren't we above such petty squabbles?"

"What about an answer?" someone shouted.

"You'll have your answer when the queen feels it necessary to share it with you. We have now tarried here long enough and her majesty has several other appointments to attend. Until the next meeting, we will be on our way," said Gauge in a tone that said the decision was final. He extended Elyse a hand and led her carefully down the stairs. Those councilors still in their seats, surrounding the chambers stood and bowed as she passed. Adein and Vicalli bowed as well, though each did a poor job of hiding their discontent. Only Illyan dared to be so bold to speak with her.

He brushed by Gauge, blocking Elyse's path. She had never been so close to the man before, and despite his small stature, he intimidated her. His face resembled something out of a children's fairy tale, ugly and hideous, like some troll that would hide under a bridge.

"Your Majesty, you would make a terrible mistake to ignore my advice. A terrible mistake indeed," said the short man, his big voice a whisper, sending shivers down her spine.

"You forget yourself," said Gauge in a low hushed tone, audible only to the three of them.

"I'm sorry, Your Majesty. I am only concerned about the state of my country," said Illyan, forcing himself to back away and offer a slight bow.

Elyse left the council chamber in a rush, wanting to be away from everyone, hoping for a moment to gather herself. Gauge hurried after her and once the two were a distance away, he spoke. "I apologize for that, Your Majesty."

Elyse breathed a heavy sigh, still a little shaken up by the confrontation. "What was that about?"

"Illyan has always been a forceful man. Perhaps he is making up for what he is lacking in height." Gauge chuckled, trying to make light of the situation.

"Perhaps. Though Adein and Vicalli were hardly any better with the looks they gave me."

"Yes. If truth be told, I am not fond of many of my colleagues."

"I need to make a decision on the matter."

Gauge sighed as they came to a stop. "Well Your Majesty, you don't really need to do anything. That being said, in light of what we discussed this morning and in the chambers just now, I don't think this is something you can put off much longer. When we meet again, they will expect an answer."

Elyse frowned. "I see. And what do you suggest?"

"As much as I hate to admit it, they both make valid points. However, I would urge you not to give either exactly what they want as it would leave the others with the impression that you can be bullied into a decision."

* * *

She closed the door and dove onto her bed, face down in her pillows. She let out a heavy sigh as she hoped to put the long day behind her. For a half second, she enjoyed the peace but then she heard a small knock at the door. "Go away," she said, her voice muffled in the fabric.

The door creaked open and a small voice sounded, "Elyse, it is nearing midnight and I have your bath ready."

Elyse rolled over to her back. Looking up, she gestured for Lobella to come in and close the door. "Midnight already? I'm no closer than I was hours ago."

Lobella approached the queen. "Closer to what, my queen?"

"Closer to a decision with the council. I've met with what seems like every Lord and Lady in the land today and yet I have no idea what we discussed because my thoughts returned to Adein's and Vicalli's arguments."

"I'm sorry for your stress. Perhaps a good night's sleep will help you decide."

Elyse shook her head. "I still have to catch up on my reading. I just wish I knew who was right," she said, sitting up. She walked to her dresser and began to take off the uncomfortable gown she wore. Lobella came over and helped her. "The decision would be so much easier if I didn't have to consider how it would affect the power of whoever I side with," Elyse continued.

"Too bad you couldn't cater to both of them."

Elyse frowned. "But then they would think of me as someone they can get what they want from."

"Well, I didn't mean exactly what they want. You know, just enough to pacify them so they wouldn't be able to argue, but then again not so much that it looks as though you are showing favoritism."

Gauge more or less said the same thing. If a servant uninvolved in such things reaches the same conclusion on only a shred of information, then perhaps the decision is an obvious one. Elyse turned, hugging Lobella. "You're so helpful."

The serving woman blushed. "My Queen is too kind. I was simply thinking of something my mother told me once when dealing with multiple suitors is all."

"Well, then give her a hug for me as well. I think I know what to do."

CHAPTER 9

Jober listened begrudgingly to Dek and Olan's constant arguing.

"Be careful, stupid," said Dek in a hushed voice.

"Don't call me stupid. I can barely see what I'm doing, it's so dark," whispered Olan.

"It's past midnight what do you expect?"

"I expected a much easier time with this between the three of us," said Olan grunting. "Maybe if we had some more light…"

"No. You know our instructions," said Dek, gesturing to the sack the three men dragged along the dark corridor. He looked up and nodded toward Jober who hadn't said a word. "Just be thankful we got this one to help. Otherwise, we wouldn't even be this far," he said as they turned a corner, avoiding tools left out from the previous day's work.

Dek was right. They all knew Jober had the biggest muscles, and intentional or not, they let him take most of the weight.

And more than likely, it's intentional.

Sneaking around in the bowels of Bazraki's palace had him breaking out into a cold sweat. *But what other choice do I have?*

He was accustomed to hard work from spending his early life training as a Kifzo warrior. Unlike other potential warriors who were weeded out and later placed in basic military units, Jober was one of the few who had thrived under the harsh physical and mental stress. That's what made his discharge from the entire Blue Island Clan military so bitter. Rather than bringing pride to his family, he had only brought them shame.

Carrying that dishonor into adulthood, he was lucky to have obtained work as a stable hand. He never understood how he found love when the entire city seemed to know his shame, but somehow his wife saw the real person beneath that reputation. She and the family they made together were all that mattered to him.

His bulging physique convinced Dek to approach him the previous week about an important job.

"And what if I'm unable to help?" he asked.

"Then don't come into work tomorrow, or ever again for that matter," was the response.

"But I have a family to support."

"We know and we'll be happy to remove that burden from you, if you like," Dek had said with a grin. "You wouldn't really need this job then, would you?"

Jober understood well those grim words. And so here he was, dragging a sack through the middle of some dark hallway, with two men he never cared to know, all in order to protect his family. He looked at them, still arguing, and shook his head.

They'll probably kill me anyway when they're done using me, but what choice do I have. Even after all these years, I have no credibility. He looked them over again. *I could kill them both now and leave. But they aren't working alone. Someone would find out and remove "my burden" as they already threatened. Better to do as they say.*

"Hey, you're not thinking of backing out?" Dek asked him, as if he heard his thoughts.

"No. Just keeping to myself is all."

"Good. I like that."

"Uhhhhhhhhh," came a noise.

Jober let go of the sack in reaction to the low moan, causing the other two men to stumble.

"What's the matter with you? You trying to get us killed?" asked Dek.

"There's someone in there," said Jober.

"Of course there is. Did you think we needed help dragging out the trash at this time of night?"

"But there wasn't a body the other nights."

Dek shook his head. "Those were practice runs. We wanted to make sure we could trust you first." He pointed down. "Now pick up your end. We've still got a ways to go."

The three men moved along the palace's winding passages, avoiding the debris that littered the floors. Jober said nothing for some time, listening instead to the two men squabble in hushed tones, just as they had every other night this week. He tried to ignore the body inside the sack but each small grunt or heavy exhale of breath that reached his ears, only piqued his curiosity. Finally, he had enough. "Who is it?"

The bickering cut off at Jober's question and the two men stared back at him.

"What's it matter to you?" asked Dek.

"Just curious is all."

Olan turned to his partner. "Yeah, who is it anyway?"

The other man grinned, eyeing Olan before turning to Jober. "How about I give you a hint? Who is the one person in all of Hesh that you would least expect to be taken by surprise?"

"Bazraki?" said Olan.

"No, you idiot," said Dek, punching the other in the shoulder.

"What are you hitting me for? You said the least likely."

"No," said Jober. "He said the one you would least expect to be taken by surprise."

"What's the difference?"

"Plenty," said Jober, pausing in sudden realization. He looked at Dek. "I don't believe it."

Dek's grin grew wider. "Look for yourself then. He ain't going anywhere."

Jober hesitated at first, but decided he had to do it. He bent over and slowly undid the knot, loosening the laces. The opening fell around the man's head and Jober heard a gasp from behind.

Impossible.

"Kaz. We've been dragging *him* around." said Olan, his voice edged in fear.

"How is this possible?" said Jober turning to Dek.

"You trying to say I don't have the skill to pull this off?" asked Dek.

Olan turned to his friend, saying what Jober wanted to say. "You *don't* have the skill to pull this off. No one does."

Dek made a face. "Fine. We bought someone off to drug his food along with his wife's so she wouldn't wake up. Then I snatched him and brought him into the hallway for you two to help with."

Jober turned Kaz's head, feeling a sticky substance on the back of it. Moving his hand away, he saw blood. "You hit him when he was already unconscious?"

"I wanted to make sure he was out."

"Why not kill him right there then?" asked Olan.

"Because, idiot," said Dek. "That wasn't what our instructions were. I was told to bring him alive."

"I don't like this. What if he wakes up? You've heard the stories. They say he can't be killed in battle and that over a thousand men have died by his hands."

"He don't look like much now, does he?" asked Dek, kicking Kaz's limp form. "He's probably not even half of what those stories say he is. Everyone just talks him up because of who his father is. Well, he doesn't impress me any." He paused. "Hey Jober, you're awful quiet again for someone who was just so curious. You're not about to try something funny, are you?"

I can't try something funny, not if I want to save my family. "No. I'm fine."

"You were a Kifzo too for awhile, weren't you?" asked Olan.

"Yeah."

"Is it true what they say about him?" said Olan, nodding to Kaz. "They make it sound like he is unstoppable."

"Do you know the Kifzo named Durahn?" asked Jober.

"Yeah. He's an evil one," said Olan. "Huge too. Looks like some giant gorilla, right?"

"That's him," said Jober.

"What of it?"

"I'd rather face a half dozen like Durahn than one like Kaz," said Jober. Even in the dark he could see Olan's eyes widen.

Dek grunted. "You're full of it. Besides, what do you know? I heard how you were kicked out."

Jober's head hung low but he didn't say a word. *Who hasn't heard what happened?*

Olan started. "But, what if…"

"I don't want to hear it. Enough talk. Close that up and let's get him to the shaman."

Shaman? That figures. It wouldn't be the first time one tried to kill him. Though, I can't think of anyone brave enough to try after the last time. I guess after a few years people forget. Jober retied the sack after closing it around Kaz's head and the three resumed their journey down the hall.

* * *

Jober descended the winding staircase while taking the brunt of Kaz's weight, more careful with the sack now that he knew what it contained. *I owe at least that much to him.*

The bottom of the stairs flowed into a circular room, empty except for a half dozen arched doorways facing them. Dek pointed toward a flickering light beyond the entrance farthest to the right. "There."

The three entered the room, sack in tow. Underground, the room was windowless. Torches lining the walls provided light. An air shaft sent a small breeze throughout the room causing the flames to dance. *A storage room.*

A figure in shadow stood near the opposite wall, hands clasped behind his back. He stepped into the muted glow and Jober recognized Nachun. Dark blue robes, covered in red symbols, a hint to the man's past, hung off his tall, thin frame.

If the whispers about his power are true, then it would take someone like him to have the guts to attempt this thing.

The shaman's eyes settled on the sack. "I take it there were no problems?"

"No one bothered us or saw us if that's what you mean," said Dek. "It wasn't easy hauling him around though. He's a heavy one."

The shaman ignored the comments. "Get him out of the sack and place him in the center of the room."

Dek removed the sack completely and Jober saw that Kaz was naked. Even in the faint light he could see the fresh scrapes covering Kaz. His massive chest heaved up and down with every breath as if seething in anger though he remained unconscious.

"Why was he not bound?" asked the shaman.

"He was drugged and in a sack. Besides I took extra precaution," said Dek with a smile, pointing to the dark fluid matting the Kifzo's long hair.

The shaman looked at the wound on Kaz's head. "I thought I was specific about his condition."

Dek shrugged. "You said you wanted him alive. He's breathing."

The shaman didn't look up, and only sighed. "So I did."

Olan leaned into Dek, whispering, "When are we going to get our money?"

The shaman pointed to a spot on the floor behind him, off in the corner. "You'll find your money there."

Dek took a step back. "It was a pleasure doing business with you. We'll just grab this and be on our way."

The shaman wheeled around. "No. Not yet."

"We had a deal," said Dek.

"We did," said the shaman. "And I've just changed the terms. Don't worry, you'll both still get your money." He turned to Jober. "And your family will be safe, but only after I'm done here." He pulled a piece of rolled parchment from his sleeve, unraveling it with care.

Dek extended his neck and peered over the parchment as the shaman laid it on the floor in front of him. "What do you need a map for?" He looked at the parchment again. "And one so old? I don't recognize any of the landmarks."

"It is none of your concern. However, it is crucial that I'm not disturbed until the process is over. You two will watch the doorway."

"For what? We already told you that no one followed us."

"I don't want to take any more chances."

Dek sneered. "What's in it for us?"

"Your life." said the shaman. A small glow formed in his hands as his gaze met each of the three men, lingering the longest on Dek.

Olan swallowed hard, then forced a smile. "Sounds fair. Right Dek?"

Dek nodded.

"Good," said the shaman. "Now take the door." He pointed to Jober. "But you, I want next to me in case he starts to wake up," he said gesturing to the floor. Kaz let out a low moan and the shaman handed Jober some cord. "Check him quickly and tie up his hands."

Jober leaned in close to Kaz, blocking the shaman's view of what he did. He checked the Kifzo's eyelids as Kaz groaned. "Forgive me Kaz," was all he dared to whisper and Jober swore he saw a glimmer of brief recognition before Kaz's eyes rolled back into his head. *Just my imagination.*

He tied Kaz's hands together using lengths of leather, betting on the fact that the shaman would not look over his work. Still, to be safe he looped, turned, and twisted the knot over and over to give it the appearance of strength.

I wish I could do more though I'm not even sure what's going to happen.

Jober stood up and nodded to the shaman that Kaz was secure. Dek and Olan had moved near the door. Neither appeared particularly interested in keeping watch. Instead they glanced back to the shaman's preparations.

Now on his knees, less than five feet from where Kaz lay, the shaman leaned over the map, eyes focused on one specific section. The shaman seemed oblivious to all else around him.

After a moment, Jober could feel a shift in the air. It seemed almost thinner somehow. He caught the worried expression from Olan's face and knew he also felt the change. Beads of sweat formed on the shaman's face accompanied by a small tremble in his lip which he attempted to stifle by biting down. Kaz's entire body started to quiver, and the Kifzo let out a deep groan. The shaman's eyes clinched tight, his jaw set in determination as drops of sweat rolled off his nose and splashed onto the parchment before him.

Having once trained as a Kifzo, Jober was not completely naïve about sorcery, yet he was far from an expert. Still, even he recognized the amount of power emanating from the shaman, and it dwarfed anything he had felt in the past. A shiver ran down his spine. The air shimmering, he struggled to keep his breathing even.

Despite the awe of witnessing such a thing, a faint sound caught his attention. He turned toward the doorway and saw Dek gasp in surprise. The body slumped to the floor, exposing a man wielding a knife and appearing almost identical in size to the warrior bound in the center of the room. Olan moved too slowly and the same blade sunk into his gut. The arm holding it thrust upward with such force it lifted the man briefly off the ground. The body fell next to Dek's.

* * *

For the third straight night Tobin had had trouble sleeping. He had been running into Lucia more than he was accustomed to during the day, and thoughts of her bright smile and warm touch filled his dreams. He should have welcomed those thoughts, a break from the horrors of war that haunted him. But those imaginings of Lucia only increased his depression. His brother's disapproving scowl woke him with a start each time and Tobin found himself covered in sweat. Then the dull throb of his ankle that seemed to plague him most when at rest, brought forth more bitter feelings. Rather than stare at the plastered ceiling of his bedchamber until morning, he had taken to walking the palace.

He found himself enjoying those walks. Absent of activity, he could look upon the work from the day before uninterrupted. And for some unexplained reason, he had always found comfort in such moments of quiet. Even after three nights, he had barely covered half of the palace's grounds as he visited a different section each night.

It was only by chance that he chose a part of the east wing upon waking from another fitful sleep. The route he had planned changed as he strode through the meandering hallways, noticing a small amount of fresh blood near a seldom used stairwell. His curiosity piqued further by several sets of footprints that appeared to be dragging something through the thick dust from all the masonry work.

A sputter of light from a doorway near the bottom of the stairs made him thankful for the time he took to arm himself. Two men stood with their backs to the entrance, their attention diverted from where Tobin suspected it should have been. Padding on light feet, he peered into the dim room without either noticing. Another man stood near the room's center. He looked familiar, but Tobin could not immediately place him. The man, like the two near the entrance watched the bent figure kneeling on the floor. He wore the robes of a shaman, though the shadow from the man standing over him blocked much of his form. In shock, Tobin 's eyes landed on the naked body lying near the shaman, wrists tied behind his back. He didn't need any help recognizing his brother.

A hundred questions ran through his mind. But rather than wait and hope for answers, he acted. He unsheathed his knives and the man to his left fell. The one to his right followed. He rushed into the room toward the familiar figure who stood near Kaz.

Tobin's arm whipped forward and the knife left his hand. The man attempted to avoid the dagger but was a step too slow and the blade took him in the side. Letting out a scream, he toppled next to the shaman. Looking to take advantage of the situation, Tobin raced forward. He halted at the sound of his name from a familiar yet ragged voice. "Tobin?"

"Nachun?"

The air took on a foul odor and Nachun looked down to Kaz, his body convulsing. "No," he whispered. "What have you done?"

The center of the room rippled, reminiscent of a raindrop striking a puddle. Tobin stared at where his brother's body had been, mouth gaping.

* * *

Still thinking of protecting his family, Jober took the opportunity to whip his leg around, striking Tobin in the ankle. The Kifzo's leg buckled, toppling him to the floor. Tobin let out a terrible scream. Jober pounced on top of him and the two wrestled for position. For a moment, Jober held his own, but his training had been long ago, and blood poured from his side. Tobin quickly overpowered him, sweeping him onto his back. The Kifzo reached for another blade at his side but Jober got a hand there first and unsheathed it. A burst of light filled the room, blinding him. The blade clanked to the ground.

Why did he stop me? Too weak to move, he knew he was finished. *This is it.*

But the killing blow never came and instead he felt Tobin roll off of him. When his eyes focused, Jober saw that the Kifzo struggled under the same symptoms, half dragging himself to lean against a nearby wall.

On his knees, Nachun breathed heavily. "I'm sorry, Tobin. I barely had enough strength to send that spell let alone ensure it did not affect you." The shaman's voice sounded faint.

The room fell silent as all three men struggled for air. He knew he should try to move as he felt strength return to his limbs but he had little motivation to do anything other than move a hand to his side, hoping the pressure would slow his bleeding. He wasn't sure why he bothered, he knew he would die.

Maybe if they kill me, they will leave my family alone. What threat is my family with me dead? They think I'm just working on some special project for Bazraki.

Jober grimaced at the lie. He remembered the sparkle in his wife's eyes, the pride she had shown when she had found out that he was specifically chosen for the task. Realizing she would discover the truth after tonight, he almost wished for death.

Better than to face her disappointment when she learns the truth. So rather than live, he moved his hand away from his side and waited to die. But death is often fickle and sometimes slow. And while he waited, he listened.

* * *

Control of his limbs slowly returned, and once Tobin had the strength, he propped himself up against the nearest wall, picking up his blade that he had heard clang to the floor following the blinding light. Prepared for the strange man to attack him once again, he readied himself. However, other than his labored breathing, the burly man lay motionless on the stone floor.

Still weak from the sorcery, Tobin decided against finishing the man, worried the stranger feigned his condition. He remained cautious, eyes searching for any sudden movement.

Tobin glanced at the shaman; a man he had thought was his friend, someone he could trust. But now he didn't know what to think. He felt betrayed, confused, and angered. Yet his concern for the shaman, a man who had befriended him when no one else would, decided his response. Nachun's eyes were sunk into an already lean face and his dark skin seemed to have paled noticeably. The features of the shaman's face even looked foreign, unlike any other Heshan he had ever seen. He squinted into the gloom and shook his head, not sure if he was still feeling the effects of sorcery. "Nachun? Are you alright?"

The shaman nodded, closing his eyes. Opening them, he seemed to look more like himself. "I will be eventually," he answered in a whisper.

"What happened?"

"I'm sorry. He had your knife and I was too weak to isolate the spell's effects." He swallowed.

Tobin looked at the man on the floor and then back to Nachun. "That's not what I meant. What are you doing down here? And what did you do with Kaz?"

Nachun coughed, then sighed. "I was trying to solve both of our problems." He paused. "But you distracted me at such a crucial point. I warned them that the results could be terrible if that happened." He looked at the two bodies lying near the doorway, each cooling in their own pool of blood, and snorted.

"That doesn't answer my questions."

Nachun nodded. "It will take time for me to explain."

"Then I suggest you hurry. Dawn is in a couple of hours and when my father wakes and discovers that Kaz is missing, he will likely kill us both."

Nachun's eyes widened. "You're right." He thought for a moment as if searching for a place to begin. "Do you remember the maps I've been researching and buying up in the market these past few weeks?"

"Yes. You said you were doing research on the land in order to aid father."

"Do you also remember that I said there were other things about them that interested me?"

"Yes."

"This was one of those things," said Nachun, gesturing with his hand as if the statement answered all of Tobin's questions. "Most think of teleportation as something found in children's stories. But I can tell you that it is a very real and powerful form of sorcery, one that is rarely used for the risks are quite high. You saw me take that risk with your brother only moments ago."

Teleportation? Impossible. "Then where is he?" asked Tobin, more confused than before.

"To be honest, I'm not sure." Nachun closed his eyes. "Let me start over." He took a deep breath and blew it out slowly. "You know my interest in history and such. Well, in my youth I came across several antique texts that spoke of powerful weapons in the cities of old. Cities and lands our people inhabited before the crossing of the Great Divide. If those weapons do exist, no one could stand in the way of the Blue Island Clan. In turn, such a thing would help me realize my own goals. Unfortunately, the locations of those weapons and for that matter the ancient cities themselves are not well documented.

"Since coming to Juanoq, I've stumbled across a new wealth of information, and coupled with what I had previously known, I'm much closer to discovering those locations than ever before." He pointed to the parchment lying on the floor. "That map is one of several I bought, detailing Hesh as it was hundreds, perhaps thousands of years ago. I've made some improvements, but that faded portion is where I believe the great city of Quarnoq once stood. It is there I hoped to find one of those ancient weapons.

Quarnoq? The capital of our people before we were forced to cross the Great Divide.

Nachun continued. "However teleportation can be unpredictable, unless attempted by someone skilled enough. But even then, other elements come into play. Familiarity with the location you are teleporting to as well as distance from one location to the next all factor into the success of the spell. I have never purposefully traveled a distance as great as the map indicates, nor do I even know with certainty if Quarnoq still exists." He shook his head. "I couldn't just send myself."

Tobin's eyes widened. "So you sent Kaz instead? You are mad to use my brother for…"

"Mad?" Nachun cut in. "Don't fool yourself. I could have chosen any beggar off the street who would have gone unnoticed. But that would have only benefited me." His voice softened. "And why would I waste an opportunity to help both of our causes?"

Tobin exploded. "I never asked for this!"

"You didn't have to ask. You yourself said that things would never change for you as long as Kaz was around. With him gone, Bazraki will learn to trust you, rely on you, and in time take pride in your accomplishments as he should have all along."

"You act like I need my father's approval!"

"I never said you did. But do not try to fool me into believing that you are not envious of the way he treats your brother, that you do not desire such treatment yourself."

Is my displeasure so obvious? Does everyone else see it? Tobin sat in silence. "Perhaps I was jealous of Kaz, but I didn't want this," he said, gesturing around the room. "I only wanted my father to respect me."

"And without Kaz spreading lies to your father and everyone else, you can have that respect, and, in time, much more." Tobin looked up and a thin smile appeared on Nachun's face. "Many things are within your grasp, my friend. One in particular would probably be of most interest to you. Lucia is suddenly available."

"I told you never to speak of her again," said Tobin.

The shaman put his hands up. "Very well. But during her time of *mourning* I'm sure she will seek comfort from *someone*."

"You speak of Kaz as if he's dead. Before you said he was *teleported*."

"He was. But due to the interruption in the spell, I'm not sure where. All I know is that he is bound, naked, without his memory, and injured thanks to these idiots," he said pointing to the bodies at the door. "So even if by some miraculous chance he should recover and stay alive, he'll probably find himself alone in some part of Hesh he's never even seen before without the slightest idea on how to return. He's dead."

"What do you mean, he is without his memory? And if you don't know where he went, then how would you have determined the spell's success?"

"I cast a spell that caused Kaz to lose his memory. I figured it was in both of our best interests to do so. I was also working on a tracing spell in addition to the teleportation one, but my concentration broke before I could complete it. If I had been able to finish, I could have determined if he'd arrived alive and in theory even return him if I wanted. But now, he's lost forever."

Lost forever or dead? Tobin stood up and began pacing as he tried to come to terms with the realization. *I should turn Nachun in. It would be the right thing to do by Kaz. Despite our differences, we are still blood. Or should I say we were? Father may even reward me for coming to him. I wouldn't even need to lie to gain his favor.* He shook his head, and clenched his hand around the blade he still carried. *No. He would blame me for not stopping Nachun.*

He glared at Nachun, hating the position the shaman thrust upon him. *He risked his own life for me more than once. Even now, he put himself in danger, and he was honest with his intentions. And now I have the chance to do the same for him. Should I reward his friendship with a death sentence?* He knew his father would expect him to do just that, and perhaps it was the right thing to do, but he couldn't.

It doesn't make sense. In the last couple of months Nachun had done more for him than Kaz ever had. They may not have shared the same blood but the shaman was more of a brother to Tobin than Kaz had ever been.

"You're right. It's done." He changed his grip on the dagger in his hand and moved toward the man still lying motionless on the floor.

"No! Wait," Nachun cried out.

Tobin came to a halt. "Why? We need to remove all evidence."

"We need a diversion to throw them off of the truth. Kaz would never just leave on his own accord and without a plausible explanation, his disappearance will raise too many questions."

"But he's dying," said Tobin, gesturing to the man.

"He's dying, but far from dead. We can use him yet." The shaman pulled a pouch from under his robes. "I'm too weak to perform even the most basic of healing spells but I always carry a few things with me, just in case," he said, grinning. "This will keep him alive until we get him to a healer."

"What makes you think he will help us?" asked Tobin.

"Oh, he will help us. He has far too much to lose, if he doesn't. Isn't that right, Jober?"

Jober. I knew the man was familiar. Of all people to be here with Kaz.

"Besides," said Nachun, bending over the man and opening his pouch, "who would turn down the chance to be a hero once again?"

CHAPTER 10

Squalor Bay, like most of Slum Isle lived up to its name. Little had changed in the two years since Jonrell's last visit. Most of the docks looked ready to collapse at any moment. Like the rest of the island, the only law a man followed in Squalor Bay was his own. Drinking, fighting, gambling, and whoring passed the time.

Ocean Spirit eased through the green water and moved past ships of various shapes and sizes. Galleys, cogs, and even longboats crowded the area around the small wharf. Many of the ships rocking in the small waves at berth looked abandoned. Tattered sails hung lifeless. Rotted railings drooped over the side of the ship like drunken sailors. Yet the swaying caskets floated alongside the occasional Cadonian royal ship that docked there.

Many would think those lesser vessels were outmatched against the better constructed great ships, but Jonrell was not one of them. He had been to Slum Isle countless times since leaving Cadonia and knew the captains of those decrepit ships could out-maneuver and out-sail many of the royal navy's commanders.

Captain Sylik maneuvered his way through the harbor, nestling into a spot away from most of the other ships. The old captain had proven his worth more than once during the voyage, first with Melchizan, and then with a series of storms, one after the other, that battered the crew. The only clear sailing since their first week out came just two days ago. Both the ship's crew and the band of mercenaries longed for the chance to unwind after such a trying voyage. Once the weather cleared and they no longer had to pull together to stay afloat, the close confines began to wear on them. Jonrell knew they needed to release some of their aggression.

One Above, help the man who dares start something with them tonight.

Men already pushed each other aside in an attempt to be first into several row boats lowered into the bay. Sylik walked up next to Jonrell, shaking his head in disgust. "The fools act like this is their last chance at dry land."

"I guess being at sea affects some more than others," said Jonrell.

"What about you, Commander?"

"Oh, I may have acted the same when I was younger but I've learned to be patient. I'll follow them on the next wave when they're done tearing each other up. I only gave them one night to themselves so I won't slow them down. Come tomorrow, we'll begin working to bolster our numbers for when we reach Cadonia. Sixty-five men aren't enough for what I have in mind. One group will recruit the north half of the island while my group works the southern half. You?"

Sylik shook his head. "I'm an old man."

Jonrell chuckled. "Even an old man can have some fun from time to time."

"Aye, but I got all the woman I need below my feet and she's in need of some attention after what we've been through. I need to see to her so she'll be ready when we meet up on the other side of the island in Mudhole Bay."

"Well, if everything goes as planned, we should all arrive at roughly the same time."

The captain chuckled. "I'll see you in a couple of weeks then. Just don't get killed in the meantime. You still haven't finished paying up."

Jonrell winked as he stepped down the rope ladder. "I'll keep that in mind."

* * *

"Forgive me, Kaz," a voice whispered in his mind. He couldn't say who the voice belonged to or when it spoke, but it repeated itself over and over until his eyes opened. He was uncertain if those words had jarred him awake, or the cool breeze that sent a shiver up his spine. The dewy grass he lay on heightened his senses, pressing against his bare skin. Regardless, he was alert now.

He blinked his eyes until they adjusted to the overcast light. His body felt like a giant wound. Small aches and bruises pulled at muscles, and cramped limbs longed to stretch out as he forced himself to a standing position. A wave of dizziness washed over him. The sudden assault to his senses brought him down to one knee. Reaching back, he felt his hair caked in dried blood. He steadied himself again, much slower than before and though his head still pounded, the dizziness waned.

A dry mouth and empty stomach told him he had been unconscious for some time. He looked down at himself for the first time, seeing his nakedness. There was no sign of any personal belongings, only the remains of loose bindings around his wrists.

Someone did a poor job at trying to bind me. He looked around his feet once more, hoping there was something nearby he could use, but he found nothing. *I'd rather have a blade than anything else.*

The thought struck him as odd at first, a weapon being so important to anyone. Then he reasoned out that with a weapon, he could hunt for food, dig for water, and skin an animal for clothing. He considered his current state and began asking himself questions.

Why wouldn't I have a blade now if it's something I desire so much? He took a step forward and his head pounded. *Have I been in a fight? I must have been. Disarmed and left for dead.*

He stared out over a wild land. Trees and brush grew in a haphazard manner around rocks jutting through the uneven ground. *I don't recognize any of this. Nothing is familiar. Where am I?* Then he stiffened and tried to think of what had led him here. He couldn't. *Who am I? I…I don't remember anything.* A whispering voice echoed in his mind again. "Forgive me Kaz," it said. The voice was deep and not his own, he realized after repeating the words aloud. Still, something about the way those words were said brought him both comfort and sorrow. Comfort when he realized the words were spoken to him and sorrow from the voice's solemn tone. *I at least have my name.* "Kaz."

Kaz hoped the voice would keep talking and give him more information but it remained silent. Still, just knowing his name improved his spirits. Rather than dwell on a poor situation, he set off to at least solve one of his problems and allowed his instincts to take over as he traveled the unfamiliar terrain.

Sometime later he found a stream nestled within a thick forest. Shallow but moving, it was more than he expected to come across. He drank heavily, slow at first so as not to upset his stomach. He washed the blood from his hair as best as he could, shivering as the cool water ran down his back. Having seen after his most pressing problem, he set off to solve the next.

Kaz wandered up the stream for several hours, stopping to drink as needed. He headed toward a stony hill where he hoped some breed of bird might make its nest amongst the crags. He looked to snatch an egg or two to satisfy his hunger after poor luck fishing in the stream.

He reached the hill and started to ascend its slope. There weren't any nests, but he discovered several bushes of wild berries near the hill's crest. He picked one bush clean, the sweet taste a treat to his tongue. When done with the first, he moved to the second.

A noise startled him and he froze, inclining his ear toward the sound. He heard voices that seemed to be coming from the other side of the hill. Being so close to the top, he decided to risk the last few steps, and peeked over the edge.

He spotted a tall warrior, some thirty feet below, with his back to Kaz. The warrior wore armor the color of blood. He held a longsword in his hand, the blade matching his armor. Five men arrayed in a mismatch of armor and weapons stood surrounding the warrior some distance back. Two bodies lay near the warrior's feet. Despite their numbers, each man seemed leery to press an attack.

A voice called out from a small set of trees some twenty yards behind the men encircling the warrior. A squat man appeared in yellow robes, stepping from behind a wide oak, his hands concealed in his sleeves. Something about the man in robes angered Kaz. The emotion triggered a piece of his memory. *A shaman.*

He could not understand the conversation between the warrior and shaman and couldn't tell what the dispute was about. However, Kaz found himself siding with the warrior below, if only because of his growing hatred for the man in yellow robes.

Kaz reached to his waist for a dagger that was not there and instead settled for a rock at his side. He quickly scanned the side of the slope and found a path which he used to descend in a quiet determination.

* * *

You've done it again, haven't you? You just couldn't let things go and give them what they wanted. What are a few coins to you anyway? But why should I? If I let every second rate thief who thinks he can use a sword get the better of me, it won't be long before everyone is trying it.

Jonrell glanced down at the two dead bodies in front of him, each pumping blood from a hole in their gut. He looked up again as the remaining five bandits closed in. They had killed his horse with a crossbow bolt through the neck. Outrunning them in full armor was not an option. So Jonrell had retreated to the rock face, using the wall to protect his flank. The two men on the ground had come at Jonrell before the others arrived, their strikes sloppy. *These others won't make the same mistake.*

Those who encircled him were a motley group, dressed in bits of mismatched armor, rusted in spots where the dirt had washed away. The grime on their faces was as thick as their smell.

Their drawn swords were in no better shape than the pieces of mail and plate crudely strapped to their frames. *It should be a crime to treat one's blade in such a way.* Jonrell imagined how odd the contrast must be between their appearance and his own. *Well if I die, at least I'll look good doing it.*

The threat of such bandits was reason enough to travel in groups, but Jonrell had decided to go out for an early morning ride to clear his head and ran right into their ambush on the way back. He had hoped that going out in full armor would have been a deterrent for such an attack, but instead it only grabbed their attention.

Stupid. I should have known better. What would a poor man be doing with such nice weaponry?

The one in the center approached with eyes flicking to the two men bleeding on the grass before him. Jonrell winked and the man froze, unsure of the meaning.

Jonrell changed the grip on his sword.

"Hold!" a voice shouted, and the five men stopped, too far away for Jonrell to take advantage of the distraction. A stout figure appeared from behind a wide oak wearing yellow robes, hands concealed in his sleeves. Sweat sat on his brow despite the cool morning air which told the commander that the mage had at least one spell ready to unleash. A smile crawled across the mage's face as his eyes met Jonrell's. He moved forward, away from the tree, and stopped. "Don't take your eyes off of him. But do not act without my command. Is that clear?"

Several men grunted in reply. *Great. Yellow or not, a mage of any sort changes things. If I was lucky, I may have been able to best the five but not now.*

"Do you know who I am?" asked the mage.

And he has an ego at that. Gotta love a mage with an ego. Well, at least I should be able to stall him while I try to think of a way out of this. "Can't say that I do, but I'm assuming I should, right?"

The mage chuckled. "Always full of jokes, aren't you, Commander?" He smiled. "Don't look surprised. I know who you are. Our little meeting was not mere chance." He paused. "But to your question, I don't expect you to remember me. It was very long ago. I was only a boy." The mage's forehead wrinkled and his voice took on an edge. "But I haven't forgotten you or your band of mercenaries, especially that old man, Krytien."

There was something about the look in the man's eyes that caught Jonrell off guard, something familiar. He couldn't place the mage but it was obvious the yellow-robed figure was well acquainted with him and his crew.

So a mage with an ego who appears to be bent on revenge. What a great morning. "Ah, so you're saying you're familiar with our work? Good," said Jonrell, trying to be indifferent. "You mentioned Krytien. Perhaps I can reintroduce you two. He's quite fond of mages who've taken such an interest in him."

"No. The old man will get his on my terms, not yours. You are simply the bait to bring him to me."

"You think so? I've already killed two of your men. Who's to say the rest aren't going to join them?" He leveled his sword, pointing it at the center man's throat. "I think I'll start with this one." The man gulped as he squeezed the hilt of his sword.

The mage laughed again. "So full of confidence, and yet the odds are not in your favor today. But don't fear. As I said, I prefer you alive for now." The mage removed his hands from his sleeves, and a small glow crawled along his skin. "However, if you won't come quietly, I can kill you now and worry about Krytien later."

Jonrell paused as a man emerged from behind an oak tree some distance behind the mage. He was unlike anything the commander had ever seen with skin as black as night. He was well over six feet tall and seemed to be carved from granite as slabs of muscle flexed with each silent footfall. Most surprising, the man wore no clothes. He held a large rock in his hand and his eyes were focused on the yellow-robed mage, inching ever closer with the grace of a panther.

A rock isn't much but I guess it will have to do. He'll probably die before he gets within five feet but maybe the distraction will be enough to give me a chance. Just need to keep him talking. "One Above, this is getting ridiculous. Will you just tell me why you want me and Krytien dead? Otherwise, let's get this over with."

"You killed my family, both my father and mother while in Thurum. It was at Asantia!" yelled the mage.

Jonrell's eyes widened ever so slightly as he did his best to hide his reaction. The look in the mage's eyes suddenly made sense. Asantia had been one of the darkest times in the Hell Patrol's history, and many of those memories still haunted his dreams. One of those images that had etched itself into his mind was that of a young boy cradling the bodies of his mother and father, staring at Jonrell with hollow eyes as he walked by.

I'm not surprised he never learned to move on, even if his parents deserved to die.

"Well, I can see how that may bother you," said Jonrell trying to keep the mage's attention as the black man continued his approach. "But that was years ago. We killed a lot of people in Asantia, and last I remember, they were trying to kill us. It's called war."

"No!" cried the mage. "That mage Krytien burned my mother alive as she tried to save my father. They were killed in cold blood. And that's not all…" The mage fell in a slump as the black man's hand crashed down on the back of the yellow-robed figure's head with the sharp crack of shattering bone. The five bandits turned toward their leader.

Jonrell rushed forward, sweeping his sword across the center man's unprotected neck, severing his head.

Well, no one can say I didn't warn him.

The man to Jonrell's left swung his rusted blade upward wildly. The sword sliced through the air. Jonrell easily moved away from the attack and carved into the man's torso.

The sound of fighting came from behind, but Jonrell had no time to look as another bandit came at him. More skilled than the previous men, he parried the first combination of attacks before dipping his blade too low. Leaving himself unprotected, Jonrell stabbed him in the chest and the man crumpled to the ground.

Jonrell spun, expecting another assault. To his surprise the last two bandits were dead and the black man stood over them holding one of the rusted swords in his hand. Despite helping Jonrell only moments ago, he looked ready to spring into another attack. The black man twisted his feet in the dirt, shifting his hands around the sword's hilt.

What is his problem? He kills three men to help me and then acts like I'm next. Does he really think a naked man is going to intimidate someone in full plate? The black man lowered his gaze and the knots on his shoulders flexed. *Well, maybe it will a little.* Jonrell then realized his own position and that he too had faced the man in anticipation for an attack. The commander lowered his sword slowly and straightened his stance. "Thanks for the help. Do you have a name?" he asked, trying to break the tension.

The black man frowned and said nothing.

Alright, that didn't work. Maybe try a different language. Jonrell tried again in several other tongues he had picked up during his travels but each was met with the same response. Then it hit him. *Idiot. Look at his skin. It's much darker but it makes more sense than anything else.* He tried Byzernian, thankful for the recent practice he had while traveling with Wiqua. "My name is Jonrell. Do you have a name?"

This time the man responded, finally relaxing a little. "Kaz."

Kaz. It's a start. Though at this rate we will be standing here until sundown. Jonrell decided to take a risk and sheathed his sword, removing his gauntlets afterward. He extended his hand slowly to the man. "Thank you for the help." After a moment, Kaz lowered his sword as well and extended a free hand in return.

One Above, the raw power in his grip. Jonrell smiled as their hands released, but Kaz did not reciprocate. Jonrell decided not to let the silence drag. "Which island in Byzernia are you from?" he asked.

Kaz seemed confused by the question and responded in a thick accent, his pronunciation barely recognizable to the commander. "I have never heard of this Byzernia or any island related to it."

"Oh, alright," said Jonrell surprised. "You are much bigger than any Byzernian I've seen, but you resemble the people from there." He paused. "Though that isn't an exact match either. Where are you from?"

Kaz seemed hesitant to answer and his brows furrowed. "I....I do not know."

"You don't know?" The commander glanced down at the naked man and decided to ask the next most obvious question. "Well, do you mind if I ask how you got to Slum Isle? You aren't exactly dressed appropriately to be traveling alone and unarmed."

Almost embarrassed Kaz responded, frustration lining his voice. "I don't know that either. I awoke some hours ago, and other than my name, I can't recall anything specific from my past." Just then, Kaz staggered a bit and the point of the sword went into the dirt. He used it to brace himself.

Jonrell reached out catching Kaz's arm, helping him regain his balance. "Are you alright?" he asked.

Kaz touched his head and when he brought his hand around, Jonrell saw blood in his palm. "Just dizzy."

"You were injured in the fight."

"No. It happened before I awoke."

"Hmm," said Jonrell, scratching his beard. "I've seen a well placed blow to the head affect people's memory before. It might be that's what happened to you."

Kaz said nothing.

"Well, uh, let's assume that's the case until we find out otherwise. Why did you help me? You're injured and aren't exactly dressed for the part—not that I'm complaining or anything."

"I was not sure whether to watch or help." He turned to the man in yellow robes. "Then I saw the shaman and made my choice."

I almost forgot. I don't know if Kroke could have pulled that off so easily. Wait a minute. What did he call him? "Did you say a shaman? I'm not familiar with that term."

Kaz looked at Jonrell as if he were a dumb child. "Those who use sorcery."

"We call them mages." Jonrell shrugged. "You know, I command a group of men and we could use someone like you," he said looking down at the dead men. "In fact, that's what I'm doing. Recruiting. Are you interested?"

"What would I be doing?"

"Mostly what you did today, but sometimes the job calls for other things. I've got a couple of people who might be able to look at that head wound of yours."

Kaz stroked the goatee on his chin, and then shrugged. "I accept." Then he bent down and began stripping the bodies of their clothing and armor.

Jonrell understood and began helping, but there was little success in finding a perfect match. "You're not exactly a common size," he said while pulling the boots off another. "These should do for now though. I'll make sure you get a better match once we get to Mudhole Bay."

Kaz grabbed the boots and slipped them on. He had already taken the trousers of another which seemed to suit him fine. He decided against a shirt or armor as the leather was brittle and the fastenings too small for his frame. Instead he picked up an old shield one of the men had carried and strapped the scabbard for the rusted sword across his back. "I'm ready."

Jonrell nodded. Even half-dressed, Kaz looked like a man who stepped right out of the legends of old, a warrior in every sense of the word. "You wouldn't know if there are any others like you waking up around here, would you?"

Kaz tilted his head. "What do you mean?"

"Nevermind. Just wishful thinking is all. C'mon we have a bit of a walk ahead of us."

* * *

During the hours it took to make it back to camp, Jonrell tried to learn more of the man who accompanied him. He had little success. By the time they had arrived Kaz remained a mystery to him. Jonrell had asked plenty of questions, hoping that something would click and help Kaz recover his memory. But Kaz could provide little more than a shrug or an "I don't know." After some time, Jonrell ceased pressing the man as he saw his frustration mounting.

Once Jonrell directed the conversation to what the Hell Patrol was and why they were on Slum Isle, small pieces of the warrior's past finally trickled out. When Jonrell would talk about the interaction between him and his men, Kaz was silent and indifferent. When the conversation moved to tactics of war and combat, Kaz spoke up, asking pointed questions and providing well thought out advice. With such insight, Jonrell concluded that he was definitely a soldier and more than likely a leader of sorts.

Probably one who did not really know or understand his men. Amcaro would smile if he knew that I still used those lessons on analyzing a person's behavior.

Despite glimpsing a small piece of Kaz's life, bigger questions remained that Jonrell doubted would be answered any time soon. *Where is he from? What army was he in? How did he get here? Why is he here?*

"Where have you been?" exclaimed Krytien, scowling as he approached. He looked at Kaz, but only for a moment before continuing. "I've got five men out looking for you!"

"Calm down. I ran into some bandits and a yellow mage. Apparently he knew us, you and I in particular. It was about Asantia."

The mage's face went pale and he shook his head. "Will that place ever stop haunting us?" he asked to no one in particular. Then he added. "And you got away?"

"Yeah, but they killed my horse first." Jonrell turned gesturing to Kaz. "And I had some help."

Krytien switched to a rare dialect from a distant part of Mytarcis, trying to hide his comments. "You sure found a big one. I've never seen someone of his color before. Where is he from?"

Jonrell answered in Cadonian. "His name is Kaz. I have no idea where he's from and apparently neither does he. I'll fill you in later. The only language we have in common that I can tell is Byzernian and even that can be a struggle. It's like his language is some strange variant of it."

"Odd. Could he be from one of the inner islands? No one really knows what the culture there is like."

"Possibly, though he is quite the contrast from Wiqua if that's the case."

"I guess we'll have to wait and ask him later. I sent him out with some of the men to search for you in case you were injured," said Krytien. He then looked to Kaz and extended a hand while switching to Byzernian. "It's good to meet you, Kaz. My name is Krytien."

Kaz looked down at the mage's hand but only scowled in return. "I will not touch this man. His robes may be faded but I can still smell a shaman."

"A shaman?"

"It's what he calls a mage."

"Yes, I know. It's just that word hasn't been used in hundreds of years and that was mostly during the Elder Age."

"Interesting," said Jonrell. "He apparently has a thing against those who practice the arts. I think the only reason he initially helped me was to kill the mage trying to capture me."

"Oh joy," said Krytien.

The two men had been speaking Cadonian so Jonrell turned to Kaz, switching to Byzernian. "Look, I really don't care what your opinion is of sorcery or of mages or shamans or whatever." He pointed to Krytien. "What I do care about are my men. If you join us, then you join all of us and that means that you will fight with us, not against us. Now you don't have to like everyone to do that, but you will do it. Understand?"

Kaz looked over the mage with disgust and after a few moments of scratching his bearded chin, he conceded. "Fine. You keep strange company but I will stay."

"Good," said Krytien trying to ease the tension. He leaned off to one side and noticed the wound on Kaz's head. "I can take a look at that for you if you would like. I know some minor healing…"

"No," said Kaz cutting in. "I will take care of it myself."

Jonrell shook his head. "No, you won't. If you don't want sorcery, we can treat it the old fashioned way." He looked over the camp of men who tried to look busy while eavesdropping on their conversation. The only one who cared not to hide her motive was Hag. *Ha. She'll do.* "Hag, get over here."

The old woman mumbled something under her breath about working too hard but waddled over anyway. "What do you want me doing now? I was busy, you know."

"Yeah, you looked like it," said Jonrell. "This is Kaz. I need you to clean and treat his head. While you're at it see what you can do about a few of the other scrapes and cuts he has."

"And why am I the one stuck doing that?"

"Because he only understands Byzernian and you've become pretty adept at speaking the language since you and Wiqua got together. Also, because he also needs to eat and unfortunately, you're in charge of meals. But most importantly, because I said so."

She grumbled under her breath looking Kaz over. "I guess it can't be all bad. At least he's easy on the eyes. Maybe I can get me a younger one on the side, huh?"

Jonrell shook his head and Krytien made a gagging sound. "You should be happy with what you got now. Besides I don't want you scaring him off. I got a feeling he'd give Glacar a run in sheer power. It's a rare thing to find someone like that," Jonrell said with appreciation.

"I was only joking," said Hag waving a hand. "Besides, I have all the man I need." She turned and spoke to Kaz in Byzernian. "C'mon, big boy. Let's get you looked at. Just keep your hands to yourself."

Kaz turned to Jonrell looking confused. The commander laughed. "It's fine. She'll take care of your head and get you something to eat. We'll be back on the road in a couple of hours and I'll catch up with you then."

The warrior nodded and followed Hag. Jonrell smirked at the contrast between the two as they walked off.

"That was mean," said Krytien.

"Probably. But he has to learn sooner or later to trust us and that means everyone. Maybe after an hour with Hag, he'll regret turning you down."

CHAPTER 11

Elyse exited the council chambers in a hurry, leaving Gauge behind to distract those vying for her attention. The patience of her advisors waned with each meeting as the pleas for each of their causes grew louder. No longer were they indifferent toward her procrastination or her silence during the council meetings. Reminders that, as queen, she had decisions to make became more prevalent and less subtle each session.

Elyse wanted to act, but a great deal of her trepidation stemmed from a lack of confidence in her abilities. Despite all her studying she felt as though she had barely scratched the surface of things she should already know.

I can almost hear Jonrell saying "I told you so."

Living on so little sleep for so long was becoming counterproductive as well. She often fought to stay awake during the day, missing key bits of information that Gauge filled her in on later which added to the belief that she wasn't fit to rule. Then at night, she frequently reread the same passages over and over, unable to concentrate. Gauge had grown concerned with her behavior, hinting that the stress appeared to be taking a toll. He offered to take on more duties in an effort to ease her load, which Elyse, seeing few alternatives, reluctantly granted.

How does he find the time to do so much?

Although she struggled with her own insecurities, a greater reason for her indecisive behavior was an effort to stall.

Elyse had made an important decision some weeks ago after listening to Adein and Vicalli's arguments. Without anyone's knowledge, including Gauge, she sent a company of nearly a thousand men from Cathyrium to Duke Conroy in order to aid in his defense of the High Pass. She felt that it had been the best way to judge if what Adein had previously said was true. If not, she figured that the troops, sent on her behalf, would deter Conroy from any further questionable behavior.

She also sent messages to Duke Bronn, offering to aid him in his search for a wife. Elyse had felt less comfortable about making such an offer to Bronn since she knew better than most his true nature. But, she could think of no better way to mend their relationship, and Lobella thought it was a fine idea.

After issuing the orders, she waited several days before telling the council of her actions. She hoped her quick thinking would please both Vicalli and Adein. Instead, it only infuriated them.

Vicalli went on about how Bronn would surely see it as an insult that the queen after turning down his marriage proposal would have a say in making a match for him.

Adein felt that sending a force from Namaris left the city vulnerable to attack should Tomalt grow ambitious. He spoke as though the queen should have known the only option was to send forces from Duke Olasi's army to aid Duke Conroy since the two shared a border and should be working together. Adein's statements caused strife among those in support of Tomalt, upset that Adein would insinuate he would commit treason. Those in support of Olasi grew upset, feeling it a great slight to imply the good duke would not do what's best for the crown.

And so these new arguments, pleas and discussions were added to those still unresolved items lingering since before the king passed. As a result, she was hesitant to make any more decisions until she had learned the results of her previous ones. But now it seemed she would be forced to act. She had heard nothing from Conroy or Bronn, and it was possible that given the distance, a reply could still be weeks away. *Yet, I cannot wait any longer.*

Elyse was so lost in thought as she rushed through the long hall that she nearly ran into Illyan. He stood, blocking her path with a devilish smile across his face, bowing slightly as their eyes met.

How did he get ahead of me?

But then she remembered that Illyan had not been in the council this morning. The realization made her nervous and set her heart racing. She turned quickly to see if Gauge had caught up to her but he was nowhere in sight. She was forced to face Illyan and return the smile.

He would not dare to do anything to harm me in my own castle. I am the queen and his ruler after all. I must remember that. Then a cold thought struck her. *My father was the king and yet Nareash struck him in his own castle.* A shiver ran up her back.

"Ah, my Queen," Illyan said bowing once more, "it is so good to see you again. May I speak with you for a few moments?"

Elyse lied. "I would love nothing more as I missed your valuable insight this morning, but I'm afraid I have much to do today."

"You are too kind. I promise that I will not trouble you long. In fact, I can speak with you as we walk to your next appointment. I'll even double my short steps to keep up with your own elegant stride," said Illyan, mocking himself.

What is he up to? Self deprecation isn't something he is known for. He continued while they walked, still smiling. "I believe you usually meet with Gillian to go over your household's administration, correct?"

"Yes," said Elyse, taken aback. "How do you know that?" *One Above, is he spying on me?*

"Oh, it is nothing, Your Majesty. I find it convenient to know many people's schedules in case I have a need to contact them about a most crucial matter. For instance, did you know that every day about this time, after his morning duties, General Grayer retreats to a small room in the back of the armory where he gorges himself on a plate of pastries? I find it quite humorous that such a hard man could have such a childish vice." He paused. "I could go on all day, you know, on the personal habits of your subjects. But that is not what I wished to speak with you about. My concerns are far more pressing."

"I don't mean to discount your concerns, but you know that these things are meant to be discussed openly in council."

"I agree, Your Majesty, but I'm sure you understand that with the all the confusion of the council chambers as of late, very little is properly addressed."

I'm sure that was meant to be a slight against me.

"It seems that many of my pleas, despite their volume, are overshadowed by those with a greater flair for presentation," continued Illyan.

"Well, you may always set up a private appointment. I'm sure Gillian could find a spot for us to meet at a more opportune..."

Illyan interrupted. "I beg your pardon, Your Majesty, but I have tried for several months to do just that, but it seems your tight schedule is hard to break into. I joked that someone as small as I would only need a little of your time but your steward was quick to point out that your time was too precious to waste. I believe you had an appointment with the seamstress that day," said Illyan in a dry tone. "Don't worry; I understand the importance of a new dress when speaking with nobles," he added with a sneer.

Elyse did not know if she should apologize for the insult he felt, or if she should point out that as queen he had no right to chastise her for her use of time. *What crime is it to take a few minutes for myself? Am I not allowed any pleasure in this life?* Rather than encourage his behavior, she said nothing.

Illyan was not put off by her silence. "But please, let's not waste any further time discussing such things. I'm assuming that you have not received word yet from your *attempts* to reach out to Duke Bronn and Duke Conroy?"

Does he have a spy in my head? "No. As I mentioned today in council, it has been too early to receive any news." Then she added. "I can have Gauge fill you in on today's discussions since you were absent," said Elyse with a smile. *I can play this game too.*

If the comment bothered Illyan, he did not show it. "No, Your Majesty, I'm sure I can guess that the discussions resemble all too closely those from the meetings before. Really, each meeting these past few weeks has become quite easy to predict. I'm sure you have been able to guess who will say what and when they will say it, too. Yes, I will take it from your look you agree.

"To be blunt, Your Majesty, I came to urge you into action, real action that is. Preparation for this war is crucial and I promise you there will be a war." He paused, punctuating the last word. "I will not talk to you about your decisions with Conroy and Bronn, though I vehemently disagree with them. Those things are done. No, instead I must talk to you about what should have been done some time ago."

Elyse felt put off by the short man. In their last conversation he attempted to persuade her through intimidation and this time he lectured to her as if she were a child. Not even Gauge, her closest advisor took such liberty and Illyan's tone began to grate on her. "Is this about your silly road, Illyan?"

Illyan's eyes narrowed but his voice remained calm. "That silly road will be an advantage when transporting supplies. But that is only one aspect of which I speak. There is much more. I thought it would be equally beneficial to build small warehouses along the road which the locals would be tasked with guarding. Then the supplies will have less distance to travel when needed. I have other ideas as well…"

"I'm sure you do," interrupted Elyse. "But what you are asking is ridiculous. The cost would be enormous and the merchant guild would benefit the most. Coincidentally you are part of the guild, correct?"

"I never denied that the guild would be one of the groups to benefit, but I dare say you are missing the greater picture. Even if war is avoided, which I doubt it will be, the economic impact would be extraordinary for everyone," said Illyan.

"If your idea is as grand as you say it is, why has no other counselor shared your view? Why is it that you are the only one to have thought of such an idea when Cadonia has been around for hundreds of years?" said Elyse, feeling confident in her argument.

"They do not support my decision because I have not allowed them to meddle in the details," said Illyan, a bitter sound to his words. "If I were to do such a thing they would twist it into their own purpose." He paused, smiling once again. "And I never claimed the idea was my own. In fact, Aurnon the First, himself, had thought of such an idea shortly after conquering Cadonia but he was never able to see the plan through to fruition. If I recall, it was about that time that he left Cadonia and marched back to Quoron to dispose of Sacrynon's Scepter. Of course," he paused, "we both know he didn't do a very good job of that, did he?"

Elyse tensed but collected herself quickly enough. "Well, it is destroyed now."

Illyan rubbed his chin. "Yes, I guess it is. I do find it interesting that an instrument of power so strong that Sacrynon himself could not control the effect it had on him could have been destroyed by his former pupil. And with

Master Amcaro in a weakened state, having already fought Nareash as I've heard."

Elyse felt a lump in her throat and she stopped. "High Mage Amcaro was a great man."

"Yes, he was. But just how great, I wonder?" asked Illyan, a smile dancing at the corner of his lips.

Is it possible? No, not even he could know. He wants me to give something away. Elyse realized it was best to end the conversation. "I have heard your advice, and as always, I will take it into consideration. It's possible that at some point later in my reign, I would be willing to embark on such a large project, but I'm afraid now isn't the time."

Illyan began to chuckle which bothered Elyse even more. She was sure he could see the displeasure on her face and yet, he continued to laugh as he spoke. "Very well said. You almost sound as if you mean it. But, I'm afraid you just don't understand, do you? You speak as if your reign has a future. I tell you, act now and you may stand a chance. Twiddle your thumbs in indecisiveness and your time upon the throne will be the shortest in this country's history, and a worse failure than your father's."

Elyse was shocked. "How dare you speak of my father? And for that matter, how dare you speak to me in such a tone? I'm warning you..."

"Come now, Your Majesty. I speak nothing that is not true. I know your opinion was not so high of him that you could be completely blind to his ineffectiveness."

"I loved my father."

"I do not question your love for him. But a ruler must be quick and absolute in their decisions, something your father hadn't been in years. I hate to see you emulate him in such a way."

"By what right do you think you may speak to me in such a way?!"

"My Queen! Are you alright?" came a shout done the hallway. "Illyan, what are you doing here?"

Elyse noticed that she and Illyan had stopped in a secluded portion of the long hallway, in the shadows of the entrance to a storage room. The realization made Elyse cringe as she had allowed herself to be cut off from the normal activity of the castle. Gauge must have understood the same thing. He was accompanied by two of her personal guards who approached at a brisk pace. "I'm fine," she answered, meeting her advisor's eyes.

"Yes," said Illyan cutting in. "Her Majesty and I were just discussing the imminent war."

"There is no imminent war," said Gauge. "Saying such things only feeds the rumors among the people. Besides, you know that no one is allowed to speak to the queen in such a common manner."

"You are right. How silly of me to forget that such activity is kept exclusively for you. I don't think I ever congratulated you for such an honor.

Let me take the opportunity to do so now," said Illyan with a mocking bow. "And as for your first point, I'll let you tell Her Majesty about the interesting news that arrived just a couple of hours ago."

"How could you…"

"Oh, it's nothing." He turned to Elyse and bowed. "Please excuse me. I hope you will forgive me for getting carried away in my passion for this great country. Maybe you will soon realize that few people have your best interests at heart," he said while glancing at Gauge through the corner of his eye.

Gauge did not miss the slight. "Are you saying you do?"

Illyan smiled. "I care only for my country." He met Elyse's gaze. "May I have your leave, Your Majesty?"

Elyse nodded. Illyan turned and left, his legs moving at a quickened pace.

After a moment Gauge addressed her. "I'm sorry that I could not leave the council chambers soon enough. If I had known that…"

"You were only acting on my command."

"Still, you must always be with your guards."

"I did not see them. Where were they?"

Gauge turned to both men. Hadan and Willum each hung their eyes down in shame. "Someone had sent them a false message. I wouldn't doubt that Illyan arranged the distraction. I'm already looking into it and if so, he will surely be punished for such a crime."

"Let it go. He talks and no one listens."

Gauge hesitated. "Very well, but I have told these two that their only orders are to come from me or you. They shall listen to no one else."

Elyse nodded.

"Now I'm sorry, but you're late for your appointment with Gillian. We must be on our way."

"Wait."

"Yes?"

"Illyan spoke of news that just came in this morning. What is it?"

"I'm sure it is something that can wait until you have seen to your duties…."

"I will hear it now."

Gauge sighed. "As you command. It appears that we have finally received word in regards to Tomalt. He has called in many of his lords, especially those along our southern borders."

"And you do not think this is important? Why would you wait to tell me such a thing?"

"I did not want to trouble you. All dukes have been known to do such things from time to time, Tomalt more than others. He has always been one to test his lords."

"That may have been well and good in times less strained but given the current situation, such an act can take on many other meanings." *Was Illyan right? Is war really inevitable? Maybe there are preparations that could be made now, though I promise none will involve new roads.*

Gauge responded as if reading her thoughts, "We mustn't do anything that would instigate a confrontation with Tomalt."

"I don't plan to do any such thing. However, I can't just sit on my hands any longer and hope the problem will go away."

"Your Majesty, let us discuss such things after we meet with Gillian," said Gauge taking a step forward, urging Elyse to follow.

No, Gillian will do little to help me with such things and, in truth, neither will Gauge. Illyan said General Grayer is in the armory now and I can't think of anyone better to talk to about such a matter. Yes, in fact, I daresay I should have spoken to him in person some time ago. "I will need you to meet with Gillian for me and handle my affairs. I must go speak with General Grayer and have his thoughts on this matter with Tomalt."

"Grayer? But I'm not sure where he is at the moment. Perhaps I can send a messenger to find him while you and I meet with Gillian together?"

"No. You go on ahead. I'm sure to find the general in the armory."

"The armory?" said Gauge, appalled. "But such a place is not meant for a queen."

"And why not? It is part of my kingdom and in my very home. Don't fret about my safety, if that is what concerns you. I promise, my guards will see to my every need, isn't that so?" said the queen turning to each of them.

They each perked up at being addressed by their queen, bowing solemnly in response. They responded in unison. "Yes, Your Majesty."

Gauge sighed, seeing it was no use to press the issue any further. "As you command." He bowed and the two parted ways.

* * *

Although it was her first visit to the armory, Elyse had passed the large stone building countless times when walking about the castle. It was plain with hard edges. Twin eight-foot great swords that crossed each other over a monstrous shield hung above the door. Time had worn the luster off the sword hilts and the royal coat of arms.

She took a deep breath upon her approach. Growing up, Elyse had no interest in swords and bows or any other weapon for that matter. Jonrell had tried to teach her about such things, but it had been no use explaining them to a young princess. At first she tried to listen, if only for her brother's sake, but she found each fact utterly boring and her mind constantly wandered to places of legend.

One more thing that I ignored in error. But then again, I never thought he would leave me. He was supposed to be king. He was supposed to protect me so I wouldn't have to worry about such things.

The memory was bitter not only because her brother was no longer with her but because it made her angry at herself.

Hadan opened the door to the armory and Elyse crossed the threshold, her eyes immediately going up to the ceiling where banners depicting the great battles of Aurnon the First in his conquering of both Thurum and Cadonia hung. Large columns supported the expansive armory in place of interior walls. To her right stood a forge, massive in size, where more than a dozen blacksmiths could work at once. A man with a knot of gray hair tied at base of his skull rang a hammer against a piece of glowing white metal. A boy no more than ten helped. To her left was an area used for fletching arrows. Again, most of the space was empty save for another old man tending to a quiver of arrows.

Both men were focused on their work and neither noticed Elyse. Choosing not to disturb them, she walked through the rows of cracked bows, rusted armor, dulled swords, realizing how immense their task was. It brought a sinking feeling to her stomach.

Everything is in disrepair. What would we use if war did break out?

Continuing on through the wood, leather, and steel, she came upon General Grayer sitting at a small table at the back of the armory. On one side of the table was a stack of papers and on the other was a stack of pastries.

Just as Illyan said.

The thought of the devilish man knowing the habits of her subjects better than she did, gave her both chills and flashes of anger. She signaled Hadan and Willum to wait as she approached the general.

Grayer sat in a sleeveless jerkin, exposing large, powerful arms. In one hand, he held a sheet of paper within inches of his face, his eyes squinted in concentration. The other hand held a lemon cake that he shoved into his mouth. A large belly folded over his lap.

The general made no sign that he had heard Elyse or her guards enter the armory. So Elyse addressed him first, "Good day, General Grayer. I hope all is well with you."

Her voice caused him to jump from his chair and come to full attention. The man resembled a barrel with skinny legs. Elyse held in a snicker as she wondered whether he would topple in a strong wind. Despite his size, he bowed fluidly at the waist as befitted a man who had spent his life in the military.

"I'm terribly sorry, Your Majesty. We get so few visitors here. If I would have known, my dress...."

"Your dress is fine, General. May I have a moment of your time?" she asked.

"Yes, of course. I can change quickly and meet you at a place more appropriate if you like."

"Here is fine. Please have a seat," she said motioning to the chairs. After the two settled she continued. "What shape is our army in?"

"Shape? Why, the army is in excellent shape as always," said Grayer, though Elyse could see his voice lacked the confidence she hoped for.

He fears what will happen when I learn the truth of things. She glanced at a rusted breast plate and shook her head. *I may have believed him only yesterday but not after seeing this.* "General, please, I need you to be as honest with me as you would with your captains. Brutally honest, in fact. I need to know that if it comes down to it, we can defend our land."

He heaved a heavy sigh. "I can give you brutal honesty, Your Majesty. In fact, I welcome the truth, though I'm afraid you won't like it." He paused. "Yes, I have heard the rumors circulating around the kingdom and I know they change daily as to who poses the greatest threat. And each day I sit here asking myself the same questions. Who will attack first? Where will the attack be? How can we defend the realm? I'm no closer to the answers. But I do know the answer to one question, perhaps the most important question of all. Can we defend the realm? And the answer is, without a doubt, no. I look at the numbers you see before you in our records and they never change. We don't have the strength or skill to win a war if it came down to it." He paused for a second adding, "Don't think that will stop me from trying, Your Majesty. I am a man with honor. I swore an oath to the crown each time I moved through the ranks. I don't take those things lightly."

It is worse than I thought. How can I not have already known about this? Why do my advisors not know about this? Even Gauge made no mention of such things.

She tried not to let it show that his words had bothered her. "Thank you, General. But I must ask, how can you say we don't have a chance to win a war? You are in charge of the Royal Army. Where are we lacking?"

He gestured to the forge. "I remember when I joined the military and I was given my first sword. Every fire burned bright in here, and you could feel the heat throughout the entire building. Masters and apprentices alike hammered away each day making repairs, and trying to outdo each other with their newest creations." He gestured to the fletcher. "The same occurred there. The warm temperatures of the forge allowed the fletchers to work the wood more easily to make bows and arrows at an alarming pace." He sighed. "This place was so efficient, we could supply fighting forces in and out of the realm, even to Conroy before he built his own armory. Now, we are barely able to maintain the weapons for the royal guard let alone a larger army."

"I don't understand. Isn't it one of your duties to ensure such things are properly maintained?"

"Yes, Your Majesty, it is. But it all boils down to money. I can yell, scream, argue, and plead, but no one works for free. A blacksmith, a fletcher, and even a soldier have their own responsibilities at home and mouths to feed."

"How is it that you lack the funds necessary to maintain your army?"

"Well again, if brutal honesty is what you want, your father cut funding greatly over the past few years. He went on about how maintaining a strong military was a waste of money as there hadn't been a real threat of rebellion outside a few minor lords since Aurnon the Third's reign. I tried to explain to him that the crown should always be in control of the strongest army in the land, but he would not listen. I daresay our forces are the weakest and our lords have been allowed to work their land without performing their duties to the army."

Is that all I really inherited from you father? A long list of mistakes and problems? And now I have just a few months to try to fix mistakes it took years to make. "How large is our army now?"

He sighed. "Large isn't the best word to use in describing the army, Your Majesty. Outside of the royal guard, we have roughly four thousand men stationed throughout our territory."

Elyse's eyes widened. "That can't be all?"

"It sickens me to say this, Your Majesty. But I'm afraid so. Most of our best men were sent to Conroy," he said with his head down, not wanting to meet her eyes.

He blames me for making matters worse. But I had no idea things were so bad. But that's it, isn't it? It is my responsibility to know everything.

"Last I heard, Tomalt could call in a full army that would be well over ten times that amount," said Elyse.

"Yes, and that would be just from his northern forces. Conroy's army isn't as numerous but his men are better trained, and far more experienced from defending the High Pass. Bronn is somewhere in the middle."

"And what of Olasi and Jeldor?"

"Olasi's troops are second in training and experience only to Conroy's. Being so close to the High Pass himself, they have to be in case Conroy needs help, however his numbers are fewer. Regardless, we would be cut off from his help if a war did occur with Tomalt. I'm not as sure about Jeldor's men since that region is so isolated from the rest of Cadonia. I do know that his army would be the smallest of any but our own, having the smallest territory. However, growing up in such a land, his men have a natural hardness about them." He paused. "Your Majesty?"

"Yes, General?"

"Well, one area we always had a great advantage in was sorcery. And if it comes to war, a few extra mages could make a big difference in our ability to defend the kingdom."

Elyse frowned. "I know, General. But Amcaro is dead and with no High Mages left alive, Estul Island is without anyone to oversee those still in training or provide council to those here on the mainland." She shook her head. "I've asked Gauge to send word to them, but so far I've not received any response."

"I see," said Grayer, looking weary.

Such talk of her army's inferiority overwhelmed Elyse but she had to do something. *My advisors want decisions, then so be it.*

"General, I want our army to grow and I want it done fast," said Elyse, raising her voice.

"Your Majesty?" said Grayer, looking up wide-eyed. "We will need money to…"

"You will have anything and everything you ask for within reason. Consider money no longer a problem." *At least I hope it isn't.* "We will meet each day at this time to discuss your progress, starting tomorrow. We have much more to go over then. I want you to be completely honest with me going forward in all things and do not be afraid to ask for anything concerning your task. The defense of this kingdom is my number one priority. Is that clear?"

"Absolutely, Your Majesty," said Grayer, his eyes springing to life with purpose. "I promise you that every waking moment will be spent on bringing this army back to its glory."

Elyse nodded, satisfied by Grayer's eagerness. As the two parted Elyse noticed that Grayer seemed to be in much higher spirits as he raced to begin work. She, on the other hand, felt more depressed than ever.

One Above, how can we ever hope to win with so small a force? Still, I refuse to run away and give up. How could I have been so oblivious to the state of the army? I'll have to talk to Gauge about the army's condition before the day is through.

Realizing her tardiness for another appointment, she rushed from the armory.

* * *

"And then what did you say?" asked Lobella as she helped Elyse undress.

"Nothing at first. I was too shocked. But then I was angry and in so many words told him that in the future it is not his place to keep things from me regarding my kingdom. Then he apologized and we bid each other good night."

The two said nothing else as Elyse slipped her gown over her head and Lobella put it away. Lobella came back and began helping Elyse with her undergarments and then with her nightgown. Finally, Elyse broke the silence. "You don't agree with me, do you?"

"It isn't my place to question my Queen's decisions," said Lobella.

"Well then question your friend's decisions," said Elyse turning to face Lobella.

The servant dropped her eyes. "I think you were too hard on him."

"Too hard on him? How can you say that? He purposefully kept information from me regarding the state of the royal army." Elyse paused, flustered, then added, "On top of that, he did nothing to remedy the situation."

"I didn't say I agreed with his actions. And frankly, I'm the last person to say whether his decisions were sound in judgment. But I think he was only looking out for your best interests. You tell me yourself that he handles a great deal of duties that would otherwise fall on you."

Elyse swallowed hard. "I do rely on him a lot, but how could he ignore something so important?"

"I've only spoken to Gauge in passing but he doesn't seem like the type of person to ignore anything that is important. You said yourself that the military isn't what it should be. Maybe he thought his time could be better spent looking at other issues that would solve the same problem?" Lobella finished with a shrug.

Some of his suggestions do lend themselves to that idea. It would make sense why he has spent so much time negotiating with those advisors sympathetic to other dukes. Now that I think about it, he started behaving that way more so after I sent those troops off to Conroy. Is he only trying to fix my mistake? I'll have to talk to him tomorrow about this. Maybe if word gets out that we are spending so much on our own army, it will deter Tomalt or anyone else from attacking?

Elyse realized that she hadn't yet said a word in response to Lobella, who now brushed her hair. "I think you're right. I'll need to apologize to him in the morning. As queen, I have no one to blame but myself."

* * *

For hours Elyse tossed and turned, unable to find rest. Her mind busied itself with the thoughts from that day. Another stressful council meeting, the worries of war, an inadequate army, and losing her temper with Gauge all contributed to her frazzled state. However, the meeting with Illyan caused her the greatest distress. She thought about how easily he set up their meeting, sending false messages to her guards, catching her alone in a secluded hallway.

And he knows my schedule and that of my aides better than Gillian does.

However, the part of the encounter that terrified her most was the knowing look and the devilish grin Illyan gave her when mentioning Sacrynon's Scepter. There was no way for him to know what had happened on that dreadful day when the castle became a killing field. Only she bore witness to those tragic events, and when recalling them to others, she had been careful about what information to leave out.

Perhaps, I remembered some of your lessons after all, Jonrell.

Yet, Illyan's insinuations gave her pause. After Lobella had left her room earlier, she locked the door and checked the floorboards under her bed. It was still there. She had no reason to doubt that the Scepter could not be found. The secret hiding spot was one she discovered as a girl and never told anyone about. At first she wondered if someone would be able to sense the Scepter's power emanating from her room, but that was apparently not how the weapon worked. She remembered Nareash saying that the scepter had originally been concealed as a simple candleholder for centuries until he had stumbled upon it.

No, someone must first know how to wield the weapon and bring forth its power.

She shuddered, knowing that she slept right above the dreadful object. Yet, what other option did she have? She refused to allow anyone to use such a thing again.

CHAPTER 12

Notch. Draw. Aim. Release.

The steady rhythm with a bow brought him peace in a way that few things could match. With it in his hand, the world around him no longer existed.

In Tobin's youth, his Uncle Cef had been responsible for schooling the potential Kifzo warriors. A harsh man, he would push the recruits every waking moment, leaving little time for them to think about anything other than their task. After Tobin's uncle died, the training of the youth shifted to the veterans. It was understood that the older warriors knew what was expected of them and so no longer were they forced to keep as strict of a schedule.

Tobin recalled hating that single-mindedness of his uncle's methods. How ironic that he duplicated such a schedule now. Without Kaz hovering over him, Tobin had become his own staunchest competitor, rising before dawn and working well past dusk.

Notch. Draw. Aim. Release.

Since the night he found Nachun kneeling before his brother's body, Tobin had only spoken to his father once, that next morning. As expected, Bazraki had wanted him to confirm Nachun's story surrounding the previous night's events which he did.

Bazraki also used the time to finally probe Tobin about what he had discovered during his time with Nachun since Nubinya. To his surprise, the discussion was not as intense as he had expected. Tobin found a way to give enough information to his father without casting Nachun in a negative light. Yet, Tobin felt relieved when he finished.

Tobin and Nachun had barely spoken since that night in the bowels of the palace. In fact, Tobin purposefully avoided him, though he never stopped long enough to consider why.

Notch. Draw. Aim. Release.

Tobin had kept his distance from Lucia as well. When their paths happened to cross, he would feign deafness or quickly seek a place to hide in order to avoid her. Undeterred by his behavior, Lucia took to sending him messages, asking that they meet for dinner. Tobin declined each offer without explanation, through the use of a messenger.

He shook his head. The thoughts he tried to shun somehow had crept back into his mind. He narrowed in on the target.

Notch. Draw. Aim. Release.

Tobin's newfound commitment to preparation was intended to separate him from the others, but in some ways the plan backfired. Other Kifzo had noted his new training habits and he found himself no longer alone in keeping such lengthy hours. Tobin didn't know if it was out of inadequacy, competition, or guilt that his fellow Kifzo joined him for his marathon sessions but the training yard beamed with activity each and every day. Yet Tobin only desired to revel in its silence.

He snorted. *When have I ever gotten what I wanted? None of it really matters. In fact, nothing matters anymore.* His eyes squinted to the farthest target out; one that only a few in his whole clan could reach.

Notch. Draw. Aim. Release.

The edges of his mouth turned up.

* * *

Tobin closed each day with the sword. Practicing while already fatigued forced him to narrow his focus. He ran through the memorized drills his uncle had taught him while seeking a way to compensate for his hindered footwork. The self-imposed challenge seemed to rejuvenate his interest with the weapon. He worked later and later each night, sometimes only by the light of the moon. He failed to pinpoint the cause to his sudden rededication.

Perhaps it's because Kaz is no longer here to ridicule me at every turn.

Sessions had begun with Tobin working on his forms alone. But as his confidence grew, he realized he needed more of a challenge, understanding that with such isolation, he only limited himself. So, putting aside his fears, he made use of the practice circles that he had shunned for so long.

Dozens of fenced-in practice circles were grouped in the southwest corner of the practice yard, butted against Juanoq's southern walls. Looming overhead, the fortifications cast long shadows over the grunting combatants below. The cacophony of clashing weapons filled Tobin's ears as he twisted the sword in his hand, dodging a flurry of blows.

Tobin knew Walor would work with him, rather than against him. As an accomplished swordsman, Walor used his compact size and quickness to dart around and between his opponent's defenses. The head scout's style challenged Tobin's hampered mobility.

Parrying one of Walor's thrusts, Tobin countered with a slash of his own. Walor ducked under the blow, then sidestepped Tobin's next swing. A grin crept across Walor's face as he leaped backward to circumvent yet another of Tobin's attacks.

The two paused, circling each other around the crude fence that enclosed the practice circle. Walor jerked his head off to the side and a loud pop followed. "Ah, there it is."

"Am I boring you so much that you can stretch during our match?" said Tobin, lifting his arm to wipe sweat from his brow.

"Actually, I was just thinking how much better you've gotten. A week ago, you would have left yourself open after the upward cut, but this time you kept pressing."

"So, what you're saying is that I've shaken your confidence?"

Walor's grin widened. "Hardly." He jumped forward, bringing his sword down. Tobin clacked his practice sword away.

Got him.

As Walor landed, Tobin moved to separate their weapons by pushing off with his boot. But Walor rolled, tumbling to the dirt, limbs snaking out in a blur of motion. A moment later, Tobin rested on his back, staring up at the gloomy night. Walor stood over him and the light from the torches lining the circle danced off his face. Walor's sword hovered inches from Tobin's face. He smiled. "You're dead."

"Again," Tobin said with a sigh.

"You're improving each time though. Before long your swordsmanship will rival your skill with a bow," said Walor offering a hand to Tobin.

"Don't patronize me, Walor." Tobin stood up and winced as he put weight on his ankle.

"I thought I went for your good leg," said Walor, looking down.

"You did. I must have twisted it when I fell," said Tobin, throwing his sword down in frustration.

"We need to keep focusing on your strengths," said Walor, as if reading his thoughts.

A deep laugh roared up from behind the two Kifzo. Tobin turned and saw Durahn leaning over a post on the far side of the practice ring, his bullish head bobbing with each guffaw.

"Look at you two. It almost makes me wish your brother was around, Tobin. I can only imagine what he would say now with Walor fawning over you like some woman."

Tobin's eyes narrowed and his hands closed into fists.

Durahn laughed louder. "Maybe a kiss will make that ankle of yours better."

If only the ankle was healed Durahn...If only.

"I was told to let you know that El Olam, or whatever your father is calling himself these days, wishes to see you," said Durahn, calming himself. "Sooner rather than later," he added before walking away, chuckling again.

"I wish Kaz had killed him when he had the chance," said Walor in a low tone.

Tobin turned away, exiting the practice circle with a heavy limp. He heard Walor call out, but ignored him. *Durahn is right. Kaz would call me weak if he saw me now.* Tobin picked up his pace despite the pain. Cursing under his breath with each step, he did his best to mask the injury. *You don't even need to be here to cause me grief, do you, Brother?*

He weaved through the maze of practice circles, skirting around the much larger areas where full-scale battle sequences commenced. Terrain, group size, and weapon choices, varied in an effort to account for as many scenarios as possible. Instituted years ago by Tobin's uncle, the younger warriors looked forward to the competitions to prove they were ready to enter battle. The more experienced warriors betted on those involved now that they no longer participated in such things.

Tobin had excelled in those competitions as a youth. He had bested Kaz on several occasions when given the chance to lead a squad on his own. Once Kaz became warleader everything changed. His uncle had always been against Kaz's harsh treatment of Tobin and wanted them to put aside their differences. But Bazraki was explicit—as warleader, Kaz answered to no one but him.

At least uncle attempted to set things right before he passed. More than I can say for my own father.

Tobin never understood why Bazraki dropped the issue of finding his uncle's killer so quickly.

We knew he was poisoned. And yet, Father never even allowed a shaman or healer to examine the body. "We have no time for the dead." He snorted, realizing where Kaz had picked up the saying.

Tobin shook his head, mulling that thought over, as he walked by the armory and into the onsite barracks used to house the Kifzo still in training.

He searched only two days for the killer of his wife's brother. Without Uncle Cef, Father would have never gained control of the Blue Island Clan. He found it remarkable that after a month, Bazraki continued his search to find Kaz.

He started to clean up before seeing Bazraki. Alone, he stared down the rows of empty cots where he himself had once slept. Memories flashed before his eyes. Few were pleasant.

* * *

Tobin left the training compound and made his way across the dirt roads littered with beggars and trash of the city's oldest district. The dilapidated buildings that filled the quarter were tucked behind the more regal structures that lined Juanoq's main street. Many chose to forget this area of the city and its significance. Long before Bazraki united the Blue Island Clan, this small borough housed nearly the entirety of the city's population. But as Juanoq expanded and the Blue Island Clan prospered, most of the original populace moved out of the old neighborhoods and into districts far more impressive. Now, only the downtrodden called this area home.

Would it kill Father to rebuild this section into something that would match the rest of Juanoq? Tobin shook his head, stepping over the corpse of a dead dog, flies feasting on its rotting flesh. *No, he never speaks of the time before he seized power. It's as if he believes it has always been the way it is now.*

Dirt roads gave way to stone avenues as Tobin turned onto the main street. Having left behind the dregs of Juanoq, it felt like stepping into a different world. Free of garbage and waste, Tobin failed to see even a piece of horse dung from the clattering merchant carts along the cobblestone thoroughfare. The walls around him stood tall and strong, covered in intricate designs. Ornamental stained glass protected first floor windows from prying eyes rather than the broken shudders of older homes. Even past dusk, no beggars dared to find a night's rest here lest the city watch throw them in jail.

Tobin had not yet seen all of Hesh, but according to Nachun, nothing compared to the beauty that Bazraki had created in Juanoq. Even Nubinya, a paradise, or so its name claimed, seemed insignificant.

And to think that most of this we created without the aid of other clans. He had to give his father credit for how far the Blue Island Clan had come in such a short time. *He was driven by anger then, embarrassed by how we were viewed by the other clans. I wonder if it is anger that still drives him now.*

Tobin passed twin watchtowers that flanked either side of the main street. Housing most of the city watch, the large towers stood at Juanoq's core. Bazraki wanted his main force in the center to more easily distribute people in case of a major disturbance. Tobin doubted the possibility of such a disturbance. With a system of stringent laws that Bazraki vehemently enforced, even the poorest citizens avoided testing them.

Such inactivity led to a force often bored, one that became easily distracted. The guards were caught on more than one occasion visiting Juanoq's more extravagant bathhouses while on shift, or gambling into the night at the garrison. But Tobin had seen very little of that behavior as of late, and tonight appeared no different.

His gaze traveled up the inward sloping tower walls and saw only a handful of lights still on. His father had devoted every spare man into discerning Kaz's whereabouts, some sent out of the city.

Amazing how no one has even come close to discovering the truth.

After a series of sharp turns, Tobin reached the palace's outer gates. One of his father's personal guards waited at attention with spear and shield in hand. He met Tobin with a bow and then led him through the courtyard and into the inner gates before traversing the network of confusion. As the two ascended and descended several staircases while taking twisting corridors that turned back on themselves, he found himself questioning the ineptitude of the palace's designers more than usual.

Why does Father allow such nonsense?

Finally, after reaching a wide staircase, the guardsmen stopped at the threshold of an open door, announcing Tobin's arrival.

Nachun acknowledged Tobin with a slight nod but Bazraki looked past his son, dismissing the guards with a wave of his hand. His father turned as if Tobin wasn't there and continued his conversation. He spoke with a different group, not his usual gaggle of advisors.

It appeared that the assembly consisted of craftsmen, predominately blacksmiths. Each listened intently as Bazraki went over a sheet of parchment while he pointed at various items spread on a table. Tobin tried to listen in, but the room was far too crowded. Since he had not received permission to join the conversation, Tobin watched from the room's entrance, surprised to see Nachun interrupt from time to time.

He grows so bold. Only Kaz would get away with speaking so freely around Father before.

Isolated from the exchange, Tobin's eyes wandered around the room. Several large maps adorned the walls, varying in size and focus. Each detailed a different clan's territory. The largest map engulfed one wall in its entirety, showing all of Hesh west of the Great Divide. Below the maps, atop shelves and tables sat neatly organized stacks of parchments.

So this must be Father's new war room.

As the meeting concluded, attendants filed out, talking amongst themselves, bowing their heads in respect to Tobin upon leaving.

Well, at least some acknowledge who I am. He and Nachun exchanged a nod before the shaman left and the door clicked shut. Tobin was alone with his father. Only then did Bazraki speak to his son. "You were late."

"I apologize, El Olam," said Tobin, bowing deep. "I was training and needed to make myself presentable before entering your war room."

"I've noticed that your time in the training ground has increased significantly as of late. I'm glad." Bazraki's eyes flickered to Tobin's feet. "But does it take that long to bathe?"

Tobin glance down and saw what his father had seen, his left ankle had started to swell from earlier. *No use hiding that.* "No, El Olam. My ankle twisted in the practice circle. It would appear that it hindered my pace more than I had anticipated."

"I see." He paused. "And you would not take a horse or a cart? Surely, it would have made your arrival more prompt."

"Horses are for plowing, battle, or carrying the sick and old. Using them to travel such short distances is for the weak. I am not. Besides the injury is minor and will not hold back my ability to train on the morrow."

"Does that include the circle again?" asked Bazraki.

"Yes."

Bazraki nodded and Tobin exhaled, knowing his answer pleased his father. *For once.* Tobin took the chance to change subjects. "What did you wish to see me about, El Olam?"

"I had intended for you to sit in on the meeting, but since you arrived late, it was not fair to stop and start over for your sake." Bazraki walked back to the table he stood near before. "I wanted you to corroborate Nachun's assertions about the new armor and weapons that you and he had been working on. But since you were late, I'll have you do so now."

New weapons? What is he talking about? Tobin moved to the table to better see the items that adorned the table. Spread about were articles of war, many different than anything Tobin had ever seen before, some completely foreign in appearance. He gestured to the table. "May I?"

Hands clasped behind his back, Bazraki nodded.

Inspecting each item, Tobin paced the table, doing his best to hide his nervousness and anger at Nachun. *Going behind my back once again?* He started with the easiest to discern, a sword, and picked it up. Longer, yet lighter, than what a Kifzo normally carried, the balance impressed him most. He spun the weapon in his hand. Bringing the hilt to his eyes, he looked down the length of the blade, carefully turning it over in his hand. He tested the edge with his thumb and drew blood with little effort.

Amazing.

"Well?" said Bazraki, a tight scowl worn on his aged face.

Well what? Should I tell you that this is the first time I've seen this sword and that Nachun has lied to you once again and kept me in the dark the entire time. No, I cannot. I decided my position on Nachun.

"Nachun and I discussed many of these," Tobin said, gesturing to the table, "some time ago. However, he is more familiar with the details than I am. Perhaps you can tell me first what he has already told you about each item so I don't waste your time with information you already know."

Silence stretched as Bazraki eyed his son with a glare that would shatter stone, one often used to break the wills of most men. Tobin forced himself to remain calm, emotionless, so not to give anything away.

His father finally nodded. "Nachun has talked about a new process, one long lost to our people that he *claims* to have rediscovered and, in his words, 'improved upon.' He maintains that no other clan in all of Hesh could compare to the quality of steel that would result from this process. The blade in your hand is his proof of such claims." Bazraki stopped.

Tobin continued his lies. "We did discuss this process at one point. It seemed beneficial if it could be accomplished. But since then, training has taken the bulk of my time and I had not given the conversation much thought until now." He placed the sword back on the table and picked up a dagger in its stead, examining it with care. "The craftsmanship is amazing. However, they are far different from what we currently use in look, size, and feel. It would take time for me to know these as well as I already know my own. Only then could I value their worth."

"You have two days," said Bazraki.

"That is not enough time."

"Two days. If what Nachun claims is true, their advantage is too great for us to ignore. Those I spoke with earlier will be in charge of overseeing the production of all that is before you," said Bazraki. "However, I told them that they must first wait two days before receiving my final order to begin. In the meantime, your task is to confirm their practical use so that I am not late in doing so."

Tobin sighed to himself. *A nearly impossible task to complete in only two days. This would have been given to Kaz. I doubt he would be held to such an inflexible schedule.*

"As you say, El Olam." Tobin placed the dagger down and picked up a device that resembled a bow, only smaller, mounted on a flat wooden frame. A mechanism appeared to control the release of the string but Tobin was unsure how.

"Nachun calls that a crossbow. He says that less time is needed to become effective with it than what is normally required with a longbow and that there will be more power behind each shot."

Tobin frowned, adding another lie, easier than the last. "I wasn't expecting it to be so bulky."

"He said the weapon is not meant to replace the longbow, but instead to compliment it and that it is not ideal for every situation. You have the same two days to determine what those situations are and just how efficient the weapon is before reporting to me."

Of course. "As you say." Tobin set the crossbow down and moved to the last two items. One appeared to be a shirt, made from small metal loops woven closely together. The other consisted of a series of metal sheets, laid out in a manner that resembled a person's body from head to feet. He liked the look of neither.

"Now I see why one's blade must be so light. This extra weight must be compensated for," said Tobin, lifting the armor and inspecting it. He grunted. "It's lighter than it looks and no doubt it would provide better protection than the boiled leather we wear now. But where stealth is needed, it seems a hindrance. No telling how much this would slow one's movements as well."

"I expressed similar sentiments. Nachun assures me there are ways to dampen most of the noise the armor would make and he admits that some may still prefer to fight without it. However, he promises the positives will outweigh the negatives. These here were made specifically to fit your build. Two days, Tobin."

Tobin nodded. *Apparently I won't be sleeping over the next several days.*

"I'll have these delivered to the training field at dawn for you."

"Send them to my room instead. Tonight. I often arrive at the training yard long before the sun rises."

Bazraki nodded in approval. "It will be done."

"Is there anything else, El Olam?"

"No. You may go," said Bazraki, turning away from his son.

* * *

Tobin swore with each shot of pain that raced up his leg. He had broken out into a sweat by the time he reached his personal chambers on the opposite side of the palace. *It's almost as if this sprawling waste of resources was designed to spite me.*

With his father's news fresh on his mind, he thought it best to try to retire early for the night. He hoped a few extra hours of rest would do his ankle some good.

That is, if my dreams don't keep me up again.

He halted in the doorway of his room, alerted to a presence at the window. A lone figure stood staring out into the starry night, hands resting inside the sleeves of his robe. "I didn't expect to see you here," said Tobin stepping over the threshold and walking over to a chair. He collapsed with a sigh, easing the stress from his leg.

The shaman turned, smiling. "I was worried I would have to wait here all night for you. I see you decided to turn in early."

"Well, I do have a long two days ahead of me now, don't I?" asked Tobin in an accusatory tone.

"Aren't you happy for the opportunity?" said Nachun.

"Why should I be happy?"

"Your father has given you an important task. He needs you."

"He only *needs* me because of your doing. And next time you advise my father and intend for me to help sway him, it would be helpful if you let me know ahead of time. I had no idea what was going on tonight." Tobin pulled off his boot with care. He reached for a jar of salve near him and slowly began to work the substance into his ankle, dampening the pain.

"I was only trying to help. I thought you would be pleased." He frowned, casting his gaze downward. "Speaking of help, I may have found a way to mend your ankle. I haven't worked out all the details yet and it would...."

"No," snapped Tobin. "I'm not sure I want your help right now. What you did to Kaz, these new weapons and armor, and countless other things. I never asked for any of it and worst of all, you keep doing these things without my knowledge. It makes me wonder who you're truly helping," he said through slotted eyes.

Nachun moved to a bare wall across from Tobin and leaned against it. He removed his arms from his robe and folded them across his chest. Staring, he said nothing. Tobin ignored him and continued working the salve into his ankle.

A few minutes passed before Nachun spoke. "I'll ignore that jibe since I understand what this is about. Better, in fact, than you do, I think."

"And I assume you are going to enlighten me as to what that's supposed to mean?"

"I believe I will. And I want you to remember we are friends. Because despite your avoidance of me, and your annoyance at my attempts to help you, I do consider you my friend."

Tobin leaned back and folded his arms.

"When I traveled with you from Nubinya, you talked a lot about things that obviously needed to be said." He paused. "Maybe you didn't realize exactly what you were telling me at the time, but by opening up in such a way, I saw that you trusted me. That meant a great deal to me. You also befriended me and accepted me long before anyone else." Nachun stopped speaking for a moment and began to pace the room, head down.

Tobin started to say something in reply but a raw emotion in Nachun's eyes took him off guard. *It looks like he's barely keeping it together.*

"I wanted to do something in return, to thank you for the kindness you'd shown me. But what could I possibly do? Then I remembered our conversations and I saw the root of all your problems. You never came right out and spoke of it but it could be inferred from almost everything you said or did. I could tell how miserable Kaz made you. I witnessed firsthand how he belittled you at every turn. He hated you."

"And so you thought his hatred gave you the right to take matters into your own hands? To remove him from my life?" said Tobin interrupting.

Nachun shrugged. "The right? No. Rather an obligation."

"An obligation?!" asked Tobin, raising his voice. "You have no obligation to me."

Nachun cut in. "It has been weeks since Kaz disappeared. At any time you could have turned me in, including the very night of his disappearance. But you didn't. You helped me cover it up. Why would you do that?"

Tobin threw up his hands in exasperation. "I've told you why. For one, my father would have punished us both. And two, we were friends."

"Were? Rest assured, Tobin, our friendship has not changed in my mind." Nachun waved a hand dismissively, "And though fear of your father may be part of the reason, the truth of the matter is that you hated your brother. Perhaps as much as he hated you. You never would have been able to bring yourself to do anything about it. It isn't easy for you to be as callous and cold as Kaz. I took care of it so you wouldn't have to.

"Now you're struggling with guilt, and its weight is something you can't handle. So, you spend most of your time mindlessly training and avoiding anyone who would remind you of that night."

"That's ridiculous," said Tobin.

"You're happier with Kaz gone, whether you agree with the circumstances or not. You don't feel any remorse for what happened and you think you should. I think you may even feel guilty and ashamed that I had to do your dirty work."

"I am not the kind of person…."

"…who would chop a man's head off? Who would loose an arrow through another's eye? Who would sneak up behind a crouching foe and slit his throat?"

"That's different. I'm a Kifzo warrior and those acts are part of war. It's what I'm trained to do."

"Since when does war end on the battlefield? War is all around us. Each and every day we make allies and enemies. And like a good warleader, we must strategize to handle each one of them. I've learned that the hard way." He paused. "Being a Kifzo is what you are trained to do. Think of all the things I've done for you as my way of providing you with a different sort of training."

"Am I an ally rather than the friend you just claimed?"

Nachun shook his head. "They are not always synonymous but a man can be both and to me you are. And so like a good ally, like a good *friend*," he said emphasizing the word, "I eliminated your biggest enemy, your strongest foe."

Friend? That word once meant so much to me but now I'm not sure. I never once considered that a friend would act this way for my benefit. After a moment, Tobin responded, his voice tired. "What exactly are you training me for?"

Nachun grinned, his eyes brightening. "A good strategist does not unveil his intentions until the proper moment, or else his plans may go awry. So, I only ask that you trust me."

Tobin snorted. "Why should I trust you, when you keep trying to run my life?"

Nachun laughed. "Who else would you trust? Who else would help you in the ways I have? Walor? A good acquaintance, yes. But what has he done to truly help you in all the years you've spent together? Has he ever stood up for you at the risk of himself?" Nachun took a step closer to Tobin, staring. "I have not given you a reason to do anything other than trust me. Can you deny that your life isn't better now than before we met?"

Tobin couldn't deny any of it. He still had stresses in his life but Kaz's disappearance had eased many of them.

I did hate him and I often wished someone would cut him down in battle. If his life meant so little to me then why do I now care how he died?

He sat for some time thinking. Finally, his mind cleared in a flood of revelation. *I don't.*

"I can see you need time alone. I will see you in the training yard tomorrow. Before dawn, yes?"

Tobin blinked his eyes. "Why would you be there?"

"To help with the testing, of course. I would not leave you to do it alone. After you do well with this task, your father will begin to see you through his own eyes and not through the eyes of Kaz."

Tobin let out a sigh. "You keep helping me. What can I do to repay you?"

"Succeed," said Nachun. His eyes darkened. "I don't speak of it often, but to you, I will admit that revenge is ever on my mind. I want to repay those that made me suffer. They deserve nothing less. Each victory of the Blue Island Clan inches me closer to my goals."

Tobin remembered what Charu had done to Nachun and his family. He walked over and rested a hand on the shaman's shoulder.

"I will do everything I can to help you get your revenge," said Tobin.

Nachun smiled. "Thank you."

Tobin smiled back and shortly after the two parted.

To his surprise, sleep came easy to him that night.

* * *

Weeks had come and gone since Kaz's disappearance, yet many on the streets of Juanoq still whispered of that night. No one ever imagined it would be possible for someone to break into Bazraki's own palace, let alone kidnap his first son, their warleader. But someone did. Or at least that's what everyone was made to believe.

Several times on the morning that followed Kaz's disappearance, Jober almost bungled his story to Bazraki. Nervous, weak from loss of blood, and genuine shame from his deception, left him struggling to keep his thoughts clear. If not for Nachun stepping in at just the right moments, adding bravado to the heroic deeds he was told to convey, he would have lost it. Tobin stood off to the side then, adding only a nod or two as needed, but nothing more.

Jober had been sure Bazraki would see through their deceit, but somehow, perhaps distracted by the shock of it all, he accepted their story.

Since then, the retelling of those events had not grown easier. Intruders broke into the palace, drugged Kaz and his sleeping wife, then stole away with him. They delivered him to a second group who then snuck him out of the city. Jober happened to see the two men returning as they passed by the stables, bragging about what they were pulling off, thinking no one was listening. He followed them and acted when he realized they were returning for Lucia.

Jober couldn't believe that anyone would believe such a story, even with all the facts laid out and neatly organized by the shaman. *Perhaps a peasant, eager to latch onto gossip would, but not Bazraki. He is far too sharp to have fallen for something so simple and full of holes.* Jober shook his head. *It had to be Nachun. I saw what he can do that night, and I heard the stories of Munai. He must have done something to Bazraki's mind.*

Even now, weeks after Bazraki had reassigned a small army of shamans and guards to scour the city, he wasn't any closer to discovering the truth.

Jober's stomach lurched. *I should have done more for Kaz. But I had to think of my family.*

Lucia had also been in Bazraki's chambers that morning, tears streaming down her face at every word. Jober would never forget that raw emotion. Struggling to compose herself, she still had the compassion to extend a hand and rest it on his arm. Wanting to provide him comfort, she had not understood that the weight of her delicate hand only added to the burden of lies resting upon his shoulders.

To compound matters, she made him her personal bodyguard. So thankful for his bravery that night, she insisted it was the least she could do. At her command his family moved from the rotted-out building they occupied in the old district to several spacious, adjoining rooms next to her own in the palace.

How is it that when I finally prosper, it is the result of so much pain?

"Are you alright?" came a soft voice that took Jober away from his thoughts.

"Oh, yes. I'm sorry. I was just thinking of my family."

"They mean much to you, don't they?" asked Lucia, touching his arm and flashing a warm smile.

"They mean everything to me."

Lucia looked away. "I understand. I feel the same."

Jober heard the lump in her throat. *She misses him so much.* "I'm sorry. I did not mean…"

"No, please, I asked the question."

Jober nodded. Unsure of what else to say, they continued walking the streets of Juanoq in silence. The sun peaked over the city's walls, a faint orange hue easing into the sky. In an hour, the streets would be alive with workers and merchants, clogging the calm roads with an urgency Jober and Lucia lacked.

"Are you sure now is the best time to be doing this? He may not even be there yet." said Jober, interrupting the soft tread of their steps across the cobblestone road.

"Tobin will be there. Lately, it seems the training ground is the only place he spends his time. He avoids every plea I make to speak with him."

"But the training ground is not a place for a woman. Bazraki will not…"

"He will not be pleased, but when is he ever? I'm willing to bet that he won't even mention this to me. As always, he is preoccupied with more important things. I am determined to do this," she said with a tone that said the conversation was over.

* * *

"First take a shot with your longbow." said Nachun.

Tobin stepped forward and aimed at the target some thirty yards away. With barely any effort, he steadied himself, found his mark, and released the shot. He smiled as the arrow landed dead center.

"Excellent," said Nachun. "Now," he continued, handing over the loaded crossbow, "attempt to do the same with this."

Tobin took the heavier object into his hands and, brought the weapon up to his shoulders. He used the crossbow's sight to find the target as Nachun had instructed. He held his breath and pulled the trigger. A click sounded and the arrow sped across the open ground, hitting the mark's center again.

"Wonderful. It looks as though your accuracy was unaffected by the weapon."

"It took longer to aim though."

"A breath, maybe two at most. But that is only because you are still unfamiliar with it." The shaman hurried toward the target. "Come. I want you to see the difference in each shot."

Nachun approached the target from the front, first examining where each arrow landed. "Very impressive, the second arrow is less than two inches away from the first." He took a step to the target's side and pointed. "Ah, but here is what I wanted to show you. Look at how much deeper your second arrow penetrated in comparison to the first."

Tobin nodded, surprised. "The weapon is powerful. You are right that with practice I should be able to find my mark just as quickly as I do with the bow," said Tobin, turning the weapon over in his hands.

"And the beauty of such a weapon is that someone can learn to wield one in a fraction of the time it takes to master a bow."

"Perhaps," said Tobin. "But first we need to finish the testing. Come."

Nachun grabbed his arm. "Wait," the shaman whispered. "It appears our plans have changed for the moment," he added with a nod.

Tobin followed the gesture and saw two figures approaching. The one in front was Lucia who, in Tobin's mind, was the pinnacle by which all other women were to be judged. Jober lumbered a few steps behind, wide but well muscled. His shaved head reflected the morning light.

Tobin wheeled around to face Nachun. "Did you set this up?" he hissed.

Nachun shook his head. "No," he said, answering back in hushed tones. "This is your own fault. I told you not to ignore her."

The shaman let go of Tobin's arm, stepping forward to greet the two visitors. "Ah, Lucia it is so good to see you," he said bowing low, adding brightness to his voice. He then turned to her companion. "Jober, I trust you are doing well." He draped his arm around the man's thick shoulders. "Come, let us allow these two a moment of privacy and perhaps you can update me on the happenings of that wonderful family of yours."

Hesitant to leave, Jober noticeably tensed at the mention of his family. Lucia put him at ease with just a touch of her hand. "I'm fine. Go." The two left with Nachun babbling away, towering over the former stable hand.

Tobin and Lucia stood there for some time, neither saying a word. Tobin was first to find his voice. "You shouldn't be here. You know women aren't allowed on the training ground," he said, averting his eyes from her stare.

"I needed to talk to you."

"You could have sent for me and…"

"Don't give me that," said Lucia, voice rising.

I've never heard her speak that way before.

"I've sent for you countless times," she added. "We haven't spoken once since Kaz's disappearance."

Tobin shrugged. "I've been busy and…"

Lucia cut him off again. "Busy or not, you've been purposefully avoiding me."

Tobin snorted. "Nachun said something similar to me just yesterday."

"Well it's good to know that I'm not the only one, even though it does little to make me feel better."

"I didn't realize I had upset you so much."

"How could you not?" she said frustrated. "They took my husband from me," she yelled, voice full of anger, nearly on the verge of crying. "And I needed someone to talk to."

"I'm sorry." He paused, head still down. "Look, I have much to do for Father over the next two days, but I can try to stop by after dinner tonight and maybe we can talk then?"

Lucia shook her head. "No. Don't pity me. Not you." She exhaled a deep breath. "I'm alright. Jober's wife, Hielle, and I have grown very close since that night. She has been a great support for me. Yes, I was mad at you before, but I understand now what's going on and why you've been avoiding me. That's why I'm here now."

Tobin's mouth filled with saliva and he swallowed. He was sick. *She knows?*

"I know this is your way of coping with your own feelings," said Lucia.

"My feelings?" *Why is everyone so certain they understand me better than I understand myself?*

"Yes. I know that you and Kaz had your differences, but what brothers don't? I see now that you miss him, perhaps even more than I do which is why you've isolated yourself from everyone."

Tobin laughed in disbelief, unable to hold in his shock.

You think our relationship was some twisted form of brotherly love? How can you be so oblivious to what we are, or what we were to each other? I don't know if I ever loved Kaz. I know he never loved me.

"I'm not sure what you want me to say," he said, collecting himself.

"You don't have to say anything. I know Bazraki has brainwashed you so that you believe expressing yourself is some sign of weakness. But I wanted to let you know that it's alright to have those feelings and if you ever want to talk about Kaz, in any way, I'm here to listen to you. Just you and me, no one else will have to know what is said." She paused, and smiled. "I would even be alright with you stopping by to talk about trivial matters. I miss our conversations."

Tobin smiled back. "I'll do my best."

"Thank you."

She leaned in close, embracing Tobin for a moment. His heart raced. When they parted, Tobin saw her wipe back tears from her cheek.

"Are you alright?" asked Tobin.

She laughed as the tears continued to come. "Yes. I'm sorry. I just forget sometimes how much you and Kaz resemble each other. Hugging you reminds me of him and I guess it hit me again."

Tobin frowned but said nothing.

Lucia took a deep breath. "I'll be on my way. I know you have a lot to do. Don't forget about me." Then she turned and left.

CHAPTER 13

Inside the dilapidated fence, a shack sat in the middle of an overgrown yard. Gaping holes covered the roof. The door hung torn away from its hinges. Jonrell assumed it had been abandoned long ago, like the others they had come upon earlier that morning. In the days since he met Kaz, they had passed a dozen such places and all were uninhabited. Although Jonrell had no reason to expect anything different, he needed to confirm his assumption.

Jonrell assigned Kaz the task of checking each homestead they came upon. He hoped that the rest of the group would be more receptive to the stranger's presence once they saw him shouldering his share of the work. Kaz set to his assignment without complaint, approaching each dwelling with a meticulous nature that Jonrell admired. The others were less amenable.

Most seemed intimidated by Kaz's size and dark skin. Those few able to overlook such things were put off by his quiet nature and the perpetual scowl affixed to his face. In Jonrell's experience, soldiers tended to be a superstitious lot, and many whispered that the black man had cursed them all with ill luck—assigning him the blame for so many abandoned cottages. Jonrell had put a stop to such ridiculous nonsense, and did what he could to smooth over their insecurities. He worried that Kaz would be able to pick up on all the mutterings behind his back.

Kaz exited the shack and signaled all was clear. As he made his way over to Jonrell, the ever-present scowl lessened and a look of confusion took its place.

"You look like something's bothering you." said Jonrell.

"There were images," said Kaz.

"Images? In the building?"

"Yes." He shook his head. "No. The images were not in the building. They flashed in my head while I searched the home."

"Do you remember anything about them?"

Kaz furrowed his brow, closing his eyes. "Fighting. Lots of fighting. A battle of some sort, I think." He opened his eyes, looking at his arm. "Everyone's skin was like mine," he added. He closed his eyes and concentrated again and after a moment said something in his native tongue Jonrell did not recognize. "Nothing makes sense," he said.

"It'll come. It may come in bursts like you just experienced or all at once, but it'll come."

"How do you know?"

"Well, I don't for sure. But I've been around people who've lost their memory before. The fact that you experienced something like that is a good thing. You're healing, and the rest of your mind seems unaffected. All of that works in your favor."

Kaz muttered something and sulked away from Jonrell without responding. As he headed toward his horse, others in the group distanced themselves from the warrior.

"A pleasant fellow, isn't he?" said Krytien as he pulled in next to Jonrell.

"Put yourself in his spot. You find yourself in a strange land, where everyone looks different, and you have no idea where you are or even who you are. I'd imagine you'd be frightened."

"Frightened isn't what I'd call his behavior. And I would like to think that if I were in a similar situation, I would be a little more courteous to those who had taken me in and tried to help me. The only person he speaks with besides you is Hag. One Above knows why."

"Probably because we're the only two who haven't treated him like he's got the plague."

"I haven't treated him like that."

"True. But he's got that hang up about sorcery."

"And that's my fault?" said Krytien. "I thought he might've bonded with Wiqua since they resemble each other a bit. But the second Kaz learned Wiqua was a healer through sorcery, that was it. It's too bad. I was hoping some of the old man's disposition would have rubbed off on him.

"It still doesn't explain everyone else's attitude toward him. I know his skin is darker than even the Byzernians but beneath that he's still a man."

"It's hard for people to get past their prejudices, Jonrell. Kaz can't get past his with sorcery, why should the men be any different?" He paused. "However, I think some would come around if he just carried himself differently. The men can see that even someone as strong as Glacar or as cold blooded as Kroke would be hard pressed if they went up against him."

Jonrell nodded. "The thought has crossed my mind. Makes me glad I sent them with the other group on the north side of the island. It'll buy me a couple of weeks."

"They'll have to meet him eventually."

"Yeah, but I'm hoping things will improve by then."

"You know, you're really taking a gamble for one man that we know absolutely nothing about. He could be playing up the memory loss thing for all we know."

"You and I both know that isn't true. And how would hiding his past make him any different than most of us? We all ran away from something when we joined up." He paused. "In fact, I know very little about your life before the Hell Patrol."

"Well, ah..." said Krytien.

Jonrell put a hand up. "Stop. I'm not asking you to tell me your reasons. It isn't my place to pry. And that's the same way we should be with Kaz. I've got a good feeling about him, and I need you to back me on this. I'll keep talking to him."

"I trust you. I always have. Just answer me one thing about that good feeling of yours," said Krytien cocking his head to one side. "Does it relate to the man he was or the man he is now?"

Jonrell shook his head. "I could care less about the man he was. I'm only concerned with the man he is now and, more importantly, with the man he'll become."

* * *

The group picked their way along the patchy terrain, avoiding the fallen limbs and rotted out trees that littered the faded road. On either side of the winding path lay tumbled stone and briars. The occasional body, stripped and left to the worms added to the somber tone of the journey.

"Here's another one," said Rygar up ahead, pointing out a corpse littered with arrows.

"Aye," said Raker coming up from behind. "I smelled this one long before I saw him." He paused. "I know it's been awhile since we've been to Slum Isle, but I don't remember the countryside being so much worse than the ports."

Jonrell pulled up alongside the two mercenaries and looked down at the remains with a frown. "A lot can happen in a couple years. He's about a week old, I'd imagine." He stared down the road with squinted eyes.

"What do you see?" asked Rygar.

"Nothing right now. Ride on ahead a little and come back if you see three boulders stacked on top of each other," said Jonrell.

"Yes, sir. Three boulders," said Rygar. It was an odd request but the young recruit didn't ask for clarification. *Just like Yanasi, loyal and trusting. I see why they get along so well. Too bad I had to send her with Kroke.*

"What's this about three boulders?" asked Raker.

"It's supposed to be a landmark to show us where to venture off into the woods," said Jonrell as he watched Rygar speed off.

"And why would we want to do that?" asked Raker, biting off a piece of chew.

"We're going to the Hideaway," said Jonrell.

"What are we doing bothering with that?"

Jonrell shook his head in disgust as he watched the mercenary wipe his dirty hands on his horse's mane. "To recruit. It's obvious we aren't going to find any takers along the road. Everyone's long since abandoned their land."

"And how did you find out about these three boulders?"

"Freeman's City. While you guys were drinking each other under a table, harassing the whores and picking fights, I was doing research." Jonrell gestured back to the rotting figure. "From what I hear, the Hideaway is responsible for all this killing. They're not too fond of any bandits looking to set up near the land they've staked out."

Raker shook his head. "Our one night off in months and the one chance we had to let loose and you worked. Talk about a shame," he said, leaning over and spitting on the dead body.

Krytien wheeled his horse around, causing the remains of his white hair to fall into his eyes. He brushed it back with his hand, revealing a face flushed with anger. "Raker, show some respect. How would you like it if someone did that to you?"

The mercenary shrugged. "I reckon if I was in his spot, a little spit would be the last thing on my mind. Besides, if he doesn't like it, then let him do something about it himself," he said with a laugh.

The mage turned away scowling and spoke to Jonrell. "I take it you aren't concerned they may confuse us as bandits?"

"The thought had crossed my mind."

Rygar came galloping back to the group. He was a little out of breath when he spoke. "I saw it. Three boulders, stacked one on top of the other, though I don't know how. It must be some kind of sorcery for them to stay up like that."

"How far?"

"Half a mile or so, just around that bend up ahead," Rygar said, pointing over his shoulder. "I didn't see anyone else around either, but to be honest, I didn't take the time to check everywhere."

"Good." He turned in his saddle to face the rest of his men. "Everyone be on your toes. We're probably walking into an ambush. Do not, under any circumstances, attack first. You are only to act by my command or if provoked. Is that clear?"

After a round of nods and grunts, he turned back to Rygar. "Lead the way."

* * *

Just as the barkeeper had described, three boulders stacked one on top of the other stood on side of the road. Off to one side of the structure, the grass was trampled and wheel ruts marked the ground.

"For being called 'The Hideaway', they sure let you know where to find it," said Raker.

Jonrell signaled Rygar into the woods first, along the narrow trail. He edged his horse after and the others followed.

A short while later Rygar stiffened in his saddle and came to a halt. His head turned to the left and to the right. Jonrell took note and raised a silent hand for the others to be on guard. His eyes scanned over the thick foliage to either side of the path, hand drifting to the hilt of his sword. Without turning round, he whispered. "Krytien."

A soft voice answered back. "I'm ready."

Jonrell decided to take a chance. He shouted, unsure where to project his voice. "We know you're watching us. We mean no harm." He paused, adding grit to his tone. "However, if you do anything to hinder our passage or hurt anyone in our group, I promise that not one of you will live to see tomorrow."

A faint chuckle came from Jonrell's left and a man appeared from behind a thick bush carrying a loaded crossbow aimed at Jonrell's breastplate. Others followed, emerging from trees and bushes on either side of the road. Some even walked out of pits dug into the ground, hidden by leaves and underbrush. Over thirty men leveled either bow or crossbow at their group.

The first one still laughed. He took a step forward and Jonrell saw how young he was. *Probably late teens, and far too cocky.*

"That's a lot of empty talk for a man in your position," said the boy.

Jonrell set his jaw and gave the youth an icy stare. "I promise there was nothing empty about what I said. I meant every word. We are on our way to The Hideaway where I'm assuming you reside. We would welcome an escort."

The boy snorted. "An escort? You've got to be the most arrogant person we've met yet. But you seem new to this area, so let me fill you in on something. The Hideaway is off-limits to anyone we don't approve of and that goes especially for a fully armed outfit your size. What are you supposed to be? Some misfit group of soldiers, or something?"

"As a matter of fact, we are," said Jonrell, allowing himself a grin, though he made sure it lacked any hint of amusement.

"Then you aren't passing this point, but you're in luck. I'm feeling generous today so I will allow you to leave here but only after each of you strips down to your skivvies. You will walk out of here empty handed, but at least you'll be alive."

I can't believe I'm humoring this kid. Probably because he reminds me of myself at that age. "I'm afraid I can't do that, son."

The boy's face turned red. Another voice, this one from the trees spoke up. "Careful, Mal. Look at that feller's robes. I bet he's a mage of some sort."

"I can see that," said Mal. "I'm not worried about any mage. That's what we got Zemiah for." His eyes darted about. "Where is he?"

"I think he's puking up in the bushes over here," someone called out.

"Well, then get him out here," yelled Mal, shifting his stance.

A moment later an old man came stumbling out of the woods, nearly tripping over a rotted stump. Jonrell shook his head. "I believe your mage is drunk."

The boy shrugged. "He might be, but it doesn't matter. Just look at those dark red robes. Even I know this here is a High Mage and you ain't got anyone to stop him."

A snort sounded over Jonrell's shoulder where Krytien waited. "The color of a man's robes doesn't make him a High Mage, son," said the Commander. Jonrell leaned forward in his saddle. "I'm willing to bet on my man. Are you willing to do the same?"

Zemiah bent over and heaved. Mal shifted the crossbow in his hands, looking less sure of himself. "We've still got you surrounded. Your guy ain't going to be able to stop all of us. I just need to…"

Mal was interrupted by his own sudden intake of breath. The point of a dagger lifted his chin up high as the blade pressed into the pale skin of his throat. The boy's eyes widened when he saw the large black man towering over him, bearing ivory white teeth.

One Above, where did Kaz come from? He's twice the size of anyone here and I didn't even see him until the dagger touched skin. He must have slipped through a dozen men to reach the boy.

Jonrell grinned at Mal as if he knew all along that they would reach this point. "You know, son, you may have something there. I'm sure you might take a few of us down, though in truth I'm starting to doubt it. But one thing is for sure. Regardless of what happens, you'll be the first one to die."

Someone called out, "He's bluffing, Mal. We can take them, including that black demon."

A slow trickle of blood crept down Mal's neck and his head rose higher as Kaz dug the point into his skin. Panicked, Mal called out. "No! He ain't bluffing. Put your weapons down."

"But we ain't supposed to give in to anyone," called out another.

"One Above, I said put your weapons down. Now or I'll kill you myself! Let Denneth take care of them. We didn't sign up for this."

Jonrell looked down as a small pool formed at the bottom of Mal's boots. He smiled. "You're not as dumb as I thought you were. Maybe there's hope for you yet."

The rest of the motley group was less eager to lay down their weapons than their once cocky leader. But after a little more coaxing, and a quick show of sorcery that embarrassed the man they called a High Mage, the others realized they weren't particularly ready to die. Jonrell was grateful that he avoided any bloodshed. The last thing he needed was to lose any of his men while trying to recruit more able bodies.

As a sign of good faith, Jonrell allowed Mal's group to keep their weapons with them, though he forced them to unstring their bows and set off their crossbows.

Mal and his men led them toward the Hideaway. Rygar, Jonrell, and Krytien rode upfront with the kid. The rest of the Hell Patrol stayed further back. All except Kaz that is, who rode amongst the Hideaway's soldiers as a reminder that any questionable move would be their end. Jonrell ensured it never came to that. He eased the tension between both groups by joking and telling stories.

The deeper into the woods they traveled, the wider and clearer the path grew with stumps lining the road. They passed over a small stream by way of a newly built bridge.

After several hours they left the woods. The trees had been completely cleared away, several miles in either direction. Off in the distance, at the clearing's center, stood a large wooden fortification with tall palisades jutting from the ground. He couldn't make out the details of what lay inside the fort, but he did note that several buildings loomed over the walls.

The land outside the fort bustled with activity as farmers tended crops and cared for livestock. Along the outskirts of the cleared land, stood small towers, each manned by a lookout.

Someone knew what they were doing here.

Mal approached one such tower and Jonrell whispered, "They've been busy."

"I guess we know why we passed so many stumps now, eh Commander?" said Rygar.

Jonrell turned and smiled at the lad. "I guess we do. Though taking a look at this, it makes me wonder how they have any trees left at all."

While waiting for Mal, Jonrell saw several workers laying stone for what he assumed would be another wall, much stronger than the wooden palisade in the clearing's center. But Jonrell guessed it would be a long time before it saw completion. He gazed back out over the open land.

The wall would need to be massive and surrounded by a moat for so few people to defend it. Hmmm, maybe their leader doesn't know as much as I thought…or is expecting a large swell in population.

Mal pointed at them, exchanging heated words with the watchman at the tower's base. After a few moments the man shouted something inaudible and took off on horseback toward the fortification. Mal kicked the dirt at his feet, head hung low as he walked back to Jonrell.

"You alright?" asked Jonrell.

Mal shook his head without looking up. "He ran off to tell Denneth what happened. I'm likely to have my command taken from me," he said, clenching his fists at his side. "Maybe that's for the best. I did exactly what I was told not to do."

"I see. I know you don't believe me, son, but you made the right choice. People would have died on both sides had you not backed down." After a moment, he added. "So, what's our next move?"

"I'm supposed to have you wait here until Denneth arrives. I can't really do much to stop you if you want to go on though," said Mal, avoiding eye contact.

"I said before that I intend no harm. If I went charging up that road now, it sure wouldn't look like I meant that." He clasped a reassuring hand on Mal's shoulder and turned his horse back to the group.

Kaz rode up to him, shifting in his saddle.

"What's on your mind?" asked Jonrell.

Kaz tilted his head in the direction of Mal. "What's wrong with the boy?"

Jonrell shrugged. "Just being hard on himself and worried about the trouble he is likely in for allowing us to pass without a fight."

"And you...comforted him. Why?"

"Because I know what it's like to second guess your own decisions. It can eat a man up if he lets it."

"I do not understand. Why would you help your enemy? He would have killed us just a few hours ago."

Jonrell shrugged again. "Seemed like the right thing to do is all." He looked back at Mal who stood with his hands on his hips, staring toward the fort, watching the guardsmen approach the gate. "Trust me, that isn't the face of my enemy."

* * *

It took twice as long as Jonrell thought it should have for Denneth and his party to head toward their position several hundred yards away.

Halfway up the tower's ladder, Rygar was the first to make out their number as he leaned out with one arm. "Looks to be forty men, all well armored and in full plate. Weapons are drawn, Commander," shouted the scout.

"Full plate? How can a bunch like this afford that?" he wondered aloud, not expecting an answer.

"I'm not sure, Sir," said Rygar. "They also have two mages with them, both yellow."

"That last one they tried to sell as a High Mage would have been better off in a yellow robe," said Krytien coming to a halt next to Jonrell. "These two must know a card trick or two then."

"Even still, just be ready for them. I know two yellows aren't much, but if they are capable, they could be just enough to slow you. Especially if they are used to working together." He looked up. "Rygar, come on down. The last thing I want is for you to be an easy target."

"Yes, sir."

"Mal," Jonrell called out. The boy met his eyes before averting them again as if remembering his shame. "You should meet them before they get here. Don't worry, I'm sure it'll be fine. I'll take over once they approach." The boy nodded and started walking up the dirt trail toward the fort.

"You don't really believe this leader of theirs is going to be alright with the boy letting us through, do you?" asked Krytien.

"Of course not. Just felt like I needed to tell him something reassuring."

Krytien grunted. "What is it with you and troubled kids?"

Jonrell shrugged. "It worked out fine with Yanasi. What can I say? I've always had a soft spot for them."

"Probably because you were one yourself."

"Possibly," said Jonrell with a scowl.

"You know that could come back to bite you one day. You may find a knife in that soft spot of yours. All it takes is for you to disappoint one of them," said Krytien.

Jonrell glanced at the mage with a puzzled look. "One Above, Krytien. I was just trying to put the lad's mind at ease. Besides, I wonder if that sour old mage who's looked after me all these years ever felt that way."

A long moment passed before Krytien spoke. He grinned. "Why do you think I sleep on the opposite side of camp from you?"

Jonrell smiled back.

* * *

Denneth and the group pulled up to meet Mal, pausing for a few moments in conversation. At their distance Jonrell could only make out a few hand gestures. None of them looked pleasant. The man Jonrell assumed was Denneth pointed with his sword back to the fort and Mal began walking. Apparently, he wasn't happy with the lad's pace as he reached out, slapping the flat of his blade against the boy's rear.

So now you embarrass the kid? I already dislike this one.

The group approached Jonrell at a slow trot before reining in less than ten feet from each other. The man Jonrell assumed was Denneth glared at him. He was not at all what Jonrell had envisioned. Short in stature, he was a far cry from the intimidating figure Mal had described earlier. His frame appeared thin under the plate armor he wore.

The group's armor had caught his eyes from a distance and up close he noted the high quality of its craftsmanship.

"You the leader of this outfit," the man said, more a statement than a question.

Once Jonrell heard the man's voice and felt its grit, he noticed the hard and weathered face. *I wonder how many times a man has been fooled into underestimating him due to his size?* "I am."

The man grunted. "Good. Then you can turn this group around and be on your way. The *boy*…" he added like a curse, "should have told you such."

Jonrell nodded. "He did. However, we persuaded him to take us here anyway. I'm…"

"I know who you are, Prince," said the leader smiling. "And I know who this group is too. My brother used to lead the Hell Patrol before you did, though I'm sure you're more capable than he ever was."

Jonrell blinked. "You're that Denneth? Ronav's brother?" *That explains the grit in his voice.*

"Aye, the fool was my own blood." He continued. "I see that look on your face—don't think about arguing with me. He was a fool but I'll say nothing more of it to you." He paused. "I know you're looking for a new bunch of sorry souls to lead to their death for some meaningless cause, just as he did."

Jonrell decided it best to ignore the remark. "As I told Mal, we mean no harm."

"Go feed that line to someone gullible enough to believe it. You take even one man from me, and you'll weaken what I've worked hard to build here. How is that not harming?"

Jonrell looked around admiring the open expanse. "I understand your point, but people should be allowed to make their own decisions." His eyes rested on the partially built stone wall. "Or is it your goal to keep these folks in a prison of their own making?"

Denneth laughed. "Of course you would see it that way. But this is safety and security to them and a chance for a better life. Here, their sons aren't killed in some bar fight along the coast, or bleeding on the battlefield for some rich noble's cause," he said eyeing Jonrell with a knowing look. "Here, their daughters aren't raped by raiders." He spat. "Would you take them away from that?"

He's a sharp one, trying to lure me into a trap. "I wouldn't take any man away from his wants, or any woman for that matter."

"I am not a tyrant, but I will do what I feel is necessary for the greater good." He spoke louder. "Any man who wishes to join the Hell Patrol and die for someone else's glory is free to do so. But remember the rules I gave when each of you first came here. If anyone leaves now, there is no coming back."

"You champion these people, try to bring them better lives, but you'd punish them for trying to do the same for themselves?" asked Jonrell.

Denneth chuckled. "Any man who leaves is a man not smart enough to know what is best for him and a man whose loyalty lies in his own selfishness. I need real loyalty. Surely you cannot deny the importance of that."

"Aye, but real loyalty isn't something you can demand."

"Sounds like something my father would have told Ronav and me when we were boys. A lot of good telling us did him. And for that matter, a lot of good telling us did Ronav. Both dead."

One Above, how can two brothers hate each other so much? Ronav spoke of him with little more affection. Jonrell pressed his lips into a thin line. Getting through to the man was like digging through sand. "Perhaps not all feel as you do. I'd still like to talk to your people at the fort."

"No. You will go no further. I'm sure word will spread." He looked up at the sky. "The sun will be setting soon. I'll allow you to make camp here, but only for the night. Tomorrow, you will leave at dawn. My men will stay here tonight and watch over you to ensure you stay put and leave on time. Is that understood?"

Jonrell shrugged. "Your land, your rules. We'll go no further than here."

"The two mages will stay as well."

"Speaking of your *mages*," said Krytien cutting in. "If they do indeed have any real skill with sorcery, I would recommend that in the future you don't exaggerate their talents. Others, such as myself, find this quite belittling and take great offense to it. If I was still in my youth, I may have reacted much differently than what I did earlier when we came across the drunkard you call a High Mage."

"I care little about your feelings," said Denneth. "Those robes give a lot of people reason to pause and most aren't as knowledgeable as you." He turned to Jonrell. "Again, the well being of my people is my concern."

Turning away from Jonrell, Denneth barked quick orders to his men for the night.

Jonrell couldn't decide whether he hated or admired the man.

Perhaps a little of both.

* * *

Dawn could not come soon enough to the men watching over the Hell Patrol that night. As the sun dropped, so did the temperature, a cool breeze punctuating the chilly darkness. With the moon rising into the clear sky, complaints amongst Denneth's men bubbled to the surface. Denneth's apparent favorites returned to the fort while the others stood watch.

So, everyone is not as equal as you would have us believe, eh? thought Jonrell.

Soon after such talk began, the more hardened of Denneth's men turned their displeasure on Jonrell, citing he was the true reason that kept them from their warm beds, not Denneth.

In an effort to ease the resentment, Jonrell had opened a spot near the fires for anyone interested, and even offered a warm meal. Only a handful of men accepted the gesture. The rest balked, turning their heads away in disgust from the stew, muttering about a lack of loyalty from those who would take such an offer.

* * *

The first rays of sunlight fractured the eastern horizon when Jonrell felt a firm hand on his shoulder. He reached for the dagger under his blanket. But another hand, steady and calloused, seized his wrist and spoke in a low tone as the commander shook off the night's sleep. "It's dawn. Denneth's men grow restless and eager for us to leave," warned Kaz.

Jonrell eyed the cold expressions of Denneth's men and nodded. "Wake the others." Then he paused, noticing the alertness of the black man. "How long have you been up?"

Kaz shrugged his broad shoulders. "Most of the night. I slept a couple of hours near Hag while everyone else made camp, but woke shortly before the first watch began."

"Why? You're going to be dragging today on the road."

"I don't need a lot of sleep. Besides, it is hard to relax when I know someone is watching over me and longing to see me dead," said Kaz in an emotionless tone.

"Well, then I guess it's a good thing we've only spent one night here."

"I wasn't talking about Denneth's men."

He knows they hate him. "Look, I had Krytien talk to the group so you needn't worry about someone taking a knife to you, if that is what's on your mind." He paused, trying to organize his thoughts. "But things aren't going to get remarkably better if you continue to be so standoffish," said Jonrell.

Kaz furrowed his brow. "You want me to change, but I don't even know who I am or if I need to change."

"Then stop forcing the past on yourself and start from scratch. Almost everyone in this group has run away from something and wants to forget their old life and be something else. You have that same chance, though better than anyone else, to be someone new and truly start over."

For a moment, Kaz sat in silence. "I'll go wake the others," he said, turning away.

Jonrell rubbed at his face as he watched him move about the camp, shoulders bunched in frustration.

* * *

Beams of sunlight found passage through the forest's canopy and illuminated the narrowed trail. There was a quiet calm about the woods with very little chatter from the wildlife. Only the sound of clomping hooves against twigs and leaves sounded in Jonrell's ears. The peace unsettled him, leaving him to the ramblings of his mind.

As his men had readied themselves, Jonrell offered anyone interested a chance at freedom, money, and adventure. All anyone would need to do is leave the Hideaway behind.

There was no need to fill them in on the bad parts just yet.

Half a dozen men joined Jonrell, less than he had hoped for, but the commander was sure it was six more than Denneth had expected. Ronav's brother had decided not to see them off that morning.

Those who would come with me are dead to him. Jonrell shook his head. *What a close-minded view.* Unsurprising, the half dozen who joined were those guards who accepted a place at the fire and a hot meal in their stomach the night before." *Never underestimate good manners," Amcaro would tell me. Though I'm sure he never thought manners would be used to recruit killers.* Jonrell laughed at the thought. *Killers?* Of those that came over, only one showed any real skill, the rest would need some serious training before he would feel comfortable calling them members of the Hell Patrol. Until then, they would stay recruits. Only after that first battle would their status as members be decided. Only then would he know if they were killers.

Jonrell stiffened in his saddle remembering Denneth's words from the day before. *Perhaps he was right. I am looking for souls to lead into death.* He thought about that as memories of past battles and the men he'd lost under his command flooded his mind. Then he remembered the men who lived on. *Just because I lead them to death, doesn't mean they have to accept it. That choice is theirs. And if they do die, my cause is far from meaningless.* His grip squeezed tight around the reins, twisting them in his hands. *And six men are not enough for that cause.*

"Wait!" A faint shout from behind eased the tension in Jonrell's body. Everyone in his group halted and turned to the sound of the voice. The men assigned to rearguard looked back at their commander with a questioning look. Jonrell nodded and the two men set off in the direction of the shout.

The riders came back into view and next to them were three on foot, carrying packs of weapons and equipment. A boy, and a man favoring a leg as he limped along, accompanied Mal.

"What are you fellas up to, Mal?" asked Jonrell.

The lad had his head down. "We've come to join."

"Have you now? Don't you think you're a little young to be running off?" said Jonrell glancing at the other boy. The pimpled young man with floppy hair did not appear to be the least bit intimidated by the situation. He boldly looked about curious. "Your friend looks even younger than you. I'm not accustomed to taking on recruits so green."

"We can help. I'll do whatever you ask, just say the word. And Drake," Mal said tilting his head toward the other boy. "He's like a genius or something. He helped design most of our buildings, that bridge we crossed, and our irrigation system."

Taking even one away will harm us. Jonrell could hear Denneth's words echoing in his head. *The decision is theirs.*

"Is that true?" asked Jonrell, turning to Drake.

"Oh absolutely, Sir. It's really not that difficult, all you have to do is…"

Jonrell raised a hand, cutting him off. "Now's not the time."

Drake nodded and to his credit added nothing further.

"So, will you take us on?" asked Mal.

"You need to look at me when you talk, son. A man needs to be able to meet the eyes of the person he's speaking with," said Jonrell.

Mal raised his head slowly, revealing a welt on his forehead and a dark circle under his eye. He said nothing.

"Denneth did this?" asked Jonrell, anger creeping into his voice.

"Yes, sir."

"I see," said Jonrell. He turned to the man accompanying the boys. "And what's your story? How can a man with a limp help me in battle?"

"Well, if it's alright with you I'll stay away from the battlefield unless I'm pressed into it. My name is Cisod and I'm a smith by trade, but I can do a little bit of everything."

Jonrell looked at the man's calloused hands and exposed chiseled forearms. "I can see that now. Are you the one who built the armor then?"

"I am."

"Impressive," said Jonrell. "Why leave? Seems like you had a pretty good setup."

Cisod shook his head. "I'm sick of being second guessed by someone who has no business doing so," said the gruff man.

"Well, if you can give us armor and weapons like the ones I saw, then I see no reason to question your work."

"Sounds fair. I've got a lot of ideas for improving your armor and weapons."

Jonrell nodded. "Grab a spare mount and we'll talk later, when we make camp."

"Aye, Commander," said Cisod as he turned and walked to a free horse.

Jonrell eyed Mal and Drake. "So I guess that leaves you two, doesn't it?"

"Yes, sir," said Drake. Mal remained quiet.

"Raker," Jonrell called out.

"Yeah?" said Raker.

He nodded to Drake. "You just got yourself an apprentice."

"What? I don't want to spend my time wiping some kid's nose," said Raker, spit from his chew dribbling down his chin.

"Too bad. He's yours. Find out what he knows and teach him everything that he doesn't. I don't know what our resources are going to be when we get to Cadonia, but there is no such thing as too many engineers. You can't be everywhere at once."

"Come on, kid," Raker said with a grunt. "Let's find you a horse," he spit a wad of chew that nearly hit the boy. Drake kept his mouth shut, but his face was covered in disgust. Still, the boy followed after him.

"What about me?" said Mal.

"I'm not sure what to do with you now, but you said you're willing to do anything, so I'm sure we'll eventually find a place for you." Jonrell gestured with his head. "Get a horse and fall into line. We'll talk again later and figure something out then."

For the first time since Mal had stepped out of the woods with that cocky smile on his face, Jonrell saw him grin again. "Thank you."

He smiled as the boy ran off. Jonrell turned his horse around and signaled ahead for Rygar to move out. Out of the corner of his eye he saw Krytien shaking his head.

CHAPTER 14

"Amazing. I knew you were making progress but…all this in less than two months?" asked Tobin as his eyes drifted from floor to ceiling and then wall to wall of the vast room.

"I know. Having free reign to ensure all is ready in time for your father's next move has ensured that both speed and quality are equally impressive," said Nachun.

"So it was your idea to have the forges running all day and night?"

"Yes. Seven days a week, working in alternating shifts to ensure there is no downtime in production. Bazraki is adamant about meeting his deadlines."

"I'm sure the craftsmen weren't happy with that."

"Not at first. The worst were the artisans I pulled away from their trades and pressed into service as blacksmiths and fletchers." The shaman paused and a grin crept onto his face. "However, it is quite remarkable how attitudes change when the matter of compensation is discussed and they come to understand that far more money would be made under my employ than peddling their wares in the market."

Tobin nodded. "Well, my friend. It looks as though you're running out of room here," he said, turning his gaze back to the rows and stacks of shields, armor, swords, and barrels of arrows.

Nachun gestured for Tobin to step back, and after he did, the shaman closed the thick door. "We secured two warehouses in other parts of the city. We'll start sending items to them tonight."

"I see," said Tobin, watching Nachun slide a heavy lock into place.

The shaman faced Tobin. "And how is the new weapons training of the Kifzo coming along?"

"Better than I expected. There was some grumbling about change at first, but it didn't take long for many to see the advantages in some of your ideas. Though, to be honest, they were loathe to admit it."

"It seems that despite my best efforts, many still haven't warmed to me."

"I've known some for close to twenty-five years and they still haven't warmed to me."

Nachun nodded and after a pause asked. "So you said that the Kifzo have only seen advantages in some of my ideas? Where have they found fault?"

"Like my first reaction to the crossbow, they don't see it being practical to the Kifzo style of fighting. It has its benefits, but I think it should be used solely by the rest of our military. The weapon is too heavy and bulky for a Kifzo to carry in the heat of battle and it would likely slow us down. And remember, we would be in the front line of most engagements where its cumbersome nature would be more of a hindrance when reloading quarrels."

Nachun nodded. "I have no argument against that. Military strategy is best left to the experts such as yourself. I'm just glad that you've been open minded to the devices and found an appropriate use for them."

Tobin snorted. "Me an expert? You must be confusing me with my father, he does the planning. We only follow his lead."

"True, but how often have you had to think on your feet and make a decision without your father's aid? Or even Kaz's instruction as warleader? I'm sure you can think of many times where your decision impacted the outcome of a mission. Your father provides a broad strategy, but you are tasked with making it work."

Hmm, I hadn't thought of that before. There were times when we all but abandoned father's original plans. And there were times I had to change new plans Kaz had given me as new information arose.

Nachun patted Tobin on the shoulder, startling the Kifzo from his thoughts. "Come. I want to show you something I've been working on. Actually, several somethings," he said, face lighting up with excitement.

"Where are we going?" Tobin asked as they entered the street.

The shaman only smiled.

* * *

A cool breeze blew off the water as wind rushed in from the north and carried itself along the bay. The docks flowed with movement. Shipwrights overseeing the activity, barked orders at men and women alike who pushed and shoved all who stood in their way.

Most of the dock's workers were captives—slaves in Tobin's mind—taken from the Orange Desert Clan after conquering Nubinya. It had been Nachun's idea to use the powerful and influential captives as labor in order to lessen the chance of revolt. Tobin had not cared for the idea then, but Nachun's argument that a growing empire needed extra laborers appealed to Bazraki. His father had wasted little time breaking in the captives during the trek from Nubinya to Juanoq. After a few days of public punishments for dissenters, no one dared question their new role in society. The captives had been tasked in many of the ship building processes.

Nachun paced the docks, explaining in great detail each of the many projects underway. Ships of various shapes and sizes, all foreign to Tobin, caught his imagination. The feeling humbled him as a member of the Blue Island Clan, a people who prided themselves on their mastery of the water.

How does a shaman from the Red Mountains of Hesh know so much?

"This one is massive," said Tobin, shouting over the clamor of activity around the frame.

"It is a transport ship, carrying more men and supplies than anything ever seen in Hesh."

"But it is too large to come ashore. No other clan has a dock large enough to handle a ship this size. You can't expect us to swim the distance while carrying supplies on our back."

Nachun chuckled. "Of course not." The shaman pointed. "Smaller boats will be attached to either side of the ship and lowered by winch. Those will be used to come ashore."

"When did you start all of this?"

The shaman looked up to the sky as if searching for an answer. "About a week after starting the weapon production. Your father was so pleased at my progress then, that he allowed me to pursue these ideas as well."

And yet this is the first I've heard of this? Am I just that lost in my own world not to see what is going on around me? "Where do you keep getting these ideas from, Nachun? How does a shaman from the Red Mountain Clan learn so much about weapons, armor, and now shipbuilding?"

Nachun laughed. "It does seem strange, doesn't it? But what can I say?" He tapped a finger to his skull. "The ideas come from here. I read something here, pick up something from someone there, and it just builds upon itself." He shrugged. "Come to think of it, I've always been that way. I remember when I was just a boy, no more than ten or eleven I came up with an irrigation system for my father's farm that soon everyone else copied and found success with. Seeing my ideas work was all the motivation I needed to try new ones."

Tobin grunted.

Nachun smiled. "There is one more I want to show you."

The two walked down a bit further, coming upon a ship much further along than the others, though not quite as large as some. "This one will be finished long before the rest. More than twice the number of workers are assigned to it," said the shaman.

"What is its significance?" asked Tobin.

"These new ships," he said waving a hand, "will take some getting used to. It will take time to learn their tendencies and how to maneuver them properly in the water. This vessel," he added, walking up to its side and slapping the hull, "will be the training tool to learn from. The sooner she gets into the water, the better."

"Father will be pleased to hear your foresight. He has always placed a great deal of emphasis on preparation."

The shaman's face hardened and eyes grew distant. "I've learned its importance as well. Never again will I assume success."

An out of breath messenger from Bazraki's personal guard arrived then and interrupted their conversation.

"What is it?" asked Tobin.

The messenger bowed in respect to Tobin and gave merely a nod to Nachun. Tobin glanced at the shaman but his face betrayed no anger by the slight. "El Olam wishes to speak with you both. I was instructed to bring you back to the palace immediately."

"Is something wrong?" asked Nachun.

"It is not my place to speak on El Olam's behalf," said the guard in a stern voice.

"Very well," said Tobin. "Lead on."

* * *

Bazraki stared out an open window with his back to the door and hands clasped behind him. He held his head high. Tobin found it odd for a ruler with such a large palace, sprawling over countless acres of land, to spend most of his time in its war room. Since Kaz's disappearance, his father had even begun taking meals there, strategizing late into the night while pouring over his maps and the piles of information received from messengers.

Tobin stood at the entranceway to the room, looking at the only parent he had known since he was five and wondered what the man had been like before his mother died. From what his uncle had told him, Bazraki had always been driven but it wasn't until her passing that his quest for power and dominance over Hesh had become an obsession.

She must have been special to him. What little I heard Kaz speak of her, I know he felt the same. And yet I remember nothing of my life during the time she was alive. Not her touch, not her voice, not even her face.

The guard announced their arrival. He could see now that his father coped with the loss of Kaz similarly to Tobin's mother. His father's goals of conquest became as grand as the walls he built around himself.

And what would you do if I were to disappear father? Tobin was afraid to even pose such a question, unsure he wanted to hear the answer.

Waving a hand to dismiss the guard, Bazraki turned to face them. Tobin noticed his father's shoulders were bunched and the muscles in his jaw tightened and relaxed with each intake of breath.

This can't be good. Is it possible that he's learned the truth about Kaz? No. Nachun swore that no one would discover anything. Why would that change now?

"There has been an uprising in Nubinya," said Bazraki, his voice flat.

"When? By whom?" asked Nachun.

"Weeks ago, though we just received word today. Some noble had remained hidden outside of the city until after our departure. He was able to rally enough supporters from the smaller hamlets to his cause. His rebellion killed over a hundred of our men before order was restored. More than double the causalities on their side. We captured the noble alive but torture does not work on the man. He will not tell us about his co-conspirators. The city is now undermanned and tension remains high. I need to send someone with a strong hand to crush any remnants of resistance before things get out of control once again."

"And you would have me go, Father?" asked Tobin. "I'm sorry," he added with a bow, "El Olam."

His father glared at his son but ignored the mistake. "No. I have other plans for you."

"What would you have me do?" asked Tobin.

"I need you to choose a Kifzo I can send to teach these people a lesson. We will send with this person twenty-five Kifzo and a hundred soldiers from our regular forces. You may choose the Kifzo only."

Tobin was confused. "Why would you have me select the Kifzo?"

"Because I've decided that until your brother returns to us that someone must act as warleader in his stead. I've had my doubts about you in the past, but since his disappearance you have shown me something with your training. The rest of your brethren have responded by following your example and are training with a renewed vigor. Since they are now under your command, you should decide which you can do without."

Act in Kaz's stead? I can't believe that after all this time with no word from the kidnappers, he still thinks Kaz will return. And me? Warleader? That can't be possible.

Memories that Tobin had not had since he was a boy flooded his mind. He used to dream about making his father proud by leading soldiers into battle and conquering in his name.

But when he was fourteen and Kaz fifteen, the Testing to choose the next warleader came. Five boys, including Tobin and Kaz, were the best among the Kifzo. Kaz became warleader by doing things Tobin would not consider.

Any dream he had of leading the Kifzo and making his father proud ended that day. *But now I can prove to my father that he had made a mistake all those years ago. I can...* A small shooting pain in his ankle jarred him from his thoughts as he shifted his weight to his good leg. He closed his mouth, realizing it still hung open in shock from Bazraki's news. "I'm sorry but how can I lead the Kifzo with my ankle?"

Bazraki nodded. "I've already thought of that. You will have it healed."

"Shamans have tried to heal my ankle before. They've all said that too much time had passed for them to heal it any better than what it is now."

"Yes, but I've been assured that those results would have been different if treated sooner."

"I don't understand," said Tobin.

"It's simple really. I'm not sure why the thought had not occurred to me before. We are going to break your ankle again and then heal it anew," said Bazraki.

"Is that possible?" asked Tobin, glancing toward Nachun.

Nachun nodded. "Yes. But, the ankle will need to be practically shattered."

Tobin cringed at the thought, and his ankle throbbed harder as if in anticipation of such trauma. *And what if this doesn't work? Will I even be able to walk?* He looked back to his father. "Do I have a say in this?"

"No," said Bazraki in a tone that meant his decision was made. "You just implied that a warleader cannot lead with only one leg."

"Then when will it happen?" asked Tobin in a low voice.

"Tonight, after you have made your selections," said Bazraki. "But first I will have your answer. Who should I send to Nubinya?"

"Durahn," Tobin blurted. *That came out with little trouble.*

His father raised an eyebrow. "Are you sure? He is a fierce warrior."

"And therefore will bring the city quickly under control."

"Will you not miss him in battle?" asked Bazraki.

"Battle?"

"Nubinya's revolt will not hinder my plans. We will push forward," said Bazraki.

I wonder if anything would hinder your plans. "All Kifzo have skill. You have always taught us that one man should not be placed higher than the rest, except as warleader. We will not suffer from the loss of one man, not even one the size of Durahn." *If anything we will be stronger. If I am to be warleader, I will not have him undermine my authority as Kaz so often allowed. Why my brother never rid himself of Durahn, I'll never know.*

"Then the matter is closed. The other twenty-five are yours to choose as well. I do not need to know their names. I have already isolated the hundred that will accompany Durahn from the rest of my army. They will set out first thing in the morning."

Tobin nodded and was ready for his father to dismiss him when Nachun blurted out a question. "Might I offer a suggestion?" said the shaman.

Bazraki inclined his head. "What is it?"

"I thought that now would be a good time to let Tobin in on your future plans, specifically those we've recently discussed."

Bazraki eyed his son with a contemplative look.

"I suppose you are right," said Bazraki, beginning to pace the room. "We will invade the Yellow Plain, conquering Actur and the Yellow Clan next."

"The Yellow Plain Clan? They are more than double our size," said Tobin.

Bazraki halted, glaring at his son. "Does their size scare you? Maybe I made a mistake in selecting you as warleader. Kaz would never shy away from such a challenge."

Tobin clenched his fists in frustration but kept his emotions from creeping into his voice. "You made no mistake. Their number could be ten times our strength and I would lead the Kifzo into battle and victory. I was merely stating fact."

Bazraki let out a grunt, its significance a mystery to Tobin. "Good." He paused. "But you are right. They are much larger, even with those warriors from the Desert Clan we absorbed into our own ranks. I do not doubt our victory, but I am also not so blind that I can't see our losses would be great and would weaken us for the future." His father continued pacing before returning to his spot by the window.

He has a plan, but he wants me to ask just so he can be smug about it. With each success, his arrogance grows. Fine, I'll humor you. "How will you circumvent such an outcome?"

"Nachun's weapons and armor should help. But that is not enough. Any man that dies today is one fewer who can fight for me tomorrow," said Bazraki, still gazing out over Juanoq and once again growing silent.

Tobin sighed to himself. *How long am I going to have to keep this up?* "What else is there?" he asked.

Bazraki turned. "The Gray Marshes."

"The Gray Marshes? I don't understand," said Tobin.

Bazraki nodded to Nachun and resumed pacing. "Tell him."

The shaman cleared his throat. "Apparently some time ago, before conquering the Orange Desert Clan, your father sent Kaz to meet with Mawkuk, the leader of the Gray Marsh Clan, and offered him an alliance. However, since your brother's disappearance, they have not responded to our latest messages. You and I are to leave for Cypronya and meet with their war council to finalize terms in person."

"When do we leave?" asked Tobin.

"As soon as the healers say you are safe to travel," said Nachun.

"You will not fail me," said Bazraki. "Is that understood?"

"Yes, El Olam."

* * *

Halfway down the staircase, safe from his father's ears, Tobin swung about to face Nachun. "So, how much of that were you already aware of?"

Nachun shrugged. "All of it, more or less."

Tobin threw up his hands. "It would have been nice to have some sort of warning."

"You're focusing on the negative. Your father is starting to understand your worth now that Kaz is out of the way, just as I said he would. Taking advantage of such an opportunity is what you should focus on." He paused and started walking once again. Tobin followed close behind. "I had thought of telling you sooner—but does it matter if you found out a week ago or today? I doubt your reaction would be any different, and a more sincere reaction is best."

"Why would he want to wait until the last minute?"

"Because he can. Power does strange things to people once they have it."

Tobin thought about Kaz's behavior as well as his father's and couldn't help but agree with Nachun. "So it does. Still, I never thought my father would consider an alliance with anyone."

Nachun grunted. "After Mawkuk ignored his messages, your father had all but changed his mind and was ready to attack instead for their slight. I had to convince him that sending an emissary to solidify an alliance would not be a sign of weakness. Then I reminded him that his plan to conquer the Yellow Plain was a more logical decision rather than have our forces isolated in the Gray Marshes with an enemy between us."

"Sound reasoning," said Tobin.

The shaman cleared his throat. Tobin followed Nachun's gaze and saw Lucia at the end of the hallway, her arm draped over one of the servants as they spoke. She wore a simple brown dress, as plain as the serving woman's.

I can't talk to her now. Just as he decided to take a different route, Lucia spotted him, smiling and waving. Tobin looked back toward Nachun, hoping for a way out of the situation but the shaman had disappeared.

Lucia hurried down the hall toward him, Jober following at a distance, head held high and short sword hung at his hip. Tobin felt a hint of bitterness as he considered that the former stable hand now spent every waking moment shadowing the woman of his desires while he had refrained from contact with her whenever possible.

Instead, I watch her from a distance, spying on her from the shadows like some thief. Why does guilt still haunt me when I know that she is better without Kaz in her life? Her smile widened as she got closer. *Probably because she hasn't reached that same conclusion?*

She embraced him with a hug. The warmth of her body and smell of her hair twisted his stomach into knots. "It's good to see you," she said in a soft voice, as she pulled away.

"It's always good to see you, too," said Tobin, trying to smile.

"Then why have you only joined me for dinner once since we spoke on the training yard?"

Because I'm not able to put aside any lingering guilt around you. "I'm sorry. I have been preoccupied, I guess," Tobin said, averting his eyes from hers.

"Will you join me tonight? I'd like to talk to you. So much has happened."

"I wish I could, but I was just on my way to carry out orders from my father. Then I'm afraid I must make preparations to leave with Nachun."

She scowled. "I do not like that shaman."

"What? Why not?" *She's never mentioned this before.*

"It's just a feeling. One that Kaz shared."

"Kaz was not right about everything." *Why is that so hard for you to see?*

Her smiled disappeared and she bit her lip. "Be careful," said Lucia.

"I always am."

She hugged him once again, abruptly ending their conversation, her touch lacking the warmth from earlier. She turned and left without another word, not even sparing a glance back. Still, Tobin saw how much their encounter had brought her down.

CHAPTER 15

Brooding, Kaz rocked back and forth in his saddle. The Hell Patrol had traveled hard for several days, moving ever closer toward Mudhole Bay. There, Jonrell said the group should have better luck recruiting. Kaz noted the commander growing frustrated at the number of abandoned homesteads.

Even though Kaz had understood almost nothing of the exchange between Denneth and Jonrell, he had developed an immediate distaste for the way Denneth carried himself. Later, Hag had translated a summary of what was said and Kaz felt his earlier suspicions about the man confirmed. He could not understand why anyone would want to live life cowering in fear with such a man as their leader.

Jonrell rode several paces in front of Kaz and talked in earnest with one of the recruits from the Hideaway that had joined them. Both men joked as if long lost friends.

Why do I not mind following this stranger to places unknown? What makes Jonrell different than Denneth?

The question had occurred to him several times over the last day. He realized it was probably due to the images and scenes that would occasionally flash in his mind. He knew that he had once been in a position of command but those briefest moments of battle provided too little of information for him to discern anything more. One thing did stand out and it troubled him. He could still see the eyes of the men he had commanded and their look more closely matched Denneth's followers rather than those who followed Jonrell.

Kaz allowed his horse to drift back, so he could ride alongside Hag.

The old woman smiled, showing her gnarled teeth. "You can't get enough of me, can you?"

Kaz ignored the remark. "Why do you follow Jonrell?"

"You aren't going to even comment?" said Hag, disappointment in her voice. "What does it take to get a rise out of you anyway?"

"Save such talk for that one," said Kaz nodding to Wiqua who rode at her other side. "Why do you follow Jonrell?"

She threw her hands up. "One Above, you're no fun at all. Now I see why you and Jonrell get along. Both of you have the same sense of humor. You

195

should think about being nicer to me since I'm one of the few people round here who'll actually hold a conversation with you."

Kaz sighed. "Are you going to answer my question? Why do you trust Jonrell?"

"Who said that I trust him? Maybe I just follow because I've got nothing else better to do with my life. Besides, there are perks involved." She inclined her head toward Wiqua who seemed oblivious to their conversation. "You get the chance to meet all sorts of people."

Kaz shook his head. "Nevermind, woman. It's no use talking to you about anything of importance."

He clicked his reins and moved up a few paces, isolating himself once again. Such behavior had become a habit after seeing how uncomfortable others got as he moved too close to them. After a moment, Hag came up beside him. "I said nevermind, woman."

"Hold up, now. I'll answer your question but first tell me why it's so important to you."

Kaz shrugged. "I see the respect in the eyes of those who follow Jonrell. Loyalty as well. I want to know what would move a man, especially men such as these to have such devotion."

"So you'll understand why you follow him?" said Hag.

"Perhaps."

Several moments passed and Hag remained silent. Kaz looked at her. "Well? Why do you pause?"

"Cause I've never thought about it before."

"So you follow a man but never question why? You're no better than those fools who follow Denneth."

Hag shook her head, dirty white hair falling into her face. "Just cause I never thought about why I follow Jonrell don't mean I don't have my reasons. Just like I'm willing to bet those who follow Denneth have their reasons too."

Kaz grunted. "Fear."

"Yes and no. The way I see it, there's a certain layer of fear in any group. The Hell Patrol is no different in that. We don't fear the physical punishment or mental abuse that Denneth likely dishes out. Don't get me wrong, Jonrell can be a hard man when he has to be, but he doesn't use those tactics often. The punishment, however it's distributed, is more emotional than anything."

"I don't understand."

Hag scratched her cheek. "What I'm trying to say is that our fear is driven by a desire to not let Jonrell down. Those who follow Denneth are driven by a desire to protect themselves. Their fear is selfish. They aren't as close of a group as we are, and that closeness starts at the top with Jonrell."

"That's what I don't understand. What causes such closeness? What causes men to be so committed to one person?"

"I'm sure if you asked each of us that question, few answers would be the same. It may be a comforting word or a pat on the back for some. It may be the challenge that Jonrell gives to another. It may be the fact that Jonrell has saved many of our lives in some way." She paused, nodding. "Aye, I'm willing to bet that would be the answer for many, especially the old hands. It may be for others that he is willing to fight and work right alongside his men and only pulls rank when he needs to. For those who know his background, that carries a lot of weight."

"His background? Your answers only bring more questions."

She chuckled. "I forget how new you are to us. Well, let me be the one to tell you that you are under the command of the Prince of Cadonia." She laughed. "Shocking, isn't it? How many princes do you know would dig a ditch alongside a thief, or sometimes pull a double watch at night so a man running away from murder can get a few more hours of sleep? I'm willing to bet you would be hard pressed to find another who'd do the same."

Kaz sat in his saddle swaying in silence. Looking up the line of mercenaries, he saw Jonrell laughing with a different man than he had before. *Royalty? And yet he treats everyone the same.*

Hag snorted. "Hard to wrap your head around it, huh? You aren't the first one to sit there dumbstruck after discovering the truth." She paused. "You know, now that I think about it, there may be a common reason among us after all. When it comes right down to it, he puts as much trust in each one of us as we do in him, probably more. What more can we ask of a leader?"

What more can you ask of a leader? He took me in knowing how different I am from the others and not once has he treated me differently. And if anything, the trust his men place in him is what keeps many from slitting my throat. Kaz replied in a low tone. "I don't know."

"Aye, me either. So, does that answer your question?"

He nodded. *I will need to work at earning the trust of these men if I ever hope to find a place among them.* "I think so."

"Good."

No better place to start than now. "But I do have one more."

"Oh?"

"Did you really come here to answer my questions or was it because you couldn't keep your eyes off of me?" said Kaz, forcing a small grin.

Hag sat back in her saddle, shocked, then let out a hoot. "He smiles! Oh, and what a smile." She laughed. "So, you decided to finally wake up?" Then she gave Kaz a devious look. "Well, now that you realize what you've been missing, don't get any bright ideas." She winked. "I'm spoken for, you know, and he is the jealous type."

He grinned. "And he should be."

Hag laughed back. "Now, if you don't mind, I'm going to head back and ease his worries."

Kaz turned slightly in his saddle. "Hag?"

"Yeah?"

"Thank you."

Hag nodded and slid back into the group while Kaz remained alone, thinking more on what she said, fully aware of the puzzled looks directed toward him after their exchange.

* * *

Mudhole Bay stood as a sight to behold, aptly named for its murky waters and surrounding terrain. If not for the unique defensive position the port offered against any serious naval attack, Jonrell wondered why anyone would want to build a city on such unfavorable ground. He looked down on the city from the top of a low-lying hill just outside of town and shook his head. The skies had been clear for several days, but a change in the air told him this night would be filled with rain. He was not anxious to travel roads overflowing with muck and debris.

The unique characteristics that gave Mudhole Bay its name were what also kept it from becoming a proper city in his mind. Unlike Freeman's City on the other side of the island, where shacks, lean-tos, and other dilapidated structures lined the city's avenues, buildings here were built on soft ground with substantial foundations. Many thought the skill it took to build such strong structures couldn't be found in a place with mud caking each building's outer walls—they assumed that was what kept them standing. However, Jonrell knew better.

Here in this cesspool of a city, there is real talent. Talent that has been underused for so long because Cadonian nobles cannot put their prejudices aside. Jonrell allowed himself a grin. *Good thing I got over such things long ago.*

After roving across the island these past few weeks with little recruiting success, Jonrell looked forward to joining up with the rest of his men to see how they fared. But first, he wanted to make one final pitch in town.

The Hell Patrol had always been a pretty small outfit, focused on quality over quantity. Jonrell had found that the few men he was lucky enough to pick up from the Hideaway fit that mold perfectly. Still, he had hoped to have better numbers by this point in his journey.

One night here may not be enough time. But what other choice do I have? One night is all I can afford.

Jonrell wheeled his horse around to face his men, a crimson hue from the setting sun danced off the blood red mail he wore. "We are not here to let our guard down. We are here to work," he said, meeting the eyes of each man he thought could potentially cause the most trouble. "Our primary job is to find others to aid our cause. Now, I'm not saying you can't have a drink or two, or that you can't take some willing woman to your bed. What I'm saying is that two drinks better not turn into twenty, and one woman better not turn into three, and willing had better mean of her own volition. And those activities had best be secondary in each of your minds." He paused, eyes piercing the gaze of each man, holding the stare until they averted their eyes from him. "If I have to bail any man out of trouble tonight, only the One Above will be able to help him come the morning. Anyone of you wishing to defy me best do it now while you're sober because in a few hours, my patience will be gone. Is that understood?"

He saw nods and heard murmurs of "Yes, sir." *Good enough for this bunch.*

He softened his glare. "Good. Krytien, you'll take Hag and the supplies to *Ocean Spirit*. Make sure they're safely aboard. Drake and Mal will go with you. Sylik should be in the harbor by now and I don't need two boys running around this place. After you're squared away there, grab a few of the greener men when you go back out into the city. I'd much rather them under your protection so they don't get in over their heads. The rest of you, can split up in any way you choose. No less than three men to a group and no more than five."

Krytien answered with a nod. With a final look over his men, Jonrell led the way down from the hill.

* * *

The night of rain started early, a slow drizzle just before the sun dipped down into the brown water of the bay. The downpour increased by the time they reached the outskirts of town. The streets quickly filled with sludge and even more quickly emptied of people. His men would have to follow the crowds seeking to pass the night with a mug of something foul in their hands.

Which means everything I said will be forgotten if they start drinking this early. I'll have a lot of hung-over mercenaries tomorrow washing away their vomit along with the sea's grime from the decks of Sylik's ship.

Jonrell decided to ride straight toward the middle of town, where the hardest of men hung out. *Raker will find me builders, Krytien will look into mages. However, few are going to convince the nastiest of men to join our group. Those men are too smart, too cunning, to come over with a few fancy words from a common soldier. No, talking those men into joining up has become a specialty of mine.* He smiled.

Jonrell pulled up to The Orchid. The tavern's name always gave him a chuckle as there wasn't a single orchid on Slum Isle, and despite the innocent name, it was a bar that only the most hardened of men entered. He stepped down from his mount, tying the animal to a post that was covered by an extended roof. Kaz, Rygar, and one of the new recruits he brought along all did the same.

He had brought Kaz with him out of necessity, as no one else wanted him along. Rygar came along because Jonrell felt an obligation to him for Yanasi's sake. *I can't imagine her reaction if something happened to him. She was upset enough at their separation. At least this way I can keep a better eye on him.*

The new recruit was Krytien's idea. The mage felt that out of all the ones picked up from the Hideaway, Senald was the most responsible.

Jonrell entered the tavern, inhaling the stale air. Conversations were scattered throughout the large single room, though it seemed as if everyone spoke in unison. Scantily clad women squealed in feigned delight as hands reached out, fondling them as they wove between the tables with mugs of foamy ale. Each burst of glee was only meant to entice the men with the opportunity to move upstairs and seize an empty room. Jonrell glanced up and saw several men returning from those rooms, dressing as they descended the stairs, then moving on to the dice games near the back wall. All in all, it was what Jonrell expected to see on such a miserable night.

A table opened near the entrance and the group settled in. A serving wench came over to take orders. Jonrell ordered ale for all. He hated the taste of alcohol but was smart enough not to try anything else in a place like this.

The wench came back with four mugs, setting each down with little care and spilling part of their contents. She paid the act no mind and instead held out a hand waiting for payment, her face twisting into a sour look. Jonrell took out a silver coin and placed it in her hand. "Keep the change," he said with a smile.

She stared for a moment at the money, puzzled. She placed the coin in her mouth and bit down. She looked at Jonrell. "I ain't one of these whores so don't think this will buy you some time upstairs."

Jonrell shook his head. "That's not my intent. I was just hoping to win over a smile from you."

She scowled. "All it will win is ale free of spit, so long as you keep your hands to yourself."

One Above, does no one appreciate a kind gesture?

She started to turn away when Jonrell called out. "Wait."

The wench swung back to Jonrell with a glare and started to speak but he cut her off. "Don't say another word. I get enough attitude on a daily basis, I don't need any more from you." He thrust a couple of coins in her hand. "This should be more than enough to buy a round of ale for everyone in the bar. See that it gets done and that they know where it came from."

She muttered under her breath about giving her more work as she stalked away from the table.

"What did you do that for?" asked Rygar.

Jonrell took a sip of ale and puckered his mouth up. *One Above. This is awful.* He swallowed and shook off the taste. "Even with ale this bad, free drinks will go a long way."

"You planning to take all of these on?" asked Senald as he scanned the room.

The commander shook his head. "No. Many are going to ignore the gesture but some will come over hoping to milk me for a few more rounds. Of that group, a few may sit down to hear my offer and if we're lucky a handful of them will be interested enough to join us."

"Those aren't very good odds," said Rygar.

"Aye," said Jonrell. "But sometimes you take what you can get."

* * *

Five hours. Five long and miserable hours Jonrell had spent talking to men of all shapes, sizes, skill sets, and personalities. Buying drinks, sharing tales, and laughing at jokes so old he had learned them as a boy. Yet despite his efforts and the steady stream of men coming and going as the night wore on, he had convinced only one man to join.

Pathetic.

He was nodding absently at the man next to him while praying the man would conclude the impossibly long tale. Out of the corner of his eye, he caught a half-dressed woman leading a man upstairs.

That's at least her fifth this night. Maybe I should be buying women instead of ale? Nah, I'm not that desperate yet…though if things don't get any better it may come to that. He shook his head in disgust as he considered the notion.

"…and I swear on my dead mother's grave that's what happened," said the man, finishing his tale and gulping down the contents of his mug.

The unexpected silence from the man startled Jonrell from his thoughts. "Aye, it sounds like quite the adventure," he said, trying to sound sincere.

The man settled his mug down and wiped his mouth with the back of his hand. "Oh, it was. And I've got plenty more." He paused looking down at the table and then to Jonrell. "I'd be grateful for another drink. You know, it helps keep the mouth wet when retelling such long tales."

I'll bet it does. "All in due time. We've been talking for some time now and I was hoping you could give me an answer to my offer."

The man's face twisted into confusion. "What offer?"

Jonrell sighed, growing agitated. "The offer about joining the Hell Patrol and journeying to Cadonia. The offer of making more money than what you'd ever expect to see staying here."

The man waved a hand. "No, I'm not interested in that. Money is great but I'd rather be alive and drunk than rich and dead," said the man with a chuckle. "Speaking of," he added, looking down at his empty mug, "I sure could use another drink."

Jonrell's jaw clenched. "Then I suggest you find another fool to support your habits. We're done."

The man's face turned to shock. "But I thought you wished to hear about my life and adventures…"

"Adventures," Jonrell said with disgust. "You've wasted enough of my time spouting off your lies. Now get out of here."

"I see," said the man. He got up and without another word left the table, moving to another nearby. He slapped one of the men on the back as if old friends, starting another tale while casually reaching for someone's ale.

Jonrell sunk into his chair and saw the others at the table looking concerned. Each had hardly said anything during the night, especially Kaz who had yet to even touch his ale. "I hate to say it but I think we need to call it a night. I knew this was the wrong time of year but we had to make the effort." He shook his head. "Spring is much better. You'll find more willing bodies after a winter of drinking and whoring their money away. They're more eager to refill their pockets."

The commander stood up and the others did the same.

"You the one buying all these fools drinks?" came a voice from behind.

Jonrell turned and met the man's eyes, but not before noticing a face full of scars framed in a patchy beard. *Now this is the kind of man I'm looking for. The uglier the better.* "I am."

He nodded. "My boss wants to see you."

"Boss?"

"Aye." He turned and began walking across the room.

"I guess we're supposed to follow him?" asked Rygar.

"It would seem so," said Jonrell.

"Be wary. This man watched us the entire night," said Kaz, speaking for the first time since entering the bar.

Jonrell shrugged and followed the man to a table in the tavern's back corner where the lamps were dimmed.

Why do these people always feel the need to be mysterious?

Two men, just as grizzled as the first, flanked the table. Another draped in shadow stood between the figures. Little could be made of his features except that he seemed to occupy more space than the others.

"My name is Jonrell," he turned and gestured, "this is….."

The man in shadow cut in with a thick voice. "I don't care."

Jonrell was taken aback. "I figured we should make some sort of introductions before getting down to business."

"I have no business with you," said the thick voice.

Jonrell felt his face flush. *I've had enough for one night.* "Hey, you're the one who called us over. We were just on our way out, so I'll be more than happy to leave you to your little spot back here if you've changed your mind."

"I haven't changed my mind about anything and you can leave whenever you want." He paused a moment. "But first, I'll have the rest of that money you keep waving around."

Jonrell sighed. "Oh?"

"I figured if a man is dumb enough to throw his money away on these useless drunks, he'd be willing to hand it over to me. I know I can find more than a dozen better uses for it than what you have."

He's got me there. "Look, you're obviously a smart man. I can tell you how to make a lot more money than this."

The man in shadow let out a snort. "How? By joining your pathetic group? And I suppose you'd be the one to lead us since you do all the talking? No, that's not my style. I don't take orders from a bunch of little men. Especially not a crew of kids and freaks," said the man looking at Rygar and Kaz.

Jonrell glanced at Kaz from the corner of his eye. His face was hard as granite, and the commander was glad Kaz hadn't learned enough Cadonian to pick up what was said. Though from the black man's stance and muscles flexing and relaxing with each breath, it seemed he was prepared for things to get ugly. Jonrell's eyes moved back to the man in shadow. "Not many people would say that about the Hell Patrol."

The man in shadow made another sound that this time Jonrell knew was a laugh. "It takes more than a silly name, an exaggerated reputation, and fancy armor to impress me."

"A man's entitled to his opinion no matter how ill informed it is. We'll be on our way," he added, making a motion for the door.

"You're not going anywhere with that coin."

Jonrell looked at the four men. "If you know who we are, then you know I can't do that. After all, I do have a lot of stories to live up to," he said with a grin. "The way I see it four on four seems like pretty good odds. But, personally, I'd rather not. It's been a long day."

The man in shadow barked a laugh. "You may want to recount your number. That green looking fellow you were sitting with snuck out the door as you walked over. That tells me all I need to know about the kind of man you are and the kind you command."

Jonrell saw that the man was right. Only Kaz and Rygar were with him. *I'm going to kill Krytien for suggesting I take Senald. Right after I kill Senald.* Jonrell's face twisted, eyes narrowing. "So be it. Three against four. That should add a bit of embarrassment to you once we're done here," he said, hearing an audible gulp from Rygar. *Just do what you can kid and try to stay alive.*

The man in shadow suddenly grew in size. The figure towered above the others at what Jonrell estimated to be near nine feet.

One Above, he was sitting the entire time. With the shove of a hand, the man tossed the table in front of him, slamming it with a crack against the nearest wall. The bar's conversations were replaced with the sound of chairs skidding across the floor and the shuffle of boots exiting the tavern. The man in shadow stepped into the light. Jonrell saw his chin and forehead were overly pronounced, jutting from his face with a steep slope. The thick voice made more sense now.

A Ghal? Here?

The Ghal grinned. "Now who is going to be embarrassed by..."

A black blur shot out from the corner of Jonrell's eye with the speed of a striking snake. The giant's head rocked back. The Ghal staggered to the side, blinking as he leaned onto the scarred man next to him in an effort to steady himself. The man couldn't move away in time, nor was he strong enough to hold the enormous body up. Despite his best efforts both slumped to the ground in a heap of tangled limbs.

Rygar already had his blade out, guarding the two others. Their eyes blinked in disbelief and their mouths hung open.

Aye, I can't believe it either. One Above, I barely saw it. "Sit them down at an empty table and keep a close eye on them for now."

Jonrell turned back to the floor after he was satisfied that the two others weren't interested in making a move. Kaz stood over the giant, ready to strike again.

The Ghal started to come around, shaking his head and lifting a hand to rub at his jaw. The scarred man underneath was out cold. Jonrell leaned in close to Kaz and whispered. "That was impressive."

Kaz shrugged. "There is a time for talking and a time for fighting. Talking was obviously not working and when it comes to fighting the victor is usually the one who makes the first move."

"I can't argue with that. Though I still don't understand how you knocked out a Ghal with one punch."

"You mean the giant?" Kaz shrugged again. "He is overconfident in his strength and so he chooses not to guard himself as he should. He never thought anyone would dare challenge him. He left himself open to several attacks, really. I picked one of them." Kaz faced Jonrell. "I think about those things all the time, often without even realizing it."

"What things?"

"Playing out an entire fight in my head, going through various scenarios based on the information available." He paused. "Those thoughts happen so fast and with such repetition that I feel as though I've fought thousands of fights each day."

Great. And how often have you fought me? He looked down at the Ghal, moaning in his native tongue. He realized that Kaz still waited for a response to his admission.

A shout sounded from behind. "What's going on? Is everyone alright?"

Jonrell turned to see Krytien rushing over. "Where were you ten minutes ago?" He paused and directed his attention to the man standing behind Krytien. "I thought you ran out on me, Senald."

"It's not like that. He came running after me a couple of blocks over, muttering about you having to face some giant," said Krytien.

Jonrell felt his face go red. "You knew?" he asked Senald.

Senald looked down. "Not at first but once I saw where we were going, I remembered hearing the stories of this giant who often hung out in town. By that point it was too late to say something so the next best thing I could think of was running to get help."

Despite being angry, Jonrell knew Senald had acted with the best of intentions so he saved any berating on how the recruit should have acted until he had a chance to clear his head. "Next time a little warning would have been nice. We'll talk more about this later."

"Yes, sir," said Senald, eyes still examining the floor boards.

"So where is this giant?" asked Krytien

Jonrell nodded over his shoulder. "On the floor."

Krytien closed the distance in a few quick steps and exclaimed. "A Ghal? What's a Ghal doing on Slum Isle?" He paused. "And what happened to him?"

"We never had a chance to find out the answer to the first question. And as for the second," the commander tilted his head, "Kaz had a word with him."

Krytien pivoted to face Kaz, who stared once again at the Ghal on the floor. "How?"

Jonrell chuckled. "Believe it or not, he knocked him out with one punch."

The mage's eyes widened. "Impossible. His hand would be shattered."

"Hmm, I hadn't thought of that. But you're right," said Jonrell. Realizing he and Krytien were speaking Cadonian, he switched languages when addressing Kaz. "How's the hand?"

Kaz raised his left hand and Jonrell saw it was already starting to swell up. "It will heal," he said as if stating fact.

"Amazing," said Krytien in a hushed voice. "It looks like he may have a couple of minor fractures but nothing as serious as I would expect."

"We'll get Wiqua to look at it," said Jonrell.

"No sorcery," said Kaz.

"You need the use of your hand," said Jonrell.

"Until it heals, I still have my sword hand. I swung with my left hand in case it was injured."

"You mean I was hit with his weak hand?" said a groggy voice from below.

"Ah, you're up," said Jonrell, turning his attention to the Ghal. "Well, I wouldn't call it his *weak* hand given your situation now. But, yes, it was his off hand."

The Ghal rubbed his jaw. "Feels like someone dropped a mountain on my head."

Jonrell grinned. "I definitely don't envy your position. You know, the offer still stands."

The Ghal looked up for the first time, blinking. "Even after what happened?"

"Why not? You aren't the first to try something like that and I doubt you'll be the last."

The giant's face twisted into something that resembled a grin. "I can't speak for my men but I'm in." He swung his head toward Kaz. "If for no other reason than to see what he can do in battle."

I'm not surprised. Has a Ghal ever turned down the chance to fight?

"Good. It's settled." Jonrell pointed at the floor. "Why don't you give the guy under you a break and sit up. Krytien will look both of you over."

The Ghal's eyes went down to the floor showing surprise. Jonrell turned back to Kaz. "I still want Wiqua to look at your hand."

Kaz shook his head. "I said…"

"I know what you said," said Jonrell, growing frustrated. He let out a small sigh. "I promise, no sorcery. Wiqua knows many conventional methods of healing as well."

Kaz nodded.

"Good. Let's head to the docks and see if we can find the rest of the crew. They should be back by now and I'm curious to see how they fared."

* * *

"Man, you guys look rough," said Jonrell, walking up to Kroke. Their group had made it in from the north side of the island some time ago.

"Yeah Boss, it was an interesting trip," said Kroke, unloading his horse.

"Trouble?"

Kroke nodded. "Just about every day we got in some sort of fight. You'd think with thirty-five soldiers in our group, we would've been left alone. Most weren't much to worry about, but it got old fast."

"Did we lose anyone?"

"Nah, nothing that bad. Besides, we found ourselves a guy early on who knew some basic healing spells. He fixed the worst of us up when we needed it. We're mostly just dead on our feet. I've been pushing them hard the past two days to make it here in time."

"After the ship is loaded up, I want your crew to take tomorrow morning off."

"No arguments from me there. I'll grab any rest I can. This trip ain't going to be pretty."

"Oh? Why is that?"

"You know the seas are always rough here during this time of year. Most people are smart enough to wait."

Jonrell nodded. "Aye, but I don't have time to be smart." He inclined his head to Sylik who barked orders to those coming on ship. "Besides, after the mess he got us through on our way here, I'm really not that worried."

"Yeah, I believe he's too stubborn to die at sea," said Kroke, flipping out a knife.

Jonrell chuckled. "And that's exactly the kind of captain I want." He paused and changed subjects. "So, how many recruits?"

"Considering the trouble we had, we still managed to bring in fourteen men." Kroke sighed. "I was hoping for more but at least they've all seen a battle or two."

Jonrell grunted. "Not much different than us. But, the ones we picked up are mostly green and will need a lot of work in the coming weeks. I'll probably put you in charge of that."

Kroke nodded then gave Jonrell a suspicious look. "I hear there's one who doesn't really need any work?"

Jonrell noticed the mercenary's eyes looking off to the left. Turning he saw Kaz being tended to by Wiqua. The old man wrapped Kaz's hand in bandages, packing some sort of herbs between the layers. "Yeah, not everyone is as raw as the recruits we picked up at the Hideaway."

"I hear he knocked out a Ghal." said Kroke. "That sounds like anything but raw."

"One Above, news travels fast. But yeah, we left Krytien back at the Orchid with the Ghal and his crew to get them ready to travel. They'll be a huge help, definitely the kind of men we need more of. I hear Raker lucked out and convinced a couple of masons to join up too."

Kroke ignored the last part, his eyes still hadn't left Kaz as he picked at his finger nails with a blade. "I don't like him."

"Not you, too. Look, I don't care what color his skin is…"

"It ain't that, Boss. It wouldn't bother me if he was blue, I still don't like him."

Jonrell was puzzled. "Why is that?"

"Just watch the way he moves." He paused. "That's the way a killer moves. He's a dangerous man."

The commander laughed. "Look who's talking."

Kroke cocked his head at Jonrell and smiled. "Thank you." His grin faded though as he turned his eyes back in Kaz's direction. "But it's different than that. I may be a killer but I'm predictably dangerous. I don't try to be anything that I'm not."

"And you're saying that he is?"

"Raker filled me in on how you found him. He seems to think that he's only pretending he don't remember who he is so he can do us in later when he's grown bored."

"And you actually believe Raker? That's a first."

"Not entirely. I bet there's more to it than that. Maybe subconsciously he does remember what he was and doesn't like it. Maybe one part of his brain is telling the other part to forget that old life and start off with something different. If that's true, then both of those voices are going to be battling it out."

"And?"

"And the killer will always win out. It's just the way things are," said Kroke sheathing the dagger.

"You haven't even met the guy."

Kroke shrugged.

"Unbelievable. Well, he's staying so get over it."

"You're the boss."

Jonrell left the mercenary without adding anything else to the conversation. He was too frustrated by everyone's treatment of Kaz and he knew he'd say something he would regret. *What is everyone seeing that I'm missing?* He shook his head to clear his thoughts and made his way up the end of the dock. Looking out across the muddy waters of the bay and into the starry night, he tried to relax and enjoy the breeze, but it was no use. The sound of activity behind him still echoed in his ears as preparations continued. They would set sail with the rising sun.

Plenty of time to rest once we're out to sea, though I doubt I'll be able to relax any.

CHAPTER 16

"When will you be back?" asked Elyse, tears streaming down her face.

"When Father isn't around anymore," said Jonrell in a voice cold and hard.

"You mean when he's dead?"

"Yes."

"How can you say that? How can you be so cruel?"

Her brother threw up his hands. "Cruel? It's the truth. I've been away studying with Amcaro for over a month and what does Father do when I return? Does he welcome me with open arms? Does he ask what I've learned? Does he tell me that he misses me? No, of course not," said Jonrell his arms shaking. "He takes the first opportunity he can to belittle me, to embarrass me…"

"Maybe he was having a bad day," said Elyse, trying to find some excuse for the king's behavior.

"Having a bad day? He struck me! For nothing!" He threw up his hands. "Every day has been a bad day for him since Aurnon died. It eats him up inside knowing that I'm in line to take the throne and not his first born. I know he blames me for Aurnon's death." Jonrell's voice trailed off. "And maybe he's right."

"Don't say that. You were only five."

Jonrell shook his head. "Don't try. You weren't even born yet. And you're only nine now."

"So. I know the story just the same."

"Then why are you defending Father?"

"I'm not. I promise I'm not," sobbed Elyse. "I just don't want you to leave me."

Her brother went down to one knee and hugged Elyse. "I don't want to leave either, but it's for the best. I know you don't understand now but one day you will."

"But what happens if Father gets mad at me too?" asked Elyse, pulling away to look Jonrell in the face.

Her brother smiled. "He won't."

Elyse hung her head and sniffled. She felt a hand under her chin pushing her head up. Jonrell reached back and pulled a necklace from his neck and put it around hers. She looked down and admired the jewel. "You're giving this to me? But you love this necklace."

Jonrell smiled again and Elyse saw a tear fall from his eye. "It does mean a lot to me, but not as much as you do, little sister. I want you to promise me you'll never take this off."

"I won't."

"Good. As long as you have this on, you'll always know that no matter where I am, I'll be with you and I'll come back home." Jonrell turned his head to the side, wiping his cheek.

Elyse reached up and wrapped her arms around Jonrell's neck and squeezed as tight as she could, hoping that if she squeezed hard enough he wouldn't leave. "Please," she whispered.

Jonrell slowly undid her arms and pulled away. "This is something I have to do." He kissed her on the forehead and turned away. He left her room without sparing a glance back.

The little girl stood there alone, grasping the necklace around her neck, trembling in sorrow.

* * *

Elyse was on her knees, sobbing just as she did as a girl of nine. As the years rolled by, she hadn't realized how hard she had worked to put the pain and hurt of those memories away. But with the reports that came in this morning, all those feelings of abandonment flooded back from the far reaches of her mind.

It took everything she had to keep her emotions under control during the council after hearing the news. Within moments of the meeting coming to a close, Willum and Hadan whisked her away, where she retreated to the only place she felt true solace could be achieved. Yet, even in the great cathedral, in the presence of the One Above, she felt little relief.

I've been away too long. Since becoming queen, I've spent my time in meetings or in books. I've rarely prayed with the fervor I once did. Is it any wonder that being here fails to bring me the peace I desire? He has forgotten me just as I have forgotten him. She put her hands over her face as her tears came on again. *Maybe if I pray hard enough, he'll forgive me.*

A slight touch on Elyse's shoulder and a soft voice made her jump. "Child, what troubles you?"

She looked up and saw High Priest Burgeone looking down at her. His face was full of concern and Elyse wiped away the tears, sniffing as she composed herself. "I'm so sorry, Your Grace. I had thought I was alone."

The High Priest smiled and inclined his head to the statue above the altar. The One Above was depicted there, embracing children who swarmed in from all sides, each vying for his attention. A smile was carved into his face and warmth resonated from his marble eyes as he looked upon the boys and girls. That image had always given Elyse comfort when she was a child, though now the effect was lost.

"You can never be alone here, child. Not so long as our creator is watching over us."

Elyse smiled back but otherwise stayed quiet. She was unsure what to say with her faith so shaken.

The High Priest gestured toward the pew and Elyse made room for him to join her on the kneeler, honored by the gesture. His bones creaked as he took up position next to her. He let out a small sigh once settled. "Each day, it gets harder to do that," he said with a grin to cover his grimace.

"If it's more comfortable for you, we can sit." said Elyse, making a move to do so.

Burgeone touched her arm. "No child, this is fine. Suffering for a few minutes each day is nothing when one thinks of all the One Above has done for us."

Elyse nodded.

After a moment the High Priest cleared his throat. "I haven't seen you here since your father's funeral."

The queen bowed her head in guilt. "I had just reached the same realization, Your Grace."

"And is that why you were crying?"

"Yes. Well, no. I mean, not exactly. Other circumstances brought me here, I'm ashamed to say."

"The burden of ruling a kingdom."

"Is it that obvious?" asked Elyse in a tired voice.

"If you know what to look for, it is. I've felt the pressure that comes with a position of power. Having so many rely on your decisions can seem quite daunting at times."

Elyse bowed her head again. "I was so caught up in my own worries that I didn't notice my own lapse in faith."

"I see."

"You must be disappointed in me." She let out a slow breath. "I know the One Above is."

The High Priest looked startled. "What would make you say such a thing?"

She shrugged her shoulders. "I don't feel as close to him as I once did."

"Then you must mend your relationship with him." The High Priest gestured to the statue again. "He embraces anyone who does his will just as he embraces those children. But we must choose for ourselves to allow him to love us." He paused and his voice softened. "Child, I have been in your situation before."

Elyse looked up, surprised. "You have?"

"I am human, after all," Burgeone said with a small chuckle. "The weight of my office can grow heavy. Overseeing all the churches in Cadonia is not an easy task and sometimes the administrative duties have a tendency to get in the way of spreading the truth, even if they are a necessary part of the job."

The queen had never thought someone as pious as the High Priest could struggle through the same problems as her. "How do you set yourself back on the right track then?"

"It's amazing," he said, a sense of wonder in his voice, "but oftentimes I think that the One Above does it for me," added the High Priest, a far off look in his eyes as if in deep thought.

"What do you mean? You just said that we must choose to follow him ourselves."

Burgeone blinked. "Yes, we do. However, he is the one who provides us with the opportunities to make those decisions. A sunny day, a hearty meal, why even a chance meeting with an old friend can all be a reminder to us on what is important in our lives. For the One Above provides all." He smiled, tapping her hand.

Elyse looked down at his hand, confused. *A chance meeting?* "Are you talking about now?"

Burgeone smiled again, his nose crinkling in turn. "Yes. I hadn't even realized it until just now when I thought about my own relationship with our creator and how I too have slipped in my faith. Though to be honest, it isn't the first time that you've inspired me."

Elyse couldn't believe her ears. *How could I inspire anyone when it seems all I do is cause trouble?* "Really?"

"I seem to remember a time some years ago when I found a little girl crying behind the altar, hiding from the rest of the world and feeling abandoned after an older brother had run away. I never told anyone this but I considered leaving the faith altogether that day."

I was just thinking of that same day. Elyse looked up to the statue of the One Above. "I remember that day, too. You spent hours talking to me about the One Above and his fight against the One Below. That was the moment I dedicated myself to the faith." She paused, realizing the implication to Burgeone's words, she added. "Were you lying to me that day?"

"Not lying. You see, as I spoke the same speech I had told hundreds of times, something happened. The look in your eyes renewed my own passion and I realized that you were sent to me not only so I could help you, but so you could in turn help me. Again, the One Above provides us with the opportunities, but it is our job to take notice."

"...and the opportunity has changed little after all these years," she whispered, thinking of her brother.

"What do you mean child?"

She let out a sigh. "We received word today that someone resembling my brother and using his name was spotted on Slum Isle."

The High Priest grunted, his eyebrows bunching as if in thought. "Haven't those reports surfaced before?"

Elyse nodded. "Yes. But there is something different this time. The message continued by saying that the man was in a hurry to return to Cadonia. He could arrive almost any day now if the reports are to be believed, and we have no reason not to trust the information."

"Well, then that's wonderful news if it's true!" He paused. "Isn't it?"

"It should be, I suppose. For years all I wished for was his return. But since becoming queen, I had finally begun to move on. I assumed I would never see him again. The thought of coming face to face with him now is bringing up all sorts of emotions." She paused, shaking her head. "And that's only part of it. The council started to get out of hand this morning when the reports were read. I think many are hoping the news is true, simply because they would rather see Jonrell on the throne than me."

"But by leaving Cadonia, your brother denounced his birthright."

"As queen I can reinstate it."

The cathedral fell silent as the two stared forward, looking in the direction of the One Above. "Which could cause its own set of problems."

Elyse shrugged. "Or perhaps resolve the ones that are present."

"Perhaps."

"You don't sound convinced?"

"I do not mean to sound so indecisive, but in truth, those decisions are not for me to make. And although I hear a few things here and there, I'm sure there are others who can provide you with better advice." The High Priest spread his hands out toward the wide open cathedral. "I'm afraid the most help I can be to you is here," he said in a solemn tone.

Now I know why the One Above chose him to come to me. Elyse reached out a comforting hand and placed it on the High Priest's arm. "That is nothing to apologize for, Your Grace. In fact, that may be the help I need most of all."

Burgeone smiled. "Thank you, child."

"Do you have anywhere you need to be at the moment?"

"No. I don't believe I do. Is there something I can do for you?"

Elyse's eyes welled up again, catching her off her guard. Quickly, she wiped her cheeks. "I have some free time myself and I was wondering if you would stay with me a while longer so that we might pray together, like when I was a girl."

The High Priest nodded and turned his head back to the altar. Bowing his head, he began to recite the prayers he first taught Elyse. After taking a moment to compose herself, she joined in, chanting melodically to Burgeone's praises. As she focused on the One Above, the stress, the hurt and the pain slowly faded away.

* * *

Dabbing her brow, Elyse walked through the armory and past the forges. The old blacksmith labored away just as he had weeks ago during her first visit. The same young boy from before was now accompanied by several new apprentices, each scurrying about at the slightest command. Eleven other smiths hammered away at mail, sword, and shield, each with their own set of aspiring helpers.

Activity to her other side mirrored their industry as a gang of fletchers churned out arrows and quarrels, others crafting or repairing bows and crossbows.

So intent on their tasks, none noticed the queen enter the armory.

Perhaps they have become accustomed to my presence and see no need to show me special treatment? Some of the nobles she knew would take that as a slight, but Elyse welcomed the anonymity after being pulled and prodded by others.

Making her way through the armory, she looked over its stores. For every row of polished and repaired mail, there seemed to be another ten rows rusted and untouched. For every barrel filled with arrows, a dozen more stood empty. Elyse could not deny the improvements Grayer had made, but she still felt sick to her stomach.

How can we ever stand a chance with so much work to do? Rather than dwelling on her thoughts as she would have just days ago, she remembered the calmness she had gained in the cathedral. Taking a deep breath, she recited a short prayer to herself, asking the One Above for strength.

General Grayer, as usual, sat in the back. Leaning over a stack of papers that seemed to grow larger with each visit, he reached for his plate of pastries, shoving one into his mouth whole.

Elyse noticed how the mountain of sweets had grown to absurd proportions. *I guess we must all find ways to handle the pressures of our jobs.*

The general wiped the sweat glistening off his forehead with the same hand, unaware of the sticky residue he left behind. She suppressed a laugh. It was obvious Grayer suffered from the heat, but since Elyse had caught him off guard, he had been more cognizant of his appearance and wore his best armor when he knew she would drop by. She appreciated the gesture but thought the decision impractical.

Elyse's footsteps were drowned out by the rhythms from behind. She was not surprised when Grayer jumped in his seat as she cleared her throat. He rose quickly from his chair and bowed low. "Your Majesty, I apologize for my rudeness."

"Please, General. Must we go through this every day?" Elyse said. Grayer waited for her to seat herself before retaking his own.

"I appreciate you being so forthright with me, Your Majesty. But I am a military man, and have been my whole life. I cannot help but treat you in the manner you deserve."

Elyse shook her head. "So be it. I'm sorry that I haven't been here to see you in several days. It's good to see so much activity. How are things?"

"Better, Your Majesty. Though we are still far behind." He gestured toward the weapon stores. "The amount of work is quite daunting and we were only able to fill out the positions a few days ago."

"Why is that?"

"Truth be told, I think people are scared and want to make sure they don't get caught on the wrong side, Your Majesty. Many are simply cautious and looking out for themselves."

No one has confidence in me then. "Then what has changed?"

Grayer shrugged. "People's worries seem to go away when you give them more money. I hate to see how much it will cost to run a second shift."

"A second shift? Is that how things were once run?"

"No. But if there were enough hours in a day, I'd even go so far as to hire enough for a third shift. But alas, the One Above saw fit to only provide twenty-four hours in a day," he said, throwing his hands up.

Elyse shook her head. *I understand his frustration but I mustn't let him shake my faith again; not so soon after rediscovering it.* She changed subjects. "Are the number of recruits improving?"

The general grunted. "That is a double edged sword."

Elyse inclined her head. "I'm not sure I follow you."

"I apologize. What I mean is that we desperately need soldiers but it seems the only ones eager to join are too young to know any better, or are so poor that they'd take a free meal and roof over their head from just about anyone. Regardless, neither group can afford their own armor, nor do we have enough ready to arm them ourselves." He shook his head. "And training them is a completely different story."

"The state of the armory is hindering your training as well?"

"Not completely, Your Majesty. We can train with wooden swords and shields. The bigger problem is a lack of competent officers to oversee the training. I'm worried these recruits are starting off on the wrong foot,' said Grayer reaching for a pastry before remembering Elyse was there and returning his hand to his lap.

I sent away his best men to Conroy. And I haven't heard a word from the Duke or from the forces I sent to him. The queen jumped in her seat as a side door burst open, slamming against the wall. A young boy came running through the door in tattered clothes, a letter in his hand. "Sir! I have an urgent message for you."

"Soldier, don't you realize you're in the presence of our queen. Show some respect or you'll have latrine duty for a month," said Grayer rising from his seat.

A Soldier? He can't be more than fourteen years of age.

The boy turned and looked at Elyse as if she hadn't been there a moment ago. His face turned red and his mouth worked up and down but his brain couldn't find the words. To his credit, he was able to muster together a bow of sorts.

The General turned to Elyse. "I apologize, Your Majesty, but now you can see what I was saying earlier." He looked back at the young boy who stood frozen in place, still unable to speak. "Let's have that message, soldier," barked Grayer.

The young boy snapped out of his trance and with a shaking arm, extended the letter to the General who snatched it away. Unrolling the parchment, his eyes scanned the document with an intense glare. As Grayer read, Elyse noticed his grip tightening, his teeth slamming shut as he finished.

"What's wrong? What does the message say?"

He dismissed the young soldier who left eagerly. Grayer let out a long breath. "It's Tomalt," he said with his head down, leaning over the table.

The queen's stomach tightened. "Tell me."

Grayer looked up with a long face. "He's crossed over into our land and has attacked Namaris," he said, handing the message to Elyse.

She started reading the news herself, hoping the General had overlooked something. It was spelled out clearly enough, the city was under siege. "We have to help them."

"I need more time, Your Highness. We aren't ready to meet Tomalt on the field of battle yet."

Elyse shook her head. "These are my people. We mustn't let them think that we've abandoned them."

"But, Your Highness, you've read the hopelessness in the letter. Namaris was undermanned. By now, Tomalt has probably taken the city."

Undermanned due to my own folly. "Then we must take it back."

"You cannot expect us to lay siege to a city where the occupying force so greatly outnumbers our own."

"Not only do I expect you to carry out my wishes, I command you to do so. If we just sit here and do nothing, what is to stop Tomalt from attacking Lyrosene next?"

"But, Your…."

"You have one week, General. Do whatever it takes to get it done. Money is no object."

Grayer slumped back down into his chair and nodded.

CHAPTER 17

While *Ocean Spirit* navigated toward the docks, Jonrell gazed out across the busy harbor to the shoreline of Floroson. *After all these years, it's barely even changed. The architecture looks the same but what of the people? How will Lord Undalain and Lady Jaendora receive me? Just like Amcaro, they were more parents to me than my father was. Thank the One Above that Elyse had them while I was gone.*

"What's on your mind?" asked Krytien.

The commander tried to hide his surprise by managing a grin. "For being an old man, you sure can sneak up on someone when the mood strikes you."

"Please. Even Crusher could have snuck up on you. You've been standing in the same spot since Yanasi spied land."

"Where is he any way?" asked Jonrell looking over his shoulder.

"Crusher?" Krytien inclined his head. "With Kaz."

As Jonrell spared a look over his shoulder, Sylik bellowed out orders and the Ghal set to hauling rope with Kaz. The commander watched for a moment before turning his gaze back out across the water. "It'd take more than half a dozen men to equal what they can do together. I wish I had a hundred more like them."

"That makes one of us," said the mage under his breath.

He gave Krytien a piercing look. "You still harping about Kaz? I really don't understand everyone's attitude about the man. "

"Really?"

"Yes, really. I've heard all the arguments several times over and they just don't hold water. He's pulled more than his share since becoming part of the crew, and lately doing so one-handed." He stopped but saw that Krytien waited for more. "His Cadonian is improving and he's spent a good portion of the voyage talking to people besides me."

"And those just happen to be two of our more eccentric members." The mage turned back to Crusher. "I can at least understand the Ghal. Those two have the same mentality, living by some warrior's code." He paused. "But it makes you wonder why Glacar hasn't warmed up to them, doesn't it? Neither of the three are what I would call a soldier in the truest sense of the word."

Jonrell laughed. "Like any of us are. That's especially funny coming from a mage who swears off any of the formal training that most others go through."

Krytien shrugged again. "I prefer to go off of feel."

Jonrell continued, choosing not to respond to the mage's last comment. "Glacar's just upset is all. He's been our heaviest hitter for years and now he's got two rivals."

The mage winced. "I'd keep that comment to yourself if I were you. He's been acting like a caged animal around them lately, especially Kaz."

"Oh, I'd never be dumb enough to tell him that to his face," said Jonrell with a grin, trying to lighten the mood. But then his face grew serious. "You're right about Glacar. He's never been very personable, but since Mytarcis he seems to have gotten worse."

"The appearance of the Hell Patrol has changed since then. First Wiqua, then Kaz, and now Crusher. He's not exactly accepting of those that are different than him."

Jonrell spat. "Everyone's different than that giant hairball. He needs to either accept my decisions or move on."

Krytien grunted. "Alright. Back to what we were saying before. Crusher and Kaz's relationship makes sense but what about Hag?"

"Hag can be a pain at times but we all like her."

"Like her, yes. But it's much different between her and Kaz. He's looking out for her almost like she's his mother."

"So? Have you noticed how much better of a mood she's been in? And you realize that the two people you mentioned both had a good enough grasp of Byzernian so he could talk to them while working on his Cadonian. On top of that, each was actually willing to talk to him. They don't treat him any differently just because of his appearance. Maybe it's because Hag and Crusher are both outcasts themselves, but they've overlooked the things that turned a lot of people off about him."

"I'm not saying I disagree with your reasons. Just passing on the thoughts of some of the crew is all."

"And what are your feelings?"

Krytien sighed. "I'm still a little uneasy with him, but I can tell that Kaz is making an effort with most of us, and I know you spend about as much time talking to him as you once did with Cassus. So, I trust you. It'd be nice if he got over his issue with sorcery though. I'd be more than willing to talk to him myself if I could."

"Yeah, I guess he and I have become closer. With the trip so calm, there was a lot of downtime to talk about those bits of his past that come up every now and then."

"Any luck figuring out what they mean?"

"Not really. Lots of fighting or time spent training to fight. Seems like he's lived his entire life with that as his sole purpose."

In silence they both stared back out over the water. Even from their distance, the details of Floroson's bone-white buildings came into view. The uniquely curved rooftops matched the up and down motion of the waves. People carrying cargo from the newly arrived merchant ships looked like ants weaving between the buildings.

It's amazing that life goes on after what happened to the kingdom when Nareash betrayed Father. He gripped the railing, thinking about how ignorant he would be if Raker hadn't picked up on the news while in Mudhole Bay. *So many friends I never said good-bye to. Friends I'll never see again.*

Boots scampered across the deck and pulleys squealed with each tug of rope. He looked up and saw seagulls soar overhead. The birds wheeled about and dove into the foamy water, coming up with their meals.

"So are you done stalling?" Krytien finally blurted out.

"What?" said Jonrell.

"I ask what's bothering you and you respond by changing the subject to Crusher, which leads to Kaz yet again. You were hoping I'd forget why I came over here in the first place."

Jonrell started to chuckle, putting his head down. "You'd think I'd realize by now I can't get away with that."

Krytien waited.

Jonrell saw the impatient look on the mage's face. "I was thinking about a lot of things. For one, what is Cassus doing? Is he alright? Will I ever see him again? I mean last time I looked upon this harbor, he and I were standing together like this, but the harbor was fading away. We were just a bunch of scared kids on our way to Slum Isle, hoping to leave our troubles behind us." He shook his head. "But I realize the difference between us is that he never really wanted to return."

"No, I guess he didn't," said Krytien.

"And here I am while Cassus is miles away doing only the One Above knows what."

"I don't doubt you miss him. We all do. He was well-liked and helped keep us in check. But I think the real issue comes from what Raker told you he heard while in Mudhole Bay. You haven't talked about it once since then, and that was weeks ago."

Jonrell stared down at the water and watched the waves crash against the ship. "I barely believed him until I overheard several others chewing over the same story. There are conflicting facts in the retelling, but the gist is the same." Jonrell's hands tightened around the ship's railing, turning his knuckles white. "You know the day I left Cadonia, I only said good-bye to two people. Elyse and my father. Elyse reacted about as I expected a girl her age would. It tore me up inside, but I did it anyway.

"My father…his reaction hurt more, even though it shouldn't have come as a surprise." He paused. "I told him I was leaving, that I had no plans of returning while he still lived, that I no longer wanted to be thought of as his son. And you know what he said? He looked me dead in the eyes and in the most even of tones said, 'My son is already dead. You killed him.' After thirteen years, he still held me responsible for something that occurred when I was five. What kind of man does that?"

"A man who wanted someone to blame for his pain. A man whose grief was so great that he couldn't move on with his own life," said Krytien.

Jonrell grunted. "And I hated him for it. I still do. To this day, I hope that he is rotting somewhere in the lowest parts of hell, acting as some puppet to the One Below." He looked up and chuckled. "In a way it was fitting that he was used before he died." He paused again. "Only…only others had to suffer with him. Men far greater than him died because of his inability to run a kingdom. One Above, Amcaro taught countless mages, and advised every king after Aurnon I. He was as much a part of Cadonia as the royal family. But now he's dead and so are the other High Mages—all of whom I knew. None of them deserved their fate. And neither did Elyse."

"You know there is little logic behind what happens in the world. It doesn't make a difference if we deserve what we get. It matters how we deal with our troubles when they happen."

The commander let out a heavy sigh. "After what Raker told me, I feel like I'm coming home to a graveyard." He grunted. "I had my doubts about Elyse's reaction before. But now…now she's likely to throw me in a cell and be done with me."

"From what you've told me, Elyse is not like your father."

"She wasn't. But twelve years is a long time. I left her a girl and a princess. I'm coming back to a woman and queen. Just think how much I've changed in that same amount of time."

"Sure, you've changed. But not for the worse."

* * *

Drake watched the city come into view with a sense of awe. He had never left Slum Isle before, so the images he had of those far away cities that populated the great continents remained dreams.

But not anymore.

Floroson didn't match any of the places he had created in his head, but it was impressive nonetheless. Buildings were mostly pale in color, and rooftops angled in unnatural ways.

The engineering required to create such structures impressed him. *I'd love to meet the ones who designed them. Even better, I'd love to learn from them.*

A grimy hand came down on his shoulder and yanked him backward. "Boy, you wool-gathering again?" came a voice in garbled speech.

"Uh, sorry. I was just looking at the city."

Raker spat and pointed. "We ain't got time for that now. Go on and get back to your station. We got work to do." Raker walked away mumbling curses. "What's that boy gonna do in battle? Liable to get his head chopped off cause he ain't paying attention."

Drake walked back to his station next to Mal. Everyone thought he was too young to be a soldier, but he would show them. *It will be me doing the chopping when the time comes.* He smiled at that.

Mal cast him a sidelong glance as Drake came over and helped him secure some rigging. "What did you see?"

"It's beautiful, Mal. Beats anything we ever saw on Slum Isle."

"Give me details."

"The buildings are all made of stone and vary in size, some even a couple of hundred feet tall. The city looks to be encircled by a simple wall that extends to the waterfront. The docks are at least ten times the size of those in Mudhole Bay."

"What else? What about the people?"

Drake shook his head. "We're still too far away for me to see that kind of detail. Besides, Raker caught me and told me to come back over here."

Mal scowled at Raker's retreating back. "Idiot. I can't understand a word he says."

"You get used to his speech after awhile, and really, he ain't that bad once you get to know him. You just don't want to be on his bad side."

Mal cocked his head. "But you couldn't stand him before."

Drake shrugged. "Better than being at the Hideaway with Denneth."

"I guess."

"Seriously?" asked Drake. "Don't tell me you're having second thoughts."

"This isn't what I expected, doing all this menial work."

"Someone has to do it, and we're the newest members. The others they picked up from Slum Isle are stuck doing the same stuff."

"Easy for you to say. At least you're learning something useful from Raker, even if he is an idiot. They want me to talk to Wiqua so he can teach me some basic healing procedures you don't need sorcery for."

"See," said Drake, "healers are important for any army."

"Maybe. But it's also boring."

"Everything can't be exciting all the time."

"It was when I was in charge of the group guarding the Hideaway. That was fun having everyone listen to me." He sighed. "I thought Jonrell would be teaching me more about being a leader but he's always doing something or talking to someone else."

"He's got a war to plan. No offense but there's a lot for him to consider."

Mal scowled. "Whatever. I'm going to see what boring work Sylik needs done next," he said, sulking off.

Drake shook his head and went back to work.

* * *

A short while later Sylik eased *Ocean Spirit* into place along the docks. Jonrell pulled his company aside one last time before stepping ashore while the crew saw to last minute preparations.

"Look, I know many of you have never been to Cadonia before. Things are much different here than on Mytarcis and even more so than on Slum Isle. Do not, I repeat, do not go running off once we get our gear unloaded. You will remain within spitting distance of each other at all times. I want to be out the gates on the other side of town by this evening. We will not wait on anyone." A few moans of disappointment greeted that news but the commander ignored them.

Ocean Spirit nudged into the wooden dock with a groan. As the gangplank lowered, Jonrell turned round. "One more thing, keep the armor and the bulk of your weapons stowed away. We want to be as inconspicuous as possible."

The commander took the first step over the side out onto the gangplank. He nearly lost his balance at the sudden cheers that erupted upon coming into view. He looked up and saw crowds of people by the unloading area with members of the City Watch frantically working to stop a full on rush of the docks. Screams of "King Jonrell, long live the king!" and "We're saved!" reached his ears. Several less enthusiastic cries of "That doesn't look like him," or "I thought he was taller," filled in the gaps between cheers.

Jonrell's mouth hung open in shock as the first few citizens broke through the City Watch's barricade, causing a tidal wave of bodies to come flooding through the crack. The onslaught of people intimidated him more than any battle charge. People pushed one another into the bay as they clamored forward.

A meaty hand closed around his shoulder, yanking him back onto *Ocean Spirit* and the commander watched Kaz kick the gangplank over the side just as the first few of the mob reached it.

Sylik yelled out, "Get those ropes and ladders up! I'll not surrender my ship to this lot."

Someone shook him. "You alright, Boss?"

Jonrell blinked. "I never expected this."

Kroke flashed a rare smile. "So much for being inconspicuous, huh?"

Jonrell looked over to where Kaz stood, peering over the side. The warrior announced in Cadonian with a thick accent, "They're climbing up the side."

The commander found his voice and called out. "Krytien, take care of this."

The mage stepped forward, pushing back the sleeves on his robe and raising his hands up high. "Watch your eyes."

Jonrell closed his eyelids just as he felt the heat from the sudden flash of light envelop him. There were several screams from below. The commander looked over the side and noticed that the mass of people had calmed.

He addressed the stunned crowd. "Where is Lord Undalain?" he shouted.

"Dead," came a woman's voice from below. "I govern Floroson since his passing."

Dead? One Above, not him too. Jonrell looked down to the blue haired woman below. Caught in the middle of the rushing mob, she stood between her own personal guard who pushed and shoved all those around them with the flats of their shields. Though she had aged, he immediately recognized her.

His chest tightened, but he smiled. "Lady Jaendora, I'm sorry to hear such bad news about your Lord Husband. Would you care to join me on deck?"

Lady Jaendora looked up, blinking. Clearing her vision, she managed a smile. "You left a boy but return a man, Jonrell."

"Not sure how true that is. Will you accept my invitation? I'm afraid we have much to talk about," said Jonrell, shouting over the crowd noise.

Her face grew hard. "Yes. I'm afraid we do."

* * *

The commander and Lady Jaendora borrowed Sylik's quarters to get out of the way of those on the ship's deck. Her personal guard accompanied the governess aboard and stood vigilant outside of the captain's door. It took some time for Jonrell to clear off a space for the two to sit and he felt compelled to apologize on the captain's behalf. He was left wondering how a man so particular about every crevice of his ship could tolerate such disorganization where he slept.

As Lady Jaendora took her seat, Jonrell couldn't help but notice how much she had aged in the time he'd been away. Nearing sixty, the intervening time had stolen the spark from her eyes. He wondered how much of her change could be blamed on the loss of Lord Undalain and what could be attributed to the current state of Cadonia.

Jaendora was the first to speak. "That thick stubble may hide your face but it does little to disguise those eyes of yours." She touched his face like a mother, turning his head. "And you still carry so much pain after all these years. I'm sorry to say that if you've returned to find comfort, you will be hard pressed to do so."

Jonrell pulled from the governess and looked away. The cold tone that she spoke with cut deeply. *She is upset with me, though who can blame her.* He chose not to address her comment. "I've heard of the atrocity that occurred in Lyrosene. However, I'm clueless to what's happened since then."

"Chaos."

Jonrell's eyes widened. "Is it that bad?"

Jaendora shrugged. "It depends on who you ask, but I feel it's a pretty accurate statement. Your sister hasn't made very many friends since your father passed away. The poor thing never had a chance, really. Things had deteriorated quite a bit in the last couple of years before your father died, especially in the last year or so when they say Nareash had taken control of his mind. I think the High Mages were all that stood in the way of open rebellion." She shook her head. "Though why Amcaro never stepped in before things turned so bad, I'll never know."

"He always felt it wasn't his place to interfere directly in such matters," said Jonrell. "It was just his way."

"Well, his way turned out not to be the best way," she said in a bitter tone. "Doing something could have saved hundreds of lives—thousands after we go to war."

"Are you certain it cannot be avoided?"

She shook her head. "Yes. Maybe if you showed up right after your father's passing, but not now. Everyone knows your sister suffered in some way from Nareash as well, and many wonder if it affected her mind."

I hadn't thought of that. "What do you think?"

"I don't know. I only spoke to her briefly at your father's funeral. Given the circumstances of our conversation, it was hard to say."

"Then why does everyone have so little faith in her ability to rule?"

"Because she was never prepared to rule a kingdom. Even after you left, your father never brought her into council, and she showed little interest in such things. From what I hear, she is trying her best, but she's in over her head. She doesn't know the relationships or who to trust and everyone is trying to use her to push their own agenda. The queen lacks the basic knowledge and confidence to rule effectively and the dukes know this."

Why didn't you continue with your studies after I left, Elyse? I tried to tell you how important they would be one day. He changed subjects. "Tell me about the dukes. What are their positions?"

"What you'd expect. Tomalt is gathering his forces under the guise of training exercises after being slighted by your sister."

"How so?"

"He wanted to be made commander of the kingdom's armies and she turned him down."

"Well, it doesn't sound like she is as foolish as you think."

"Jeldor made an appearance at your father's funeral but was insulted by just about everyone and no one has heard a thing from him since he returned to Ithanthul."

"Typical."

"Bronn…"

"Bronn?" said Jonrell cutting in. "Don't tell me Duke Alnane is dead?"

Jaendora nodded. "I'm afraid so and Bronn is definitely not his father's son. He is as arrogant as ever," she said in disgust.

"Alnane was at least someone you could reason with," Jonrell said in frustration.

"Not Bronn. You know he was once betrothed to your sister, but the King called it off after some questionable behavior on his part. He took the king's funeral as an opportunity to make a play for the throne by marriage, but to your sister's credit she turned him down. Probably one of the smartest things she's done since taking the throne, though few others see the kind of person he really is."

"Unbelievable."

"It gets better. There are rumors that he and Conroy have become close since Alnane's passing."

"Really?"

"Those are the rumors."

"Interesting."

"Yes. And Conroy's been the most mysterious of all since the king's death. He didn't come to the funeral, citing his duties at the High Pass. Since then, little information has made it out of his lands." She paused. "He is the one I fear most."

"No argument here, but he isn't my concern now. You haven't mentioned Olasi. I assume he is still loyal to the crown?"

"As loyal as ever," Jaendora said with a nod.

Jonrell let out a sigh. "Thank the One Above. He's just strong enough to give Conroy reason to pause. Besides, knowing Conroy, he'll sit back and wait before making any moves. Tomalt is my real worry for now. If I hurry, maybe I can help Elyse mend that relationship and avoid any bloodshed."

"Then I take it you won't be staying for the night? I was hoping you'd fill me in on your interesting choice of company."

He chuckled as Jaendora's hard exterior finally showed signs of softening. "They definitely make fools of themselves in any formal setting, but I wouldn't trade them for anything."

She raised an eyebrow. "Now, you've really piqued my interest."

"I'm afraid you'll have to wait to hear those stories until this mess is sorted out."

The governess nodded but said nothing else. *She's waiting for me to stand up first. I'd completely forgotten what it felt like to be of royal blood.* He rose and helped Lady Jaendora to her feet. *I'm suddenly remembering how much I hated the formality of my station.*

The door burst open and the commander's hand immediately moved to his sword hilt before recognizing one of Lady Jaendora's guardsmen. He bowed at the waist. "I'm sorry for the intrusion, My Lady," he paused, glancing up, "and My King."

"Prince," said Jonrell, correcting the guardsmen. "My sister is our Queen."

"Yes, My Prince," the guardsmen said in response.

"What is the matter, Lieutenant?" asked Jaendora.

The guardsmen extended his arm and handed her a message. "Best if you read it yourself, My Lady. It just came in."

She gasped as she read. Despite his curiosity, Jonrell waited patiently for her to finish. She looked up, her face more pale than a moment prior. "It looks as though I won't be hearing those stories any time soon. Tomalt has claimed Namaris and the queen intends to take the city back. She is planning to march any day now. You must hurry before she does. Last I heard her army isn't capable of laying a proper siege."

Jonrell's heart sank at the news.

Welcome home.

* * *

After the gut wrenching news, Jonrell excused himself from Lady Jaendora to attend to his company of men. The governess stayed near the ship, out of everyone's way. A string of messengers had come and gone during the time it had taken to unload the ship and secure their provisions. The governess handed slips of paper to them before each went scurrying away.

The Hell Patrol set off down the main thoroughfare where the throngs of people lined the streets in a much more civilized manner than before. It didn't appear as though news of the attack on Namaris had spread as quickly as the commander would have thought. Most in the crowd wore a wide smile with hopeful eyes and shouted words of encouragement. However, Jonrell noticed several times where whispered words changed that expression to one of despair and their cheers to pleas. He glanced at the City Watch, who in full armor, formed a protective barrier from the eager masses.

The sooner we leave here the better.

Jonrell looked about at his soldiers, proud how they handled the crowd, refusing to encourage the masses for the good or the bad. *They've never experienced anything like this before. Now that I think about, when have I?* He spotted Yanasi off to one side. She wore a frown as she scanned the crowd of strangers. Her frown grew deeper as she glanced at Rygar.

Jonrell allowed his horse to drift back from the front, nudging his way alongside her. "You hanging in there?" he asked.

Her head whirled around, snapping her ponytail like a fiery whip. "Sorry, Sir, you startled me."

Jonrell flashed a reassuring smile. "I didn't think that was possible in all of this," he said gesturing with his hands toward the masses. "Tell me what happened."

"What makes you think anything happened?" she asked.

Jonrell tilted his head and gave her a knowing look. "Yanasi."

"I feel so out of place. It's like everyone is staring at me."

"They're staring at all of us, but at me especially."

"That's different. They're supposed to look at you." She paused, her voice barely a whisper, causing Jonrell to strain to hear each word. "But they stare at me, just like they do with Kaz and Crusher…only different." Her eyes moved back up to Rygar before drifting down to her saddle once again.

The commander looked up and saw Rygar carrying a wide grin. The mercenary dipped his head toward the crowd several times and Jonrell noticed a group of young girls, decked out in their finest, on the receiving end of each gesture. As they passed the girls, they scowled while the older women ignored Yanasi altogether. On the other hand, men of all ages had noticed the female mercenary, dressed in tight leathers. They gawked and leered and whispered.

Jonrell felt himself become flushed with anger. He met each of the onlooker's eyes with an icy stare until they averted their gaze in shame.

"Do you see what I mean?" asked Yanasi, her voice full of dismay.

The commander caught himself, realizing his hand drifted to the dagger at his belt. *One Above, what's the matter with me?* Despite the lewd comments from Raker and the attention drawn by other soldiers, he hadn't been that protective of her as she grew older. She could take care of herself. But seeing her hunched over and helpless to defend herself against an enemy she was unaccustomed to brought up all the protective instincts he had when he first found her. *She was so young and fragile then.*

"Did I do something wrong?" she asked.

Jonrell shook his thoughts away, remembering where he was. "No. Of course not. You did nothing wrong. The young girls are jealous of you because deep down they wish they could just run off and do what they wish with their life."

"Then why don't they?"

"Opportunity. Money. Other reasons that can be overcome. All except their own fear. And they see you, a soldier, able to live without relying on anyone else. And they realize they'll never have that. You're living their dream whether they realize it or not."

"Really?" she asked, her face lighting up.

He nodded. "And the older women? Jealous as well. They see a woman both young and beautiful and they know you have your whole life ahead of you. They can never recapture that. So they choose to ignore you so they don't have to come to terms with the decisions of their past."

She smiled, something she was often too shy to do. "You really think I'm beautiful?"

"Of course. Why do you sound so surprised?"

"It's just… you've never told me that before."

Jonrell stopped for a moment trying to remember the last time he said as much to her but couldn't. *One Above, forgive me. I guess Cassus was right, she needed my approval more than I realized.*

"Well, that's my fault and I apologize. Maybe it's because I know how much you hear that stuff from Raker and some of the others when they joke around with you. I guess I didn't want you to assume I was doing the same."

"Raker's never called me beautiful," she said with a pause. "And it's different coming from you. You're like a brother to me. I don't even like to think about where I'd be if you hadn't taken me in," she said.

The commander felt his eyes watering and quickly coughed into his hand. "What do you say we don't think about that then?"

She nodded. "Agreed."

"Good. Why don't you go keep Hag company in the back with the wagons?"

"Why is that?"

"Well, it'll keep you out of sight some, especially from the men. I'm afraid their motives are much less innocent than the women," he said, glaring at a man in the crowd.

"I think I'm fine now," she said with a grin.

I don't know if I've seen her smile this much in a week, let alone a day. "Good." He looked up at Rygar who was now throwing an occasional wave toward the crowd and he frowned.

"It's alright," said Yanasi.

"No. No, it's not," he said, shifting in his saddle.

"What are you going to do?" she asked.

He set his jaw. "Go be a big brother."

* * *

The Hell Patrol finally neared the other side of Floroson after a slow and arduous journey through the city, its main avenue winding through each district in a haphazard pattern. The once boisterous crowds had faded away with the exception of a few stragglers who contented themselves to walk alongside the band of men.

"Has your people's excitement worn off already?"

Jonrell recognized Kaz's deep voice masked in broken Cadonian. "Perhaps. More likely they've heard of Tomalt's attack on Namaris and their optimism wanes."

Kaz grunted. "A fickle people."

"They've been given little reason over the years to be anything but that. Hopefully, we can help my sister change their view." When Kaz did not respond, Jonrell looked over to him. Through narrowed yet distant eyes, the warrior stared at a large cathedral, sunlight bouncing off of its bright, stained-glass windows. Jonrell recognized the look. Something sparked within Kaz's memory.

Upon passing the building with intricate stonework, Kaz shook his head and rubbed his eyes. Jonrell waited.

"The patterns built into the walls are very familiar," Kaz said.

"How so?"

His hand moved from his eyes to the goatee at his chin where it rested while trying to recall his thoughts. "It's very odd to remember this way. I'm not sure what I can trust as being real or if my mind is making these things up."

"Just take your time. Don't force it."

"Tell me about that building we just passed. We passed others similar in appearance today. What are they?"

"Cathedrals. Places we go to worship our god, the One Above."

"And they are all built the same?"

"More or less. It gives people comfort to have a familiar place during their travels."

The warrior worked the space between his bottom lip and chin, massaging the area with force. "As a boy, I helped build places like that."

"A place of worship?"

Kaz shook his head. "I don't think so. I don't know any gods from my past." He paused. "But those symbols built into the stonework.... There were buildings lined up, one after the other in patterns of blue, far more detailed than those we just passed."

Jonrell was confused. "Did you design the buildings?"

"No. I just helped build them. I think it was part of my training. The labor acted as a form of conditioning." He shook his head. "Sometimes I see these memories as an outsider would, watching myself move about. At other times, it's like I'm reliving the memory. This was one of those times. I was a boy and I was with many others near my age. I felt the chisel in my hand and the vibrations from the hammer shooting up my arm as I formed the stone block. I felt the sweat bead on my forehead as I lifted the stone into place and smelled the mortar as I joined that stone to the others."

"Were you building a large city?"

Kaz looked to either side of him, then turned in his saddle. "Not like this. At least not then. But I did see a brief glimpse of something bigger and more grand much later. It was like the end result of years of work, yet it was still growing."

"And you were still working on the city?"

"Maybe, I'm not sure. I was much older then. I do remember watching hundreds of others working, though many were not warriors."

"Interesting."

"Yes. But it still tells me so little new of my past," he said, frustrated. "I was a warrior whose life seemed to revolve around fighting."

"At least it's something."

"But it's as if that's all I ever was."

Jonrell opened his mouth to respond but closed it upon sight of Lady Jaendora reaching the city's gates. He slapped Kaz on the shoulder. "I'm sorry. We'll talk more on this later."

Kaz nodded in the gate's direction. "Go."

The commander clicked the reins of his horse. *A city of blue and larger than Floroson? And from what I can guess has grown quickly over the past twenty years. I have never heard of such a place.* He considered his extensive travels and, more so, his extensive study of the world of Hyron under Amcaro. Then he found his thoughts taking a turn to the more skeptical. *Could he truly be making all this up? If so, he's a great actor.* A scarier thought struck him then. *Could the blow to his head have damaged his brain permanently? Could he end up crazy?* He looked back at Kaz who was feeling the grooves in the wall of a tanner's shop, concentration lining his face. *No. I will not condemn a man who has given me no cause to do so and has become a friend. The others will come around. I know it.*

* * *

Lady Jaendora forced a smile as Jonrell came up beside her, the stress from Tomalt's attack still obviously fresh on her mind. She had led the way through Floroson, continuing to send messengers throughout the journey. "Lord Undalain would be proud of you, My Lady," said the commander.

The comment took the governess off guard as she leaned back in the saddle, raising an eyebrow. "How so?"

"I've watched you at times during our passage through the city. A word or simple gesture from you seemed to put the masses at ease. They love and respect you. I remember your husband was held in similar regard. I always admired that about him."

She smiled. "Thank you. Undalain was always mindful of the people. I try to be the same. It was something he and I both learned from your grandfather. A good king and an even better man, he deserves the credit."

"I wish I could have known him. He seems like someone I would have gotten along with."

"Your father was at one time very much like his father."

"So, I've heard. Yet, I never knew that man," said Jonrell bitterly.

"Just so," said Jaendora. "You do remind me of your grandfather."

Jonrell raised an eyebrow. "Really?"

"Yes. When you weren't watching me, I was watching you," she said. "I can see the way your men treat you. They would lay down their lives for you without pause. It takes a rare man to command such loyalty. Your grandfather also had such effortless skill and would be proud of the man you've become." She paused and nodded toward Kaz. "I must say I've never seen anyone like the black man you were just speaking with. I can tell his friendship is important to you. Though by the behavior of others around him, it seems many do not share your opinion. Why is that?"

The commander shrugged. "His complexion, the way he carries himself, his unmatched skill, a mysterious past."

"Yet he is made to feel as important as the rest?"

"Because he is. I look at the man underneath. And all of my soldiers are important whether they know it or not. Otherwise, they wouldn't be under my command."

"As I said, much like your grandfather."

Jonrell let out a small sigh. "Thank you. I just hope Elyse sees me in such a way."

Jaendora frowned.

"What's wrong?"

"What you said about your sister. Jonrell, she will be angry with you, with good cause and especially at first. You hurt a lot of people by leaving. Undalain and I were heartbroken, as were countless others, noble and common. But you were young and never saw that." She hesitated as if trying to find the words. "You know, after you ran off, your father would not allow Elyse to stay with us any longer for visits. And then as Undalain's health declined, we weren't able to travel to Lyrosene as often to visit her. When he passed away, I tried to reach out to her again but she had isolated herself from most everyone. I think she was afraid to let anyone in again," said Jaendora, her voice filled with regret.

Jonrell remained silent.

Lady Jaendora cleared her throat. "I know that isn't what you wanted to hear right now, but I needed to say it so I can forgive you. But there, it's done."

She reached out and touched his hand, causing him to meet her moist eyes. "I know it is all true. I don't know what I can say to that. Only that I'm sorry and I won't let you down again," said Jonrell.

She cleared her throat. "I know you won't, My Prince. I can see that. However, others may not be as understanding at first. Elyse most of all."

Jonrell nodded.

"Well, then," said the governess, removing her hand and placing it on her saddle, "enough of that. I think we should discuss this business of Tomalt. What would My Prince have me do?"

Jonrell chuckled at the sudden change in conversation. "Well, I'm afraid I haven't conferred with the queen just yet on the matter. However, I do have several suggestions that I believe she would find most agreeable. As a matter of fact," he said, reaching into his pocket and pulling out a rolled piece of parchment, "I have a certain letter I believe you should have."

Jaendora accepted the letter and began reading its contents. She nodded.

"That is for your eyes only. Make the preparations as outlined there, but tell no one about its intent. I'll contact you when the pieces are in place."

"And in the meantime?"

"Do whatever you have to in order to prevent Tomalt from raising a blockade. I convinced Sylik, the captain of *Ocean Spirit*, to stick around and aid you in any way. I know he doesn't look like those you'd normally employ, but I've never seen a better captain. Utilize him any way you see fit, the more impossible the job, the better with him. He likes money but deep down, I think it's the challenge that excites him."

"It will be done."

Just then several wagons rolled into view from a side alley, trailing several dozen warhorses. "Ah, here they are," said Jaendora.

Jonrell raised an eyebrow. "What's this?"

"A governess must learn to multi-task as well," she said, smiling once again. "It's not a lot, but it's the best I could muster on such short notice for your journey to Lyrosene. The horses may be the most important of all, I'm afraid. You'll find that your father let many things fall to the wayside in his later years. Maintaining a proper cavalry was one of them. I only wish I could offer more."

"You've done more than enough." He leaned over, and kissed her on the cheek. "Thank you, My Lady."

She touched her cheek.

He slipped away quickly as her eyes welled once again and a faint smile trembled at her lips.

CHAPTER 18

Strapped tight on his back against the hard wooden table, Tobin tightened his hands into fists. Sweat beaded on his skin and his nostrils flared with each rapid intake of air. He gripped a dowel of wood between his teeth.

He hoped for a hint at what was happening beyond his vision, but saw nothing. A face appeared before him, hooded in blue and red. It smiled, though the gesture brought little comfort. "I'm sorry," it said, casting a glance toward Tobin's ankle. "But it must be this way."

Sudden movement caught his attention. Torchlight bounced off the head of a large hammer, looming high. Tobin thought he heard voices talking, but the pounding of his heart drowned out any coherency to those words. His eyes widened as the hammer dropped out of sight. He never saw the impact. He only felt it. The dowel snapped in his mouth and he let out a terrible scream. Pain shot up his leg and then into the rest of his body. His mouth filled with bile and his eyes with water. He choked on that scream as the world around him turned black...

* * *

Tobin awoke with a start and gasped for air. He sat up and wiped sweat from his brow, trying to calm himself. A figure stood several paces away. He blinked away the remaining sleep. "What time is it?"

"Near midnight. We've dropped anchor and preparations have started." Nachun paused. "I was able to keep the others from hearing your screams."

Tobin stood up and began dressing without looking at the shaman. "Thank you."

"Was it the same dream?"

"Yes."

"What are you going to do after leaving the ship?"

"I'll be alright. Now that we're here, I think my mind will be focused on meeting with Mawkuk."

"If you would let me come..."

"No, you were right earlier. I need to do this alone so I can prove to my father and to the other Kifzo that they can have confidence in me as

233

warleader. Besides, I don't want Mawkuk recognizing you from when your family traveled through here before."

Nachun tilted his head. "Actually, my father approached Mawkuk alone when we petitioned the Gray Marsh Clan. I had remained behind with my family in order to protect them in case he failed to return. Mawkuk does not know my face."

Tobin grunted. "Regardless, it's best for you to stay with the ship."

The shaman extended his hand. "Then I wish you luck."

Tobin slung his bow and a quiver of arrows over his shoulder. "Let's hope I don't need it," he said, clasping Nachun's hand.

And let's hope I don't regret having you stay, my friend.

* * *

Leaving the Gulf of Eurinul, the Kifzo entered the Gray Marshes through the Dylis River. The river branched off in several directions and they used many of these tributaries and adjacent canals as they worked toward their destination. Alternating shifts, moving day and night, they wove their skiffs through the maze of muddy waterways in order to reach Cypronya. Travel was slow as the maps used to plan their route did not take into account every twist and turn.

Tobin woke at the slightest touch from Walor on the early morning of their fifth day in the swamps. The sun had yet to rise, but the black night had softened to a light gray. Other Kifzo stirred in their boats as well. They spotted lit torches inside what looked to be a small inlet. Impossible to judge from such a distance, the torches appeared to surround several larger campfires burning bright despite the coming night. Without that glow bouncing off the water's surface, access to the canal they sought would have been more difficult to spot. Large cypress trees stood with branches hanging low, and moss hanging lower, on either side of the waterway. They cast an ominous shadow as the party ducked under them.

Even at midday, I think this place would be difficult to find.

Tobin stood at the bow of the lead boat with his arms raised out to his sides, his chest exposed in the Heshan sign of peace. A voice called out from shore and Tobin saw a clansman from the Gray Marsh Clan urging the Kifzo onward. Tobin lowered his arms and gave commands to follow their guide.

Well, at least it looks like they aren't going to kill us right away.

As they continued on down the canal, the passage broadened, exposing the entrance to a city most travelers would not have expected to find in such an isolated area. *Father's spies outdid themselves in discovering this place. But their description does not do the place justice.*

Several types of watercraft were moored at the docks. Most flatter and better suited for navigating many of the swamp's shallow canals than the

Kifzo boats. Nets, traps, and rods adorned the sides of the fishing vessels. Tobin realized that like the Blue Island Clan, the Gray Marsh Clan depended greatly on the sustenance they found in their waters.

But our similarities stop there.

He looked down at the stagnant murkiness and grunted. The water here was thick and still, a stark contrast from the clear, moving ocean he had always known. He inhaled deeply, nearly choking on the foul odor.

There is nothing as awful as the air here. It is something I hope to never grow accustomed to.

Stepping ashore, Tobin turned his gaze toward Cypronya. Looking back only to ensure the others were following, he pursued their guide who had made no effort to slow down or speak. Tobin was sure he should take offense to such a move, and he knew Kaz and his father would have.

The city slowly exposed itself in detail as the first rays of sunlight pushed away the soft veil of gray covering the landscape. The architecture was unusual in comparison to other cities and villages he had visited. Massive trunks of giant cypress trees constituted Cypronya's foundation. Thick branches provided the city's framework for buildings constructed high above the ground. Walkways of rope and wood connected the city above, just as sidestreets separated the main thoroughfares of Juanoq. Few structures stood at ground level and those sat atop poles sunk into the ground. Tobin thought the design peculiar.

The guide turned back and grunted. "You will walk only where I walk."

Tobin nodded.

Footsteps sounded from behind, softly padding the matted reeds covering the path. "How's your ankle?" asked Walor.

"It's fine," said Tobin, pausing briefly. The journey south provided Tobin more than enough time to grow accustomed to the full use of that leg.

"Come," the guide called out impatiently. He walked faster than before in contempt.

Tobin spared a glance back at Walor.

"I like them already," Walor said, smiling, cracking his neck with a sharp twist.

Tobin grunted and set off down the trail.

As the sun peaked over the horizon, Cypronya continued to impress. Craning his neck to look at the massive trees, he saw the first glimmers of movement on the open decks and swaying walkways. The city itself was deep, an alley with no visible end in sight.

The rows of trees are so straight it seems like someone carefully planted each one by hand.

Their guide stopped in front of a large bonfire with flames slowly dying. Wisps of smoke danced through the air. On the other side of the fire sat an old and frail man on a throne erected from driftwood. The throne was pieced together haphazardly and carved into the images of hideous beasts foreign to the Kifzo. The man's wrinkled eyes narrowed as the guide whispered in his ear.

Men and women stood on either side of the throne. The servants could only be distinguished from the man's advisers by studying their mannerisms. The old man shifted in his seat of moss and pulled away from the guide.

The old man cleared his throat and leaned forward. "You're late."

That was not what I had expected to hear. "I did not realize I had an appointment, Mawkuk, Leader of the Gray Marsh Clan." He bowed as a sign of respect. "I am Tobin, Warleader of the Blue Island Clan, son of El Olam, our ruler."

Mawkuk nodded in acknowledgement. "You had an appointment the day your boats reached our lands." His tone was accusatory.

"We have good reason for our visit," he replied.

"Good reason? We may be isolated here among the swamps and the other clans may look down on us, but we have not been deaf to the dealings of your people." He shook his head and chuckled. "El Olam? Is that what he calls himself now? Full of arrogance, your father. He is proud to have united the Blue Clan through the spilling of his own people's blood, isn't he? No matter that I, and others, found more peaceful solutions to rule." He paused. "But that wasn't enough for him, was it? He claimed the Orange Desert Clan as his own and enslaved many of those he'd conquered. A clan that was once considered the weakest in all of Hesh, slowly becomes one of the strongest." He paused again, before continuing in a patronizing tone. "I must say that I find it interesting for a man with such success to approach me not once, but twice now. What could we offer someone so much greater than ourselves?"

"Maybe this isn't the best of places to discuss such matters," said Tobin, aware of all the eyes on him. "Perhaps there is a more private setting to continue our conversation?"

"No. Here is where we will discuss whatever it is you would bring before me and my people. But now isn't the time. I am both tired and hungry. We shall continue this when I am ready."

"I was looking to conclude matters quickly. El Olam is awaiting our return."

"Your father can wait. You are on our lands and before my throne. Not his."

Tobin opened his mouth to respond but Mawkuk raised a hand and spoke to the guide. "See these men to our guest quarters and provide them with food and drink. They've had a long journey."

Tobin's jaw clenched to bite back his anger. *Father would have exploded at such an insult, but I will do this my way.*

He bowed.

* * *

The same guide, who had brought them into the city, led them to a large wooden cage resting on the ground beneath a colossal cypress tree. Tied to the cage was a thick rope that stretched toward the sky. Their guide said nothing as the twelve Kifzo warriors followed him into the cage. The guide gave two short tugs to a smaller rope inside the cage. They ascended, swinging to and fro.

Tobin watched Mawkuk leave his throne. Several women led him to a smaller cage further away. Gazing down from such a height caused him to break out in a cold sweat. He distracted himself by turning his attention to the dwellings they passed during their ascent.

The cage stopped at the top of the cypress. Tobin saw the enormous pulley the rope was set to and the locking wheel system used to lift and lower the wooden cage. A handful of men worked the system with apparent ease, despite the weight from the men the cage held.

The guide led them across a long and narrow walkway where they entered a large single room. Wooden pallets covered in straw lined the room's walls. A wooden table, filled with various food and drink stood in the room's center.

They were more than ready for our visit it seems.

Tobin addressed the guide. "When will Mawkuk call for us?"

"When he is ready," said the guide, closing the door.

From a small window, Tobin watched him cross the walkway and hop back into the cage before it was lowered. Shortly after, the cage returned and half a dozen men joined those already near the wheel system. Though they tried to conceal it, they were each warriors, weapons hidden beneath loose clothing.

"Looks like they don't trust us very much," said Walor, looking out an adjacent window.

"Why should they?" asked Tobin with a shrug. "My father is not making a name for himself by being a peaceful man."

"So then what do we do?" asked Walor, moving away from the window.

"We wait." Tobin gestured toward the table. "And for now we eat and get some rest. Same shifts as before, day and night."

A man hissed at the comment, snatching a leg of some roasted bird from the table, collapsing onto a pallet.

"Do you have something to say, Ufer?"

The assassin grunted, biting into the leg with a savage, ripping motion. "I need not say anything. We saw with our own eyes how you would lead us, *Warleader.*"

The disgust in Ufer's voice made Tobin's skin crawl. The way he said it reminded him of the way Kaz called him brother. *Kaz would have given them*

blood, even if it meant our eventual deaths. He remained calm, speaking in an even voice. "That's right. You saw exactly what was meant to be seen."

The dissatisfied looks of his men turned to confused ones. Tobin ignored them all, including Walor's. He returned back to the window and continued his watch.

* * *

Two days had passed since the Kifzo's arrival and yet Tobin still waited for Mawkuk to summon him. For all outward appearances they were being treated as guests, staying in reasonable quarters and their basic needs cared for. Different servants changed waste pails and provided food and drink. Tobin had yet to see the same one twice. He tried to ask them questions on the first day, but quit after he realized their ramblings were a waste of time and full of misinformation. Tobin took to ignoring them.

Late that afternoon three new servants entered with their meal. He found himself gaping at one in particular. *She looks like Lucia, only younger.*

As the servants set about their duties, he tried to distract himself with the constant activity on the dizzying walkways, watching people scurry about like squirrels bouncing from branch to branch. Yet, his eyes kept drifting back to the center of the room, watching the young woman lay out fresh food on the large table. His last glance told him that he wasn't the only one to notice her beauty as several other Kifzo stared at her with devilish eyes. He grew angry at the thought, knowing that many of those warriors would be quick to rape the woman had they been here conquering the city rather than seeking an alliance.

And even then, the hunger in their eyes makes me wonder how well they will control themselves.

Only after the door closed and the servants vanished out of his sight, did Tobin push himself off the wall and help himself to the food. He grabbed a half loaf of bread and some water, and then returned to his spot near the window. The rest of the Kifzo settled on their pallets, eating in relative silence. Tension filled the room.

Tobin was not blind to his men's growing displeasure, though Ufer had been the only one to voice his opinions. The way each warrior moved, the looks they gave him, the faint whispers when they thought he slept was enough to show Tobin that they blamed him for their current situation. He wondered how long their patience with him would last.

Would they dare defy me here and now?

The sound of rain falling from the surrounding tree branches onto the slated roof distracted Tobin from those grim thoughts. His eyes caught the quickened pace of the people below as they ran for cover. Watching others struggle to maintain their composure while being struck from every possible direction brought him a brief moment of satisfaction. He lost count the number of times he had felt as they did.

He stood there for some time, motionless, until dusk came.

Walor relieved his watch some time later and Tobin saw the strain in the scout's face when doing so. "Do you question my decision then, too?" Tobin whispered out of earshot of the others.

Walor sighed. "Question? Yes."

Tobin grunted. "What would *you* have me do then?"

"It isn't for me to say. You are warleader now, not me. I don't understand what you're doing. Your approach is so different than your brother's. But I do trust that you have your reasons."

"And the others?"

"The others do not share my confidence."

"How long do I have?"

Walor shrugged. "No telling." He paused. "Two against ten. The odds would not be in our favor."

Tobin met Walor's eyes and nodded. Nothing more needed to be said.

I'm glad that I brought him with me. I wonder if it was a mistake to have left Nachun behind after all.

Tobin lay down in his pallet and tried to relax in the quiet night. Sleep evaded him.

* * *

Eventually sleep did come, though Tobin could not say when. He knew this only when he awoke with a start late in the night. A sound caused him to jump and his hand moved toward one of his concealed daggers to prepare for the mutiny he was sure to be upon him. Walor stood in the door, speaking softly to a messenger.

Tobin got up and introduced himself to a young boy whose dress consisted of pelts from the giant nutria that inhabited the swamps.

"Tobin, Warleader of the Blue Island Clan, I greet you. Mawkuk, Ruler of the Gray Marsh Clan seeks an audience with you and your men this night," the boy said in a quivering voice, barely above a whisper.

The messenger had not looked up to meet their eyes and Tobin saw the trembling in the boy's limbs as he awaited a response. "Take us."

Riding in the cage at night was a far different experience than during the day. Rather than searching the trees and taking in the city's details, they focused on the ground below where torches and fires burned bright. Despite the time of night, half of Cypronya looked to be up, crowding around the fires and awaiting the outcome of the anticipated exchange.

The Kifzo were led to the center fire, where Mawkuk sat upon his contorted throne. Shadows danced off his thin frame, giving him the appearance of a corpse.

When all were settled, Mawkuk gave a slight bow which Tobin returned. "I am ready to speak to you about our terms."

"Terms?" said Tobin confused. "I was under the impression that terms had been discussed previously."

Mawkuk waved a hand. "You would be wrong."

There was a hiss from behind that Tobin knew came from Ufer. He ignored it. *I will not let him provoke me now.* He stood motionless with his arms crossed in front and eyes focused on the Gray Clan's ruler.

Mawkuk continued. "Our people have always been looked down upon by the other clans of Hesh just as your people once were. So when Bazraki used his Kifzo warriors to unite the Blue Island Clan, we took notice. Other clans dismissed his actions despite the tales of your warriors' skill in battle. I became intrigued and monitored Bazraki's subsequent actions with keen interest.

"We watched the construction and fortification of Juanoq that made it a city almost impenetrable from invaders. We watched him absorb several of the smaller nomadic tribes into his own. I see what Bazraki intends for the future.

"Your brother came to us, offering *terms,*" said Mawkuk. "He claimed such an offer was an alliance, but those terms seemed hardly fair. And so we waited to give our answer, eager to see just how powerful the Blue Clan had become.

"Then we heard of your father's conquest of the Orange Desert Clan. How he acquired the talents of a shaman whose powers are said to be unmatched in all of Hesh. It is also said this shaman has learned secrets from the old ways and created new weapons for your father."

"I fail to see your point." said Tobin.

"It sets the stage, if you will, for the reason you're here now," Mawkuk said with a knowing grin. "Despite all the advantages the Blue Clan has acquired, your numbers are still lower than the other clans. Folding in warriors of the Orange Clan did not completely solve this problem since their casualties were so great."

"And?" asked Tobin.

Mawkuk snorted. "Very well. My point is that you are here for our answer to those pitiful terms your father offered us. Your father would have us fight for him and help him conquer Hesh while in return we receive what? A fraction of the spoils? A small portion of land?" He paused and smiled. "Bazraki needs us, but we do not need him. No one bothers us here—our land is next to useless. We could live here as we always have and be content.

Your father, on the other hand, needs greater numbers if he is not only to conquer, but also occupy the rest of Hesh."

"It is as you say," said Tobin with a shrug.

"Good. Then I think it only fitting for him to meet our terms rather than the other way around."

"And what are those terms?" asked Tobin, his patience starting to crack. Another hiss of displeasure from behind caught his ear.

"Nothing too grand, I assure you. We simply divide Hesh down the middle. Your father would keep his land, of course, along with what he took from the Orange Desert Clan. We would then help him overthrow the Yellow Plain Clan and in turn, he will help us with the Green Forest Clan and the Red Mountain Clan which I will rule over. Very reasonable, don't you think?"

"And the White Tundra Clan?" said Tobin, trying to appear indifferent.

Mawkuk waved a hand. "Let them be, I say. Their land is even less desirable than our own."

"No argument here."

"Then you will convey my terms to Bazraki?" asked Mawkuk.

"Actually, I have been given leave to speak on my father's behalf," said Tobin in a smug tone. "I would think we could work out the details here and now.

"Tobin, please. You mustn't make this deal. El Olam...," said a small whisper from behind.

Tobin quickly whipped around. "El Olam is not here, Walor. As warleader I speak with his voice, not you." Walor noticeably flinched back at the brush remark. Tobin met the eyes of several other of his Kifzo. "Nor does any anyone else." He turned back, the piercing hatred of his warriors' eyes traded for the greed in Mawkuk's eyes.

"Excellent," said Mawkuk, grinning ear to ear. "Then we have a deal?"

"Wouldn't you like to hear my father's terms again?"

"Seems like a waste of time."

"I don't think so."

Mawkuk chuckled in a raspy voice. "Very well."

Tobin nodded. "Yes, my father is looking to make use of your warriors. In return, he would be willing to give you one third of all spoils. Of course, he must have first choice." Mawkuk let out a snort which Tobin ignored. "Second, he would extend your lands by half into those lands currently held by the Yellow Plain Clan. You would still be required to pay tribute each year to him as will each of the other clans. However, if your men prove themselves worthy on the battlefield, I think he would be willing to reduce the tribute required of the Gray Marsh Clan."

Mawkuk laughed deep and long, nearly choking. "Obviously, I must refuse your father's terms."

"I thought you might say that."

"So then we are agreed that my terms are fairer?"

"Fairer? Possibly. Acceptable? No. Your terms are an insult."

Mawkuk's face grew dark. "An insult? You dare talk to me like that in front of my people? We've given you every courtesy and treated you hospitably!"

"How did you treat us hospitably? You kept us up high in your trees, where we were guarded by poorly disguised warriors. You made us wait, to wear us down. Now, you make ridiculous demands without even the simple respect of hearing our terms first. Then you *dare* speak to me as some servant in front of *my warriors*," said Tobin seething.

Mawkuk's eyes widened at the sudden change in tone. "So, the son thinks he can intimidate me as well as his father? You can tell Bazraki there will be no alliance and he will have to be content with the land he already has."

Tobin started to laugh. He noticed Mawkuk's men shift nervously, tightening the grip of their weapons as he did so. "For a man who claims to know so much about my people, you sorely misjudge my father. He would ignore everything else he had planned to bring his full might upon this treehouse you call a city. Even if it set him back years, he would destroy you."

Mawkuk laughed back. "You talk brazenly for a man with only eleven others watching your back. I've heard the tales of your brother's fierceness on the battlefield. I've seen firsthand the savagery behind his eyes. I see little of that from you." His leaned forward. "You are not your brother," he said in a condescending tone.

Tobin seethed. *It always comes back to Kaz.*

Mawkuk waved a hand. "We are done." He paused and looked at his men. "See them to their boats. But if our guests give you any trouble, kill them."

Tobin snarled as a man near his right stepped forward. "Enough!" He moved in a blur, pulling free two daggers. The throws landed where intended. *Let's see if my men understand the gesture.*

He rolled under the lunging marsh warrior and reached over his shoulder for another concealed blade. In less than two long strides, he was at Mawkuk's throne, the dagger's point resting on the skin just below his sunken left eye. "Everyone stand down or he dies," Tobin snarled.

The Gray Marsh warriors halted. After a moment, one chanced a step and Tobin pushed the tip of his blade into Mawkuk's skin, just enough for a single bloody tear to run down his cheek.

"Stop!" the ruler screamed, his voice cracking. The warrior froze.

A strong stench filled Tobin's nostrils as Mawkuk relieved himself. Tobin spared a glance toward his own surprised men. *Good, they understood me.*

Several Kifzo crowded around the two daggers he had thrown in the dirt. They understood the targets Tobin marked and knew not to harm them without his command.

After a moment he spoke, eyes glaring at the frail old man. "You are right. I am not my brother. Kaz would have long ago lost his temper at your endless slights. He would have killed you before your warriors could have stopped him." He grinned. "Even now, I could do the same. But I see little value in that.

"For all your talk, you cannot hide your fear of the Blue Island Clan. Isn't that why you would only meet with us in front of your people? Little good that did you," he said grinning wider. He gestured with a tilt of his head toward the two people his daggers had marked. "It's also why you dressed your daughter and son as servants and mixed them with the others waiting on you. You assumed you could hide such things from me." Tobin leaned in close, his voice barely a whisper as he slightly twisted the point of his dagger, drawing forth more blood. "But I know things. I know they are your weakness. You see, my father has spies too and they are much better than yours. I could have killed them. I threw my blades at their feet to let you know how helpless you really are." He leaned in even closer. "So tell me. Do you see the same savagery in my eyes that you saw in my brother's?"

Mawkuk trembled, he wheezed with each intake of breath. "What must I do?" he finally rasped. "I will accept your father's terms then."

Tobin clicked his tongue. "I'm afraid I can't do that. Those terms were meant for someone who would help our cause willingly. Things have changed. No, rather than one third of the spoils, you will be rewarded with one fifth instead."

Mawkuk's eyes shot down to the blade at his face. "Agreed," he said with a quick intake of breath.

"Good. And since you've proven that we cannot trust you, your children will be coming with us."

"No! Wait, I…"

"You had your chance. Don't worry. As you said, I am not my brother. I promise you they will stay safe as long as you uphold your end of our deal. Betray us in any way, and I will see that they suffer in ways you can't even imagine."

Mawkuk noticeably sunk in on himself, seeming even more frail as Tobin pulled back the knife from his face. "I will not betray our deal," he said. A heavy sadness filled his voice as he eyed his children.

"Good. Tell your people to clear a path for us."

Mawkuk straightened in his throne, trying to appear more authoritative. "The Blue Clan will not be harmed. Anyone caught doing so will face not only their own execution but that of their family's," Mawkuk shouted, his voice growing stern once again.

The people reluctantly parted as the anger and confusion upon their faces slowly turned into despair.

Tobin suppressed a smile. *A better deal without any bloodshed.* He looked down at his dagger and then to Mawkuk's face. *Well, maybe a little. Kaz could not have done this, and neither could my father.*

"Walk with me down to our vessels. You and your warchiefs. We will discuss what is expected of you, and when it is expected to be carried out."

Mawkuk nodded, eyes never leaving his children's faces.

* * *

Bathed in moonlight, Tobin moved one foot in front of the other. He shuffled backward and then hopped forward. The sword in his hand slashed, stabbed, and spun while he teetered on the narrow railing of the ship. His balance was improving, though it was taking him longer than he liked to relearn proper technique with two strong legs beneath him. Three quick steps and then a front flip. Landing softly on the ship's deck, he sheathed his sword.

"After coming in so late this evening, I thought even you would have tried to catch up on rest," said a voice from behind.

Tobin spun around. "You know I don't sleep well. Besides, it's the first real chance I've had in some days to go through my forms uninterrupted."

Nachun looked down. "And the ankle?"

"I know it is as strong as it once was but I still find myself favoring it out of habit."

"It'll come. I can already tell a difference in the way you move." He paused. "That means your body is becoming more accustomed to the change."

Tobin raised an eyebrow, glancing around at the clear star-filled sky. "So, you stayed up to check in on my ankle?"

Nachun smiled. "Not exactly. I haven't had a chance to speak with you in private about what happened with Mawkuk. Walor filled me in, though, and said that you surprised even him on how you handled yourself."

Tobin walked over to a skin of water and drank deep. "I hope he isn't angry with me for keeping my plans from him. I haven't been able to talk to him about it."

Nachun shook his head. "I think he understands. You were wise in not telling anyone. Your men are looking at you differently now?"

Tobin nodded. "I'm not sure how much of it is respect."

"Some, I'm sure. But respect will come with time. What I'm talking about is that look of uncertainty in their eyes. I can see it, so I know you can too. Even after all the years together with your men, they only cared enough about you to know what Kaz told them. Now, they are second-guessing that. They wonder who you really are, and they're going to compare you to Kaz even more until they realize you are his better."

Tobin spat and balled his hands into fists. "The hunger he had for death and destruction I do not share. I did things…but only when I had to."

"In time, you'll be able to right some of those wrongs and you'll have my help in doing so. But you can't expect to do it all at once." He paused. "I also heard from Walor about what happened with Mawkuk's daughter."

Tobin nodded. "On our first night out of Cypronya, I had to stop a warrior who thought to force himself on her." *And I had to refrain myself from killing the man because she reminds me so much of Lucia.*

"Walor said the others backed you up there. Isn't that a start in the right direction?"

Tobin shrugged. "They heard me give my word to Mawkuk. That and Odala's station make her case different than raping some peasant. I doubt they would have seen my point if we were raiding a village like Munai."

"Eventually, I think they will. Use the time on our trip back to improve your relationship with those here. Once these are on your side, you'll have help in swaying the others at home."

Tobin grinned. "Since you seem to have all the answers, how am I to do that?"

Nachun shrugged. "Fight. Train. Joke. I don't know. I did not grow up with these men. You did. Even if they don't know the real you, it seems like you know the real them."

I do know the real them and that's the problem. I probably like them less than they like me.

* * *

The first thing Tobin noticed as the ship pulled into Juanoq's docks was the progress made in the shipyard. Workers swarmed around Nachun's creations. Those massive vessels, some capable of holding hundreds of warriors, according to the shaman, dwarfed the smaller ship Tobin was on.

At such a pace, Nachun will far exceed his timeline of completion. Tobin wondered how quickly captains could be trained to pilot such vessels, and how soon they could be put to use. *For Father, probably not soon enough.*

"The shaman surprises us once again, Warleader. I wonder how someone can know so much," said Ufer walking up beside him. He matched Tobin's gaze on the nearest ship with three masts looming high overhead. Workers dangled from various pieces of rigging and swung precariously in the cool breeze coming off the water. "It seems unusual."

"He is an intelligent man. One who's learned a lot from the old ways."

"So he says. Yet, I find it odd that he's so much better at understanding the old ways than anyone else. He has not been the only intelligent man in Hesh since crossing The Great Divide. Others have attempted to study those texts for centuries."

Tobin turned, not liking the accusatory tone in Ufer's voice. "He is our ally," careful not to call Nachun friend. "What has he done to show us otherwise?"

"Perhaps there isn't one specific instance, but his behavior does not seem right to me. Even in Munai, how he came upon us, and then was later accepted so quickly by El Olam. Kaz felt unease about him too. He wanted Nachun dead."

"Yes, he did, and without ever knowing him. And if we had listened to my brother we wouldn't have had the weapons and armor we now wear, would we?" he said gesturing to the sword at Ufer's hip. "Or these ships?" he added with a wave of his hand. "Or many other things, including the Kifzo lives he saved by using his sorcery in battle. I think it is safe to say that Kaz was wrong about Nachun."

Ufer shrugged. "As you say." And after a moment he added. "I'll grab the boy and girl. You will want them for your meeting with El Olam, I assume?"

"Yes." After Ufer turned his back and headed toward the hull, Tobin took a deep breath. He had found himself holding much of it in as his anger rose due to Ufer's voiced concerns. *The influence of my brother runs so deep.* Still, he felt that he had maintained his composure on the matter and for that he was pleased. The fact that Ufer came to him in such a way was a step in the right direction, and something that would not have happened even a week ago.

As Nachun said, it will take time.

* * *

Marching shoulder to shoulder, shield arms cleared a path along the busy dock as a half dozen of Bazraki's personal guards greeted Tobin as he stepped off the ship. Tobin noticed each of them was adorned in a deep blue breast plate. Gauntlets and shin guards were of a lighter hue.

I see everyone is making the most of our new armory.

Like all of his father's personal guards, they held an air of superiority, even toward Tobin, who officially outranked them. Rather than acknowledging him as warleader with a bow, their captain emphasized the need for haste in reporting back to El Olam. Tobin knew he should have used the opportunity to make a point to the captain that he was the guard's superior, but out of habit he let the moment pass and realized his error too late. He cursed to himself for the mistake.

They must learn to show me the same respect as they showed Kaz.

The group set off through the crowded streets of Juanoq surrounded by guards.

Tobin's eyes shifted to the boy and girl whose wrists had been chained together. The captain of the guard hurried them along at a steady pace.

Despite the small ship, he had spent little time talking to Mawkuk's children on the journey home. Each seemed far too young to be the children of someone as old as the shriveled Gray Clan leader. Soyjid was sixteen but looked younger as he was cursed with the same small, thin frame as his father. His attitude had surprised Tobin during the little time he had spent with him. He had never once been intimidated by the situation or his captors. Even now, his head swiveled around with wide eyes that took in the sights.

In contrast to her brother, Odala, walked with her head down and shoulders hunched forward. She seemed more cognizant of her situation. Tobin ventured that she must have resembled her mother as her soft face and shapely figure contrasted the appearance of her father. Though she lacked the strength and confidence at seventeen that Tobin had admired in Lucia, he was amazed at how much Odala favored his brother's wife. The guilt he felt at the thoughts that raced through his mind was the main reason he had avoided the two captives.

Bazraki waited for them in the upstairs dining hall where he sat alone at the head of the table eating from plates of baked fish, roasted fowl, and steamed vegetables. His father stayed seated as the group entered. The guards announced their arrival and then quickly left.

An uncomfortable silence hung in the air as Bazraki's stare bore holes into Tobin. "I do not recall instructing you to take prisoners," he said in a hard voice.

"I have my reasons for doing so," said Tobin, trying to appear confident.

"Tell me."

Standing firm in place, with shoulders back, Tobin told him all that had occurred during the entire trip. By the time Tobin finished, Bazraki had completed his meal and stood before him.

"I see," said Bazraki, breaking his silence. "Your brother would have killed Mawkuk for such conduct. That would have been a wiser decision."

"I thought this would be a more effective method, Father."

A hand lashed out, slapping Tobin across the face. "El Olam," his father said. "Acting as warleader does not give you a pass on showing me respect. I will not remind you again." He continued. "So you think that you are wiser than I am."

"Of course not, El Olam," said Tobin in a low tone, trying to disguise the bitter anger rising in the back of his throat.

Bazraki grunted. "Maybe I should take part of the blame here for assuming too much from you. I am too used to thinking of Kaz as an extension of myself. You however, need more guidance."

Kaz again. Tobin felt his anger growing, the muscles in his arms tensing. A light touch on his arm calmed him though. Nachun stepped forward between father and son. "El Olam, let us not forget that an alliance was made between the clans and by lesser terms than you intended," said the shaman.

"And to do so, we showed weakness by allowing Mawkuk to live." He paused and looked to Tobin. "Are you certain that we can trust him?"

Tobin gestured with his hand. "I promise you he will do nothing while we hold his children."

"Is this true?" asked Bazraki, his eyes piercing Odala.

Nachun nudged her with an elbow to get her to answer.

She jumped and croaked, "He cares for us deeply. He will not do anything that may cause us harm."

"Very well," his father said turning to Tobin. "We should learn soon enough if Mawkuk intends to uphold his end of the deal. Until then, they are your responsibility. We will talk again on the morrow after I've had time to think on what was said." He paused. "Kaz never took such liberties with my instructions. Going forward, I expect you to act as he would." And with a wave of his hand, Bazraki dismissed the group.

CHAPTER 19

Elyse knelt in the pew praying, her eyes fixed on the likeness of the One Above. The statue radiated the love and tenderness she longed for. Her neck, knotted up from the council's morning meeting, slowly relaxed, and the calmness she prayed for spread throughout her limbs like a warm bath over her skin.

Messengers confirmed several days ago that Jonrell had indeed landed at Floroson and traveled toward Lyrosene. The reports were initially questioned when it was discovered that he commanded a well known group of cutthroats that killed for money. Elyse shivered at the frightening thought. She could never imagine the brother she once knew doing such a thing, and she was reluctant to believe such reports. But Lady Jaendora had sent a personal message, sealed in wax, and baring her signet that confirmed many of the early details.

What are his motives in returning now?

She was surprised to realize that what she had always thought would provide her comfort now scared her. *What will he do when he arrives? Will he cast me aside and take the throne?* Despite all her hard work to be a good queen, the thought of relinquishing such responsibility appealed to her. *I think the first thing I would do is sleep for a week.* Her next thought took her off guard. *What if his rule is filled with blood, death, and oppression?*

Footsteps echoed across the great cathedral. She turned as Hadan and Willum approached, their giant shadows stretching across the polished floor. "My Queen, I'm sorry to interrupt your prayers," said Hadan.

Elyse stood. "I was just finishing up. What is it?"

"A messenger, Your Highness. Your brother was spotted down the road. It's expected that he will be here on the morrow."

A flutter of nervousness caught her in the stomach and she took a deep breath. "Does anyone else know about this?"

"Not yet, Your Highness."

An idea struck her. *I need to speak with him in private before anyone else does.* She started walking up the center aisle toward the large double doors, her long green gown twisting around her.

"My Queen, shall we send out a formal party to greet your brother?" asked Willum in his higher voice.

"No. Send a messenger to Gauge right away. Tell him he must meet me in my private study, but tell him nothing more. Send another messenger to General Grayer and have him do the same. But first, have him prepare his fastest and most trusted horseman for travel outside of the city. Do not tell him why."

"Yes, Your Highness," said Willum, armor clanking as he ran off. Hadan remained at her side as they exited the cathedral, making for her private study.

* * *

Gauge sat in the corner reading a book that discussed the legendary events surrounding the fall of Quoron while sipping on a small glass of brandy. Considering its lack of relevance to Elyse's current situation, the book had moved to the bottom of her reading list. Gauge selected the ancient tome several hours ago and had been engrossed ever since. He stopped only once to comment on a passage relating to the discovery of Sacrynon's Scepter during Aurnon the First's conquering of Thurum and settling of Cadonia.

Elyse dug her nails into her palm as Gauge had read aloud about the weapon's power, remarking on how such a force would quickly solidify her reign. Elyse felt sick remembering that day in the castle and the horrors caused by the scepter. Gauge had read the text like it was a new piece of information, once lost and newly discovered. It was as if he had forgotten what such a thing meant to Elyse. With an obvious lack of malicious intent, she could not bring herself to be angry at Gauge so she quickly changed the subject to something lighter.

Scribbling at the table in the center of the room, General Grayer busied himself preparing messages, counting supplies, and balancing the military's funds. Elyse had sent someone to retrieve his things once she realized that without doing so, her meeting would put the general far behind in his daily duties. After watching him work so diligently, she couldn't help but admire the man more.

He works so hard for a queen so incompetent.

Elyse marveled at each of the two men, jealous of their calm demeanors as she paced the room. Her feet began to throb after spending so much time pacing, but the constant movement eased her mind.

When Gauge and Grayer had first arrived after her summons, she informed them of her intentions and both aided her in crafting the invitation Grayer's messenger sent to Jonrell.

Hours later, while waiting for a response, Elyse's guilt began to gnaw at her for keeping the two men away from their duties. But she was too anxious, too nervous, to be alone.

I may need their knowledge before the night is through.

A sudden knock at the door caused her to spin around quickly, taking in a deep breath as her eyes went to the door. She glanced at Gauge who marked his place in the book and looked up. Grayer set his quill on the table and waited for Elyse's response as well. "Hadan?" she called out in the direction of the door.

"Yes, Your Highness. May I enter? I have a certain guest to see you," he answered back, the door muffling his voice.

She nervously straightened her dress, not sure what else to do in an effort to compose herself. "Please come in," she said, her voice quavering.

Willum stepped aside as Hadan came through the door, trailing a tall man in a large black cloak, hood pulled up over his head. The man reached up with both hands and pulled back the hood. His appearance took Elyse off guard.

Is this my brother?

His head was covered in the same auburn hair that she remembered from her childhood, though it had grown long. He wore a well-kept beard now, touched by the faintest patches of white, despite his age. She marveled at the weathered look on his face and studied the lines that led her to the man's gray eyes. She knew for certain it was indeed her brother.

His eyes used to comfort her as a girl, but now she only felt trepidation.

Elyse stood there staring and realized everyone was waiting for her to respond. Yet, she didn't know what to do. *Do I embrace the brother I once knew? Do I ask for homage from the tattered soldier before me?*

Almost as if Jonrell could read her thoughts, he bowed his head and took a knee. "My Queen."

She was stunned by the gesture, but also found herself angry as well. Gauge cleared his throat which caused Elyse to respond. "Everyone, please leave us for a moment. You can wait in the adjoining room."

"Your Highness?" said Hadan with a confused look on his face.

"You and Willum as well. I would speak to my brother in private first. I will call for you when I'm ready."

Hesitant, he exited the room last and shut the door behind them.

When Elyse turned back to her brother she saw him still on his knee, head staring at the floor. "What are you doing? Stand up," she said in an agitated tone.

"Yes, Your Highness," said Jonrell, rising.

"Stop that. There is no one else here for you to put up a visage for. Treat me like your sister," she said, starting to pace once again.

"I'm sorry."

She stopped. "Sorry?" She turned to face him. "What exactly are you sorry for?" she said in a bitter tone.

He gave her a wounded smile. "For everything. I made a mistake leaving you. I want to make up for that now."

"A mistake? Is that what you call it? I've lived in constant misery since you left! All alone with no one to talk to and a father who wouldn't let anyone near me. I could only watch him as he fell further into insanity." Tears started pouring out, smearing much of her make-up. Yet, she didn't care. "And just when I thought things couldn't get any worse, Nareash came along."

"I've heard how he manipulated Father and then killed half the palace staff."

"Don't act like you know what happened. He kept me trapped in my own body and didn't allow me to so much as bathe myself for months. It's a wonder I haven't lost my mind as well. I maintained my sanity by focusing my thoughts on a better time, a better place. Do you know when that was?"

"No. I don't."

"It was when I was with you!" she yelled. "I thought about how much you made me laugh and how much you loved me when I needed it. And I thought over and over about your promise. That you would return when I needed you most. I needed you most then, Jonrell," she paused, lowering her voice. "I've needed you in the months since then as I did everything I could think of to ensure Cadonia didn't go to war."

"Is that why you took the necklace off?" asked Jonrell in a hurt tone.

Elyse reached up to touch her neck and nodded. "After Father's funeral, I knew I was on my own and I figured it was time to stop acting like a little girl counting on a promise that would never be kept." She chuckled. "But now here you are," tears streamed down her face, "only it's too late. Tomalt has taken Namaris and we must go to war. I have failed. I guess I am just a little girl, after all, and not the ruler I've been pretending to be."

Her body shook as the tears flowed. She felt weak and her head throbbed. Dizziness began to take her. But she couldn't stop crying and she started to lose her balance.

Arms enveloped her with a familiar embrace and secured her tightly. She finally felt safe. After years of hoping and waiting, her brother had come home and Elyse's prayers were answered.

* * *

For nearly an hour they ignored the kingdom's turmoil and focused on each other instead. Considering the short amount of time and the years spent apart, Jonrell was surprised to see how well they reconnected. But when the conversation shifted back to the current state of Cadonia, the laughter and tears they shared ceased. They could not ignore their duties forever.

"I want you to know why I'm here before you send for your advisors," said Jonrell.

Elyse shrugged. "To take the throne, right? I admit, I wasn't sure what kind of man you'd become after hearing you were commanding a mercenary outfit. And don't think you've gotten away with not explaining that to me," she said. "But now that I have talked to you, I realize more than ever you're more suited for this role than I am. I mean, you were always so loved by the people when we were younger. I've never had that kind of support from even the nobles, let alone the commoners." She looked up. "Besides, you already know the things I should know."

Jonrell shook his head. "I don't want the throne. I never have."

"Neither have I." she said, exasperated.

"Maybe not. But once things settle, you'll be a far better ruler than I ever would be. I left when things got tough, but you've stuck it out. Even now you've sacrificed yourself for the kingdom's well being when you could've taken the easy way out. It takes someone like that to rule Cadonia."

Elyse threw her hands up. "But I'm not prepared. I've been running myself ragged just trying to read all the books you wanted me to read when I was a girl and never did, all while trying to keep up with the affairs of everyone and make decisions I have no business making. Tomalt has already taken one city. What's to stop him from taking another? Or to stop others from following his lead? That happened while I sat on the throne. And with war all around us, I'm the person least qualified to wear the crown. I feel like I'm hanging at the end of a rope that could snap at any moment."

Jonrell spoke in an even tone. "You're much smarter than you give yourself credit for. I'm here now to help you get through it. You can do this. You just lack the confidence."

Elyse turned away. "You know, I can step down as queen and reinstate you as heir. That's what everyone expects me to do. Besides, I read that Aurnon the Fourth's mother, Queen Anne, did just that when he tried to avoid the crown. So, I know there's precedent. Then you won't have any choice but to take the throne."

Jonrell raised an eyebrow. "Well, I can see you've gotten something out of those books after all."

"I'm serious."

"I am too," he said in a low tone. "The last thing Cadonia needs is instability in its ruler. There was enough of that with our father. You may hear whisperings from the people that I should be king but that is only because I haven't done anything yet for them to gripe about. I am not anyone's king, Elyse, and I don't ever plan to be."

"You really mean this, don't you? Isn't there a way I can change your mind?" she asked in a pleading tone.

"I'm sorry. No."

She looked defeated. "I don't want this."

"I know," he said with a heavy sigh. "And after how I've let you down before, I can only imagine what you're thinking about right now." He paused. "But you have to trust me. Can you do that?"

Silence hung in the air. Finally, Elyse let out a deep breath. "Alright." Her green eyes met his and she continued. "I trust you," she said.

Jonrell heard the words but her eyes betrayed a lingering doubt.

And can I blame her?

* * *

She closed the door to her room and in several quick strides dove onto the bed, landing face first into her pillow. It was late, past midnight, and Lobella wasn't there. Elyse had given her the night off once she knew her brother would be coming. But now she selfishly wished she hadn't, if only to talk to someone and clear her thoughts.

The night had not gone as she expected it to. Her brother swearing off the crown and pressing her to keep it was the last thing she thought would happen. She was so sure he would reclaim the throne upon his return.

But now, he expects me to rule and even thinks I'll be better at it than him. She shook her head. *That can't be right. He only said that last part to ease my mind and convince me it was the right thing to do.*

She rolled unto her back and began to disrobe, throwing her clothes on the floor. She was too tired to bother with anything more. *He said to trust him. And I told him I would. But did I really mean it? Even though we bonded tonight, I don't know him as I once did.*

She took off the simple jewelry she wore, placing it on the nightstand next to the bed. *And really, I only knew him as a little girl knows her brother.*

She slipped her feet into the bed and pulled the covers up to her chest. *How can I trust someone who left me alone?*

She thought of Adein, Vicalli, and that snake Illyan bickering in the council, each attempting to sway her opinion for their own personal gain. She thought of the condescending stares from Vulira and Phasin she received each day, making her feel incompetent in her role. Then she thought of Bronn belittling and embarrassing her, and Tomalt attacking his own people for the sake of power. She worried about what Conroy planned in secret and the kingdom's lack of strength to stand up against them.

Elyse had voiced those concerns to her brother, but he only hinted at some of what he intended when they met with Gauge and General Grayer. He felt it was better to discuss such matters in greater detail on the morrow and rode back to his camp to ready his men for their entrance into Lyrosene. *"Trust me. And tomorrow be the queen I know you can be."*

She rolled over, dimmed the oil lamp near her bedside and closed her eyes. *I don't really have a choice but to trust him. I need him. Cadonia needs him. And he kept his promise to me.*

She smiled in the dark.

* * *

Jonrell made his way toward a small hill with the bitter wind tugging at his cloak and watering his eyes. Though a couple of hours remained before dawn, the clear and starry night provided plenty of light. He strode over the wet ground with a long and deliberate gait. He came to a stop at the hill's crest and pulled his cloak tight around his body. *Winter is on its way.*

He cocked his head at the sound of footsteps. "You're losing your touch. I actually heard you coming this time."

"I had no reason to conceal my movements," said Kaz.

Jonrell grunted. "I thought you were Krytien for a second."

"Sleeping."

"Hmm. So, are you on watch?"

"I couldn't sleep so I took an extra watch," said Kaz.

Jonrell nodded. "Even after the long ride, my mind is restless too."

"Did your meeting not go well?"

"In some ways it went better than I expected. In others, worse."

"I don't understand."

Jonrell chuckled. "Neither do I." He paused, shaking his head. "Krytien and Cassus are the only ones I really talked to about my past. Few in the Hell Patrol talk about their pasts. It never felt right to complain about my life of privilege." He paused again. "That's not really what I wanted to say. What I mean is that leaving my sister behind was the one mistake in my life I've regretted most. I could have come back at any moment for her sake, to make things right, but I chose not to for whatever reason. And now I have this chance to make it up to her. I'm just worried that we've spent so much time apart that she won't allow me the opportunity."

"So, she hasn't forgiven you?"

Jonrell shrugged. "I think she has but I can tell she is hesitant in trusting me."

"It makes sense," said Kaz.

"Thanks."

"I only speak the truth. She could have had you killed, right?"

"Well, yeah. I guess so," said Jonrell dumbfounded.

"Then I think things went better than you realize. You're still alive."

Jonrell turned to face Kaz, expecting some sort of grin or smile but the warrior's serious face hinted at neither.

At least Krytien isn't so blunt. "Well, when you put it that way, I can see your point."

"Good." He faced Jonrell and clasped the commander on the shoulder. "Then I will return to my rounds."

"Sure. I'll speak to you in the morning."

Kaz nodded and disappeared into the night.

Jonrell shook his head thinking about how far Kaz had come. *He actually sought me out to comfort me. Just a couple of months ago, I was worried he would kill me.* He shrugged. *If only things in the wider world were so easy. With such turmoil in the land, a lot of hard decisions will need to be made tomorrow. I hope that Elyse remembers what I asked of her.*

* * *

Kroke leaned against the wall in the dark alley. He had a knife out and flipped it end over end, catching the blade on one pass, the hilt on the other. He wasn't watching the knife, though he knew where it would be.

I always know. His head swiveled back and forth between the alley mouth where he kept a lookout, and behind him where Glacar roughed up someone Jonrell had wanted them to deal with.

Along with a few others, they had been spying, intimidating, and gathering information all day.

Kroke caught his blade and sheathed it as Glacar came strolling out of the shadows wearing a sneer. "Where is he?"

"Where is who?"

"Where is who? The guy we chased here half an hour ago. The guy you've been working over while I've been keeping watch."

"Oh, I let him go," said Glacar, brushing by Kroke as he walked toward the alley's opening.

Kroke followed him into the light. "You did what?"

"You heard me. I let him go. He was the wrong guy."

"But the boss said …"

Glacar wheeled. "I know what Jonrell said. I was there. He had the wrong guy."

"He wasn't wrong about the other ones."

"Well, he was wrong about this one. Even though you and every other member of the crew seem to worship the ground he walks on, Jonrell is known to make mistakes."

"Not often."

"Too much as of late."

"You still all worked up about the new members?"

"And you ain't?"

Kroke shrugged. "The old Byzernian is harmless, Crusher acts like every other Ghal I've known…

"…and the black devil?" said Glacar cutting in.

Kroke worked his mouth. "I've got my doubts like others do but I trust that Jonrell knows what he's doing."

"And that's where you and I differ, Kroke," said Glacar, walking off.

"What's that supposed to mean?"

"Figure it out for yourself. I'm done talking."

Kroke knew he probably should have pressed the big oaf further but he never was one for words. So he set to thinking about what Glacar had meant while tapping the hilt of one of his daggers.

* * *

Kaz sat atop a swaying beast as the Hell Patrol passed through the cobbled streets of Lyrosene. He rode near the back with the supply wagons. Despite his sparse memories, he felt confident in assuming that before joining the band of mercenaries he had rarely ridden on horseback. On Slum Isle, he just started to get over the soreness when they set sail and now the process had begun once again. He dared not show his discomfort to the other soldiers. He worried the weakness might separate him even further from them.

Crusher rode in the rear as well. Unable to find a horse big or strong enough to carry his heavy frame, he rode in the back of an open wagon. He leaned over the side when he spoke. "For such small men, they build a city large enough to house even my people." He chuckled, gesturing around them. "Though their efforts pale in comparison to the colossal structures my race built centuries ago, I will at least acknowledge their effort was admirable. What do you say?"

Kaz looked around at the buildings on either side of the main avenue. Rooftops several stories high jutted into the sky. Tall spires sat at their points, seeking to pierce the clouds above. The blackened shingles contrasted against the white, polished stone walls. For a city so large and heavily populated, the warrior was impressed by its cleanliness. "Its size is greater than Floroson. I have little else to compare it to."

Crusher nodded. "That it is," he said in an understanding tone.

The Ghal often spoke to Kaz about the people in Cadonia as if they were nothing like the two men. And in some ways, Kaz knew this was true, he with his dark skin and Crusher with his size. Any differences in appearance never seemed to bother the Ghal and maybe it was because he knew there were others out there like him. He knew his past. But for Kaz it was not so easy. Such talk reminded him that not only was he not with his own kind, but that he had no clue where to even locate others like him.

The looks of curiosity, disdain, or even revulsion he found in the eyes of each passerby only fed on Crusher's comments. Even among the soldiers he had attached himself to, few spoke to him unless out of necessity.

So, why do I stay with them? He seemed to be asking himself that question more often than not. *I have clothes and weapons. I could steal food and money along my way.* But he knew how impractical that would be. Where would he go? Even if his skin matched these people he would surely stick out. Crusher had suggested that they could skip out on the group and return to Slum Isle to sell their services for gold, women, and fame. "A life all our own," he said. *But it would still not bring me back to the life I once had. I would be no closer to learning who I am or how to return to my people.*

Crusher continued to ramble on and on about the city and its architecture. Kaz nodded occasionally, though he rarely listened to the giant when he started to carry on in such a manner. The Ghal was capable of going on for hours about even the most mundane of topics. Kaz looked over at Hag, who must have recognized his nods as she gave him a wink before turning away. Kaz suppressed a grin.

Up front, his commander discouraged shouts of "King Jonrell" by working the crowd to support the Queen and her cause. Many were confused by his remarks, while others simply ignored his requests. The few who changed their shouts were drowned out by the others. Despite the daunting task, Jonrell had told Kaz earlier that he was confident he would sway the people's opinion in support of his sister. Kaz admired the fact that Jonrell had the opportunity to seize such power in an instant and yet turned it away unselfishly to secure another's rule.

Crusher. Hag. Jonrell. Maybe even a couple others. They numbered few but that would have to be enough. For now, he had reason to stay.

* * *

At the queen's command, Jonrell and his men rose from their knees. He would have hoped for a louder reaction from the crowd, but their disappointment in his gesture wouldn't allow it. Bending a knee in front of the entire city for all to see had been his idea the night before. He not only wanted to dismiss any thoughts that he was after the throne, but he also hoped to show his confidence in his sister in an effort to strengthen her support.

Elyse had hidden her nervousness well during her speech. Following his advice, she was brief and direct. The commoners needed to hear words of encouragement after the news of the fall of Namaris. Her message was clear. Tomalt would be stopped and a plan was already in place to do so.

That wasn't completely accurate. Jonrell had a few things rolling around in his head on how to handle the situation but he wouldn't be able to work out the details just yet, not until he had a better understanding of what he had to work with. Even then, he would probably have to make some things up as he went along.

I've been away too long to understand the clandestine maneuverings within the kingdom.

After rising from his knee, the queen kissed him on the cheek, a gesture for the crowd mostly, though Jonrell was happy to recognize the sincerity behind it. "You did well," he whispered.

"But now the hard part," she said in a worried manner.

"You'll do fine. I'll be there. Just remember what we talked about."

She nodded.

"Good. Then let's go, My Queen," he said smiling.

Elyse forced a smile as well, waving to the crowd before striding back into the castle. Before joining her, Jonrell met the eyes of several of his men, nodding to each one. They answered back in a similar manner. Satisfied, the commander followed.

* * *

Heated conversation filled the council chamber. Advisors seated behind the black dais that encircled the space shouted at each other. Those who had not found their places yet argued in the room's center. Jonrell walked in unnoticed and strode across the floor to take a spot below Elyse's seat. To Elyse's right, Gauge strained with effort to calm the fury of voices.

One Above, they would have never thought to act in such a way when my father was alive. Have they forgotten him already? The old fool might have been insane but he demanded respect.

He shook his head in disgust and then met the queen's gaze with a comforting wink he was sure no one else noticed. His sister looked troubled, helpless in her seat, not the regal image he wanted her to portray. She acknowledged the gesture by straightening her posture. Jonrell gave her a slight nod of approval before turning back around to face the room, drawing his sword in one fluid motion.

Heads turned in his direction at the sound. Conversations ended in midsentence as the hiss of steel resonated throughout the chamber and echoed off the walls. "It is a sad day in this kingdom when a drawn sword is what it takes for lesser men and women to remember the company they are in," he said, pointing with his sword at those still standing. "None of you would have dared to act in such a way in front of my father. Your Queen, has tried to rule differently than him and chooses not to use fear to gain respect as he did." He paused. "I, on the other hand, lack my sister's patience. I have no qualms in handing out any necessary punishment."

Faces paled at the implication and seats were taken with haste. Jonrell turned back to Elyse. "Your Highness."

All eyes went to the queen but she failed to move.

C'mon Elyse. This has to start now. Just a few words. Remember, you rule over them.

As if hearing Jonrell's thoughts, she slowly rose. "I think your point was made, Brother. Please, sheathe your sword."

Good. "Yes, Your Highness," he said and obeyed.

A throat was cleared to the left and a man stood. "Your Highness, if I may. I would like to apologize for our…behavior and take the opportunity to welcome Jonrell back home after such a long time away. His return has caused us to forget ourselves."

"Your apology is noted, Phasin. Have a seat," replied Elyse in a flat tone.

Very good, Jonrell thought. Then he saw a slight shake of the queen's hands and watched her quickly move them to her sides to conceal her nerves. *Just a little longer.*

"To Phasin's point, I know everyone is eager to discuss the return of my brother and what that means. That was addressed moments ago outside the keep. Jonrell is dedicated to bringing peace back to our kingdom and has returned to aid us in the war I had hoped to avoid. I have given him command over all our armies and resources. He answers to no one but me. That is what his return means and there will be no further discussion on the matter." Heads turned as whispers hissed through the council.

"Now," Elyse continued, "My brother has already determined our first steps in response to Tomalt's capture of Namaris. I will let him comment further on the matter." Elyse took her seat.

"Thank you, Your Highness," said Jonrell with a slight bow in the queen's direction. "I will keep what I have to say brief for we have little time to accomplish the many tasks that need to be done. I have heard good things about what General Grayer has been able to accomplish in such a short period of time. Therefore, he will stay here in defense of Lyrosene and continue to train and prepare the bulk of our army. I will take with me a smaller force and any necessary supplies to Cathyrium. We will strengthen their garrison and that is where we will make our stand against Tomalt."

"But wouldn't it make sense to keep our forces together as one unit here since he is likely to march on the capital?" blurted out Vulira.

"No. It wouldn't. Tomalt has greater numbers than we do and by splitting our forces he has no choice but to meet us at Cathyrium. Otherwise, he would have an army harassing his rear while he tried to take Lyrosene. Such a strategy would only work in our favor. By attacking Cathyrium, he then has a better advantage in numbers. Also, he wouldn't have to worry about his lengthening supply lines," said Jonrell.

"I beg your pardon, Your Highness," said Vulira interrupting, "but this is madness. Our Prince is practically admitting that he will lose Cathyrium with this scheme."

"That is always a risk," said Jonrell, cutting in before Elyse could respond. "But I do not plan to lose anything. Cathyrium can be defended against Tomalt."

"It sounds as though you already have worked out some of the details," came a voice to Jonrell's left.

Jonrell turned. "I have."

"Perhaps," said Adein, standing. "You could be more specific in regard to your strategy?"

"No."

"But how can we advise you and the queen on such things if you would not share with us the details of your plan?" asked Adein. He gestured around the room to others who nodded in agreement to his question.

Jonrell chuckled. "You don't understand. You are here to advise in your areas of expertise. You are not rulers. When it comes to matters of war, I take my advice from those men and women with experience I can trust."

"Are you implying that we cannot be trusted?" asked Adein outraged. Several shouts rose in agreement.

Jonrell raised his hands and hushed the audience. *Good, they are learning.* "Not all of you have been tainted but indeed there are spies here in this very room." Whispers broke out once again at the statement made.

"You've just arrived this day, Prince. Spies? You haven't had time to gather the proof to make such accusations," said Adein.

Jonrell suppressed a smile. Adein already worked to undermine his authority and turn the nobles against him. *No doubt he was a catalyst in doing the same to Elyse.* "On everyone? Perhaps not. However, my men are in the process of pulling information together on two of the most notorious offenders, nobles I had warned my father about years ago before I left Cadonia."

"Well, please, you must tell us who these conspirators are," demanded Adein. "I'm sure I speak for everyone here when I say that these people deserve swift justice for their actions." Several nods were seen throughout the room.

"As you wish, my lord," said Jonrell with a mocking bow. "My men are currently confiscating your estate and the estate of your dear friend Vicalli."

Adein's face grew pale as his mouth hung open in shock.

Vicalli stood up in a rush of anger. "This is outrageous. How dare you compare me to this imbecile? I will not tolerate this conspiracy being led against me."

Adein gathered himself and bolted toward the door. But as he reached the handle and swung the door wide, several guards greeted him. Two others came in to grab Vicalli who hadn't stopped yelling, though his language had grown more colorful.

Jonrell called to the guards. "Please place the men in separate cells for questioning."

One of the guards looked to the queen. "Your Majesty?"

Jonrell turned to Elyse and saw the shock on her face. She recovered quickly and composed herself as she cast a sidelong glance at her brother. "See to it, Captain."

"Yes, Your Highness."

"Wait!" cried out Adein. "What of my possessions?"

Jonrell answered his question while facing the rest of the room. The message served as a warning. "Due to the treachery of these men, all of their wealth, land, and titles will revert back to the crown. Their punishment will be determined once the extent of their treason has been discerned and their cooperation evaluated. This punishment will be extended to anyone else found guilty of similar crimes." He paused for effect, letting his words sink in as he waited until the guards led Adein and Vicalli out of the chamber and shut the door. "Now, I want to reassure everyone here that if you are not guilty of anything you have nothing to fear. In fact, I would say that you have plenty of opportunity for gain. You only need to prove yourselves."

"What exactly do you mean by that?" asked Phasin.

"The queen has decided to accompany me to Cathyrium."

This time Gauge was the one to voice his opinion. "Cathyrium? Your Majesty, is this true?"

Elyse paled at the question and turned to Jonrell searching for an answer. However, he had to remain quiet. All eyes watched them. Any gesture would be noticed too easily, and to answer in her stead would only weaken the power he was trying to build back into the crown.

It all hinges upon these next few moments. How much is she willing to trust me?

"Your Majesty?" asked Gauge once again.

Elyse blinked away the confusion in her eyes, puffing herself up in her seat. "Yes, it is true. Once preparations are made, I will be accompanying our Prince to Cathyrium."

"But Your Majesty, the queen's place is in Lyrosene," said Gauge

"My place is wherever I chose it to be. This is my kingdom, is it not?" Elyse asked in a stern voice.

Jonrell suppressed a smile once again. *I couldn't have said it better myself, Elyse.* Gauge squirmed in his seat and Jonrell noticed the other advisors looking smug at Gauge's discomfort. *Interesting, I'll have to talk to Elyse about his position at a later time.*

After a moment, Gauge found enough words to respond. "Yes, Your Majesty. This is your kingdom. I did not mean to infer anything otherwise," he said, bowing his head.

"I'm sorry, my Prince, but you spoke of opportunity," said Phasin. "I don't understand."

"Well, I think it should be obvious, really. Those in this room will have far more time on their hands since these council meetings will be suspended in the queen's absence."

Another series of shouts erupted from the advisors and Jonrell was forced to calm the group of nobles once again. Vulira was the one to speak up this time. "These council meetings have been in place for over four hundred years. Would you abolish something instituted by Aurnon the First?"

"No. However, Her Majesty and I have discussed the validity of suspending such meetings for a period of time. After all, you can't expect to hold a meeting with the queen in another city, now can you?"

"I suppose not," Vulira answered after some hesitation.

"Of course not. But not to worry, we will not be parting to Cathyrium for several days. Before we leave each person in this room will be given a crucial task. While we're gone, it will be necessary for each of those tasks to be fulfilled. And that," he said, turning around the room to meet everyone's eyes, "is where the opportunity lies."

"The success each of you has with these duties will influence the likelihood of being assigned such tasks in the future. Naturally, if someone is unable to complete an assigned duty, well, we would have to question not only that person's support of the crown but even their overall competence. And Her Majesty cannot have people like that share a seat on her council."

Jonrell watched mouths hang open in shock and shoulders hunch forward. He also received several piercing glares that only made him chuckle.

If that is supposed to intimidate me, you are sorely mistaken.

He finally came to his sister's eyes. "Your Highness, I believe that covers everything I wished to discuss at this particular time. Do you have anything to add?"

Elyse's look was one of confusion even as she stood and dismissed the meeting.

* * *

What just happened?

Elyse sat back into her seat with as much dignity as she could muster, remembering her brother's advice from last night. She and Jonrell had spoken briefly about what needed to happen today – how she should act and what topics to cover. *"Trust me," he said. "I'll do as much of the talking as I can without taking away your authority. I only need you to trust my judgment and support me openly before the nobles."*

Despite the exhaustion from tossing and turning the night before, she had felt confident about what to expect. Once the meeting was under way, it occurred to her how few of the day's details they actually discussed the previous night. She expected Jonrell to take some of the pressure off of her and buy time with the nobles as they formulated a plan.

But he did that and so much more, she thought, watching a disheveled group of nobles shuffle from the chamber. *He completely turned the tables on them.* The same group who had pushed and pressured her every chance they had since her father died were taken so off guard by Jonrell, that they simply crumbled before her eyes. *They saw what happened to Adein and Vicalli. He set this whole thing up as an example to them. But how did he act so quickly?*

She had so many questions she even found herself fighting not to argue with him. *Cathyrium? What was he thinking?* Yet, she kept her emotions in control, remembering what he asked of her. She backed him up when needed and did the best she could to hide her surprise when each new bit of information was revealed. *He asked only for my trust, but it feels like I'm giving him so much more.* She wasn't sure why she went along with what he said, but she knew that if she did otherwise, it would have only made matters worse.

Elyse noticed that none of the nobles dared to meet Jonrell's eyes as they left the room, except for one. *Illyan.* It was only at that moment that Elyse realized his booming voice had remained strangely silent throughout the council meeting. *What is that snake up to?* she wondered as Illyan approached her brother. The man had always made her uneasy, but after their latest confrontation when he brought up Sacrynon's Scepter, she had grown especially distrustful of him. *He seems to be everywhere and know everything.*

The short man pulled a rolled letter from his robe and handed it to Jonrell while he whispered something that Elyse couldn't make out. Jonrell nodded but otherwise gave little away as the advisor smiled with a devilish grin and left. He made eye contact with Elyse upon leaving and gave her a wink that sent a chill up her back.

I wonder if he is another of the spies that Jonrell mentioned, earlier. I'd be sure of it.

Jonrell turned back to his sister and smiled. "Gauge, would you excuse us? I would like to speak with my sister in private."

"Certainly, my Prince," said Gauge rising.

Elyse laid a hand on his arm. "No. I would like for you to stay." Then turning to Jonrell, she added. "He is my chief advisor."

"I understand, Your Majesty. However, I would feel more comfortable discussing certain matters with you first. If you wish to share our discussion with him, then that is your choice to do so."

Elyse eyed her brother. "Very well. Gauge, I apologize."

"There is no need to apologize, Your Highness. I will be waiting for you outside the chamber door," he said.

After the door was closed, Jonrell smiled again. "That went well, don't you think?"

Elyse stood up. "What just happened?" she asked, realizing how angry the show in the council meeting had made her.

"Well, you took the nobles off guard and sent a message that you won't be pushed around. They won't know what to expect next and that is a good thing."

"You keep saying 'you' as if I was the one responsible for their change in behavior. You said everything while I just sat here and nodded and chimed in like some puppet. Is that why you don't want the throne? Because you can just as easily rule through me without any of the blame?"

"Of course not. We talked about this last night. You can be a great ruler but I thought it best if you had help today. I can help you further while traveling to Cathyrium."

"Yes, why am I to go to Cathyrium? Isn't my place here?"

"That isn't what you told Gauge."

"I had to think of something."

"You did well thinking on your feet. That was the perfect answer and it's an attitude you need to have more often."

"But I embarrassed Gauge. He didn't deserve such treatment. He has been a huge help to me since Father's passing."

"I'm sure he has," said Jonrell. "I find it odd that a man who was dismissed by Father years ago is all of a sudden your top advisor."

"You said that Father was an awful ruler."

"True. However, I don't like how much power you have given him in such a short time."

"Is that why you wanted him to leave the room?"

"Yes. I want you to think about how you distribute information. You should share only enough for your aides to do their jobs."

"What if I choose to share more with certain individuals?"

Jonrell sighed. "Then so be it. You are the queen and I am at your command. Just be careful and remember all those things I used to tell you as a girl about how people manipulate each other."

Oh, I haven't forgotten. And after today, I wonder how much you're manipulating me. "You still never answered my question about Cathyrium?"

"I'll give you an answer later. Not now. You have to trust me Elyse."

So, you keep saying. Yet you don't trust me enough to let me in on your plans. "What did Illyan want? I saw him talking to you," asked Elyse, changing the subject.

"Oh," said Jonrell. "This," he added holding up his hand to display the letter, "is a plan he has for bringing in supplies to Cathyrium. He said he would like to discuss some ideas he has on strengthening our lines."

"I hope you aren't actually considering his ideas."

"I don't see why not. I haven't reviewed what he gave me yet but I told him I would meet with him. Stockpiling supplies during a siege is crucial to our success."

"Maybe *you* should remember what you said about people manipulating each other. His plans always give him an edge and fatten his purse."

"I would hope so. Otherwise, I would really be suspicious. No one does anything for free. Everyone has an ulterior motive. The sooner you discover that motive, the better. Considering the risks Illyan will have to take to accomplish his goal, it only seems fair he is well paid."

"Well, he also says he has the kingdom's best interests."

"I'm sure he does to some degree, but few men and women are that loyal to an ideal."

"Gauge is."

"Is he?" asked Jonrell, raising an eyebrow.

"Yes."

"Interesting," said Jonrell.

"Now what does that mean?" asked Elyse, growing agitated.

"Nothing, right now," said Jonrell. "I've stated my opinion."

Yes, you have. How can you claim to know someone so well when you've barely spoken to him and been gone for so long? The thought reminded her of another question, tugging at her mind. "How did you know Adein and Vicalli were spies?"

"They were spies twelve years ago. Only Father failed to do anything about it. To prove they hadn't changed their ways, I sent a couple of my men into the city a bit earlier and had them feed Adein and Vicalli some false information to see what they would do with it. We intercepted their messengers carrying the information to Bronn and Conroy."

Elyse's stomach twisted. "Are they planning to attack as well?"

"I doubt it, but no one can say for sure. Regardless, my move accomplished two goals. It removed the worst of your council and sent a message to the others."

"You said you know who the other spies were as well? Is that true?"

"Yes and no. As you said, I've been away too long to know all the dynamics of the nobility. I'm just giving them something to think about that may sway their loyalty. However, I have ideas on a couple I may be able to feed false information to and add to the confusion."

"Oh."

Jonrell paused. "I'd like to leave in two days and that doesn't give us much time to prepare for the journey and see to the kingdom's affairs. I hope you weren't planning to get to bed early."

Elyse shook her head. "I don't sleep well anymore."

"I understand." He let out a sigh and continued. "Well, then let's go. I want to look over what you and Grayer have accomplished. Then we can see to…"

Jonrell kept talking as he went over the agenda for the next couple of days. Elyse missed half of what was said as she focused on one thought.

How can he be this organized and have everything down so well after being gone for so long? I never left and I feel like an idiot.

CHAPTER 20

Tobin strolled through the market, eating steamed fish wrapped in banana leaves. He shared a conversation with Lucia as she looked over the day's ware. It was the second time in as many days that the two had shared lunch and he felt at ease in her company for the first time in months.

Jober was courteous enough to give them privacy, but never far enough away where Tobin felt that he was truly alone with Lucia.

The disdainful way he looks at me makes it seem like I was the one responsible for Kaz's disappearance. Tobin gave the former stable hand a sidelong glance. *Has he forgotten how much better his life is as a result of that night? He never did thank us for what we did for him.* "What do you think of this material?" asked Lucia.

He looked at the roll of light blue fabric mixed with shades of maroon. He imagined he was alone with her, and she stood before him in his bedchamber wearing a fine silk dress made from the thin material. He imagined it hugging the contours of her body.

She would have been mine if Kaz hadn't stolen her from me.

"Do you hate it that much?" she asked.

"What?" Tobin said blinking away his desires.

"I asked you a question but all you gave me was a blank look."

"Sorry, I was just thinking of how beautiful you would look in a dress made from the material."

Lucia put her head down and despite her dark skin, Tobin could see she was blushing. "It is lovely," she said.

"I think the material would be so lucky to have you wear it. Of course, no other woman would dare wear it afterward since they would never do it the same justice as you."

She blushed again but this time looked up at Tobin and smiled.

So beautiful.

"I think I will buy the material then. I've never cornered the market before," she said giggling. "You know, I think I forgot just how much you used to cheer me up."

Tobin moved closer to her so they were only a couple of feet apart. "I only speak the truth, Lucia. You are an amazing woman. Anyone unable to recognize that would be a fool."

"Kaz used to tell me the same thing," she said, her voice distant as if remembering some past moment she had shared with Tobin's brother.

The mention of his name extinguished some of the hope Tobin had felt a moment earlier.

"I miss him so much."

"I know it is hard to do, but you must let him go."

"You speak like he's dead." she said looking up at Tobin, her face filled with betrayal.

"It has been months and we have heard nothing about his abduction or disappearance. Not even a letter seeking ransom," said Tobin, feeding his previous lies. "I see no other possibility."

"How can you believe that? You are his brother. You know the kind of man he is."

A cold, callous, evil man, Tobin thought, though he dared not say so. "He was not invincible," said Tobin, settling on a response.

"He's not dead. I know him. He will come back to me," said Lucia. There was a certainty to her tone that said she would not be swayed. "I know others think I am a fool for believing so, but your father thinks the same."

Tobin winced at the bitter reminder. Even if his attitude toward Tobin had improved, Bazraki still had not shown him the same level of respect he had shown Kaz.

At least more of the Kifzo are accepting my command each day.

Because of these small improvements in his life, Tobin had finally convinced himself to see Lucia again. She was the last piece of the life he had always wished for. He was not foolish enough to think that something would develop immediately between them, but Tobin also hadn't realized his dreams lay so far outside his reach.

She clings to Kaz's memory as if he is all she had. What about me?

"My father is a fool in denial," said Tobin.

"Does that mean that I'm a fool, too?" she asked, hurt from the comment. "Or Jober for that matter?" she said pointing to her bodyguard, leaning against a nearby wall, watching their conversation. "He thinks it's possible for Kaz to be alive."

"Of course he would," Tobin muttered under his breath, shooting Jober a look that caused the man to turn away.

"What was that?" asked Lucia.

"Nothing," snapped Tobin, turning back to Lucia. "Don't live your life for a ghost, Lucia."

Tobin stalked away before Lucia could respond. *It only stands to reason that what I want most out of life is the thing that still alludes me. Kaz, you haunt me even in death.*

* * *

The two Kifzo Tobin personally chose to watch over Odala and Soyjid, greeted him as he approached the lone entrance to the captive's rooms. The guards were less aggressive than most of the other warriors. Such an attribute caused Tobin to select them for their task, wanting to ensure that none would question his visits, especially as their frequency increased.

And why? There is no need for me to be here now.

The warriors stepped aside from the door and Tobin knocked. He was sure that they found it odd for him to announce himself when he had every right to barge into the room. He saw little need to intimidate someone who was already uneasy in their surroundings and posed no threat to him. After some noticeable shuffling from behind the door, a muffled voice called out for him to enter.

Furnished as lavishly as the rest of the palace, the room contained a pair of padded chairs around an ornate table and a stone fireplace. A canopied bed covered in blue silk sat near a doorway that led to an adjoining room. Along the wall, in the middle of the room, a large bay window with curtains drawn up, allowed sunlight to spill into the space. Odala stood by the window.

He was ashamed to admit that she was the reason for his regular visits. *The way she stands, the shine of her skin, the grace in how she carries herself. But like Lucia, she is beyond my reach.*

Tobin lowered his gaze, ashamed of the lustful thoughts for one so young. He knew in many ways it wasn't Odala that he lusted after, but such a revelation did little to ease his mind. *After all, I am here to torture myself once again—to remind myself what I will never have. Why do I do this?*

"Does your father wish to speak with me?" she asked.

As always, Tobin was surprised to hear such a mature voice from the young woman. "No," said Tobin.

"Then why do you come?" she asked, tilting her head.

That look. It is so much like Lucia. Tobin shrugged in an attempt to appear indifferent, even though he felt the knot forming in his stomach. "You were there when my father charged me with your well being. And of your brother's," he said leaning forward to look into the doorway of the adjoining room. He did not see anything of importance from that angle. "Where is Soyjid?"

"Avoiding you," she said bluntly. "He has much pride for his age. He may have accepted our current circumstances, but he does not like them."

"And you have accepted them?"

"What other choice do I have? Would you send me home if I asked?"

"You know the answer to that."

She shrugged. "So I have accepted it," she said, turning her gaze back out the window.

Tobin frowned, unsure what else to say. "I will not disturb you any longer then."

At least there are no mixed signals with her. She shows her displeasure openly.

He turned and left the room.

* * *

Odala flinched as the door slammed shut behind him. Tobin was obviously upset with her but she couldn't understand why. *Why does he keep coming to see me? And what does he want? Is he looking for gratitude for saving me when one of his men tried to attack me?*

He had saved her the first night of their captivity. But she had been too angry and scared to show him any gratefulness then. Even now, weeks later, her feelings toward Tobin hadn't changed.

He acts like he is a good man, someone trustworthy. But I saw the malice in him when he threatened Father. I saw the rage in his face. Her body shuddered as she recalled the look in his eyes that night. She hadn't seen that look from him since, but it was one she would not forget. *The look of who he really is.*

"He didn't stay as long as last time," came a voice from behind.

Odala spun round, startled. "I told you to quit sneaking up on me like that."

Soyjid shrugged. "We have three rooms to share. It's not like I can hide."

"Then what were you doing when Tobin was here?"

"I was in the other room, listening. He was not here to see me, Sister."

"What is that supposed to mean? Father's little genius has all the answers again, doesn't he?"

"As a matter of fact, I do. It means he isn't interested in anything *I* can offer him." He grinned. "I see you catch my meaning," he added.

"No," she gasped.

Soyjid laughed. "You really couldn't tell? The way he looks at you? He cannot take his eyes off of you."

Odala shook her head at the thought. "Everyone has looked at me differently since I've become a woman. He is just another man."

"His look isn't some whimsical lust. No. I think he has feelings for you."

Now it was Odala's turn to laugh. "That is ridiculous. You saw the way he threatened Father and how he struck fear into the man who attacked me. Someone like that does not love. He takes what he wants."

"Then why hasn't he taken you? He is warleader. No one would know if he made you his. And none would care, either. There must be something else behind that look of desire in his eyes. Something more."

Odala didn't want to believe what her brother was telling her, yet the more she thought about it, the more things began to make sense.

Checking in at random hours of the day and night, trying to make conversation, never seeming to have a purpose for his visit. It was so obvious, she couldn't believe she never thought of it herself.

"What should I do?" she asked.

"Embrace it, Sister. Show him that you care for him."

"How could you say something so cruel?" she hissed.

"You must use him to our advantage."

"What are you talking about?"

"Act like you care. Get him to talk to you. Maybe in time you can influence his decisions and hurt him as retribution for hurting Father. I promise that night was only the beginning. They will continue to take from us. They will push us around until we are no better than any other clan they've conquered. Isn't it proof enough that he already took away part of what was originally offered to us in the alliance."

"It was only after Father insulted him," she said

"It was a poor deal to begin with and Father knew it. They rule over all of Hesh and in return we get a bit of extra land and money. We would still be subservient to someone not of our own clan."

"What makes you think Tobin would be so easily influenced?" asked Odala.

"People do stupid things when they are in love."

Love. The word in connection with that monster made her skin crawl and her stomach turn. "What do you know about love?"

"I know enough. I watch and I listen. You may have gotten mother's looks but I inherited her mind. It's a good thing too, because with Father getting older it will soon be my turn to lead our clan. That is, if we make it home alive…." His voice trailed off, but after a moment he continued. "I don't know why the idea seems so repulsive to you. You've been manipulating suitors for over two years now." His eyes narrowed. "And last I remembered, you enjoyed doing it."

That was different. It was fun then to flirt and have people give me nice things. None of it was serious. She'd even let them steal a kiss if she was attracted to them. "It was a game," she said, sounding disheveled. "If I did this, I may have to do *things* with him," she said.

"Perhaps, but not right away. That would be too suspicious."

"But eventually…" she started.

"Eventually, you may come to find him tolerable. He certainly has the look of the men you used to gawk over with your friends. If you must, when the time comes imagine you are with one of them."

"I don't know how you can say such things. Father would never want me to do that," she said.

"Father isn't here. He never has to know. This can be kept between you and me. Besides, if you are to succeed, who knows what could happen.

Perhaps our clan will be the one to conquer Hesh, and Father could become ruler. Wouldn't you want to give that to him if you could?" he asked.

Odala hugged herself and closed her eyes trying to imagine herself with Tobin. But even if it was an act, she couldn't bear the thought. "I can't do it," she whispered. "I just can't."

"You always were selfish," he said in an icy tone. He turned and stalked back into his room.

* * *

Tobin saw his opening and moved in for the kill. But his opponent spun away from the attack. Walor feinted high and struck low. Tobin whipped his blade down and the dulled practice swords banged together. From the look on his opponent's face, the noise came as a surprise. Having expected his strike to find its mark, the Kifzo took two quick steps back in retreat.

Tobin cut off his path each time Walor looked to gain better positioning. He sidestepped with balance and precision using an ankle that no longer held him back.

Walor's uncertainty was evident and Tobin seized the opportunity by pressing his opponent with a flurry of moves, lashing out recklessly in wild swinging motions. He dodged or parried each of Tobin's strokes while smiling the entire time.

His sword slid off as he shifted and turned his blade for a thrust to Tobin's gut. Tobin recognized the feint and made no effort to counter the strike. Tobin turned his shoulder and slammed into the smaller man while sweeping his back leg. Walor fell. Tobin placed his blade against Walor's cheek.

"You're dead," said Tobin between breaths.

"You set me up, didn't you? The whole thing? Swinging your blade like some young fool eager to end a fight. I can't believe I fell for that," said Walor.

"And yet you did," said Tobin with a grin.

"What is that? Four straight matches you've won?" asked Walor.

"Five," answered Tobin. "Do you want to make it six?"

"No. I would however, like to get up," said Walor, his eyes focused on the blade.

As he helped Walor to his feet, Tobin noticed the gesture warranted him a few looks from the Kifzo watching the match.

I help up my brethren. There is no reason why I have to keep you beaten down like my brother did. He and my father saw weakness in such a move. I only see respect.

Walor stood up, working his shoulder with a freehand.

"Do you need a healer?" asked Tobin.

Walor cast him a sidelong glance.

I shouldn't have asked him that in front of the others. "I didn't mean…" said Tobin, starting to correct himself.

Walor held up a hand, cutting him off. "I'm fine, Warleader." He rolled his shoulder again, changing direction until there was an audible crack. Walor let out a sigh of relief. "Better than ever."

"Is that so?"

"Don't get any ideas," said Walor. "I think next time we spar, I'll wait until after you've been worn down a little first."

As they left the practice circle, Tobin whispered. "How do my skills rank in comparison to the rest of the Kifzo?"

Walor grunted. "Even with your injury, you were above average. Now, you're becoming one of the most skilled with a sword."

"But not the best?" asked Tobin. "Not as good as Kaz once was?"

The two walked in silence for a moment as the question hung out there unanswered. "No, not the best. Not yet anyway," said Walor. He nodded over to a different practice circle at a man facing off against three opponents at the same time. "Some of our best, such as Guwan, spar with multiple Kifzo. Your brother went against three or four of our best men, sometimes more. I'm sorry Warleader, but Kaz was the best I've ever seen with a sword."

Tobin shook his head. "Then I need to practice more."

"Why? You may not be our best with a sword but no one can come close to your skill with a bow or a throwing ax. Your brother never could either. What does it matter if you are our best swordsmen?" asked Walor.

"You know why. They compare me to Kaz in everything I do. It matters little to them how well I can shoot a bow because I was that way before Father made me warleader. Now, I need to be something more. Kaz set a precedent that a warleader must lead his men into battle at the front of the lines. Therefore, I must be better at a sword than any man here, just as he once was. In fact, I need to be better than even he was. That is the only way I'll get them to forget the man Kaz made me out to be."

Walor nodded. "I see your point. But you need to make sure you aren't showing any shortcomings in front of the others. I can help you with this if you would let me."

Tobin turned to face the man. "Thank you. You have always been a good friend to me."

Tobin saw the comment took Walor aback. *A Kifzo doesn't show appreciation. A Kifzo doesn't have friends. Both are signs of weakness.* He could hear his uncle's words in his head from when he trained them as boys. From the silence, Tobin thought he had made a mistake. *He is not Nachun. I shouldn't have said anything.*

Walor nodded and even smiled. "You have no need to give thanks. I always knew you to be the better son. In time, others will see the same."

Tobin nodded in appreciation. He wanted to tell Walor that those words meant more to him than he would ever know, but he dare not expose himself further. He took a gamble by opening up to the man just as Walor took one in responding so openly back to him.

Best to leave things as they are for now.

The two parted company. Nothing else needed to be said.

* * *

Once Tobin became warleader, Bazraki no longer kept his plans hidden. Tobin attended the strategy meetings with his father and advisors. However, he was often relegated to the side and only on a rare occasion was he asked to provide his own input.

But at least I'm here. That's far more than what I was ever allowed before. Besides, when the arguing is done and everyone is dismissed, Father gives me, not Kaz, his final decision. And I am allowed to distribute such knowledge amongst my warriors as I see fit.

However, there was a downside to the position that he hadn't expected. Receiving Bazraki's plans, unfiltered from Kaz, cast his father in a different light. The battle strategies were often riddled with holes and full of obvious weaknesses. They even contradicted some of the most basic principles of warfare Tobin's uncle had taught him as a boy.

And maybe this is why Kaz never told anyone what Father's entire orders were. He was probably changing the orders himself but Father was never near the action to know better. Before Uncle Cef's death, he must have also covered for Father.

His suspicion regarding his father's inadequate military strategy only grew with each meeting he attended. Even now, as talk focused on the conquest of the Yellow Plain, Bazraki crushed each well thought out concern that Nachun brought up.

And Father's lackeys support him without question. They prematurely celebrate his victory over a clan nearly double our size as if the matter has been decided. Watching the events unfold, he found himself appreciating Nachun's tenacity even more in getting Bazraki to agree to his previous ideas.

At the meeting's conclusion, the room emptied except for Nachun, Tobin, and Bazraki.

"Nachun, fill Tobin in with the news we received today."

Tobin shook his head. *Father can't even be troubled with giving the information himself.*

"We've received reports that the Gray Marsh Clan has begun harassing the outer villages on the southern end of the Yellow Plain. So far, it appears that Mawkuk will uphold his part of the deal," said Nachun.

Tobin nodded. "I had not doubted he would." *I saw his fear.*

"Yes, well he still has much left to prove before I share your confidence. I do not trust as easily as you," said Bazraki.

Tobin did not miss the insult.

"I'm sending word to him about our plans to start the campaign. His orders are to continue his raids until instructed otherwise," continued Bazraki.

"And also your strategy?" asked Tobin.

"He will not know anything that was discussed tonight. Do you take me for a fool? I'm not one to share such things with anyone I do not trust," said Bazraki.

Good. Then Mawkuk will not realize how ill informed you are, Father.

"I did not mean to imply you were a fool, El Olam. I just assumed it would be best for us to leave our plans open ended for any changes that might be needed from now until we meet the Yellow Clan in battle."

Bazraki met Tobin's eyes. His lips formed a thin line. "What changes?"

Did Kaz never tell him that even the best laid plans require adjustments when in the heat of battle?

"Not changes, El Olam. I'm sure what Tobin meant to say was any last minute fine tuning to the details is all." said Nachun trying to deflect the rising anger evident in Bazraki.

Tobin knew it would be easier to just agree with Nachun. But for some reason, he couldn't bring himself to do so. "No, Nachun. I meant that there are some things that as warleader I may need to adjust before we go into battle. I think that Nachun's distribution of supplies and troops was closer to how I would align our resources given what your scouts have reported back."

Bazraki seethed. "Your brother would never dare question my authority."

My brother. The sudden thought enraged Tobin. "Never to your face, perhaps. But what little I've known of your original plans in the past were often far different than those Kaz issued to us, Father."

A thick hand shot out, snapping Tobin's head to the side as one of his father's rings caught his bottom lip. Tobin tasted blood.

"El Olam…" started Nachun.

But Bazraki cut him off, raising a hand in warning. "Silence. I do not need your advice when it comes to this."

Tobin licked his lips to wipe away the blood. He said nothing.

"You will call me 'El Olam,' you insolent fool," continued Bazraki as he stared down Tobin. "First you disrespect me and question my decisions. Then you speak ill of your brother who is a man far better than what you have become. I don't know why I made you warleader," said Bazraki.

Despite his rage, Tobin thought to calm the situation. *I can swallow my pride and apologize.* "Father, I…"

A hand whipped out again but this time Tobin caught it. And he squeezed, digging his fingers deep into his father's wrist as he forced the hand down. His father's eyes grew large from shock and his other hand shot up toward Tobin. But Tobin caught it as well, pinning both of his father's wrists.

Despite the predicament, Bazraki's glare never wavered from Tobin's eyes, almost as if he was in denial of what was happening.

This isn't what I wanted to happen, Tobin thought. But he knew it was too late to go back and so he pushed on with what he started.

"You will not raise a hand at me ever again, *Father,*" said Tobin, spitting the word out. "And you made me warleader because you had to. Choosing anyone else would have been an insult to your pride. Removing me from command would be even worse."

He slowly eased the grip on his father's wrists and to his surprise Bazraki left his hands at his sides. "Do what you want on a larger scale, *Father.* Conquer your land, form your alliances, and build your cities. That is your legacy. But the battlefield shall be mine."

Bazraki stood there, his face hard and chest heaving with each massive breath. He stared at Tobin. Tobin was sure that his father would call for his guards at any moment or take matters into his own hands and reach for the dagger at his belt but he did neither. "Get out," he said finally. "Both of you, get out of my sight."

Tobin and Nachun left without another word.

* * *

Roaming the palace halls, Tobin contemplated what had led him to lash out at his father. It didn't take long for him to figure out. Neglect. Ridicule. Unrealistic expectations. Lack of love. His father was a callous man and standing up to him for the first time in his life seemed to clear Tobin's mind to face those harsh realizations.

He has never loved me so why do I care if he starts now?

He found himself wanting to talk about these things, but given the late hour, he decided to keep walking instead, up and down stairs, in and out of rooms and hallways.

Tobin would normally seek advice from Nachun first. However, the two had parted rather abruptly after leaving Bazraki's war room and gone in separate directions. The surprised and questioning look on the shaman's face still bothered Tobin as well.

He sighed. *I may have ruined all he had worked for to gain my father's confidence.*

He could seek out Walor. He and the head scout shared a bond unlike what Tobin had with the other Kifzo, though neither would openly admit it. *And that's why I can't go to him now. Besides, I should not show such weakness to him for I am still his warleader…at least for now.*

An image of Lucia then popped into his mind. *She said that she would be there for me if I needed it. She would not ridicule me. She is too good of a woman for something like that.* He shook his head. *But then she will likely bring up Kaz. I'm sure he never cried like a little boy on her shoulder. I can't go to her now and give her another opportunity to compare us.*

"Warleader?" came a surprised voice.

Tobin looked up blinking. He was so preoccupied with his thoughts, he had drifted along the darkened corridors with this head down until coming to a stop outside of Odala's room. He hid his own surprise by keeping to the shadows, away from the flickering torch near the door. "Have the prisoners gone to bed?"

"Some time ago, I believe. It is very late," said the guard with a questioning tone.

"It is," replied Tobin. He added nothing more, letting the guard wonder at the purpose of his visit. He wasn't sure what they assumed, but he would not give them an answer. He was warleader after all. His reasons were his own and none of their concern.

They stepped aside and Tobin knocked on the door. *What am I doing here? Lucia. Thinking of her must have led me here.* He waited patiently at the door. It was too late to turn around and appear indecisive. After a moment, the door crept open and Tobin pushed his way inside.

* * *

Tobin turned and closed the door quickly, leaving the guards behind and exchanging one awkward moment for another. He knew Odala would be upset at him for waking her. *And what excuse do I give her for this visit?*

He turned to face her and froze. The moonlight from the open window illuminated the outlines of Odala's body through the almost transparent night gown she wore. His heart raced. *She looks like Lucia in my dreams.*

She moved suddenly, reaching for a robe that she draped over herself, hiding the details of her body. But it was too late, the vision had etched itself into his mind, and he felt shame once again. He blinked his eyes, hoping to clear those thoughts. His gaze met hers and the look on her face was not what he had expected. He assumed she would be disgusted but she seemed almost concerned.

That can't be right.

She took a step forward and raised her hand. Tobin flinched away out of reflex but his reaction did not deter her. Her hand only moved slower, until it rested on his face, her thumb on his lip. Despite the chill in the air, her touch was warm, comforting.

"What happened?" she whispered.

Tobin noticed the tone in her voice had changed as well. *Is this some sort of trick? But what could she gain by deceiving me?*

"Where you in a fight?" she asked.

Tobin shook his head, still unsure what to say or whether to say anything at all.

Her hand drifted away from his face while her other reached out and grabbed his own. *So delicate and caring. Just like Lucia's*, he thought.

"Come," she said leading him to a bench near the window. "Tell me."

Tobin wasn't sure why but he let his guard down then and opened up to her in a way he had always wanted to with Lucia. In a way he never had to anyone else, not even Nachun.

He talked for hours while Odala listened and occasionally offered a word of comfort or encouragement. Though he barely remembered half of what he said, he doubted he would ever forget the look of genuine care on her face when he left.

* * *

A warm, red light from the rising sun bled into the room. Odala watched it reflect across the bronze door handle as Tobin exited her chambers. She was exhausted. If only for today, she was glad to be a captive. At least here she could sleep the day away and not be ridiculed for doing so.

"I never thought he would leave."

Odala jumped in her seat and gave her brother an evil look as he peered through a cracked doorway.

He held up his hands as he stepped into her room. "Sorry."

"Were you eavesdropping the entire night?"

He nodded. "He was so engrossed with you that he was unaware of what was happening around him." He paused, his voice taking on a serious tone. "You did the right thing."

She shook her head. "He frightens me. You heard the things he talked about."

He nodded. "I'm surprised he spoke so openly about his training."

Odala shivered. "If all of their Kifzo suffered through such things, it is no wonder they are unmatched on the battlefield."

"Yes. And he barely scratched the surface. Even still, for him to talk so freely with you says many things."

"Such as?"

"He wants to talk. And you are the person he wants to talk to. And most important is that he trusts you."

"I do not wish to hear about such things. I had to suppress my own reactions several times upon hearing his monstrosities."

"Is that why you barely spoke?"

She nodded.

"Then change that. Learn to direct the conversation into areas that can help our people. I will help you practice."

"He'll know I'm playing with him."

"He didn't know last night. He is unstable and that makes him someone easy to manipulate," said Soyjid, smiling.

* * *

Tobin wiped his brow and rammed the practice sword point-first into the ground with a grunt. He snatched up a skin of water and drank deep. Even with a cool breeze blowing, sweat poured from his body. Although he tried to hide his fatigue, his limbs felt numb after a day's worth of Walor's drills and sparring, always against two opponents at a time.

"I think that's enough for today," said Walor.

Tobin shrugged as he tried to look indifferent. In truth he was thankful for the respite. "Where did you learn all of these drills?" Tobin asked, after taking a moment to catch his breath.

"Some came from Kaz. Others simply came from trial and error."

"I think even my uncle would have been impressed by your techniques," complimented Tobin.

"No offense, but I never liked the man," said Walor.

Tobin grunted. "Few did. But he was effective in training us. Same as you. I can feel the improvement in my skills already."

"You always were a fast learner, even when we were boys."

Tobin heard the bitterness in Walor's voice, though he knew it came from recalling those rough times from their youth, rather than anything Tobin had done. Few Kifzo spoke about their childhood, but Tobin was certain that many felt as he did about it, though none would ever admit such a thing. They were all pushed into a life of bloodshed and were never given the opportunity to experience joy.

Another reason to hate my father.

The two men looked up as Nachun approached from a distance. He noticed the shaman's new robes were red with few markings of blue. *He is so bold to reference his previous life.*

Tobin nodded in greeting as the shaman came closer. They had spoken little since Tobin stood up to Bazraki. It was not abnormal to spend some time apart as each had their responsibilities to see to. However, once they were together again, Tobin could feel the closeness, the bond two friends shared. Tobin set out to meet the shaman away from the other Kifzo.

"I bring news from El Olam," said Nachun.

"My father treats you as a messenger now?" asked Tobin.

Nachun shrugged. "He sees it as a way to punish me, just as he punishes you by giving you information second hand." He let out a heavy sigh. "Now you know why I hid so many of my plans from you. It was not that I was necessarily being secretive, I just didn't want you to see that side of your father."

He snorted. "It's too late for that now." After standing up to Bazraki, Tobin had waited for some punishment to come down but nothing happened. Rumors of Tobin's actions had reached many of the Kifzo and he heard their whispers when they thought he wasn't paying attention.

No doubt Nachun's doing as I haven't said anything.

He had assumed many would be upset he stood against his father, their ruler. However, many had become disenfranchised with Bazraki, and Tobin's outburst had only increased their level of respect toward him.

"What news do you bring?" asked Tobin

"He wanted to confirm that all preparations have been made." said Nachun.

"They were finished days ago," said Tobin.

"Good. Then we leave in the morning for the Yellow Plain."

CHAPTER 21

Elyse stared out of the carriage, watching the landscape drift by.

"Is there something wrong, Your Majesty?" asked Lobella.

Elyse smiled. "Just lost in thought, I'm afraid. I hope I'm not bringing you down as well."

"Oh, of course not. In fact, I was doing the same. I was thinking of Lyrosene. It may sound silly but this is the first time I've ever been outside of the city."

"Really?" asked Elyse sounding a bit too surprised. *Of course she wouldn't have traveled as much as I have. She never had access to the resources that I did.*

"Oh yes, Your Majesty. My entire family is from Lyrosene so we really never had much of a reason to leave the city. Well, except my mother that is. But her family passed away from the plague when she was barely my age."

"I've heard stories of that time. I'm sorry for your losses."

Lobella smiled. "Thank you, Your Majesty. You are too kind. She only has me now and a few distant cousins we rarely see."

"You miss her already, don't you?"

"Very much so."

"I'm sorry you had to come with me. I tried to find another way but I needed someone I could trust to attend me while away from the city."

"Oh, I understand. Your brother hired nearly half a dozen servants to replace me in caring for my mother in my absence. He said that not only would she be cared for, but that he would see to her home being repaired to look as new as the day it was built. I told him not go to any trouble but he insisted."

Elyse was surprised to hear that. She knew Jonrell had made arrangements for Lobella's mother, but she was unaware of the extent. Though to hear Lobella tell the tale, it sounded as though they had needed the extra help for some time. She wasn't sure what else to say, so she went with the first thing that came to mind. "Well, you are definitely worth the effort."

Lobella blushed. "The prince said the same thing, Your Majesty," she said with a sparkle in her eye. "You are both too kind."

Elyse smiled and they both turned back toward the road to Cathyrium. *She is already smitten by him and barely even knows the man.*

However, she realized that without even trying Jonrell had taught her another lesson. She had always assumed that by asking how things were, Lobella would be honest and speak of any needs. Elyse realized that the young woman would not speak to her about such things.

I should have looked into it myself. I took her kindness and friendship for granted.

Staring out the window again, Elyse saw the signs of winter well under way. Branches swayed in the harsh winds as leaves blew to and fro across the ground. The faces of soldiers and servants reddened from the whipping air. And in the middle of it all, her brother moved among the men, talking to every one of them, treating each one as equal, regardless of station. And as her brother left, all stood a little straighter and seemed a little less bothered by the unruly weather.

They don't want to let him down, she thought. *If he can stand the weather and elements, then they have no right to complain.*

She sat back and frowned. Thick blankets covered her while she nibbled on hard cheese and sipped a cinnamon tea.

The little I thought I had learned about leadership over the last few months was only me fooling myself. In one day he put the nobility in their place, and in just a short amount of time on the road, he's gained the confidence of every man and woman not already his own. I haven't accomplished a fraction of that.

She looked down at the book in her lap, an exposition on the daily life of a soldier. She had hoped it would give her insight into the men she would be around during the journey to Cathyrium. She closed it and peered back out the window. She watched Jonrell talk to one of his own men and saw the respect that was in the soldier's eyes as they shared a laugh. She had made her decision.

Some things you just can't learn in a book.

* * *

Jonrell looked over to his sister bundled up tight in her thick wool cloak. Water ran down from her eyes as the wind battered her face.

"Are you alright, Your Majesty?" he asked.

Her eyes met his, determined. "I'm fine. Who's next?" she asked.

"Cisod. He's a blacksmith I picked up on Slum Isle. We'll talk to him and the other smiths we picked up from Grayer," he said.

"Then let's go."

He nodded and smiled, kicking his mount into the wind. He was proud of her. She had come to him that morning and said that she wanted to meet those they were traveling with. At first Jonrell thought it was a nice gesture and suggested she would be more comfortable in the carriage. He never expected her to go through with his offer. To her credit, she stood firm and commanded that he let her go with him. They had been at it all day, and other than their break for lunch, she hadn't left his side. She didn't say much which for now was probably for the better since the troops were unsure how to act around their queen. Shocked at seeing someone of her station brave the elements was the most common reaction.

Jonrell finally saw that she truly wanted to be a good ruler. He felt better about the decision he had made before leaving Lyrosene.

I hope that she sees the value in such a decision.

* * *

Jonrell rode his mount through the arched gatehouse and into the castle at Cathyrium. He did his best to hide his displeasure with the awful condition he found the fortress in.

One Above, there is even more work to be done than I imagined.

Lord Caliva stood near the entrance. He was an older man, bald except for a wreath of white hair that blended into a short and well kept beard. Despite his age, he appeared in good health. A number of aides and servants, who appeared eager to serve, surrounded him.

"I thought the messenger you sent ahead was telling lies when he told me of your arrival, My Prince," Lord Caliva said with a bow. He glanced around Jonrell's shoulder as the queen's carriage made its way through the archway. "But now I see it is true. Not only were the rumors of your return true, but the Queen herself has come to grace our presence."

"Aye, it is all true, my lord. My apologies for arriving in such an abrupt manner but I'm afraid there is little time to observe the proper formalities when the fate of the kingdom is on the line."

Lord Caliva nodded. "I heard the news of the fall of Namaris. These are dark times indeed."

"Yes, they are," said Jonrell. He looked around at the gathering crowd of people.

Lord Caliva forced a smile. "My household," he said gesturing to those around him, "will get everyone settled. Dinner can be ready in about two hours if that is fine with you, My Prince"

"Yes, that'll be perfect. If you would, please keep the affair a private one. We have important matters to discuss."

Lord Caliva nodded. "I'm sure some of the hopeful attendees will be upset. But they will understand the need for privacy."

* * *

The heat emanating from the roaring fires of the dining hall was a welcome relief to Elyse. Leaving the cold winter temperatures in exchange for the warmth of the room made her a little drowsy at first. She also realized just how tired and sore she felt from spending the last several days with her brother on horseback.

But it was well worth it.

She had used the time to pick her brother's brain about a number of subjects, even regaining a bit of the closeness she had once shared with him in their youth.

She forgot about her drowsiness as the scent of roasted pig permeated her nose. Stomach growling, her mouth watered as she took in the small feast laid before her on the wide table.

She noticed everyone waiting for her to find her seat. She smiled, and lowered herself with a small sigh onto the plush chair, its soft cushion another comfort she missed.

"Everything looks wonderful, Lord Caliva. I must thank you for your hospitality and allowing us into your home."

He smiled. "It is an honor, Your Majesty. My home is yours." He paused. "If you would allow me to do so, I would like to lead us in a word of prayer to the One Above before we begin our meal."

"I cannot think of a more appropriate thing to do, my lord," she said, bowing her head.

It was a short, but fitting prayer. It spoke about being thankful for each day granted to them and how during times of great stress, they should remember what is most important. In fact, given their current circumstances, she couldn't think of a better prayer to offer.

When Lord Caliva finished giving thanks, the servants began presenting the meal, to her first, and then to others in order of station. Despite her desperate hunger, Elyse remembered her etiquette and ate as a queen should with small portions and even smaller bites. The food tasted delicious, but she found herself distracted when she looked at the way many of the men at the table simply attacked their food, especially those from Jonrell's group of mercenaries. She didn't know whether to be disgusted by their lack of manners, or jealous that they could get away with such behavior.

The large rectangular table held over two dozen people. Lord Caliva sat on the other end from her, in keeping with the northern custom for the lord of a city to sit opposite their ruler.

It is an honor for a lord to be allowed to look their ruler in the eye, she thought, recalling a lesson from her youth.

Jonrell had been seated to Caliva's right. Several of Caliva's captains and his mages were interspersed with the men Jonrell had brought to the meal. During introductions it was quickly evident that many of the men from either side held a particular area of expertise.

No doubt Jonrell and Caliva want the men to grow accustomed to each other as soon as possible.

Other than a polite comment from Lord Caliva's men, few engaged her in conversation. Elyse felt so out of place that she kept to herself and enjoyed her meal while she watched the interaction of the others. During their journey, Jonrell had brought up many of his old lessons, emphasizing those on how to judge and learn from the behavior of those around you. It was a lesson she had heard many times as a youth and often dismissed. She had learned quickly while on the road that it would be a mistake to take her brother's advice for granted again.

The first thing that became evident to her was just how out of place Jonrell's men looked in comparison to the well groomed men of Lord Caliva's council. Despite the boisterous conversations he partook in, Krytien appeared ragged. His faded black robes contrasted sharply with the vibrant colored robes of Caliva's mages.

Her eyes turned to Yanasi and Rygar. Though rarely seen apart, Elyse wondered how two people so different had found happiness with each other. Yanasi had barely looked up from her meal except to whisper something briefly to Rygar. He on the other hand took in all the sights and sounds of the hall. Rygar tried to work himself into several ongoing conversations. Both were near her age, yet she felt little connection to either. In many ways, she was jealous as she watched them. They were each able to hold onto a piece of youth that Elyse never got to enjoy.

Cisod spoke with one of Caliva's captains about the condition of their weapons and supplies. Raker leaned over and butted into the conversation at awkward moments, oblivious that neither was particularly interested in what he had to say. Their snide remarks and looks of frustration did little to deter Raker from giving his opinion. Each comment he accentuated by pointing a half gnawed rib. Elyse shook her head as she watched the exchange.

From what Jonrell had told her, Raker was an engineer and would be crucial during the siege but all she saw was a man who needed a bath and change of clothes. She had only spoken to him once. The conversation ended abruptly when Jonrell cast an icy glare that sent the man cowering away. The look was in response to some passing comment the mercenary made during their official introduction about rolling in hay. Elyse didn't ask why it had aggravated her brother but based on his reaction, she later decided that she probably should have been offended by it.

Elyse was surprised that Jonrell had brought along the two young boys from Slum Isle. Drake seemed to be having a grand time listening to everyone and even laughed at Cisod's frustration with Raker. Jonrell called Drake a genius and had put him under the tutelage of Raker. Their personalities reminded her of Rygar and Yanasi.

Two more people who couldn't be more different. Mal, on the other hand, sat in silence with his shoulders hunched forward while he played with his food. Elyse's heart went out to the boy. Her brother mentioned that Mal had left his father behind to join up with them. Elyse watched the boy look up toward her brother before turning his gaze away in frustration. She wondered if he regretted his decision to leave Slum Isle.

No, I think he looks up to Jonrell. Perhaps he is upset that he is not closer to the conversation with Lord Caliva? It was a guess since she had only spoken with him once and he had seemed uncomfortable speaking to her.

There were a couple others from Jonrell's crew that her brother had brought along but Elyse was ashamed to say that she could not recall their names. *No wonder when I try to learn so many in a matter of days.*

The last of Jonrell's men fascinated her. She had met Kaz more than once since he usually hung around her brother. But despite their frequent meetings, he often acted as if Elyse wasn't there when he spoke to Jonrell. Initially, she found the behavior jarring. Later, she grew more understanding when Jonrell had explained to her how he had come to know the man and how Kaz had little recollection of his past life up until a few months ago.

Noticing that he had not spoken once during the meal, and had been excluded by the others, she ran through several scenarios in her head to strike up a conversation with him. She wasn't sure what had piqued her interest more, his appearance, which was darker than any Byzernian she'd ever seen, or the wonder of starting one's life over, free to leave behind all the pain of the past.

Now I only have to figure out what to ask.

Elyse racked her brain for several minutes, feeling foolish, until she finally blurted out, "So, how do you like Cadonia?" She grimaced, but it was too late to take the question back.

Kaz looked at her from the corner of his eye, and turned with a questioning look. "Were you speaking to me?" he said in a thickly accented voice.

"Yes," she said, trying to recover. "I was wondering if you have enjoyed your stay so far."

He shrugged his massive shoulders. Even through thick winter clothing, Elyse could see the hard lines of the man. "I have very little to compare it to. And with battle looming, I haven't really thought about my enjoyment," said Kaz, looking back at his plate.

Of course, she thought feeling deflated. *That was a pretty stupid question, Elyse.*

To her surprise, she could see that he attempted to continue their conversation, struggling to find the right words. "It is nicer than the island we came from. Larger and far cleaner."

She had to strain to decipher his speech but she smiled all the same, excited to talk to the mysterious man. "I've never been to Slum Isle before, but I've heard a lot about the place. Could you tell me what it is like?" she asked, hoping to keep Kaz talking.

"Yes, if you would like."

* * *

Kaz felt odd describing an island he had visited only once, but he did so anyway. And when he was done, he talked about what it was like to walk through Floroson and Lyrosene for the first time. He felt foolish droning on and on while Jonrell's sister barely said a word except to quickly ask another question. But she seemed interested enough, so he continued.

After some time, he finally thought of a few questions to ask in return. He didn't know why, but Elyse smiled when he did so and then talked for some time herself. Later, he even said something funny or at least he assumed he did. The queen had let out a loud sincere laugh that caused him to grin in return.

He wasn't sure what followed in the few minutes after that laugh as he had a brief glimpse of something, someone in fact, from his past. He swore he heard two laughs then, one inside his head from long ago and one outside in the warm hall. The softness of Elyse's voice and the look in her eyes seemed familiar, too, but he didn't know why.

Will these memories frustrate me forever?

As the night wore on, Kaz could see why Jonrell talked so favorably of his sister. She was a good woman, and like her brother, treated him as if he was no different than anyone else. It surprised him that two people who held so much power appeared to accept him, yet so many others did not.

When the meal concluded she thanked him for his company, and to his surprise found himself returning the sentiment, even referring to her as "Your Majesty," something he had avoided earlier since she was not his queen. Yet now, she had earned his respect.

* * *

She awoke with a quiet knocking, so soft she thought she still dreamed until a voice called out.

"Elyse, are you awake? It's Jonrell. I need to speak with you right away."

She stumbled out of bed in a rush, turning up the oil lamp on the night stand near her bed. Careful not to trip over the books on the floor, she grabbed her robe. "I'm coming," she called out. She slowed as she reached the door as she realized that an attack from Tomalt was impossible since he was weeks away in Namaris.

She cracked the door and saw her brother near the entranceway. "May I please come in?"

She allowed him to enter and caught an odd look from Hadan who stood near her room. Closing the door, she faced her brother. "What's wrong?" she said as she wiped the sleep from her eyes

"I need to talk to you about what Lord Caliva and I discussed."

"You said that could wait until morning."

"Technically, it is morning," he said with a grin.

Elyse didn't return the smile.

Jonrell took the hint. "Most of it is of little interest to you right now with the exception of one area. We are sending a messenger to Duke Jeldor in Ithanthul. We hope to forge an alliance with him."

Elyse shook her head. *I must still be groggy.* "Jeldor? Why would we seek an alliance with him? Even I know he's a cantankerous old man."

"His disposition is not important to us. What is important are his troops. People underestimate him because his lands aren't as large or as well populated as others, but the men that live there are hard. They have to be to live amid that terrain. And their winters are harsher than what we experience in the worst of times. I know. I got caught in one while traveling back from his capital as a boy. Three men froze to death on the journey home." He paused. "Besides, without any word from Estul Island, we are short handed on mages. We can't afford to be short on soldiers too."

Elyse shivered. "If we need troops, then why not seek aid from Olasi? He has always been a friend to the crown."

"True. His men are better trained since they serve as a backup to Conroy when defending the High Pass but we need him to stay put in order to keep a watch on Conroy."

"Then I grant you permission to form an alliance with Jeldor. Can we finish this conversation in the morning?"

Jonrell smiled. "I'm glad you agree but I need more from you than just approval. We need to send someone right away if we hope to get Jeldor's troops here in time."

"Then what do you need me for?"

"I need you to go."

Silence.

"Elyse?" asked Jonrell.

"You're serious?"

"Absolutely."

"Then you're also crazy. Why do I need to go to Ithanthul?"

"Because, as you said, Jeldor is a touchy man. A messenger is not going to get him to form an alliance with us. We need someone to convince him it is in his best interests to join our power."

"And you expect me to do that? You didn't see him at father's funeral. That man doesn't like me at all."

"He doesn't like anyone. That's my point. We can't just send anyone to talk to him. Otherwise, he'll be insulted."

"Then why don't you go. You're better at this sort of thing."

"I can't go. I need to be here. There's too much work to do."

"Send someone else then."

"This is too important for me to trust with someone else," said Jonrell, almost pleading. "If Jeldor listens to anyone, it would be either you or me. I'm the only one who can command an army so it must be you that goes to Ithanthul."

"Are things so bad, Jonrell?"

Jonrell let out a deep sigh and ran his hand through his hair. Suddenly he seemed much older, and she saw for the first time the stress he hid so well. "Yes. This is our best and perhaps only chance." As if sensing Elyse's sudden dread, he forced a smile and rested his hands on her shoulders. "Look, in front of others, I have to keep any reservations hidden lest they creep into the hearts and minds of those I'm trying to help." He paused. "Your subjects will mirror the way you carry yourself. A soldier, especially, must be able to look for strength in those he's fighting for. Otherwise, he is as good as dead. Remember that."

"Then why are you letting your guard down now?"

"Because I need you to understand the severity of our situation. I never intended for you to sit here and wait for Tomalt. If Tomalt captures Cathyrium, being with Jeldor will give you a chance to escape back to Lyrosene or at least find safety somewhere outside of Cadonia. Don't look surprised. The worst is always a possibility, though I don't believe it will come to that." His face grew hard once again and all the doubt Elyse had glimpsed washed away. "I won't allow it to happen."

"Then why make such a big production about me coming here?"

"In a way you're extra bait for Tomalt. We need him to attack us while Grayer strengthens the army at Lyrosene."

"Well, he's going to know I'm not here anymore once everyone sees me leaving."

"Not if you leave now. Only the night watch is up and we can easily keep them from spotting you. Plus, if someone does, they'll never assume the queen is leaving, especially to seek aid from Jeldor in the middle of winter."

"I'm sure they will find out eventually. After all, you can't tell people I'm in the tower sleeping forever."

"No, but if you came down suddenly with a strange illness…I mean, you did look under the weather this evening. I said so myself, didn't I?"

So that's why he made such a big deal about me needing rest.

"But," he continued, "if no one even catches a glimpse of you, people will begin to ask questions. That's where Lobella comes into play."

Elyse cocked her head. "You expect her to impersonate me? We look nothing alike."

"Oh, I wouldn't say that. You two are practically the same height and build. It is the hair that throws things off. But Hag has something that will dye her hair to match yours. Then all we need her to do is walk in front of an open window from time to time or have a servant catch a quick glance through a dimly lit doorway and we should be alright."

"But won't people question her disappearance?"

"Not likely. We've only just arrived today. And with so many among our party, it will be hard to keep track of who was who. But that may be different come tomorrow. Which is why you must leave tonight."

"What makes you think she'll go along with the charade?"

"I just informed her before coming to you. In fact, she should be on her way up shortly."

"That is an unfair thing to do to her. She is a friend."

"War isn't fair. But everyone must play their part in the game if we ever hope to win, including Lobella."

What am I supposed to do? He told me to trust him. "Fine. Then who am I going with. Surely, you don't expect me to travel for weeks across the country by myself."

"Hadan and Willum, four others they've selected from the army, and then two I'm personally selecting from the Hell Patrol."

"Who exactly from your crew?"

"Rygar. There are few others with sharper senses and you'll need those in order to watch out for any bandits on the road."

Bandits? This is crazy. "And the other?"

"Kroke."

"The one always playing with the knives?"

"That's him."

She shuddered. "I don't like him. He frightens me."

"He doesn't look like much, but he frightens a lot of people and with good reason. He has an area of expertise you'll need while traveling."

"What area is that?"

"Killing."

Elyse swallowed hard.

"Don't worry. I've known the man for years. I promise he will not harm you. In fact, he will do whatever is necessary to ensure your safety."

"I wish you would choose someone else."

"You have someone in mind?"

"Kaz, perhaps. He seems very nice, and besides, even I can see he would be just as able of a protector."

Jonrell raised an eyebrow. "Hmmm."

"What?"

"I've just never heard Kaz described as nice before." He paused. "I saw you talking to him at dinner. That must have been some conversation you two had."

Elyse blushed. "What are you saying?"

"Nothing. Forget about it. But yes, you are right. Even though others would disagree with me, I would trust Kaz to do this as well."

"Good," said Elyse, satisfied that Jonrell saw her point.

"But I need him here with me to defend the wall. Besides, you are going to stand out enough as a woman traveling with more than half a dozen men. Adding someone to the group who looks as different as he does will only raise more questions, and possibly cause more trouble. No, it has to be Kroke."

Elyse didn't say anything, defeated.

"Look, I know this is hard to put on you at the last second, but I know you can do it. I wouldn't send you otherwise. We need Jeldor's troops."

"And what's to stop him from just taking me hostage himself?"

There was a knock at the door.

"That must be Lobella," said Jonrell. "Shall I have her come in to help you with any last minute preparations?"

Elyse nodded.

"Good. Remember, you'll need to travel light. Only the essentials."

Jonrell walked up and hugged her tight. "I'm proud of you. I know this isn't easy."

He was right, it wasn't.

CHAPTER 22

Elyse sat on an old, rotted out log next to a low fire. The log was anything but comfortable but still better than sitting in the snow. The fire barely kept away the chill. Worried about attracting undue attention, her companions dared not build anything larger.

Since leaving Cathyrium two weeks ago, each day seemed more miserable than the one before. Weather alternated between ice and snow, making the road that much more difficult. The only constant was the wind which gave Elyse a nagging chill.

They traveled at a furious pace, despite the elements working against them. The only rest came when Rygar needed time to scout ahead or they made camp.

As others set up camp, Kroke muttered something about looking for a stream to clean and sharpen his knives in. It seemed the mercenary was always doing something with a knife and Elyse had grown tired of his habits. The thought of those grim habits probably would have produced a shiver if she wasn't already shaking from the cold.

She looked down at the borrowed brown trousers she wore, and found herself even more aware of her situation. All of the clothes she brought with her came from her servant.

I think Lobella may have gotten the better end of this deal.

The queen watched the men tend to the horses and sighed as she resigned herself to the faint heat of the flames. The journey had so far been a lonely one. She had tried to talk to the men as she did with Jonrell on their trip to Cathyrium, but most were not inclined to speak with her. Rygar was an exception, and the two often shared a laugh before settling in for the night since he often scouted ahead during the day. Her own personal guards, like the others, had avoided any conversation at all. The prospect of talking so casually with their queen seemed to make them uncomfortable. That only left Kroke.

And it is obvious he dislikes me. Only the One Above knows how he and Rygar manage to get along.

So Elyse spent most of the time alone with her thoughts, trying to come up with a plan to convince Jeldor to form an alliance with her. She wondered if Jonrell really thought she stood a chance of gaining the duke's support, or if he simply wanted to get her away from Cathyrium. For some strange reason, her brother seemed to believe in her. And that only depressed her more. Letting down a kingdom when everyone expected it of her was one thing, but now that her brother was so sure she would succeed, she couldn't bear to see him again if she failed.

* * *

The large oak at his back blocked the wind. Kroke glided the blade up and down a whetstone, working its edge to a perfection that few others would be able to appreciate. In fact, most would not have even known the blade needed any attention at all. But he knew.

He knew every detail of all his blades, and over time, they each became an extension of him. Keeping a knife in his hand never seemed an odd thing to him like it did to others. It suited him fine that few understood the habit.

People seem to bother you less when a knife is already pulled. Steel scraping against stone brought him a level of peace that he could not explain. He loved the sound. *There is only one other sound I enjoy more.* The thought brought a devilish grin to his face.

His habits had kept him a step ahead of his opponents and saved his life more than once. He turned the blade over in his hand, tilting it back and forth, and smiled. Its reflection caught the movement of two men slinking behind him on either side of the tree. They were obviously unaware that he had heard them long before this moment. They had tried to mask their boots crunching on the packed snow by walking in time to the scrape of his blade, but Kroke heard the difference right away.

Flipping the knife back and forth in his hand from hilt to blade, he grinned again. The movement served as a distraction to the two men approaching as he set the whetstone down and slid his other hand down to his belt, removing another dagger from its sheath.

In one fluid motion Kroke ducked a swinging ax that slammed into the tree at his back and rolled to his feet. He threw his knife at the man farthest from him.

One of Elyse's guards.

Willum fell with a thud to the ground while he clutched at the knife in his neck. His legs kicked up snow as he struggled to breathe. Kroke saw the other man had abandoned his ax and reached for his sword. Before the soldier's hand made it to his scabbard, Kroke stepped forward and jammed his other knife through the man's palm and into his hip.

The soldier screamed. Kroke flung him to the ground and sat atop his chest.

Kroke brought another blade to the attacker's throat. "Why?" he asked, showing no emotion.

The man shook his head and tried to catch his breath.

Kroke moved the blade from his throat to the man's crotch, adding pressure to the point. "Why?"

The soldier's eyes widened. "The queen."

"What about the queen? Did she order this?" Kroke had seen how nervous he made her. She didn't seem like the kind of person to order his death, but not many people ever seem like the kind of person they really are.

The man shook his head. "No. We were told to kill the queen." The man's eyes drifted to the knife near his groin. "Please, I have a family...." the man started.

"Then you won't need this anymore," said Kroke, shoving the blade through his groin to the hilt. The man let out a howl. Kroke slid the knife out and swung it forward through the center of the man's chest. The move silenced the chilling sound that echoed through the woods. The blood gurgling in the man's throat made Kroke smile.

He knew it took a sick man to be so pleased about things but there was always something about the sound of death he enjoyed.

What in life could possibly be better?

A high-pitched scream coming from the camp interrupted his dark thoughts. He cursed to himself and set off into the woods.

* * *

Elyse found a stick and stirred the ashes in the fire, keeping it going as best she could since the others were too preoccupied to bother. It was the least she could do. Actually, it felt like the only thing she could do. She fed a few sticks to the small flames, conscientious about making sure the fire did not grow too large.

I feel even more helpless out here than I did in council.

Footsteps crunched across the snow nearby and she looked up. Hadan wore a troubled look on his face and his hands trembled.

"Is something wrong? Maybe you should warm yourself by the fire," she said, hoping for a little company.

Hadan stopped a few feet from her and drew his sword.

Elyse looked around, noticing that others moved toward her with their blades drawn. She looked back up at Hadan. "Is something the matter? Have we been discovered?"

"No, Your Majesty, we are isolated from the world. And that's why this is the perfect spot," he said, voice quavering.

"A perfect spot?" she said looking around, not understanding. "What are you talking about?"

Hadan glanced over his shoulder. "Don't make this more difficult than it has to be, Your Majesty," he whispered, facing her again. "Let me end this quickly. The others want to make use of you first and I told them I would allow them to only if I was given the chance before them. But I will not do that to you. I am not completely without honor," he said taking a step forward.

Elyse watched him raise his sword.

She understood.

She screamed and with the stick in her hand threw hot ashes into Hadan's face. He dropped his sword and gasped. The others came at her and Elyse ran. Looking over her shoulder, she watched in horror as a sword erupted from Hadan's chest. Blood hissed into the snow.

She stumbled off toward the woods. Footsteps closed in and a cold hand wrapped around her arm, flinging her to the ground. She screamed as the man straddled her. His look of satisfaction vanished as an arrow sank into his chest. Gagging, he pulled the arrow out and his blood sprayed across her face. She scrambled away as Rygar galloped past, taking down another of the men who had turned on her.

An arrow struck the scout just as his shot found its mark. Rygar toppled from his mount and fell into the snow. The man who fired the shot drew out his sword and walked over to the prone scout. Elyse screamed at the soldier, too far away and too helpless to do anything more.

He snarled at her. "Don't worry, Your Majesty. I'll see to you in a moment."

His smile dropped as a look of confusion took its place. The man looked down to see a dagger buried in his chest. He blinked rapidly, mouth falling open as two more blades sank into his torso inches from the first. The snow muffled his fall.

With the last of her attackers dead, Elyse hurried over to Rygar. Her hand moved to the arrow but stopped suddenly at a shout.

"Don't touch it!"

Elyse jumped and looked up to see Kroke running toward her.

"Move. Let me take a look at it," said Kroke. He got down on his knees and examined the wound. "Rygar, you alive?" Rygar moaned as Kroke turned him over. "I'll take that as a yes."

"What am I doing on the ground?" asked Rygar.

"You were hit by an arrow and fell from your horse," said Elyse.

"That explains why my side is killing me."

"What doesn't make sense is why you didn't have your mail on. Jonrell would have your hide for that," said Kroke as he started to cut away the clothing around the arrow.

Rygar winced audibly with each jostle. "Be careful. Mail makes too much noise. It's easier to scout without armor."

"Easier to die too," said Kroke.

He pulled away the last bit of clothing and Elyse saw the wound. She paled, but took a deep breath to calm herself.

"I'm not feeling too good, Kroke," said Rygar.

"You're losing a lot of blood."

"Will I make it?" asked Rygar.

"I'm pretty sure it didn't hit anything important," said Kroke.

"How do you know?" asked Elyse.

Kroke shrugged. "I don't. But he's alive and talking. That's gotta be good for something." He paused. "I still need to get that arrow out and cauterize the wound. But first I have to move him."

"What can I do to help?" asked Elyse.

Kroke gave her a look.

"Please. He saved my life."

Kroke nodded. "Go build up that fire."

"What about keeping it low so we won't be seen?"

"We can't worry about that now," he said, gesturing to Rygar. "Clear away as much snow from around that log you were sitting on. When you're done, place one of those blankets on the ground."

Elyse nodded and ran off. Despite their situation it felt good to be useful.

Shortly after clearing a spot, Kroke came over and set Rygar down next to the fire. Kroke unsheathed a knife strapped to his chest and handed it to Elyse. "Stick the blade in the fire but do not let it touch the ash."

The fire was too strong now for Elyse to hold the knife in place, so she set up a few pieces of wood to prop up the blade. While she did that, Kroke filled a pot with snow. He pulled a pouch from one of their bags and poured the contents into the melt.

"What is that?" she asked.

"Herbs to fight off infection and help with the pain," Kroke answered.

Once the mixture came to a boil, he removed the pot from the flames and set it into the snow to cool. Handing a cup of the liquid to Elyse, he said, "It's still warm but I need you to help him drink this when I prop him up."

She nodded and though he struggled to swallow, Rygar got the liquid down.

"Better?" asked Kroke, looking at Rygar.

The scout managed a slight nod.

"Good." He placed a stick in Rygar's mouth. "You bite down as hard as you need to on this, but whatever you do, I need you to stay still. Understand?"

Rygar swallowed hard and managed another nod.

Kroke looked over to Elyse. "You still want to help?"

"Yes."

"Alright then. I need you to keep him still because no matter how hard he tries not to move, he's gonna start jumping the second I start pulling and tugging," said Kroke, ignoring the scout's whimper. "The more he moves, the worse it gets for everyone. So I need you to hold him down like your life depended on it, understand?"

Elyse nodded. "Just show me where to be so I'm not in your way."

Kroke showed her how to hold down his arms and chest. He then sat on Rygar's legs. "Look away. I saw how pale you got when you first saw the wound. This could get messy and I don't need you passing out on me."

She looked away and swallowed as Kroke gave her one last bit of instruction.

"Oh, and breath through your mouth."

Elyse knew Kroke had started when she felt Rygar shaking and heard him grunting. She watched helplessly as tears streamed down Rygar's face and she began praying to the One Above in part for help and in part to drown out the slew of curses sputtering from Kroke's mouth as he worked. When the hissing of hot steal against skin replaced the curses, she knew the arrow was free. By that point, Rygar passed out from the pain.

The smell of burning flesh reached her. She took three quick steps and emptied the contents of her stomach, nearly falling over as she heaved.

She turned back to Kroke where the mercenary pulled out a white bandage. He didn't look up. "I warned you, didn't I?"

"Yes, you did," Elyse muttered.

"If you're done, get over here. I need to show you how to take care of this in case I'm not able to."

Elyse hobbled back to Kroke as he put some sort of salve on the blackened skin and wrapped the bandage around Rygar's wound. She grimaced and felt her stomach turn as she saw the size of the gash.

Kroke noticed the gesture. "If you're going to throw up again, you better get up now."

"No, I'm alright." She paused. "What happened? The wound is so much bigger."

Kroke sighed. "A piece of the arrow broke off and I had to fish it out as best I could." He shook his head. "I did a number on him though and I ain't a healer. Now, we'll just have to wait and see."

"So in the morning, he'll be able to travel?" asked Elyse.

"Absolutely not."

"But you stopped the bleeding?"

"For now, yeah. But it'll start back up again if we try to put him on a horse and jostle him around."

"So, then what do we do?"

"We get comfortable. I don't want to travel for at least a couple of days."

"But Jonrell told me we had to get to Ithanthul as soon as possible."

Kroke pointed. "There's the road." He gestured toward their supplies. "And there's a pack. Grab a horse and go if you feel like you need to."

"By myself?"

"That's the only way you're leaving here tomorrow."

"But…"

Kroke cut in, his voice raising. "We leave when he is safe for travel."

"How long will that be?" asked Elyse, startled.

"As long as it takes." He turned his back to Elyse and started walking toward the woods.

Fear gripped her. "Where are you going?"

"Firewood," he yelled back without turning around. "We need more to get through the night."

"What about me?" she shouted back.

Kroke didn't answer as he ambled out of sight. She became aware of the stillness around her, quiet except for the crackling fire. She shivered as she caught sight of the lifeless corpses of the soldiers. She felt numb, not from the cold, but because she realized how close she had come to dying.

She looked back at Rygar who lay still, his chest slowly rising and falling. She found two spare blankets and covered him. She stoked the fire higher and looked at the bloody snow near Hadan's body. Kroke hadn't returned and the sun started to drop below the treeline.

Images of wolves or bears that would smell the fresh blood gave her a shudder. She needed to move at least his body away from the fire. The prospect of sleeping feet away from a dead man did not comfort her either.

She grabbed Hadan's body by his boots and pulled. The job was harder than she expected. Eventually she realized she could tie a rope to one of the horses and use it to drag the bodies away.

Elyse settled back down next to the fire just as the last bit of light faded to black.

After checking on Rygar, she nibbled on a hard biscuit. She leaned back against a fallen log and waited for Kroke.

Elyse stared into the black beyond the fire and wondered if she would ever sleep again.

* * *

"Mmm, that's good. Definitely your best yet, Your Majesty," said Rygar, taking a bite of the stew she handed him.

Elyse dipped her head, embarrassed for some reason by the compliment. "Thank you. I'm not sure what I did though. I just dumped a bunch of stuff we had into a pot."

Rygar shrugged. "Whatever it is, keep doing it," he said taking another bite.

Elyse smiled and spooned out another bowl to take to Kroke who sat a few steps back sharpening his knives.

That's the third time he's checked their edges today.

Kroke sheathed his blade, set down the whetstone and took the bowl from Elyse's hand without looking up. She stood there for a moment, waiting for any sort of comment but he said nothing.

Since the attack and the subsequent tending to Rygar, the only words Kroke had spoken to her were a few harsh instructions when dissatisfied with what she was doing. And that seemed to be just about anything, tending the fire, caring for Rygar's wound, her cooking, and so on. So, she decided to take the initiative herself and sat down next to him. As she expected, he continued to ignore her.

"How do you like the stew?" she asked.

"It's edible," he said with a grunt.

She started to open her mouth to try a different approach, but failed to utter a word.

"What do you want?"

"I just wanted to see if you liked the stew."

He set his bowl down and looked up at her for the first time. "Don't give me that. You want to say something, so say it."

Elyse frowned. "I want to know if we can leave tomorrow."

"No."

The brusqueness of his response reminded her of why she hadn't initially liked the man. Her feelings toward him had softened after he had helped to save her life and as she witnessed the concern he had for Rygar. But with each day, she found her old feelings for the man returning. "Why not?"

"Because I said so."

"But Rygar is doing better each day and we've been here for almost a week."

"He's not healthy enough to travel."

"Her Majesty is right. I'm feeling much better," said Rygar.

"That's because all you've done is lay there and eat. As it is you want for a nap almost every time you get back from taking a leak. You really think you can stay on a horse all day? Don't be stupid, kid."

Rygar lowered his voice. "I can manage."

Kroke grunted, then turned back to Elyse. "Like I said, no." He picked up his bowl and started eating again but when he saw Elyse hadn't moved and still looked at him he set it down with a sigh. "What?"

It was only then that she noticed how Kroke never addressed her as a queen or showed her proper respect. She guessed it was because her mind had been preoccupied, but now that she noticed the slight, it bothered her and even made her angry.

Even Hadan had addressed me properly before trying to kill me.

As she thought about it, she realized that she hadn't been acting much like a queen since they had left Cathyrium. Before the attack she had been sullen about being on her own, and nervous about her meeting with Jeldor. Since the attack, she had been acting more as a servant to Rygar and Kroke. Where Rygar showed constant appreciation, Kroke seemed to expect such behavior.

She decided that helping out was not something she would change. After all, Jonrell often pitched in where other commanders would not have, and the men respected him more. However, she had forgotten how important her task was. An entire army, a city, and in the end, a kingdom, depended on her success. Before, she worried under the weight of such a task, but now she felt a sense of urgency.

"I command you to leave with me on the morrow to Ithanthul," she blurted out.

Kroke's face twisted in shock and then the mercenary let out a low laugh, the first she had ever heard from him. The laugh was far from comforting. "You command me, do you? I don't care if you are Jonrell's sister, you are not my queen. I take my orders from only one man."

"But he gave you orders to listen to me," she said, trying to sound stern.

"Sorry, lass. But he only told me to keep you alive. The way I see it, I have a better chance of doing that here than anywhere else, and while we do that, Rygar can get himself healed up."

"But don't you care about my people?" she pleaded.

"You said it. They are your people, not mine. No, in fact, you're the reason I'm not with *my* people."

"But the longer we sit around, the more people will die."

The mercenary shrugged, turning away.

"And what about the Hell Patrol?"

"What about them?"

"Don't you care about their lives?"

Kroke sneered. "I care about little in this world."

"Don't lie to me. I know you don't like being stuck with me but you've said over and over again that you want to make sure Rygar is alright. That means you care about him. Just like you do about the others."

Kroke cocked his head. "What's your point?"

"My point is the longer we wait here, the more of your men will die."

The mercenary's eyes widened slightly but quickly resumed their normal emotionless expression. And just like that, she knew that Jonrell was right. If you pay attention to people long enough, you can learn a lot about them. And now, she knew how to motivate Kroke.

Kroke shrugged her comment off. "They'll get out of there before things get hairy. I'm not worried." He didn't sound convinced.

Elyse shook her head. "No they won't. You know my brother, and this is too important to him. Otherwise he wouldn't have come halfway across the world to get here. He won't just get up and leave. He'll die fighting. And I know just enough about his men to know that they'll all die right alongside him without him ever having to ask them to." She paused, watching her words turn in his head before saying what she guessed he was thinking. "And if you're here with me, you won't be there to help them, will you?"

Kroke was about to say something in return, but at the sound of a grunt they both turned back toward Rygar who had stood and leaned on a stick they had given him for support.

"What do you think you're doing up?" said Kroke.

"The queen is right, Kroke. She may not have convinced you, but she has me. I'm not going to be the reason everyone dies. I'd never be able to look Yanasi in the eyes if that happened," said Rygar, obviously missing the point that Yanasi would be dead along with everyone else.

"Sit down," Kroke hissed. "We ain't going anywhere now. It's too late in the day. We'll start first thing in the morning. Satisfied?" he asked, casting Elyse a look that could freeze water.

She nodded. "Thank you."

He picked up his bowl and turned away from her, grumbling. "Then leave me to eat in peace. Let's see how much you're thanking me when we all end up dead on the side of the road on account I'm dragging a woman and half a man along with me into areas I know nothing about."

* * *

An elbow from Kroke, whether intentional or not woke her as the black night turned a dull gray. He stood after glancing down each side of the road. He muttered something about checking on the horses. She winced first at the cold air against her body where the mercenary had lain, and winced a second time as she shook the night's stiffness from her limbs.

They had spent the night huddled in an empty ditch, a mere two day's ride from Ithanthul, using the sunken pocket of earth to block out the wind and provide cover from travelers. They spent the previous night without a fire. Without the extra blankets taken from the traitors, Elyse was sure they would have died during the night.

She wrapped one of the blankets around her as she watched Kroke disappear into the woods. Despite her fingers and toes feeling numb, her back hurting her from sleeping in such an awkward position, and just an overall sense of exhaustion, she found herself smiling at the white landscape, branches and fallen trees covered in a soft snow. Taking in her surroundings, it was the first time in days she had even bothered to give herself a moment of peace, so focused she had been on her goal to see Jeldor.

Elyse turned to the low snapping of twigs and the crunch of snow as Kroke led the horses toward her.

We'll probably just eat dried jerky as we ride again, she thought with a sigh. Bending down, her hand fell on Rygar's shoulder. "Wake up, lazy. We've got to get moving."

Nothing.

She shook his shoulder this time, speaking louder. "Rygar. Let's go. We can't just stay here all morning."

Still nothing. Elyse moved his head where she could see him and saw that his mouth hung open and his breathing was shallow. Panicked she called out to Kroke. She heard the mercenary covering the distance to her with a quickened pace. He muttered a curse. "Keep your voice down. What's the matter with you?"

Elyse looked back at him. "It's Rygar. Something's wrong."

Kroke handed her the reins. She stepped away, wrapping them around a nearby tree. By the time she came back, Kroke had pulled up Rygar's shirt and inspected his bandage. It was soaked in blood.

"What happened?" she asked.

"It must have opened up last night and the fool didn't say anything," said Kroke.

"But I thought it was better."

"It was better but it was never healed. I warned you this could happen," he said, cursing himself. "Start getting some wood together. We'll need to build another fire and cauterize the wound again."

"But I thought you were worried someone would see us."

"And they still might. Then again, it is early. Maybe if we keep the fire low enough, the smoke won't be as noticeable."

Elyse didn't argue. Even if they got caught, she owed too much to Rygar to risk his life any further. She wouldn't see him bleed to death because of her own fear.

Some time later, the embers of a small fire faded. Elyse and Kroke packed in tight around it as they tried to make use of what little warmth they could draw from it. They had given Rygar their blankets to stay warm. They had been able to stop the bleeding again and rewrap his wound, but he had broken out in a fever and Kroke was out of herbs.

Elyse decided she had enough of feeling helpless. She stood up and headed toward one of the horses.

"What do you think you're doing?" asked Kroke.

"Going to Ithanthul."

"Are you mad? He isn't fit to travel," said Kroke with a gesture to Rygar. "Or do you not even care what happens to him?"

She snapped her head around and felt her anger rising. "Why do you think I'm going? If I make it, I can send help and possibly a healer to you. Neither of us can do him any good right now."

"The roads are too dangerous for you."

"I'll manage," she said, though not completely convinced.

Kroke let out a sigh and cursed. "Let me go then. You can stay with Rygar."

She shook her head. "No. I'll be able to talk to Duke Jeldor, you won't."

"You have to get there first. Do you expect to just waltz right through the miles of land between here and the city without anyone stopping you? Something can happen at any moment if you aren't careful."

Elyse opened her mouth to argue but was cut off.

"The man is right, woman. Anything can happen."

They both turned at the voice and saw a soldier with a drawn bow standing over them on the road. The arrow was pointed at Kroke. Two others stood on either side with arrows notched as well. "You can get your hand away from that belt."

Elyse caught Kroke lowering his hand, cursing yet again. She took the opportunity to speak first, not sure what else to do. "Please, kind sirs. We need some help. We are on our way to Ithanthul…"

"To meet with Duke Jeldor, eh? Aye, I heard you. Talking loud enough to scare away all the game around here. And who do you think you are that he would want to see you."

"Don't say…." started Kroke but Elyse shouted over him.

"I am Queen Elyse. Your Ruler," she said, trying to sound as regal as one could covered in filth and freezing.

The soldiers laughed.

"My ruler, you say?" said the man. "I only have one ruler." He let out a loud whistle and moments later the sound of hooves clicked closer along the dirt path.

A voice that sounded strangely familiar called out. "You found something?"

"Yes, my lord, something you may be interested in."

"What is it?" said the voice as a man familiar to Elyse strode into view.

"This commoner claims to be the queen. In fact they were arguing about who was going to stay with this one while the other came to speak with you. He looks pretty bad," said the soldier pointing to Rygar.

"My lord, surely you can see who I am even despite my appearance," said Elyse.

"All I see are potential spies," said Jeldor.

"Aye, my lord, They were probably sent by Lord Bronn," replied one of his men.

Jeldor looked down at Rygar. "Bring the wagon for this one and have Osher look at him for now until we get back to the castle. Tie the other two up."

"Tie us up? What for?" asked Elyse.

Jeldor quickly hid the smile pulling at the sides of his mouth, but could do nothing for the sparkle in his eyes. "To be put in the dungeon for questioning, of course," said Jeldor. "I'm sure if given enough time we can get to the truth of things."

CHAPTER 23

Jonrell scribbled in a large ledger, recording the latest shipment of supplies from Lyrosene. He trusted no one else to track the things so crucial to an army's success. Any mistake would be his, and anyone brave enough to tamper with the supplies would have to be smart enough to change multiple books of record.

Still, Jonrell couldn't be everywhere at once, forcing him to rely on someone else to check in the goods as they came in from Lyrosene, as well as those produced and consumed each day in Cathyrium. Lord Caliva handled those tedious tasks for him.

Caliva rattled off more numbers while Jonrell's quill scratched at a furious pace to keep up. "...ten bushels of mixed beans and barley, two hundred quarters of corn, fifteen quarters of wheat malt, twenty quarters of oatmeal, five barrels of vinegar, ten barrels of wine, and twenty barrels of salt. That does it for the food."

Jonrell flipped several pages, dipped his nib into ink. "Go on."

Caliva ran down the lists, detailing the amounts of iron, lead, bolts, and cable that came in on the wagons that morning. "...and the last wagon contained twelve barrels full of arrows."

Looking up from his ledger, Jonrell raised an eyebrow. "Arrows?"

"Yes, my prince. Illyan sent a note with today's shipment saying that they are compliments of General Grayer. Apparently production amongst the fletchers has increased at such a rate that he could spare sending them our way. He goes on to say that Grayer hopes to have twice that many on the next shipment."

"Excellent news. I was not expecting them to catch up so fast. It's not a lot, but One Above knows we could use all the help we can get."

Caliva nodded.

"Does Illyan say when we can expect the next shipment to arrive?"

"No, My Prince, he does not give a date. He only says that the roads may allow one or possibly two more shipments before the snow makes them unfit to travel."

"Aye, and then we'll be on our own," said Jonrell, his words hanging dead in the air. *It'll be all up to you, Elyse.*

"My Prince, I really wish you would consider recalling Krytien before the roads become too treacherous. He is a huge asset to us here."

"I know. But he is already well on his way to Floroson. We will need to make do without him."

Caliva grunted. "An army of eight thousand, including those you brought from Lyrosene. Another ninety-six soldiers from the Hell Patrol and a couple hundred commoners to act as support. That's only a fraction of what Tomalt fields."

"I've faced worse odds," said Jonrell in an even tone.

Caliva seemed disappointed by the response but bowed all the same. "As you say, my Prince."

* * *

After Caliva excused himself, Jonrell locked away his ledger and put on his heavy winter cloak, dyed a crimson red. *Blood red*, he thought, remembering the words Ronav had told him.

"Most men wear black, hoping to look like the Angel of Death himself but I say why bother? Anyone who has seen the fool is already dead by that point. Doesn't serve much purpose to strike fear in a dead man. But blood? Even the simplest of men knows blood is what gives us life. That's why the Hell Patrol wears red as bright as fresh blood pouring out a man's chest. It's a reminder, Jonrell. A reminder that their life is in our hands. They may not come to that realization when we first meet them in battle but I promise you, when they're crawling over the mangled corpses on the battlefield, watching that crimson flow spilling out upon the ground, they'll look up and see me smiling. Then they'll understand."

Jonrell wasn't sure why those words had come to mind, but it acted as a bit of a wakeup call to his attitude. Ronav had been a man that exuded confidence and walked with a swagger that few dared to call him on. Those that did, rarely lived to tell about it. When Jonrell had first assumed command, he had adopted a similar swagger, trying to emulate his former commander. Over time, it seemed more natural and less of an act. He opened and closed his fists before exiting the room, once again looking over the color of his clothes. *The Hell Patrol. A name that struck fear for years just about everywhere in the world. Except Cadonia. There wasn't a need here before. But now there is.*

* * *

Jonrell made his way down the tower's stairs. When not burdened by the administrative duties of preparing an army, he made it a point to be seen several times throughout the day.

Several people bowed and acknowledged his passing as he descended. He was as courteous as time would allow, but was careful not to pause too long. His mind was too focused on the task at hand. He hoped to make his first set of rounds early today so he could tend to other matters after lunch.

Stepping into the practice yard the renewed wind whipped his coat around him. He suppressed a shiver as the cool air crawled down his neck.

Jonrell watched Yanasi lead the archers, firing two shots off for every one of theirs. Despite her speed and the wind working against her, her arrows found the center of her target each and every time. She barked at the rows of archers as she drew another arrow.

"Faster! You've each got five more quivers at your feet, all of them untouched." She let an arrow fly and didn't bother to follow it with her eye. She turned to the man next to her as her arrow found its mark thirty yards away. The man had been in too big of a hurry and fumbled an arrow from his grip. He bent over frantically to pick it up.

"Take your time to aim," she said. "You can't let yourself be flustered by what's going on around you. You need to be able to do this as easily as putting on your boots each day."

Jonrell shook his head. *I never imagined our talks on the way to Cathyrium would have increased her self esteem so much. She's like a drill sergeant with her men.* He smiled at that. *I should have listened to you long ago, Cassus. Giving her more compliments and pushing her harder has done wonders for improving her confidence.*

The man threw his bow to the ground in frustration and looked up at her with fire in his eyes. "Make up your mind. Is it faster you want or accuracy?" he snarled.

"I don't want either. I *demand* both," said Yanasi.

The man took a step forward and glared down at the red-headed woman. The others stopped, and all eyes turned to the confrontation. None noticed Jonrell working his way forward, scowling.

The soldier stood a head taller than Yanasi and outweighed her by a good fifty pounds. He leaned in close with a look of disgust. "I'm sick of taking orders from some low-rent, hired sword, especially from one who's got to relieve herself while sitting down. What do you think of that?"

Jonrell tightened his fists at the comment but forced himself to walk slower so as not to give away his approach. He didn't want to interrupt. This was the first time he had trusted Yanasi with any sort of command. She was the best archer he'd ever seen, and if they were going to be ready to defend the walls, he wanted the men to learn from the best. Jonrell had warned her that this scenario would probably happen at some point.

This is her battle, and if she doesn't put the man in his place now, it will only get worse.

Yanasi just stood there staring in silence, her eyes leaving his. *One Above, girl. Now isn't the time to give in to them.*

The soldier smiled as if sensing he won. "I tell you what. Why don't you go work in the kitchen with the other women. Better yet, there are plenty of beds that need warming during these cold nights," he said with a chuckle. Several others joined in at the comment and Jonrell saw Yanasi twist her hands around the black bow and shifted her feet.

She slammed her bow up between the soldier's legs with a force that Jonrell hadn't seen her use even when dealing with Raker. The man doubled over and let out a gasp that was cut off as Yanasi's fist crashed in under the man's chin and rocked him flat on his back. Yanasi jumped on top of him, knee thudding into his groin as she leaned in close.

"I reckon there will be one less bed that'll need warming tonight. Seems like it might be several nights before that swelling down there resides I'd say. In fact, you may have to sit down to relieve yourself for awhile. Ain't that something?" she said with a grin, though there was nothing playful about it.

Jonrell walked up just then. "Everything alright here?"

Yanasi jumped to her feet and got a bit of her old sheepish look to her face as she started to speak, almost as if someone caught her picking their pockets. "Well Commander, what happened was..."

Jonrell cut her off. "I saw what happened. The man should be punished for disrespecting one of his superiors. Usually a man would receive three lashes for such behavior. But I'll leave that decision to you," he said, making sure everyone heard him.

Yanasi looked back at the man who groaned on the ground. She shook her head. "No. I think he's learned his lesson."

Jonrell nodded. *Atta girl. Be forceful but not cruel.* "Good." He turned to the others. "Anyone else have a problem with the way training is being run here?" Heads hung low, eyes averted. "Speak up now if you have an issue. Because I won't entertain it after today. This is your last chance, no repercussions."

A throat cleared. "Well, Sir. It's just that with all this wind, we can't shoot straight. Most of us never practiced like this before. It's not that we don't understand the reason behind it. It seems harsh is all."

"If you think it seems harsh now, how do you think it's going to feel when someone's shooting back at you? If you think the wind is a distraction, what do you think a man dying next to you is going to be like? There are no perfect conditions in war. Practice should be as miserable as you can make it, because it will better prepare you for the real thing. You all need to understand that as a unit, your skills will be crucial once things get under way. The man next to you needs to be like your brother, your commander, like a parent. That is what you need to think about in this yard. Bettering yourself however you can, so you can save the men around you.

"I know you men are mostly part-time soldiers, and haven't seen what a full-scale battle is like. It isn't pretty. In fact, it's nothing you can fully prepare yourself for. That's why you need to trust me and your captains. We've lived that hell."

Jonrell scanned the faces looking at him and waited for an argument. Someone might mutter something about it "not being their war" or some other excuse he had heard dozens of times in the past. Yet, he got none of that. Instead, there were a few nods, a few more "yes, sirs" and one by one each man resumed training arrows on their targets, with an intensity he hadn't seen before.

He placed a hand on Yanasi's shoulder. "Keep it up," he said, giving her a small wink. As he turned his back, he heard her shouting orders again. The low grumbling that had followed her orders before was replaced with a determined twang of a bowstring and the thud of another target being struck.

* * *

Leaving the archery field, Jonrell made his way to the top of the inner walls. As he crossed a catwalk that connected the inner wall to the outer, he saluted several guards near the top. He passed under the arches of several smaller drum towers on his way to the much larger one that sat at the corner of the eastern and southern walls.

Jonrell saluted another set of guards bundled tight against the weather, and ducked into a doorway, thankful for the dead air inside. Even over the roaring wind outside the nearest window, he heard Raker barking instructions to his men.

He reached the top step of the tower and paused outside of the door to observe Raker's group of engineers. Jonrell watched the confusion on the men's faces as Raker, with a mouthful of chew, quizzed them on how to operate the newly constructed mangonel. Despite repeating his questions after spitting a big wad over the side of the parapet, Drake had to interpret. Jonrell chuckled as he watched Raker grow more frustrated each time Drake stepped in. It always took people some time to grow accustomed to the mercenary's garbled speech.

After a few moments, Jonrell joined them. A strong gust of wind slammed into his chest. The soldiers immediately saluted except for Raker who nodded.

Raker has earned that.

Jonrell had never cared for all the pomp and circumstance that a man in his position often received. But he knew that those small gestures and insignificant formalities helped stabilize the chain of command and build into the psyche of each man an inherent level of respect and trust in their superiors.

Or at least that's what Amcaro always told me. And the man rarely steered me wrong.

Jonrell nodded back to Raker and then looked to Drake. "Go ahead and continue on with the men. I'd like to speak with Raker in private." He thought about adding a bit of encouragement to the men but could see that unlike those at the archery range, these men didn't need it. He and Raker returned to the stairwell, shutting the door behind him.

"How's the boy doing?" asked Jonrell.

Raker spat on the step and Jonrell let out a sigh that went unnoticed. "He's getting there. I hate to say it, but the kid had some good ideas. He's come up with ways I haven't even thought of to improve the range on the weapons without increasing their size. He's sharp, but he still hasn't gotten it in his skull that he doesn't know everything there is to know about everything."

"Well, he is a boy."

"Yeah, but he's also a soldier now. He needs to understand that this ain't no game. He thinks he understands war because he saw a man or two die back on Slum Isle. I been telling him he don't understand a thing until he watches the man next to him drop his sword so he can use both hands to keep his guts from falling out."

Jonrell felt his mood turn grim. *As if I needed to be reminded myself.* "Did it work?"

"A little, I think. But who knows for sure."

"Well, keep working on him. During the battle I'm not going to be able to keep you together. I'll need you and him at opposite ends to work the crews. You can't be everywhere at once."

"Aye, I'll make him understand."

"How about the men's knowledge of the equipment?"

"Good thing is they definitely know their way around a hammer and a saw. Good craftsmen, all of them. Things are coming together fast. I wanted to start drilling them in two days on each of the machines we have. They need to know them better than they know the back of their hands."

"Where at?"

"For now, on the two trebuchets between the inner and outer gatehouses, and then the catapult here and on the opposite corner. I'm not satisfied with the other equipment just yet."

"I'm guessing you want to fire real shots?"

"Don't see why not."

"Well, there are still people out there working, for one. Not to mention all the homes and buildings outside the outer walls that may get crushed."

"More than likely they'll get burned or crushed when that army gets here anyway."

"True enough, but they don't need to know that just yet. For now, have them go through the motions with empty buckets. Once we get word Tomalt is moving, then we can talk about filling them."

Raker shrugged. "Whatever you say."

"I'll catch up with you later."

"Yeah, I need to get back to that boy before he fills the heads of those men with who knows what."

* * *

A wave of heat struck Jonrell as he stepped into the sweltering forge. He removed a glove and wiped at his face as he watched the men and boys covered in dirt and grime run about. He was amazed that a moment before, the cold had seeped through his marrow, and now he couldn't stop the sweat from pouring.

Jonrell made his way through the forge amid the incessant pounding of hammer on steel to find Cisod near a large door separating the forge from the armory. He was personally examining every piece of armor, sword, shield, chain, down to even the smallest of nails.

He held a shin guard, his face no more than inches from the metal as he turned it about. He gave the piece of equipment to a boy waiting next to him. "Send this back to Kirkell. His seams are sloppy."

"Yes, sir," said the boy as he spun round, dodged a man with an armful of lumber and ran off. Cisod started to shout after him but caught himself and shook his head in resignation. He noticed Jonrell. "Sorry, Commander. I didn't see you come up."

"It's alright. That seems to be a common theme today. If I was a prideful man, I may be hurt. But, I'd rather believe everyone is too busy to worry about that."

The blacksmith smiled. "Busy is an understatement. We still aren't where we should be. Yesterday, I finally felt comfortable to leave someone in charge while I slept, so we're running around the clock now. Hopefully, that'll help things move along."

"That's good to hear. So I take it the men are improving?"

"Aye, things were rough at first. I'd never seen such poor standards. But after they got with the program and started taking care of what they produced, well, I found a few diamonds in the rough." He gestured to a spot behind Jonrell. "Take a look at the second shelf from the bottom, third from the end."

Jonrell saw and reached down to what Cisod referred to. He was far from an expert on making armor but right away he noticed the craftsmanship in the breastplate, it stood out like a giant oak in a field full of flowers. He ran his fingertips along each seam. "This is amazing. It looks very similar to the armor Denneth wore on Slum Isle."

"It's the same technique. Only a few have been good enough to pick up on it. You're looking at the best one there. Unfortunately the process is slow, so until we've caught up, I've shifted their attention away from perfecting it."

"Makes sense." He paused, still looking at the breastplate. "Is this the man you have working for you at night when you sleep?" asked Jonrell, looking up.

"Yes," said Cisod, tilting his head.

"How hard would it be to find another to take his place?"

Cisod let out a curse and looked down. "I knew it."

"Sorry, but I need someone with considerable skill. The extra steel came in from Lyrosene this morning."

"The portcullis?"

Jonrell nodded.

Cisod blew out his breath hard. "I'll meet with him tonight and give him the details."

"So you can find another then?"

"Yeah, I'll make due. That's what we all do any way, isn't it?"

"More or less," Jonrell smiled. "You know I appreciate all your work."

Cisod raised a hand. "Don't get all emotional on me. I'm just following your orders. If you appreciate my work so much, then I'd just as soon get back to it." He waved a hand. "As you can see, it is only piling higher."

Jonrell nodded. "You're the commander here."

"Is that so?" he asked, a slight grin forming around his cheeks.

"Well, within reason that is."

"Always a catch." He picked up a gauntlet and began looking over the work. "I'll see you at dinner then."

"See you at dinner," said Jonrell.

* * *

It was almost time for lunch but Jonrell had much left to accomplish before worrying about a meal. Lunch usually consisted of a heel of bread and some dried meat that he could grab and eat on the way while making his rounds. Today looked to be no different.

He had set up the medical building next to the armory so that patients would benefit from the forge's heat. Wiqua was placed in charge of organizing and training the medical staff. At first, the Byzernian was adamantly against taking command since he was uncomfortable with being in charge. Yet, when Jonrell told him it was not up for discussion, Wiqua bowed his head and submitted.

With that on his mind, Jonrell walked into the building. Wiqua sat cross legged on the floor near a wood burning stove in the middle of the room. In front of him several rows of men and women sat in silence as Wiqua explained key information of the human body. Jonrell shook his head. He had half-expected that the brown-skinned man would face the same adversity that Yanasi did with the archers, or the bitterness Kaz had dealt with since arriving. Yet here, no one seemed to notice the short man's complexion. They were only interested in his knowledge. Such a sight gave Jonrell hope for Kaz.

Maybe if he dyed his hair gray, spouted off bits of wisdom, and bowed his head in humility it would help? He thought of the look Kaz would give him if he even suggested that he act as Wiqua and chuckled.

"Ah Commander, I apologize. I did not see you enter," said Wiqua looking up from the eager faces. He stood and bowed before his students. "Please excuse me for a moment. In the meantime, do your best to review what I just went over."

To Jonrell's surprise, each of the heads gave Wiqua a slight bow in return. *Amazing.*

"I see that leadership suits you after all."

The old man smiled. "Leadership? Not in the way you're thinking. I simply teach what I know and they listen. I must thank you for sending me such an eager bunch of minds. They thirst for knowledge in a way that makes me smile. I only wish that I was not teaching them to prepare them for war."

Jonrell shrugged. "You'll have no argument from me. I wish I wasn't doing any of what I've been doing day in and day out but I see little choice."

"So you say," said Wiqua in a hushed voice.

Jonrell ignored the comment and inclined his head back toward the group who quizzed each other in small circles. "It looks like their studies are coming along well. That gives me one less thing to worry about. What about your other responsibilities?"

Wiqua sighed. "Far less enjoyable than teaching eager minds, but I've made sure to lend them my attention. Our supplies here are fully stocked as you can see."

"And the other medical outposts?"

"None have completed construction and are ready for me to begin stocking."

"We need them ready in time. Having those smaller pavilions set up near the outer wall can make a huge difference in saving a limb or life."

"You have my complete agreement. But I keep being told that these things take time."

"I'll look into it."

"Thank you," Wiqua said with a bow.

"Do you need anything else? I know I haven't spoken with you much lately."

"It would be a huge benefit to our staff if you could provide us with even one mage."

Jonrell shook his head. "I'm sorry but I can't spare anyone to come to your aid. We will be at a huge disadvantage against Tomalt as far as sorcery goes. I'll need all the mages I have along the wall in defensive support. I'm afraid you're it."

"You do understand that without sorcery, many more may die. Other methods of healing only go so far."

Jonrell sighed. "And many more will die if the men are not protected from the attacks. It is not an easy decision to make Wiqua, but one I am burdened with."

"And one I do not envy, Commander." Wiqua bowed. "Very well. I have voiced my concern. Is there anything else you require of me?"

Jonrell shook his head. "No, you may return to your students."

Wiqua bowed again. "Good day, Commander."

* * *

His sword sliced through the air in fluid motions, parrying each attack. Kaz shifted, pivoted, bobbed around each stroke. A glimpse of the blunt weapon, void of any edge, reminded Kaz that this was all supposed to be a drill and that he wasn't supposed to kill these men. However, the set in their shoulders, the determination in their jaw, made him wonder if they understood that the battle had not yet begun and this was simply an exercise. He was not their enemy.

Kaz jumped lightly over the soldier diving at his knees, bringing the dull blade down as he landed, striking the fallen man's back. "Dead!" he heard someone yell. A growl of frustration lined another's voice as a new man was pushed into the ring, joining the five others still circling. "Here, have another then," shouted Glacar. "The last one died too quickly," he said laughing.

It was the fourth straight day that Glacar had coaxed him into fighting the men they were supposed to be training. Glacar and he did not share the same opinion on how best to train a group of men with little base skills. Though Kaz understood the value in sparing, he felt it best to build the men up with the fundamentals and then slowly increase the speed of the drills. As it was, most could not even maintain a proper grip on their swords. Glacar, however, preferred to throw a man into the fire to see if he would burn bright or fizzle out.

The two had butted heads on the issue more times than not. To prove his point, Glacar boasted that he could beat any number of men because of the way he learned to fight and challenged Kaz to do the same. Kaz could not back down from the challenge.

The first day he fought two challengers, the next three, and then four. Today, it was six and to make the situation harder, the first three men Kaz had eliminated were quickly replaced.

Kaz's approach so far had been to allow the men to attack him first so he could counter their moves. He was barely winded, but it looked like Glacar would keep replacing men until Kaz tired and fell to someone's sword stroke. Kaz knew he would be ridiculed for his defeat, regardless of the odds. If he was going to succeed he would have to change to an offensive approach.

He ducked under a sword blade, dashing forward into the press. He dodged away from an inept sword blow and shouldered the chest of the man who swung it, knocking one attacker into another. He raked his blade across the stomachs of both men as they fell. Using the momentum of his blade, he swung around, low to the ground, and clipped another soldier's leg. The man let out a yelp as he fell.

The last three men were crouched and ready for Kaz to strike. However, he startled them all by backing up and looking away. Kaz raised his sword and pointed it at Glacar's throat. "Stop," Kaz shouted. The bearded warrior turned in surprise, just as he was ready to push two others into the ring. "This is pointless."

"Are you saying you can't win? You admit you were mistaken?"

"No. If you want to prove a point, then step into the ring yourself and quit hiding like some coward. I do not wish to hurt those we should be training. But you," said Kaz, his anger rising, "that is a different matter."

"You black devil," said Glacar unlooping his battleaxe. "I'll kill you for that," he added, stepping into the ring and kicking one of the fallen men aside. "All of you get out of my way."

"Your ax has an edge. You can't do that," shouted one man.

"Yeah," said another. "That isn't fair."

Glacar ignored them as he rushed Kaz, howling obscenities with each step and throwing all his weight behind an overhead blow. The mercenary was quicker than he appeared and much faster than the men Kaz had been training with. Kaz stepped away. He swung toward Glacar's back but the mercenary swiftly recovered. The shaft of his battleaxe slammed into Kaz's practice sword.

"You'll have to do better," said Glacar. He twisted his ax down and over in an attempt to dislodge the sword from Kaz's hand. Kaz jabbed his elbow hard into Glacar's stomach. He followed the elbow up with a punch to Glacar's kidneys and then a headbutt to his face.

Glacar only grunted, pushing Kaz back a few feet. Blood ran from Glacar's mouth and into his ratty beard. He spat. "You'll pay for that," he said in a low voice. His shoulders heaved with each breath.

The two men circled each other, each probing for an opening. Shouts, boos, and curses from the onlookers reached Kaz's ears. He was surprised to hear some of the anger directed at Glacar. He wondered what caused even one man to cheer for the grimy mercenary.

Why would anyone stay loyal to such a man? Even now he is pushing his men aside with no regard for their well being. Apparently when the alternative is me, a great many would stay loyal.

"I'm waiting," said Kaz. He spun the practice sword in his hand and coiled up to prepare for the next attack.

Kaz saw the shift in Glacar's hips and readied himself. Sure enough, the mercenary let out another yell, but as Glacar brought his ax up, a man carrying a large shield smashed into him and knocked him to the ground. Kaz watched Glacar roll and bounce quickly to his feet.

The mercenary stopped short of attacking the new opponent when he saw the sword point at his face and the man who wielded it. "What in the name of the One Above is going on here?" The training yard fell to a hushed silence as their commander spoke. Jonrell's voice was full of anger, his eyes as cold as a sheet of ice.

"Why aren't you asking that black devil what's going on?" asked Glacar jabbing his ax toward Kaz.

"Because you are the one I placed in charge. What happens here is ultimately your responsibility. And when I find two of my men fighting each other, I've got a major problem with that. Now, do you care to tell me what's going on? Because if you can't even follow the simplest of commands then maybe I need to put someone else in charge here."

Glacar's eyes narrowed at Jonrell and then flickered over to Kaz before turning back to their commander. "Ten years I've been with you." He shook his head. "No, I don't think I feel like answering your question right now." He nodded back to Kaz. "You want someone else in charge, let your pet do it. We all know you'd rather have him at your side."

If Jonrell was surprised at the response, he failed to show it. "If that's your wish then so be it. Tomorrow, you can report to Crusher and work on clearing the woods. I'm sure he can use a strong back. For now, take the rest of the day to cool off. This will not happen again."

Glacar glared at Jonrell and turned to Kaz, spitting at his feet with a grunt. "This ain't over," he muttered as he left the practice circle and pushed his way through the crowd.

Jonrell looked around. "Maybe it would be best if everyone had a break. But before you leave, understand this: Kaz will be your instructor. He will speak with my authority and therefore any slight to him is a slight against me. I do not tolerate such behavior in my army. If you cannot abide by my rules, then leave tonight and join Tomalt and the other cowards and traitors who would turn their back on their own country." He paused. "Training will resume after lunch. You may go."

Several men cast each other looks but eventually the group dissipated and mumbled conversations broke out.

The whole castle will know the story before the next group arrives for training.

Jonrell resheathed his sword and approached Kaz. "You may want to put that away now. I doubt I'd beat you in a fight," Jonrell said with a slow grin creeping across his face.

Kaz followed Jonrell's glance and realized he still held his sword at the ready. He stood straighter and lowered his sword.

"Better. So what happened?"

Kaz thought about telling Jonrell that if it wasn't for the obligation he felt to him for all of Jonrell's help, he'd have slit Glacar's throat long ago. He finally had enough of the ridicule from Glacar and he was unwilling to take it any longer. He thought about saying many similar things but decided against it. Still, he owed his commander a response. "Glacar hates any man who he feels threatened by, especially one whose color is so different. Today, I had enough."

Jonrell stared at him for a moment. "Is that it?"

"What more is there?"

"So you were ready to kill him?"

Kaz shrugged.

Jonrell shook his head. "I'll talk to him again later tonight after he's cooled off. I'll make sure he stays as far away from you as possible. I need you both."

"You need every able body you can find. So move me and keep Glacar here to train the men. I think many will take you up on your offer and leave."

"Perhaps. But it is a chance I'm willing to take. I've watched you both instruct the men. Glacar is a fierce fighter, but that does not make him a great teacher. He fights from pure passion and instinct. You fight off of instinct as well, but there is a reason behind what you do. You don't waste a single move. Right now, these men need that structure. They need something to fall back on when things get heated."

"I will do my best."

"I know you will. That's why I'm talking to you now and not Glacar."

* * *

Fluid as a gentle stream, the blade swept around his body. The sword sang with each slice. His feet padded lightly across the yard like that of a prowling wolf, twisting and turning, in balance with every stroke. Each thrust was as quick as a striking snake. He was at peace.

Kaz could not recall where the memories had come from, but it didn't matter because where his mind had forgotten, his body remembered, flowing from one sequence to the next. He recalled countless forms that simulated the various scenarios of a sword fight. Some one-handed, some two. Others required the use of a shield or dirk held in the person's off hand. He knew hundreds of them, all tucked somewhere in the depths of his mind.

Each night after he finished training the men, he practiced in isolation. Each time he lifted his sword at the ready he would remember another drill, dancing to and fro across the open ground, jumping over obstacles, ducking, bobbing, and weaving. Many nights he didn't even need to imagine an opponent for one often presented itself to him. Flashing images from what he assumed was his past faded in and out of his conscious. The only commonality was that his old life was a bloody one.

He knew the images were real. They had to be. The smell, the feel of warm blood touching his skin, the yells, and cries of battle ringing in his ears. There was too much detail for it to all be his imagination. Yet his recollection always stopped at those desperate faces dying under the stroke of his sword. His former life seemed to be one that was entirely filled with death and destruction.

Yet, each pleading voice, each distorted image of pain, suffering, and anguish never deterred him from returning night after night to his forms. Maybe he was reliving those harsh moments to come to terms with who he truly was. He hoped deep down that something would spark a different memory.

There had to be more to my life than just blood.

He was here now in a strange land, set to go about killing a new host of people. The only difference was that their skin was unlike his. He remembered the men he killed on Slum Isle while saving Jonrell.

He assumed that if he ever could return home, he would not be a welcome sight since all his memories dealt with destruction. *Would it be better to be hated among my own kind where it would seem they have reason? Here, any hatred seems to stem from one thing.*

He had a couple of people he could call friends, especially Jonrell who had stuck his neck out for him on many occasions. But those relationships were few. He could see how hard it was on anyone who showed him the slightest bit of kindness. His presence often seemed to do more harm than good, even with the men he trained. Some had come around a little since the confrontation with Glacar. They listened more intently to him than they had to Glacar, but what did that mean?

Probably just trying to understand my accent is all. Either that or they are doing it out of fear for what Jonrell will do to them. Outside of the training ground, none of them even acknowledged his existence and he wondered again why he was still here.

The answer was another reason he practiced each night. While others found joy in drink, song, and fellowship, Kaz had resigned himself to seeking his own form of happiness in the feel of steel in his hands and the memories of battle. Those haunting images of his past seemed the only time in life he knew joy. Battle. War. Death. Three things it seemed he had a knack for. Maybe that's why he stayed on with the Hell Patrol then. With an army approaching, perhaps he would be truly happy again.

Kaz spun and stepped onto a fallen barrel, launching himself into the air. Gripping the sword with both hands, he prepared to chop into the log lying on the ground. Only the log was partially covered. So lost in his own thoughts and the repetitive motion of his forms, he failed to notice when the boy had taken a seat there. Kaz heard a loud yelp as he saw the boy fall backward in terror. He turned his body away from the boy as he crashed into the ground, jarring his shoulder on impact.

Kaz gritted his teeth and rolled to his knees, crouched and ready with sword in hand. His recovery was instinctive. It wasn't that he feared the boy so much as he had little reason to trust him. "What are you doing here?" he hissed.

The boy uprighted himself with legs flailing about, looking embarrassed. "I'm Drake."

"I did not ask who you were. I know you are Raker's student. I asked why you are here."

"Oh. Uh, I was just watching."

"For how long?"

"Tonight? Or in general?"

"You've watched me more than just tonight?"

Drake nodded and Kaz felt his anger rise that he hadn't noticed such a thing. *Perhaps I've been too focused while training. That could be my end.* Drake must have noticed Kaz's displeasure. "You misunderstand. This was the first time I've come down to the yard to watch. Before, I would steal…er, borrow a spyglass and watch you train from one of the eastern towers. I would lie and say I was checking on equipment though, if anyone asked what I was up to."

"Why lie?"

"I didn't want Raker to know. He uh, he isn't very fond of you."

Kaz started to relax and stood up. "Few are." He shoved the blade into the ground. "So why come down to watch now?"

"I couldn't get a spyglass and I didn't want to miss you train."

Kaz inclined his head. "Why are you spying on me? Are you trying to figure out a pattern to my style?"

Drake waved his hands. "No no. Nothing like that. I've been trying to learn."

"To fight?"

Drake nodded.

"Raker has not taught you anything?"

"Well, he is of the opinion that I should be focusing on the siege equipment and castle fortifications rather than fighting. But that doesn't necessarily take all my time."

"And what does he expect you to do, if the fight comes in close? You cannot load a catapult and shoot it at a man who is three feet from you."

"I made the same point. He just told me to find something heavy and hit them on the head if that happens."

"A mace? Similar to his."

Drake nodded.

"That seems too large of a weapon for you to handle."

"My point. I want to learn to use a sword but I have no idea how and no one will show me."

"And you want me to teach you?"

"Well, you are the best fighter."

"Are you sure? Wouldn't you rather go to Glacar?"

Drake shook his head. "Trust me. I may be small but what I lack in size I make up for here," he said pointing to his head. "I know what my eyes tell me." He smiled.

"What about my skin?"

"What about it?"

"Does it not bother you like it does the others?"

Drake shrugged. "Makes no difference to me. I don't see how the color of someone's skin makes them a bad person."

Kaz grunted. "And what will Raker say if he finds out?"

"Well, I hoped he wouldn't. At least for now anyway. He doesn't have to know, if you know what I mean."

"I see. So, I teach you how to fight. What will you do for me?"

Drake shrugged his shoulders. "I don't know. What can I possibly offer you in return?"

Kaz thought for a moment then grinned. "This. What we are doing now."

"What? Talking?"

"Yes. I still struggle with the language and my accent. I want you to help me with that. While we train, we talk. It doesn't really matter what we talk about, so long as I can practice."

"So you're going to teach me how to fight and all I have to do is talk to you?"

"That's it."

Drake smiled. "Deal."

"Good. Grab a sword. We will begin now."

* * *

Drake shuffled through the inner courtyard, doing his best not to fall over from exhaustion. *What was I thinking?*

For the tenth night in a row Kaz had trained him. Hours spent working on forms and drills left him barely able to walk, let alone fight. He was sore in places he didn't even know existed. Keeping his fatigue hidden from Raker during each day was nearly as exhausting as the time spent sparing with Kaz at night. He began to wonder if all his effort would even be worth it. He sure didn't feel like a more capable fighter. Yet Kaz told him that he had potential and in time his efforts would pay off.

I can't quit, not after what he's been doing to help me, and the things he's shown me he hasn't shown the other men. Maybe I can ask Wiqua for some sorcery to loosen things up. He doesn't ask a lot of questions so no one will know why I need the healing anyway.

He decided he would do just that in the morning but first he needed to grab a few hours of sleep. Looking up, he realized someone was crossing his path from the left. The figure's head was down and he seemed to be muttering something under his breath.

"Mal?"

The figure jumped. He saw Drake approaching him and noticeably relaxed. "Drake, what are you doing up at this time of night?"

"I could ask you the same thing."

"Yeah, but I asked first."

Drake shrugged. "Training. What about you?"

"You're lucky. They have me running errands like some little message boy. Nothing important either. No, it's trivial things to cater to the needs of Lord Caliva and his stuck up household."

"At least it's something."

"I want to fight and train. Yet, I get moved from one person to the next."

Drake shook his head. *I'm getting so tired of this same conversation.* "You keep getting moved because all you do is complain about the person you're taking orders from. No one is going to teach you anything of importance until you pay your dues first."

Mal scowled. "What do you know? You're just some pet doing whatever someone tells you to do."

Drake felt his face turn red. A moment before he had considered asking Mal if he wanted to train with him and Kaz but he quickly changed his mind. *He would complain the entire time, give half efforts, and not appreciate any of it. Kaz would never put up with that. And neither would I.*

Drake started walking again and purposefully brushed his shoulder against his friend. "When you grow up, let me know. Until then, try to learn a little humility."

* * *

Jonrell rubbed at his temples and narrowly avoided a passing servant as he left the war room. He wasn't sure what time it was, only that it was late. He moved his thumb and forefinger from temple to eyes.

He waved a hand at the apologetic servant, unable to do much else. All he cared about was crawling into his bed under the warm furs. He hoped to catch a few hours of sleep before dawn jarred him awake and he started another long day.

He blinked, focusing his eyes in the dim lamplight coming from the metal wall sconces that illuminated the staircase and hallways. His blurry vision told him he had pushed himself more than he should have, but he saw few other options. Caliva was a good enough man but being a good man meant little in a war. Many good men knew little of the boring, but necessary administrative tasks of a commander. The endless parade of requests and meetings made his head hurt just thinking about them.

He thought of Amcaro, a man, who despite his age, never seemed to tire and was always eager to learn and work even harder. "There will be plenty of time to rest when I'm with the One Above," the High Mage used to say.

I wonder how well he's sleeping now.

Dark thoughts. Nothing good ever came from them. Yet, it was hard to think of anything else when one of his old mentor's teachings or sayings would pop into his head.

He shook his head again. *Keep your head straight, Jonrell. Almost to your door. Then, you'll have at least a few hours to relax and escape. One Above knows you deserve it.*

But apparently the One Above didn't know. Jonrell jumped at the sound of a cough. He turned and drew the dirk at his side. "Who's there?" he said facing the shadow of a corner.

Mal stepped out with hands raised, and lip trembling. "I-I'm sorry. I didn't mean to startle you."

Jonrell sheathed his blade. "Mal? What in the name of the One Above are you doing in the shadows?"

"I was hoping to talk to you," he said looking down.

Jonrell sighed, rubbing his eyes. "Mal, I'm exhausted."

"It won't take long, I swear. Besides, you were up late talking to your captains anyway," said the boy, growing upset.

"Aye, I was. But that's different. I'm preparing for a war," said Jonrell walking up and resting a hand on the boy's shoulder. "You understand, right?"

"I understand that you never have time for me. You promised you would sit down so we can talk about my future with the group but I keep getting shuffled around from one person to the next." He looked up, pleading. "I want to help you."

"Look, I'm sorry. I've got a lot on my plate right now. I heard just this evening that Tomalt is on the march and will be here in a matter of weeks, earlier than we expected. Things are going to get even more hectic than before. I just don't have time to take you under my wing and teach you right now. After the battle things will change. I promise, we can talk then."

Mal shrugged Jonrell's hand away. "Things won't change. And I'm tired of your empty promises." Jonrell watched a tear fall from his eye. "I should never have left the Hideaway," said the boy as he stormed off down the dark hallway.

Jonrell thought to chase after him but he just didn't have the will to make his legs move. *Maybe Krytien was right. My soft spot got the best of me.* He shook off the thought as he remembered how happy Drake seemed to be working with Raker. *Nah, he'll be fine come morning. A boy at his age has emotions that change with the wind. Still, maybe I can get Cisod to find a use for him tomorrow. Perhaps that had been my mistake all along. Mal probably should be with someone he knew before joining up with us.*

Jonrell sighed as he made his way to his room and closed the door behind him. *One more thing to remember for tomorrow. Who in their right mind would ever want to lead an army?*

He eased into bed, clothes still on, nestling his head onto the pillow just as the bells chimed for the change in watch. *Three rings. Well, I guess three hours of sleep is better than none*, he thought, dimming the lamp near his bed.

CHAPTER 24

Elyse never thought she would find herself in a dungeon. Drab stone walls, rusted steel bars, a bed of straw to lie on, one lone stool, and a chamber pot in the corner. No plush furnishings, no fire to keep away the chill, not even a window to provide fresh air. Though in some way she was thankful for the latter as a window would have only made the place that much colder. Regardless of how she tried to find the positive in her situation, she couldn't escape the fact that she had failed.

When they arrived at the castle, Jeldor placed her in the dungeon. "You can rot with the other liars until we find out who you really are." he had said.

There would be no alliance, but it was not due to lack of trying on her part. During their journey back to Ithanthul, Elyse had tried numerous times to plead her case to Duke Jeldor. Each time he dismissed her with a snide comment and refused to even acknowledge that she was in fact the Queen of Cadonia. Her plain attire surely didn't help her argument, especially with it caked in dirt and blood.

How could he not know me?

Despite her bleak situation, her worries went to Kroke and Rygar. All alone in the dank cell, huddled under her coat on the bed of straw and left to her thoughts, she realized how much she missed the company of the two mercenaries. Even the uneasy looks and harsh silence of Kroke appealed to her over the emptiness of her current surroundings.

Her hand wiped away a tear before it fell. *Am I cursed to live my entire life so alone?* She sat down and squinted in the dim light with her legs tucked under her body and placed her head on her knees. "I'm sorry I failed you, Jonrell," she whispered.

Elyse jumped with a start at the sound of a heavy steel door closing. The noise echoed down the long corridor. Footsteps followed, growing gradually louder.

This is it. They're going to torture me. I just know it. Her stomach twisted into knots and she swallowed the bile that crept into the back of her throat.

The footsteps stopped at her cell door. She kept her head down, afraid to look up and face the fears running through her mind. "Shall I come back then?" said the grave voice. Elyse recognized it immediately and looked up to see Jeldor.

"Good. You're up," he said, pulling out a key and twisting it in the lock. The hinges squeaked as he entered the cell. He seated himself on the lone stool opposite her and heaved a heavy sigh. He struggled to settle his large frame on the small stool. After a minute he stood up, frustrated. "Bah. I'd just as soon stand then." He turned to face Elyse. "I feel the need to apologize to you."

Elyse was confused by the Duke's attitude. "Apologize?"

"Well, I'm sure you would prefer accommodations befitting your station."

"Wait. So you believe me now?"

"I always believed you. I just chose not to let anyone else know that."

"My lord?"

Jeldor waved a hand. "Don't give me that 'my lord' nonsense. We are in private. Let's put away the titles."

She thought about a lesson Jonrell taught her regarding respect, but realized she was in no position to push the issue. So, she nodded.

"Good. Now, why are you here?"

"I told you before. Cadonia is in turmoil. Tomalt has seized Namaris and is intent on marching against me. We suspect Bronn and Conroy are plotting against the throne as well. I've come to offer an alliance with you."

Jeldor chuckled. "An alliance with me? You must be desperate. How much pride did you have to brush away to come seeking my aid?"

"Actually, none. I know you think that others look down on you but…"

"Think? I know!" he cut Elyse off. "First Aurnon the First slighted us and only the One Above knows why. He gave us this bitter land that no one would even bother with. Then because of a mistake made by a distant ancestor, there are minor lords who seem to live better than I do. I don't *think* anything. My family has never been respected. But now that you are in trouble, you want my help? Why should I? The chance of you defending the throne against Tomalt is amusing enough. And if Conroy and Bronn are working together, the odds are not in your favor."

"Olasi is aligned with our cause," said Elyse, not sure what else to say.

"Olasi," he said the name as if it were a curse. "He's not a bad man but he is surrounded by enemies. He may hold out for awhile but in time, he'll fall too. Besides, he's too far from you to be much help."

"Which is why we need you. I do not care about the past. I care only about the present and the future. You said yourself that the other dukes still look down on you. Do you really think they won't turn their eyes this way after destroying me?" Jeldor's eyes widened and Elyse knew he hadn't thought about that. Jumping at the chance, she continued. "Align with me and march to Cathyrium to aid my brother in the defense of the city against

Tomalt, and I will see that all extra taxes instituted by Aurnon the Third are removed from your lands and holdings."

For a moment, Elyse thought she had struck a chord and found herself hopeful as she watched the man pace the room in silence with his hands clasped behind his back. "You make a good point, I'll give you that." He paused and stroked his beard. "But no. It will not happen."

"But they will come for you…"

"Oh, I've no doubt they will if I just sit here and let them. However, I now have something to bargain with," he said, smiling at Elyse. "Perhaps, the victor would be interested in marrying you himself to solidify his claim to the throne."

Elyse felt her heart sink.

Jeldor looked around. "But if that's the case then there is no need to continue this charade. I hardly consider you a threat to me physically. I'll see that you are moved to more favorable quarters. I may be a hard man but I am not completely lacking in compassion."

Elyse started to argue further but Jeldor raised a hand before she could even speak. "Don't bother wasting your breath. My decision has been made."

Her shoulders sagged as Jeldor exited the cell and locked the door. She suddenly remembered a question she hadn't asked. "The two men I was traveling with. Are they well?"

"Yes. The injured one is recovering and the other is unharmed as well. We had to remove nearly three dozen knives from his person before we placed him in his own cell." Jeldor shook his head. "They will remain down here."

Jeldor's footsteps faded.

There is no hope left. It happened just as I knew it would. Just as I tried to warn Jonrell. If he were here, perhaps there would be another way. She began to rock in place and tears fell unheeded.

* * *

Elyse slept very little in her new surroundings, though a lack of comfort was not the cause. After weeks of sleeping on hard ground and later a straw filled cell, the soft bed covered in thick furs was a welcome alternative. The constant dread of what was to come next kept her awake and sobbing most of the night.

I had another chance with Jeldor in the dungeon and failed again.

Despite the reputation Jonrell had garnered for himself in the years he'd been gone, he would be badly outnumbered facing Tomalt alone. Even if her brother could manage a victory, their forces would take a beating, and little would be left to defend the lands still under the crown's control.

And how many soldiers will die as result of my failure?

For some reason she thought of the warm conversation she had enjoyed with Kaz. She knew she'd likely never learn more about the mysterious man who seemed to hold so many things behind his dark eyes. Even more likely, she would never be able to apologize to Jonrell for her failings. In the end, she would be alone. Solitude should have been familiar to her by now, since she had lived so much of her life that way. But the thought of it caused her to breathe out an audible groan.

She remained in bed, past mid-morning. She saw little point in readying herself, knowing she'd never leave her quarters. Breakfast still sat untouched on a small table. The simple room held little majesty. She remembered Jeldor's words and knew the Duke did not exaggerate.

Indeed he is poorer than other lords.

Her chamber resembled the rest of the castle, plain and ordinary. Servants wore clothes in similar condition. It was apparent that the harsh taxes over the years had hurt more than Jeldor's pride. If the duke hadn't taken her captive then held her for ransom, she may have felt sympathy for the man. Under present circumstances, his lack of wealth brought her a smile. It was a small comfort, though she was ashamed to admit it. Although another enemy to her, the One Above would frown on such selfish behavior.

Disappointing the One Above yet again, only made her more depressed. *Can I not do anything right?*

She remembered her lessons from High Priest Burgeone and immediately threw off the covers, hopping out of bed and dropping to her knees, slightly embarrassed to approach the One Above half-clothed.

She began reciting one of the first prayers she had learned as a girl. The words were more familiar to her than any other. The prayer's design asked for strength to cope with life's turns, humility to deal with things not going one's way, understanding that everything was part of the One Above's plans, regardless of how bad something appeared. The last part was an area Elyse struggled with the most and like so many times before she said the verse emphasizing that plea over and over.

Despite the goose pimples forming from the touch of a cold draft, she felt her heart warm as she so often did when approaching the One Above.

"Thank you," she whispered, finishing the prayer and climbing to her feet.

A sharp voice and loud knock preempted the door flying open and slamming against the stone wall. Elyse shrieked and darted behind the bed.

Duke Jeldor strode through the door, mumbling to himself, reading over a paper.

"My lord!" she squealed, reaching for the nearest bed sheet to cover herself.

He slammed the door closed and waved a hand in her direction. "I have a wife and two daughters. You've nothing I haven't seen before."

His dismissive nature crawled under her skin and she fired back. "I know I am your prisoner and am at your mercy, but I demand to be shown some sort of respect. I am still a descendant of Aurnon the First and until someone rightfully takes my throne, I am the official ruler of Cadonia."

Jeldor stopped in his tracks, taken aback. He looked up from his letter surprised, and he stammered in response. "Uh, yes. I see your point." He turned his back. "I'll wait here for you to cover yourself," he said. "I haven't the time to leave and come back."

Elyse saw a robe draped across a chair near the fire. She carried half the covers from her bed as she moved toward it. She realized after fighting with the garment she would need both hands to get it on. She dropped the sheets and flung the robe over her shoulders, punching her arms through the sleeves and binding the opening with a thick belt.

"Alright. Now what are these pressing matters?"

Jeldor turned without any acknowledgement of her change. "A message just came in," he said thrusting the letter into Elyse's chest. "That pompous prick has taken my iron mines."

Elyse scanned the letter. "It says Bronn attacked and captured Arcas Island."

"That's what I just said! I can see that smug idiot grinning and making jokes behind my back," said Jeldor. "My main source of income…gone like that," he pounded his fist into his hand.

It took everything she had not to smile. She had another chance to save her kingdom and help Jonrell. *The One Above heard my prayers.*

"I'm not sure why you came to me with this," she said, handing the letter back to Jeldor. "I have no role to fill in this squabble of yours with Duke Bronn."

"Of course you do," said Duke Jeldor. "The alliance you spoke of."

"I seem to recall you dismissing an alliance just yesterday while I was locked in one of your cells as a prisoner." She waved her hand in a sweeping motion across the room. "And although my surroundings have changed, I thought it safe to assume my status in your home had not."

Jeldor waved a hand and shook his head with a chuckle. "Your Majesty, that was only a jest. My apologies if I hadn't made that clear before."

Your Majesty, eh? I see we are suddenly back to titles. Very well, I'll play this game. "My lord, then I owe you an apology. I guess I am unaccustomed to such wit."

"No need to apologize. An honest mistake is all. But now back to that alliance we spoke of. You will need to send immediately for your troops. I will assume command of them if we are expected to recapture Arcas Island and retaliate against Duke Bronn."

Elyse shook her head. "I'm sorry, my lord but that was not our arrangement. I've spoken of the dire situation at Cathyrium. That is where you will need to march in order to lend support to my brother. And in fact, you will take all your orders from Jonrell who has command over all of my armies."

Jeldor's eyes narrowed and his smile vanished. "Your Majesty, I hardly think you are in a place to be negotiating, given your current circumstances."

"You are mistaken, Duke Jeldor, I am not negotiating at all. I am issuing you a command. You just said that I had nothing to fear, that I was still your queen, and not a prisoner. Therefore, you must follow my orders. But, even if you were to treat me as a prisoner which of course you are not, then what difference does it make if I listen to your suggestions. My kingdom would be lost anyway for I'd have given my little remaining power to you. Frankly, the option I gave is your best chance." She paused. "However, if standing alone against Bronn and perhaps Conroy, is preferable, well, I cannot stop you from doing so."

"Just like every other time before, my family is being walked over," Jeldor muttered.

"No. Not like before," said Elyse. "I promised I would release you from the extra taxes. I still intend to do that. I will also return your island. And," she added, "fight for me, and I'll see that your lands are increased and Bronn's are reduced."

Jeldor's eyebrows raised. "Will you put that in writing?"

"I'll sign it this very day. However, you need to understand that those things will only come to pass after Cadonia is secured."

Jeldor nodded. "Fair enough. I'll have my steward write it up immediately and send it to you. In the meantime, I will make preparations to leave as soon as possible." He looked down at Elyse's robe and blinked as if noticing for the first time. "Uh, I'll see that you are brought garments more suited to your position, Your Majesty. I hope we can move on from all what's transpired these last few days…"

She nodded. "There is a war developing. There are more important things to worry about than my feelings."

He nodded in acknowledgement and left the room. As the door closed Elyse clasped her hand over her mouth to hide her excitement.

Jonrell, I did it. Just as you said I could.

She sighed as her excitement faded. *Now I only have to make it there on time.*

* * *

Elyse hadn't thought it was possible for so much to be accomplished in so little time. Even though Jeldor's men and sworn lords were already on alert due to the tension in Cadonia, many had been called into Ithanthul earlier to make plans to protect Jeldor's borders. None had expected to march in such a short amount of time and especially not before spring.

At least the worst of winter should be over. But Tomalt will know that too and if what Jonrell said about him is true, he will want to secure Cathyrium before we're better prepared for him.

Jeldor's ability to quickly organize his army impressed Elyse. After signing the papers sent in by his steward, Elyse made it a point to shadow Jeldor at every step. At first the sour duke seemed perturbed by her presence. However, he quickly grew accustomed to her and he even took care to include her in conversations and decisions. Before long, the queen found herself learning a great deal from what now amounted to her most crucial ally. If Jeldor did not come through for her, Cadonia would be lost.

She was pleased to see the rumors about his capabilities were false as she watched him lead his men. His style was different than her brother but was effective nonetheless. He did not ride and talk with his men as freely as Jonrell did. However, she could see from the look in their eyes that they respected him all the same.

It seems that there is more than one way to rule.

Elyse found the whole situation odd. Her emotions had been a constant up and down battle since taking the crown. Confident one moment, she was lost and hopeless the next. These last few days had been no different. Yet, since her time with Jonrell, then traveling with Kroke and Rygar, and now working with Jeldor, she began to understand the big picture. She could not lead like someone else. She needed to be herself, only a much better version of herself. *Now I just need to learn what that version is. I cannot be the hard man Jeldor is to his men, nor the friend to his soldiers that Jonrell is. Yet, how can I inspire the same loyalty, respect, and honor that they do?* She shook her head. *It seems that each answer only brings about more questions.*

* * *

Kroke sat atop his mount working a blade in steady strokes. It felt good to have his knives back. He'd only been away from them for a few days, yet the time apart had him feeling like some drunk giving up wine, complete with the shakes. Probably wasn't healthy but he didn't much care. They were back in his hands once again and that's all that mattered.

Rygar reined in beside him and coughed.

"What is it?" asked Kroke looking from the corner of his eye.

"Just wondering if you were going to do that the whole ride back to Cathyrium is all. It's getting a bit obsessive, even for you."

"Just making up for lost time is all," said Kroke sheathing his blade. "So what's really on your mind?"

"What do you mean?"

"That's the first time you've ever said anything about my blades. Sounds like someone trying to say something they don't really know how to say."

Rygar watched all the activity that, until a few moments ago, Kroke had done his best to block out. Not like it was hard for him once he got to sharpening his steel though.

Supply wagons were hitched to mules. Sergeants and captains shouted orders. Women sobbed and said their farewells.

Rygar gestured out to the organized chaos. "I just never thought it would work. I didn't think she could convince Jeldor to support her."

Kroke chuckled. "I thought you were on our fair queen's side."

Rygar shrugged. "Sure. I thought she was nice enough, and she was Jonrell's sister, so I figured she couldn't have been all bad. But, well, I guess deep down I thought this whole trip was a hopeless waste. She just surprised me is all."

Kroke looked over to Elyse who sat atop a white horse. She was quiet and looked to be in deep thought. Though Kroke couldn't help but notice that she held herself a little higher than before, more confident.

"Yeah, to be honest, she surprised me as well. She even made time to check up on me to make sure I didn't need anything."

"Yeah, me too. I guess Jonrell was right about her. Maybe she can be as good a leader as he is."

Kroke spat. "Let's not get carried away. Sure she did good here, at least as far as we know. But she's also got a long record of mistakes from what I hear. The way I see it, she's got a lot still to prove."

"Yanasi was right, you can be a real optimist sometimes."

"Realist. You'll learn not to trust so easily in time." Kroke spared one more glance at Elyse who now talked to Jeldor. She made herself heard, no longer cowering.

Definitely some changes there.

CHAPTER 25

The small village was hardly a threat with no more than thirty families calling it home. Yet, when Tobin received the report of its existence, he knew Bazraki would expect action. After all, his father had always believed that the key to victory was being the first to spill your opponent's blood, even if that blood came from villagers instead of an opposing army.

Accustomed to sniping off people from a distance with bow and arrow, Tobin had forgotten what it was like to lead a charge with sword drawn. Despite his initial trepidation in attacking an outmatched village, his heart raced at the thrill of striking the first kill. He cleaved a man from right shoulder to left hip.

Only a hunting knife in his defense.

Tobin wiped his blade on the fallen man's shirt before sheathing it once again, satisfied that his sword had been baptized in blood. *Let others do the same to their blades. I have other things to watch for.*

Watching the slaughter reminded Tobin of the Kifzo's past destruction. *We've always been the knife used to disembowel Father's enemies. When killing the elders who threatened his power amid our own tribes, Father never dirtied himself. And yet he is the one who leads us.* Tobin allowed these thoughts to fester as he watched the mass of Kifzo swarm into the village, moving from one sod house to another and reigning death on all who stood in their way.

Tobin's dark thoughts were interrupted by movement to his left. A young warrior, having just earned the right to be called Kifzo, held a small girl while fumbling with the laces of his armor. He had thrown her to the ground and straddled her.

In a few quick strides Tobin backhanded the young warrior, sending him sprawling into the dirt. The warrior stumbled to his feet, ignoring his half laced armor and reached for his sword. When his eyes met Tobin's, the warrior's hand moved away from his hilt, though his look of anger did not waver. "My apologies, Warleader. I did not think she would interest you. I shall find another like her."

"No. You will not. She is but a girl."

"A girl? She has reached womanhood," said the warrior, pointing to the girl's partially exposed chest. "She is ready to bare someone's child. She should consider herself lucky that I would allow her to bare mine."

"You are wrong. She's a child. And there will be no raping of children. Nor of anyone else for that matter."

Another voice shouted a question. "Warleader, what are you speaking of? It is our way."

Tobin looked around and saw that in those few short moments, the slaughter had ceased and many sets of eyes were on him and the young warrior. "And I say it is our way no longer."

"Warleader, it is our right to…" started another voice.

Tobin cut in. "Your right? By whom? I do not recall anyone saying that such a thing was our right. I know it came not from my father and it came not from me. Do you think it was a right because Kaz allowed it? He is dead. I am now warleader."

Just then a whisper. "Tobin, what are you doing?"

Tobin recognized the voice as Walor's who was now beside him. "We've talked about this before. We are not animals," said Tobin.

"I understand but now isn't the time. Look into your warriors' eyes. You have just begun to gain their respect and confidence. Do this, and risk losing them again."

"I am warleader," Tobin hissed under his breath. "They must obey."

"You know as well as I do that the title alone does not warrant their obedience. Kaz knew that as well."

"I am not like my brother, Walor."

"I know, but these men are also not like me."

Tobin looked up and locked gazes with several men, their weapons still drawn. He saw in those eyes that Walor was right. If he was to take everything away at once, he would lose them forever.

One spoke up, "Do you mean to take away our right, Warleader?"

Agat. So with Durahn in Nubinya, you now question my command. "I mean to change things, Agat. We will not rape children nor will we rape the elderly. You speak of spreading your seed and producing children with these women, then I say only choose those who are in their peak of fertility, the prime years of motherhood. We will not waste our time on those too young to bear the burden of childbirth or with those too old to bear children at all."

Agat snorted. "Why should we show these people any mercy when they have long disrespected us?"

"Because there are better ways to seek your retribution if that is what you are truly after. For the women you take to bed, you will pay them for their warmth."

A clamor rose up from the warriors. Agat spoke over the noise. "We must give them of our plunder?"

"Yes," said Tobin. "We will pay them like one would pay a whore so that the children we leave them with will grow up strong and fight for us one day if the need arises."

Agat laughed. "You are trying to fool us into believing that your sympathy for these people is disdain. Kaz would say you were showing weakness, compassion even…"

The voice trailed off into a slow gurgle as Tobin's dagger thudded into his neck. Tobin lowered his arm with eyes wide as he watched Agat grasp desperately at his throat before going limp.

I don't even remember making the decision to act. It just happened. And now I have to act like it was something intentional. "Anyone else believes that I am weak?" asked Tobin, head cocked to one side. "I have given my order." He gestured to Agat. "And here is my *compassion* for those who disobey me."

Tobin left, not once looking over his shoulder, doing his best to appear confident. He expected a knife in the back. To his surprise it never came.

* * *

Unmoving in the faint light of the setting sun, Tobin stared out over the plain. The sea of tall grass swaying in the gentle breeze reminded him of waves lapping against a sandy beach. Far outside of camp, only the chirping crickets kept him company. He needed time to think. He had killed a Kifzo in cold blood, one of his own men. Killing one of your own on a field of battle, even if a lowly one, was something that had happened only once before. His brother was the one who had done the killing then.

Tobin spat. *Am I no better than him now?*

Tobin knew he had good reason to end Agat's life. He saw the defiant look in the warrior's eyes and knew it would spread into the eyes of others. If he had let Agat continue, it would have only festered into something greater. He knew that, but the thought did little to ease his mind. Removed from the situation, he saw now several other possible scenarios he could have taken when handling the situation. Yet, he had chosen none of them.

The light padding of footsteps sounded from behind. He did not turn to face them. "What is it, Nachun?"

Tobin heard the faint pause in the shaman's stride as if surprised, before the footsteps continued on. Nachun stopped beside Tobin. "I forget how hard it is to come up quietly on you."

"What need is there to do so?"

"I only wished not to disturb you."

"It is too late for that. Are you here to ridicule me for taking the easy way out today? There is no need for it. I am already well aware of my mistake."

"Mistake? When?"

"Today. The Kifzo I killed."

"That? What of it?"

"I was wrong."

"I was not there but I spoke with Walor and he explained what happened."

"It was the easy thing to do."

"Easy because you reacted on instinct? Maybe so. But more times than not those instincts lead you to the right decision. Many of the old hands are rallying behind you, Tobin, and bringing the new blood to your side. Your support grows each day. I might even venture to say they respect you in ways they never respected Kaz."

"I don't understand."

"Simple. They knew to expect a hardness unequaled and a cruelty unmatched from your brother. With you, they once assumed the opposite, but when you do something as you did today, or something as you did to Mawkuk at Cypronya…well, they don't know what to expect. They fear and even respect what they do not know."

Tobin pondered Nachun's words.

The shaman continued. "And that move with the women. That was brilliant."

"Brilliant? Dozens of women were raped this night."

"And at least they were well paid for it. More than they would have received otherwise. And your men did not abuse them as they normally would have. The Kifzo did not wish to provoke you any further."

"Listen to you. I thought you agreed that such things were beneath men."

"They are, but you cannot expect to change things all at once. It would be the death of you."

"Being warleader is not an easy thing. I hate to say this, but perhaps Kaz was more suited to this role after all."

"Nonsense. You saved children and older women a lot of pain tonight, maybe even saved their lives. You did good while still eliminating the enemy."

"Enemy? We faced no army. Only families, helpless families."

"Sometimes your enemy is who you least expect it to be."

Nachun turned and left Tobin to consider the meaning behind those words.

* * *

The command tent roared in upheaval as each advisor fought to be heard over the others. Panic and, to a lesser degree, fear, gripped them and they pled with Bazraki to heed their advice. Tobin stood at the back of the tent and chuckled. He could see the scowl on his father's face, growing as the seconds waned. The others were so caught up in their own emotions they were oblivious to Bazraki's displeasure.

"Enough!" Bazraki shouted. The room fell silent as Tobin's father bared his teeth and met the eye of each man. "You are all weak. Pathetic. Get out," he snarled. "All of you."

Tobin turned to leave when his father called out. "Not you, Tobin. You will stay."

Surprised, he stepped back from the entranceway and allowed the others to file out of the tent. He came forward and stopped a short distance from his father who paced, breathing deep. Now that the tent had emptied, his father changed. He seemed worried. Something Tobin had never seen in him.

I wonder if Kaz ever saw him this way. Tobin suddenly felt awkward as he realized he hadn't been in his father's presence since their altercation weeks ago. *He needs me.*

"The Yellow Plain Clan is less than half a day away from us. We will have to meet them in battle tomorrow."

"Yes, I heard you relay the news," said Tobin.

"I was right about Mawkuk. You should have killed him and placed another in command. Maybe then, the Gray Marsh Clan would not have failed in drawing away the Yellow Plain Clan's army," said Bazraki.

"The Yellow Clan is not as gullible as the Orange Desert Clan was. Didn't I hear you say that the Yellow Clan was not at full strength?"

Bazraki grunted. "That was for those fools to hear," he said gesturing toward the tent flap. "The small force left behind to harass Mawkuk, slowing him from joining in the battle, will hardly matter tomorrow. Walor said the Yellow Clan's camp is more than double our size."

Tobin's eyes widened.

"Yes. So do you now want to defend Mawkuk?"

Tobin ignored the question. "We have time to adjust our plans, especially since we know where the battle will be."

"Yes. Across open land. And the advantage will be theirs."

"I will…"

"You will follow my plans," said Bazraki, cutting his son off. He wheeled about, snatching a rolled piece of parchment from atop the table and handing it to Tobin. "Here are my orders." He paused and sighed as he met Tobin's eyes. "I have so little left in life. After your mother died, my attention turned to goals of conquest. And with Kaz lost, my desire to rule Hesh has only increased. I have my goals and I have you. Nothing more." He placed a hand on Tobin's shoulder. "I'm counting on you tomorrow, son."

Tobin caught himself from staggering. *Son. He has never called me son. At least not with the sincerity I see now.*

So taken aback, Tobin bowed his head, lower perhaps than he ever had, and took the parchment from his father. "I will bring you victory."

* * *

Tobin looked down at the piece of parchment again, at least the fifth time in as many minutes. Rolling it tight, he squeezed it in his fist. He lifted his head and stared out over tomorrow's battlefield.

"This will be much different than any battle we've fought before. This land is not kind to the Kifzo style of fighting," said Tobin, staring out across the expansive valley floor. "We don't have the mounts or the men to match the Yellow Clan on horseback."

Nachun gestured to Tobin's hand. "And your father's plan?"

"Useless. I couldn't draw up a weaker positioning of our forces if I tried. And we still have their shamans to contend with."

"Yes, their shamans are quite powerful. From what I gather, they are adept at making use of the land and life around them."

"And yet, you do not even factor into my father's strategy."

Nachun raised an eyebrow. "I think your father no longer trusts me. Though after all I've done for him, I haven't the slightest idea why."

"His distrust will add to the Blue Island Clan's slaughter."

"You aren't making any changes to Bazraki's plans?"

Tobin shook his head. "I don't know. I promised him."

"You said that you promised victory. You didn't commit to how that victory would be achieved."

Tobin sighed. "He called me *son*, and I saw he meant it. Just like you said he would. He has realized my importance. How can I defy him after that?"

"Do not consider it defiance. You have thousands of men counting on you now. All of them expect you to lead them to victory. You have to do what you think is best for them. If they succeed, so will your father. Do you really think he would prefer you follow his plans and lose, rather than mold them into something better so that he can accomplish his goals? You told me yourself that Kaz altered Bazraki's plans as he saw fit to ensure success. Do you recall your father ever being upset with your brother's decisions? Now that he is recognizing you for who you are, why would he treat you differently?"

Tobin mulled over Nachun's words. He sighed again and nodded. "You're right. Find Ufer and then meet me at my tent."

"Ufer?"

"Yes. He's proven that I can trust him. I'll get Walor. Tell no one else. I don't want one of my father's advisors to hear of our meeting."

* * *

Tobin pushed aside the flap of his tent and set off into the cool, starry night. Nachun, Walor, and Ufer left several minutes earlier to carry out his orders and ensure all was set for the imminent battle. Tobin stayed behind to go over his plan at least half a dozen times more in private. He wanted to make certain that he hadn't missed some crucial detail.

Too easy how quickly everything became clear to me. Yet father spends days, weeks, months, agonizing over the smallest of details, only to have them changed later.

With head held high, he strode through camp, his face hard as stone. Tobin offered a nod to those warriors' who met his eyes. A Kifzo would not need encouragement or motivation for what was to come.

War is their life, and if they are not ready now, they will never be.

"The only thing worse than failure is cowardice. A man who is afraid to fight is already dead. By killing those who are frightened, you make room in line for those who are still alive, eager to taste victory." Another lesson of Tobin's uncle that was etched into his mind.

Tobin usually felt nothing on the day before a battle, but a sense of anxiousness twisted his stomach into knots. *It is because I have so much to lose now. The respect of my men. Of my father. And Odala.*

Now outside of Juanoq, Tobin's duties had increased, becoming much harder to spend time with Odala. Still, late each night when the camp was asleep, Tobin would go to her tent and stay for hours, talking with her and sometimes holding her. The lack of sleep had worn on him little—his body had learned long ago how to survive on a small amount of rest. Besides, each visit to her tent only seemed to renew his energy and carry him through the next day.

The day before a battle most warriors spent their time sharpening edges, checking gear, resting, making peace with their thoughts, or recalling events from the past around a blazing fire. Yet Tobin stood at the entrance to Odala's tent.

And there is no other place I would rather be.

* * *

Odala was shaken awake with force.

"What are you doing? Wake up," said Soyjid.

She rolled over and rubbed away sleep as she faced her brother. "Leave me alone. I'm trying to sleep as much as I can before Tobin arrives."

"And you think I'm not tired? Remember, I have to stay awake to listen to all that babbling so I can try to glean any information you might miss."

She sighed and turned back over, closing her eyes. "Just leave me alone."

Soyjid ripped the covers from her grasp. A gust of air sent a chill down her. She sat up with a start, furious. "Soyjid!"

Her brother smiled. "Good. You're up." He threw something at her. "Put this on and get ready."

Odala picked up what looked like a jumble of fabric. The blue material was silky beneath her fingers. She looked from the dress to her brother. "Where did you get this?" she asked in a whisper.

Soyjid lowered his voice. "Well, rather than sleep the day away like some people do, I've been busy."

"Busy with what? Eavesdropping on guards?"

He waved a hand. "They are a waste of time. However, the servants are a much different matter. One in particular secured your dress. I have several others that keep me well informed."

"How?"

"Let's just say that you're not the only one who knows how to use charms to get what they want."

Odala raised an eyebrow. Her brother's thin frame brought even more attention to his oversized head. *Perhaps they feel sorry for him.*

She kept her thoughts to herself though, knowing her brother liked to keep his secrets. She stood up, draping the dress in front of her. Dangerously revealing, a slit reached as high as where her waist would be. The cut in front, descended like a V, and would expose most of her chest and even part of her stomach.

"I can't wear this," she said, appalled that her brother would even suggest such a thing.

"Sure you can. I don't see what the big deal is. Your nightgown may cover more but reveals almost as much as the dress."

Odala shied away. "That's different. I sleep in that. This is more...alluring." She paused. "I can't do this."

"You may not have a choice, sister. I overheard the guards complaining that they would have to stay behind and watch over us during the battle tomorrow. The Yellow Plain Clan has come out to meet the Blue Island Clan. It appears they are not willing to wait for Bazraki to attack Actur."

"Then why bother with this?" Odala asked, pointing to the dress. "Tobin may die tomorrow and then I won't have to worry about this ruse any longer."

"Shh," said Soyjid, holding a finger to his mouth. "You better hope he doesn't."

"What's wrong?" asked Odala, seeing her brother grow somber.

"You don't get it, do you? The Yellow Plain Clan should be busy with Father and our forces to the south. The fact that they are here means that they did not fall for Bazraki's deception."

"And?"

"And, I was told that Bazraki blames Father for the failure of his plan. Now they must face the Yellow Clan with their armies divided and hope that Father gets here in time."

"I still don't understand.

Soyjid shook his head. "Odala, I was told that orders have already been issued to kill Father after the battle tomorrow, regardless of the outcome. You must convince Tobin to change Bazraki's mind."

Not Father. He is so old. He deserves to pass on in his own time. "How am I supposed to do that?"

Soyjid nodded to the dress. "Any way necessary."

Odala stood there, biting her lip in thought. As always, she could see Soyjid's point. *He is too smart for his age*, she thought. *Still, am I ready for this?*

A voice called out. "Odala?" Both their heads turned.

Tobin.

In panic she looked at Soyjid. He gestured at the dress and then scurried behind the flap dividing their adjoining tents. Odala cursed to herself as she slipped off her nightgown, and threw the dress over her head. On her way to the door she paused for a second in front of a full-length mirror Tobin had brought for her, admiring herself.

Maybe tempting him will be enough?

She pulled the flap aside, careful to stand away from the entrance so that the guards would not see her.

Tobin slipped into the dim room, tying the flap in place. He faced her and froze, mouth falling open.

The dress did its job then.

"I was expecting you later tonight," said Odala.

To the warrior's credit, he recovered. "I'm sorry. I couldn't wait to see you." He paused. "You look amazing."

Despite her discomfort, she still blushed at the sincerity in his voice. Rather than thank him, she took his hand and led him to her bed. If Tobin was surprised at the strange gesture, he didn't show it. Odala had always made it a point to stay as far from the bed as possible.

She tried to hide her uneasiness as they seated themselves.

"You look troubled," said Tobin.

"It's about tomorrow."

"You've heard about the battle, then? I'll be fine."

"I'm not worried about you. I mean, I know you can take care of yourself," she said, trying to cover her poor choice of words. "Actually, it's Father."

"What about Mawkuk?"

"Well, we've heard talk that Bazraki plans to kill him tomorrow after the battle, win or lose. It is his punishment for not drawing away the Yellow Clan army."

"Who told you that?"

"Soyjid overheard whisperings behind his tent earlier tonight."

"I see."

"You must save him. I promise you he did not fail purposefully. It is not his way."

Tobin sighed. "Whether I agree or not, it is my father's decision. I can do nothing to change his mind."

Odala shook her head. "Yes, you can. You can easily do this. You are warleader and have more than enough power to sway your father if you choose to use it."

Silence stretched and Odala could see that Tobin struggled with the decision, so much so that he had even cast his eyes away from her exposed body and stared at the matted floor. She remembered Soyjid's comment. *"Any way necessary."*

She swallowed hard, trying to hide her nervousness and went to him.

* * *

Tobin left her room two hours before dawn, having barely slept.

Odala lay in her bed with eyes shut tight as the tears she had held in during her time with Tobin ran down her face and soaked her pillow. She had never been with a man and she had always hoped for something far different than what had occurred.

She had given herself to Tobin physically in an attempt to sway his mind. Yet he still hesitated. So she tried something different, another lie. She leaned in close, whispering into his ear that she loved him. And that made all the difference. Tobin promised her that he would protect Mawkuk and even whispered his love in return, though the name he said wasn't hers.

It sounded as if he said Lucia. Who is that? No matter, Father is safe now. He promised.

She cried harder as a red haze flitted through the cracks in her tent. She had tried to separate her mind from her body during the experience, but it had not worked. Visions of Tobin holding a dagger near her father's eyes, coupled with the countless other atrocities he shared with her in private had flooded her mind and she struggled not to curse him as the night crept on.

Next time I need to do better at hiding that. Her body and mind felt numb at the prospect of their next meeting. *But at least I succeeded. Maybe I can do some good for our people. Maybe I can make Tobin suffer as much as he has made me suffer through this lie.* It wasn't much, but the thought brought her enough comfort for her body to relax and drift into a deep sleep.

CHAPTER 26

The first hints of an early spring began to find their way through the unforgiving northern landscape. The melted snow covering the roads created a slick mud that hindered the progress of Jeldor's troops. The temperature still dipped at night, but the sun now peeked through the thick clouds with more regularity. Elyse thought the additional warmth would be welcome, but she soon changed her mind as she watched soldiers with legs caked in mud struggle through the poor road conditions. She cringed with growing frustration as two squads of soldiers worked to free yet another wagon wheel caught in the muck.

At this rate, we'll never get there.

She moved her mount around the wagon and found Rygar who had recently returned from scouting. "Any news?" she asked.

He shook his head. "None worth mentioning, Your Majesty. No signs of anyone from Tomalt's army. Granted, we are still some length away from Cathyrium."

"How much longer?"

Rygar glanced back at the wagon as it lurched forward, into another hole created by the wagons preceding it. "At this pace, three weeks at least," he said, looking discouraged.

We can't wait that long. "Thank you."

The scout bowed his head as Elyse left him. She noted the distant looks on the soldiers' faces as she weaved through their masses.

She found Jeldor in front of the army, peering out over the long twisting road ahead. His hand was over his eyes to deflect the glare off the remaining white snow. "My lord, is there something you see?"

He turned in the saddle. "Oh no, just thinking about how much land we still have left to travel and how long it's taken us to go this far." He muttered a curse. "The weather has not been very cooperative."

"No, it hasn't."

Jeldor threw up his hands and gestured back to the train of supply wagons. "There is little I can do given the conditions of the roads."

"We can leave the wagons behind and move the bulk of your force ahead."

"That's not very sound practice. Besides, the men themselves are beaten enough just fighting this slop. Pushing the pace will only tire them further. The last thing you want is a tired army entering battle, Your Majesty. Aurnon the First said as much, if I recall."

"He did, but the last thing I want is to arrive at Cathyrium and find out we are too late." She paused, remembering a passage on military strategy from her studies. "Aurnon the First also said that a soldier will fight hardest for a cause he believes in. Well, it is hard to believe in a losing cause, my lord. If we are not there in time to aid Jonrell, that is exactly what we will be facing."

Jeldor grunted and Elyse held her breath as she watched the man stroke his wild beard. Their relationship had improved a great deal and Jeldor seemed to humor her less and respect her more each day. *Yet, these men are his. I do not have the ability to persuade them to follow me rather than their lord if Jeldor refuses my command. Perhaps Jonrell could do such a thing, but he isn't here.*

Jeldor glanced up the road ahead and back to his men. He nodded. "We'll leave two thousand behind to guard our supplies. If we don't arrive in time and are forced into a withdrawal they will be fresh if they have to be brought in for relief." He turned to face Elyse. "Not that I think that will be necessary. Still, it doesn't hurt to plan for the worst."

She suppressed a smile. "Sound reasoning. Thank you."

And thank the One Above.

"Don't thank me yet. There will be a lot of soldiers angry with us at the quickened pace. I hope it will shave nearly a week off our expected time of arrival."

She shrugged beneath her wool cloak. "It isn't our duty to be liked, is it?"

Jeldor grinned. "No, it isn't." He snapped his reins and rode back to his men, barking orders to his captains and cursing at every sidelong glance cast his way.

* * *

From the top of the castle gatehouse, Yanasi lowered the spyglass. She stared blankly over the city, into the hills, where Tomalt's army spilled over their sides. Strong vision helped her shot with a bow, but at times she wished herself blind.

Maybe then someone else could be the bearer of bad news.

"Is it that bad?" asked Jonrell.

She handed him the spyglass, finding her voice. "Worse, Commander. I've never seen such a large army before. The scouts underestimated its size."

I wish Rygar was here. He wouldn't have misjudged their number. She closed her eyes for the briefest of moments, remembering the warmth of his touch. She missed him.

Jonrell raised the spyglass to his eye. She held her breath, waiting for his response as he surveyed the masses.

"How many you guess?" he asked.

"Fifty thousand, Commander."

"That sounds about right."

She knew it was right, though she wished to be wrong.

Fifty thousand.

"The largest army we've fought since I joined The Hell Patrol was half that size. And the army we were attached to had close to that number themselves," she said.

Jonrell lowered the spyglass and put his hand on her shoulder. "You sound unsure if we'll win."

She shrugged, not wanting to admit the truth. "The odds are better that Raker will win at cards first."

Jonrell removed his hand from her shoulder and slapped the stone wall. "This will make up for our difference in numbers," he said with finality to his voice. "It takes far fewer men to defend a wall than it does to capture one." He smiled.

Yanasi couldn't help but grin back. Jonrell had a way of making her feel better, regardless of how somber her mood turned.

That's what men like him do. Like all heroes, they rise to the occasion.

"Good thing for them they've got a lot of men to throw at us then."

Jonrell grimaced and looked over his shoulder. "You're not helping the situation."

Raker spat over the side. "She ain't no young pup anymore and she's seen more than enough killing over the last ten years to know this ain't going to be easy."

Yanasi scowled at the engineer but he gave no sign of noticing.

Jonrell nodded to the rest of the army who began gathering on the outer walls. Conversations filled with doubt started as they watched Tomalt's army make camp. "And what about them?" he asked in a low voice. "Most haven't seen battle before."

Raker looked over to Yanasi and then Jonrell, grinning with a mouthful of brown teeth. "I reckon that'll change soon enough."

* * *

As Jonrell expected, Tomalt led a small contingent of a dozen people away from his growing camp, stopping just on the outskirts of the main city. The banner man held a white flag that flapped in the breeze. The duke wanted to offer terms.

Always by the book. I wonder if any good will come of it.

He took one more look through the spyglass before handing it back to Yanasi.

Only one way to find out.

* * *

Kaz flicked the reins of his horse and joined Jonrell as they rode through the empty city. Only the whipping wind populated the streets now as the remaining citizens hid safely behind the great walls of the castle.

"Shouldn't you be meeting Tomalt with twice as many men as he has? I don't think a prince would just take me along." asked Kaz.

Jonrell chuckled. "Probably. But, I haven't really considered myself a prince for some time. As a commander, I don't need all those people sucking up to me like he does."

"So you just need one?" asked Kaz in an accusatory tone.

Jonrell laughed this time. "If so, I made a poor choice with you. No, I usually take Krytien with me as back up to these sorts of things, but with him gone, I needed someone else to fill in."

"So you think Tomalt may try something then?"

"I doubt it. Tomalt is very official in everything he does. Not following protocol at a parlay would be about as bad as stealing from his grandmother." He paused. "Still, I don't like to take chances, and I know I can trust you to let me do the talking."

"So, I'm supposed to stay quiet and look menacing."

"More or less. Is that going to be a problem?"

Kaz grinned. "No. I can handle that."

* * *

Jonrell saw a brief flash of surprise from Tomalt as he and Kaz reached his group. The duke, as expected, wore his finest armor. He sat rigid in his saddle, straight as a plank, with head held high. Jonrell suppressed a grin as he remembered a childhood joke concerning the duke and an arrow.

"So, the reports are true. You have returned. Your Majesty," said Tomalt with a bow. The rest of his men did the same.

"Stop. My sister rules Cadonia. Not me."

Tomalt raised his head. "So the other reports are true as well. You haven't come to reclaim the crown?"

"No. I renounced that right when I left Cadonia. I have no desire to take it back."

"A shame."

Jonrell inclined his head. "Would that matter? Would such a thing cause you to turn your army around and return to your lands?"

Tomalt stared intently for a moment as if pondering the thought. "No. I don't think it would."

"I didn't think so."

"Your father harmed this kingdom too greatly. You've been gone too long. You aren't close enough to the problems to understand how to fix them."

"My sister, has been here the entire time. Yet, you wish to steal the crown from her."

"She is not fit to rule. Even in the short time since you've returned, I'm sure you see that." He drew a deep breath. "I want to make something clear. I am not doing this thing for personal gain. I am simply looking out for the good of the kingdom."

"How noble of you," Jonrell guffawed. "Then let's hear your terms as I'm sure they're more than fair," he sneered.

Tomalt took a scroll from one of his men and handed it to Jonrell. "The details are all inside but essentially you are to open the gates to Cathyrium on the morrow and all its inhabitants will swear fealty to me. The queen, if she is still inside as originally reported," said Tomalt with a knowing look, "is to accompany me to Lyrosene where she will recognize me as the new king of Cadonia. She has the night to accept my terms."

"And if she refuses?"

"We will take Cathyrium by force and then do the same to the rest of the lands under direct control of the crown. But please, don't let it come to that. I know your numbers and you cannot win."

Jonrell cleared his throat and glanced over to Kaz. The foreigner wore a menacing scowl, flaring his nostrils with each breath. Jonrell turned back to Tomalt's group and noticed that many of them stared nervously at Kaz, shifting in their saddles with hands near their swords.

Perfect.

Jonrell lied. "I will take your terms to the queen, but I was given strict orders not to accept any beneath our own. Would you care to hear them?"

Tomalt nodded.

"You will leave your entire army under my command with the exception of one thousand men who may accompany you back to Bolysius. You will remain there while we settle matters with the other dukes. After that time, the queen will make a decision in regards to your punishment for transgressions against the city of Namaris."

"And if I refuse?" asked Tomalt, wearing a smile hinting of amusement.

"Then you will forfeit all your lands to the crown. And we will kill anyone who stands in our way of claiming them. In the end, you will face death."

Tomalt's smile thinned at the last comment, turning into a scowl.

One of his men grunted in amusement. "We outnumber you, six to one, Commander," said the man. "Even with the walls of Cathyrium, you cannot hope to win."

Jonrell leaned in his saddle, glaring at the soldier. "What are you? A captain? Have you ever even seen battle, before?"

The man said nothing.

"I didn't think so." He looked over the rest of the group. "I bet none of you have." He nodded back to Kaz. "The kind of men I have manning my walls are just like him. They've seen battle. Six to one odds you say? I think those favor me greatly." He looked back to Tomalt. "Battle is something I know well, better than any of you. Refuse my terms and you will die. Even if I have to kill you myself. I expect your answer tomorrow."

Jonrell spun his mount toward the castle. Kaz rode next to him.

CHAPTER 27

Raker leaned over the tower's parapet and spat. He watched the tobacco-filled juice fall and hit a mangled corpse—the helm of which was imprinted with that of a mace. Hitting the mark brought a hoarse chuckle from his lips.

Raker had been so busy working the mangonel to harass the opposition from a distance, that he had neglected to notice the scaling ladders the enemy flung against the castle's walls until men started pulling themselves over the ramparts. He had just enough time to race down the drum tower to help the guards struggling there. His mace struck a soldier's head as it peeked over the top rung of the ladder. Raker watched the man take three others with him on the way down. Men pushed the ladder over and he cackled as several others let out a scream.

After another short assault, Tomalt had pulled his men back, settling for another failed attempt, the fourth in as many days. Tomalt tried something different with each one, probing the castle's defenses before retreating to the safety of their camp, just out of the range of trebuchets.

Or so they think.

"Raker."

The mercenary turned. "Drake, what're you doing here?"

"Jonrell told me to run over here during a lull in the action. He told me that you needed to place someone else in charge for now and that it was time to ruin Tomalt's day."

Raker spat and revealed a rotted out grin. "About time." He turned to his right. "Senald, you ready for this?"

"Ready for what, Sir?"

"To man this tower, boy."

"I guess so."

"You better do more than guess. Look, I'll be down in the yard by the trebuchets. But don't think I won't be able to tell if you ain't running my baby here like she should be run," he said slapping the mangonel. "And if she ain't treated right, well you and me are gonna have words later," he said, moving his hand to his mace. "You with me?"

Senald gulped. "Yes, sir."

Man, I love that scared look. "Good. Then she's yours."

Raker followed Drake down the drum tower's stairs when he grabbed the boy by the shoulder. "What in the name of the One Above is that you got round your waist?"

"A sword."

"What have I told you about swords? Engineers don't need some fancy sword to do their fighting. If he ain't manning his equipment, all he's got time to do is swing something heavy and hard. I thought I gave you a mace of your own."

"Uh, you did. It's just that well, it was too heavy and hard for me to use. I'm only fourteen. Maybe in the future..."

"So instead you gonna stab yourself with that thing?"

"No, I've been getting lessons."

"Lessons from who?"

"Uh, no one important."

Raker cursed. "You been learning from that black dog, ain't you?"

"Kaz isn't a dog."

"Close enough I say."

"Well, you're becoming the minority then, because all anyone's been talking about is how well he's been doing leading sorties out into the city and harassing Tomalt's men. They say he's saved at least a hundred men's lives and put a hundred enemies in the grave himself."

"Bah, that's nothing. I'll do more damage than that once I get to my babies."

Drake inclined his head. "What do you have against him? Who cares what his skin looks like?"

"To tell you the truth, his color don't bother me as much as it used to. I just think he's got a twisted sense of humor is all."

"I've never heard him tell a joke," said Drake, looking confused.

"That's just it. Something ain't right about a man who can't laugh, especially around all this fun," said Raker. He slapped the boy around. "Now quit squawking and let's get going before Jonrell has us on latrine duty."

* * *

Jonrell stood between the two massive trebuchets that were positioned between the inner and outer walls of the castle. He watched Drake lead Raker down a set of stairs and hurry over to where he waited. "Took you long enough."

"You can blame the boy for that. Kid will just talk your ear off rather than get to a point," said Raker.

Drake shot the old hand a look but said nothing.

Jonrell grinned. *Aye, I know the truth lad.* "Well, let's quit wasting time. They took decent losses on that last assault and I want to add to their misery while they're already hurting."

"I don't know why you wouldn't let me use the old girls sooner. They're nearly done building their towers," said Raker.

"That's the point. I'd rather destroy the towers now after all the time and effort Tomalt has wasted on them. Besides, if you're right about the range of these they'll have to push camp further back and save what supplies they can, all under a hail of stones."

Raker spat. "Right you are." Raker looked up to the gatehouse. "Who's calling my distance?"

"Yanasi is calling distance for both of you. So don't get her riled up. From up there she just may put an arrow between your legs."

Raker muttered a curse then reached over and knocked the oversized helm from Drake's head, mussing his hair. "C'mon, boy, let's see what you got. I got five pieces of gold says I can bring down more than you."

Drake had been looking sour until he heard the challenge. He flashed a smiled. "You're on, old timer." He quickly ran off.

"Old timer? That little…" said Raker.

Jonrell grabbed him by the shoulder. "Later. Let's give Tomalt something to think about."

* * *

Sergeant Lanard sat at a table in the mess hall with several other young officers. His body ached and his eyes had trouble focusing. The exhaustion was so intense he had to talk himself into taking every bite of stew and crusted bread. He longed for a place to rest his head.

I gotta get something down first.

"Craziest thing I ever saw," said the man next to him. Sergeant Moren shook his head in disbelief.

The other officers at the table looked up with heavy eyes, but cast them right back down at their bowls, paying Moren little mind. They were all feeling worse for the wear after the last few days of fighting, and no one wanted to hear another of Moren's wild embellishments.

"What are you yapping about this time, Moren?" asked Lanard, immediately regretting his mistake. *Now, I'll never eat in peace.*

Moren leaned in close and whispered. "I'm talking about Kaz. He ain't human."

Another officer clicked his tongue. "Of course he isn't. You've seen the way he looks."

Moren shook his head. "That's not what I'm talking about, Brock. I'm talking about the way he fights."

"Yeah yeah, we've all seen him in the practice yard showing off," said Lanard, wanting to get back to his meal.

Moren shook his head again. "No. This is different. You weren't out running sorties with him. I'm telling you it was the most amazing thing I've ever seen, watching that man fight. I nearly got my own head lopped off by not paying attention," he said pointing to a clipped ear. He started laughing. "You should have seen Tomalt's men. They were actually running away from him. Not us, but him. Craziest thing I ever saw."

"Don't tell me you're another one with some kind of a crush on the man," said Brock. "You said yourself, he ain't human."

Moren ignored the jibe and took a bite of stew. He then jabbed the spoon at each man at the table. "I'm telling you, boys, I don't care what he is or where he's from. I'd follow that man in battle against the One Below himself after what I've seen."

"Aw c'mon," said Lanard, having enough of the conversation he had encouraged. "Just the other day, you and Railen were going on and on about how you couldn't wait to see Glacar take Kaz down."

Moren chuckled. "Not anymore. And Railen's singing Kaz's praise to anyone who will listen in the infirmary. More than I am, for sure. And who can blame him? Kaz carried the man almost three hundred yards over one shoulder after Railen took an arrow in the side. Kaz was fighting Tomalt's men with one arm the whole way back to the castle." He paused, losing himself in the memory. "Anyway, before I came here, I checked in on Railen and that brown-skinned fellow, Wiqua. He said that if it weren't for Kaz our fellow sergeant would be dead."

Brock waved a hand. "Bah, so I'm supposed to jump down and worship the devil just because you two are impressed with his skill."

Moren laughed. "Where have you been? Under a rock?"

"No, I was working the trebuchets this afternoon with that crazy one from the Hell Patrol. Raker."

"Then you'll see soon enough. Me and Railen aren't the only ones. I'm telling you, Kaz is for real, and the rest of that crew is alright in my eyes too."

Lanard pushed himself away from the table. "I've had enough of this."

He handed off his food to Moren who eagerly snatched it away. After a hard day, the last thing he wanted to do was hear more about the Hell Patrol and their band of misfits. Yet as he strode through the mess hall, he heard snippets of conversations all relaying stories about the various members of the group. Some were about that fine red-headed woman with the fiery temper, others about that maniac, Glacar, or the giant, Crusher. And the list of names grew with each table he passed.

One name kept popping up over all others. Kaz. Lanard wondered if everyone in the whole hall had either been saved by the black devil or watched him save someone else.

Lanard shook his head. *No one is that good.*

* * *

If Tomalt had been confident in victory, Jonrell was sure that after the hard lesson Raker and Drake gave him, the duke had to be second guessing himself. The trebuchets had pounded his camp, reaching spots well beyond what most would assume possible from standard siege equipment. Jonrell had joined Yanasi on top of the gatehouse to watch the competition between the two engineers. When he had finally called a ceasefire, Jonrell could hardly determine which of the two eccentric members had earned the five pieces of gold.

The good news was that their efforts had set Tomalt back days, perhaps longer. Eight large siege towers had been completely destroyed. Supply wagons and tents were also turned into rags and splinters. The bad news was that Tomalt had lost few men during the bombardment.

Apparently his men are fast runners.

"Things have been too quiet. He hasn't attempted to attack even once since we used the trebuchets."

Jonrell turned, startled. "Lord Caliva. You surprised me." He turned back over the field, gazing upon the smattering of white tents. In front, stood newly erected siege equipment, almost twice as many as before. "Yes, but he's been busy in other ways."

"Yes, I believe all we accomplished was to stir the hornet's nest. Before, all he dared to do was probe and test our defenses."

Jonrell nodded. "Tomalt is a methodical man."

"But even a methodical man will run out of patience. I believe with his next assault, whenever that may be, he will come at us with everything he has."

"You're probably right."

"Well, let us hope the queen was successful with her efforts to win over Jeldor's support," said Caliva, leaning over the merlon next to Jonrell. "Even with the losses Tomalt's taken so far, he outnumbers us five to one."

Jonrell gave Caliva a sharp look, gauging the distance of those within earshot.

Caliva laughed. "Don't worry commander. The men figured out long ago that the queen is not ill and residing in the tower. They know her servant is standing in her place."

Jonrell sighed. "When?"

"I think they suspected some time ago, but when you met Tomalt for parlay without Her Majesty, they felt confident you were hiding something."

Jonrell sighed again. "As did Tomalt. Another reason I expect him not to dally any longer with his next assault."

Caliva grunted. "Then again let us hope that your sister was successful."

* * *

Jonrell watched the city burn from the top of Cathyrium's large keep. Tomalt had begun to set fire to the outskirts of the town yesterday, and before long flames engulfed everything outside of the castle's walls. A day and a night later the fires continued, whipping brown smoke into the air. Flames danced recklessly between the shattered ruins. The city's cathedral, no longer recognizable in its blackened state, fell in on itself with a loud crash. Ash soared into the air like a flock of angry crows.

Why did it have to come to this?

Jonrell had evacuated most of Cathyrium's inhabitants to surrounding towns long ago. He ushered those who stayed inside the city's walls days before Tomalt's arrival. They first used the city's alleys and abandoned buildings to stage ambushes and sorties to harass enemy troops. Glacar, Crusher, and Kaz had each led men against Tomalt's advances where it was said the Duke had taken heavy losses.

Jonrell knew Tomalt's newest tactic was sound, but watching the city destroyed at the hands of one of his countrymen, ripped his heart. *War is a cursed thing.*

He pulled out his spyglass and found a line of sight between the billowing smoke. Lines formed in Tomalt's camp and the siege equipment received last minute preparations.

This will be the big push.

A scribe sat next to Jonrell, jotting down his orders before handing off each slip of paper to a messenger. Even after more than a dozen orders went out, Jonrell's eyes had not left the burning pyre that had been the city of Cathyrium.

* * *

"Keep it up!" Yanasi shouted. She watched the man next to her fumble with an arrow from his quiver. Blood ran down his hand where a blister had burst open. "Don't think about how much it hurts. Don't think about how tired you are. Just think about driving an arrow right through everyone of those whoresons who wants to take your land from you. Show them no mercy, for I guarantee you will get none in return."

A roar lifted from her men and she noticed that their pace quickened. She smiled and returned to firing her own sleek, black bow. Her men had hated her at first, and she had been sure Jonrell made a mistake in giving her command. But over time, her men had grown to trust her, and now she wouldn't give up her company for anything in the world. These men were hers and she relished fighting by their side.

Jonrell, you were right after all. She allowed herself a slight grin despite the swarming lines of infantry edging toward the castle's outer walls.

Siege towers came into view, rolling down the wide avenues and parting the rising smoke. Water soaked hides covered the towers and the fire arrows her archers had switched to were of little affect. She noticed that the mangonels and ballistae stationed around the castle's outer walls were having trouble bringing them down as well. Hurled stones flew from the towers, narrowly missing the drum tower to her right.

They've got catapults on top of their towers.

She yelled to her men. "Concentrate your fire near the tower's wheels where the hide is coming away. We need to stop as many of those things as we can before they reach the walls."

* * *

Drake ducked as a rock sailed overhead, nearly soiling himself. He wanted to cower behind the merlon until the fighting was over but the battle had just begun.

This is the worst we've seen yet.

Men had come at the walls before with ladders, but he hadn't been under much pressure himself, save for a few stray arrows. But now siege towers armed with mangonel or ballistae lurched forward. They didn't seem to have the same force as those he and Raker had constructed, but the smaller equipment fired faster rounds and prevented him and his men from taking proper aim which allowed the towers to inch ever closer.

The soldier next to him raised a shield and one of the stones crashed into it, knocking the man from his feet. The corporal cursed and cradled his arm.

"We gotta get below and take cover." Drake heard another mutter. "This is useless."

They looked at Drake and he knew he should say something encouraging, or something that would strike fear in them and make them stay at their station like Raker did. However, looking out over the hellish inferno that flared beyond the castle's walls, all he could think about was the comforting calm of the green forested Hideaway that he had left behind.

* * *

Raker stood defiant atop the merlons. He bellowed orders to his men as they stayed under steady fire from the approaching siege towers. He spat over the side of the high drum tower, daring them to take him out. A missile sailed past his head and he felt the rising wind on his face.

They're getting better.

He cackled maniacally. He faced his men, dropping his trousers and wagging his backside at the enemy. His men joined him in laughter.

"That thing ready yet, Senald?" yelled Raker as men rushed the wall's base.

"Aye, Sir."

"Then fire away and show those pretty boys what we got."

"Aye." They all shouted again as the mangonel arm slammed into the cross beam. The pitched rock was flung in a high arc and landed on top of the tower he had targeted. With his breaches still around his ankles, Raker watched splinters fly through the air and men topple to the ground. He let out a holler as an arrow whipped by his head.

He looked down as ladders slammed against the sides of the wall and decided to relieve himself before the fighting got close.

Nothing worse than a full bladder while trying to kill a man.

* * *

Drake's men stared at him and he stared right back. None of them knew what to say or what to do. He glanced over the ramparts to the drum tower on the opposite corner where Raker stood relieving himself over the wall. A flash of lightning illuminated the scene. Crashing thunder followed. He blinked and shook his head at the absurdity of it all. Arrows flitted all around the man but he paid none any mind until he shook himself off and pulled his trousers back up.

How does he do it?

Drake realized his men had been talking to him. In fact, one shook him. Yet he couldn't find the words to answer the questions being asked. All he had heard were the sounds of men dying and steel clanging.

"C'mon. Let's get out of here," said the corporal, slapping one of the other men in the arm. His voice alone heard over the chaos around him.

Drake looked into the eyes of the rest of his crew and saw that each had already made up their mind to do the same. They turned toward the stairwell but quickly came to a halt as a giant shadow pushed itself through the arched doorway, a great broadsword painted in blood was in its hand.

"Where is everyone going?" asked Kaz in a deep, accented voice.

The men gaped.

Kaz met each man's eyes until he settled on Drake, still on his rear, leaning against the parapet. The massive bulk came forward and yanked Drake to his feet. "You aren't hurt. What's wrong?"

"I-I can't move."

"You're afraid?"

Drake nodded.

A dark blur slapped Drake across his face. His eyes widened.

"What do you feel now?"

His hand drifted up to his face. "Pain. That hurt…"

The hand slapped him again. "And now."

Drake's heart raced and fire burned in his eyes. "Anger," said Drake in a low tone.

Kaz nodded. "Good. Now use it," he said pointing out at the field. He sheathed his sword and ran over to the mangonel, pushing aside the men who hadn't found the nerve yet to move again. Kaz gave each a look until they joined him at their stations.

Drake looked out to the siege towers struggling forward. Without thinking, he began shouting coordinates. He ducked under his shield as another hail of rocks flew toward their position.

"By *your* command," said Kaz. Drake looked back and saw his men had gotten the message.

This tower is mine and no one is leaving unless I give the order.

His arm came down. "Release."

* * *

Sergeant Lanard's arms felt like lead.

Tomalt's men had swarmed the walls with such overwhelming numbers that before long they failed to push away all the ladders thudding the hard stone. The enemy clamored over the sides and overran his section. The strong cluster of his experienced veterans dwindled beneath the onslaught. He already killed half a dozen men since the first had crested the walls, but their numbers only swelled. Each swing Lanard used to counter their attacks got sloppier, and as the minutes passed he knew his time was coming to an end.

A man as large as an ox with a face as ugly as one came at him in a rush. The man growled like an animal each time his warhammer crashed down on Lanard's shield. Lanard's knees buckled. Another thunderous blow hit him so hard his arm went limp. His shield clattered to the walkway, stuck to the dead weight of his arm. He tried to raise his sword arm in preparation for the next blow but couldn't find the strength. With the warhammer looming overhead, he closed his eyes and resigned himself to his fate.

He heard the sound of the weapon whistling through the air and a loud clash, but Lanard felt no impact. He opened his eyes and saw the beast of a man struggling against another equal in size.

Kaz? Where did he come from? The black man's sword had caught the warhammer as it descended. The enemy struggled to overpower the mercenary, but Kaz would not budge.

The white of Kaz's teeth peeked through parted lips as a war cry erupted that sent a shiver down Lanard's spine. He could have sworn he heard the oxman whimper. With a shove of his shoulder, Kaz flung the man from the wall. Four quick slashes followed and four more bodies fell.

Kaz grabbed either side of a ladder. Another sound that seemed to have come from the very bowels of hell erupted from the black man as he heaved the ladder from the wall by himself.

A flash of lightning raced across the sky.

One Above, I'll never doubt Moren again.

Kaz turned to face Lanard and yelled over the surrounding mayhem. "Will you make it?"

After that, what can I say? I dare not tell him no. Lanard nodded.

"Good," said Kaz as he reached down and picked Lanard up with one arm. The strength of the mercenary both humbled Lanard and renewed his strength.

"I've got things here," said Lanard. "Thanks."

Kaz nodded and turned without another word, carving his way through anyone who dared stand in his way.

* * *

The smell of death hung in the air and filled Kaz's nostrils as he hacked his way through the press of bodies. Blood splattered across his cheek as he opened a man's throat, then turned in time to avoid the thrust of another. With a grunt, his sword pierced a weak spot in the man's armor and he fell, blood spilling on the cobbled wall-walk.

Kaz had been running from one part of the castle to another, drawn to wherever the fighting seemed most intense. He stayed until he got things under control, and then moved on to the next area, wreaking havoc on anyone who came against him.

As far as his memories told him, he never smiled much. Yet with each parry, thrust, bob, and weave, the corners of his mouth seemed to lift into a half-smile. For the first time since waking on Slum Isle, Kaz felt at ease, relaxed. If the few glimpses of his past told him anything, it was that he found solace in war.

Things started to fall into place when Jonrell asked him to lead sorties into the city before Tomalt torched all the buildings. He had harried Tomalt's forces with a small group. Yet, he had always been victorious. Victory felt different, better even, than those flashes of his past. The eyes of the men he fought alongside in the city did not hold the same fear or disdain as those in his memories. He saw respect and in some cases awe. Even now he could see many with those same looks. Yes, some still seemed resentful toward him for how different he appeared. But overall, he felt accepted and even acknowledged. Men gave him a shout or a nod as he passed, where before he would have been ignored or greeted with whisperings behind his back.

Kaz wasn't sure what kind of a leader he used to be to cause such hate. Neither did he know why the attitudes of the men he fought with now had changed. He only knew to continue doing what he had been doing since Tomalt started his attack and hope for the best.

* * *

Jonrell gripped the stone merlons, digging his fingers into their grooves until his knuckles turned white.

As commander, there were many things he hated, the endless paperwork, the juggling of personalities. But watching the men he once shared a meal or a joke with slaughtered before his very eyes quickened his breath in anger.

He knew he could leave the top of the keep, run across the courtyard, and through the inner gate. From there he would only need to climb a set of stairs to join those fighting on the outer walls where the battle had raged for hours. But he also knew he shouldn't.

Some commanders thrived, fighting with their men for the length of battle. Others preferred to sit back and watch the events unfold, moving men and resources around like pieces of a giant game. Jonrell often thought of himself somewhere in the middle. He had been known to lead a cavalry charge or help form a shield wall like any other common soldier when the need was dire, but he had learned long ago from Amcaro and later Ronav how to recognize what a situation called for. He was more valuable monitoring the battle's progress from a distance. He knew all these things, yet it did not stop his nails from bleeding as he dug them into the granite. He watched helplessly as arrows and stone beat against both man and castle alike.

One Above, Tomalt's men are relentless.

He knew Tomalt had the advantage in numbers, but watching the endless swarm of men crest the walls, only to be thrown back over sent a chill up his back.

What is he doing to motivate them so?

"We just got reports from Sergeant Lanard that the northwest wall was briefly overwhelmed between the second and third towers. It was the worst infiltration yet. But according to his report, Kaz reached their position and led those units in throwing back Tomalt's forces. The area is once again secure," said Lord Caliva.

Jonrell turned and saw the lord reading from a message handed to him by an out of breath runner. "What is that, the fifth such report? One Above, that man is everywhere."

"Aye, I wish I had half his energy." He looked down at another message. "This one says much the same. Sergeant Brock added that Tomalt's men are starting to believe that our mages have somehow conjured up a black demon." He paused and chuckled. "They are running from him in fear."

"And our men?" asked Jonrell.

Lord Caliva grunted. "Most are shouting his name."

Despite the chaos, Jonrell managed to smile. *He finally did it. There still may be a few dissenters, but after this day, many would gladly follow him to the abyss and back.*

A loud thud sounded. Jonrell pulled the spyglass to his eye and looked toward the main gate. "They managed to maneuver one of the towers to the wall. The blasted thing is right over the gate. We can't let them raise the portcullis."

Rather than wait for his scribe, Jonrell turned to a runner and scribbled on a piece of paper before handing it off. "Go," he said, slamming the paper into the runner's hands. He repeated the process half a dozen times more, then turned back to watch the gatehouse.

* * *

A massive hand fell hard on Kaz's shoulders. So substantial was it that he knew not to turn around and run its owner through with his sword. He glanced over his shoulder and saw Crusher cocking his head behind him. "Just got word that Jonrell wants us at the gate. He thinks it can go at any moment. There's a tower stationed against it and Tomalt's men are flooding onto the walls."

Kaz turned back to Tomalt's men coming up the ladders. He looked to Crusher. "Can you do something about these ladders first?"

The giant smiled and with a massive swing of his club knocked three ladders from the wall, pushing them into three more. They all toppled to the ground in a heap of splintered wood, dented armor, and contorted limbs.

"Good?" asked Crusher.

Kaz nodded and smiled as they sped down the wall-walk. Thunder sounded above them. Kaz led the way, weaving between men, helping quickly where he could with his darting blade. Several screams came from over his shoulder and he glanced back to see men sailing over the wall. Crusher caught Kaz's eye as he sent another soldier flying and grinned. He couldn't help but smile back.

They moved through the tight press and passed under the arches of the last tower nearest the gatehouse. Tomalt's men fought their way across the gangplank of the siege tower and forced themselves onto the castle's walls. The defenders were losing ground.

With Crusher at his heels, Kaz made his way forward, tossing even his own men aside to reach the front where he could stand against the pressing wave of the enemy.

Kaz swore in his native tongue as the sky opened up. Torrents of rain cascaded and the water hindered the footing of men on both sides as it coalesced with spilled blood.

Kaz joined the heaving mass of soldiers, each side fighting to gain even another inch of ground. Kaz and Crusher acted as a rallying point for the men around them.

Tomalt's men crumbled. They did their best to retreat into the siege tower itself, cursing and shouting something about the black demon.

Kaz led men after them, hacking unabashedly and slaying with no mercy. Bodies rolled down the twisting stairs and Kaz followed. He reached the bottom and paused, eyes locking on what must have worried Jonrell.

The gate had been blown apart and the steel portcullis bent inwards as a man in black robes faced it with arms extended. Three dozen heavily armed soldiers encircled the mage in a tight formation. Kaz guessed them well-trained. On the other side of the portcullis stood four mages, two in green robes, the other two in yellow. They buckled under the power of the black-robed man as they fought against him. Kaz felt a cold and familiar hate burn through him.

He looked over his shoulder and saw his men hesitate, unwilling to get close to the sorcerous power. Kaz and Crusher exchanged a nod. The giant filled his lungs with air and yelled out. "C'mon, you bunch of cowards."

The forces charged the shield wall but unlike before, these men did not falter. Crusher roared in anger, swearing profanities at the enemy as he too struggled to penetrate their defenses. The circle of men stood their ground, stabbing methodically with their swords.

"That blasted mage did something to them. It's like trying to push over trees," said Crusher.

The portcullis creaked under the sorcerous strain. A yellow-robed mage collapsed in exhaustion. The other three mages shook under the added pressure. A green robe went to his knees.

The black-robed one will break through any moment now.

Kaz deflected a blow from one of the heavily armored men and stepped back. The circle of men would not break formation to launch an attack of their own.

"Crusher," Kaz called out as he closed the distance between them in several quick strides. "Up!"

Crusher grinned in delight. The giant plowed a massive leg into the thigh of the soldier facing him. The man went down and Crusher crouched, bracing just as Kaz reached him. Kaz leaped to the Ghal's thigh, then to his shoulder, as Crusher suddenly straightened, boosting Kaz's jump and sending him sailing over the soldiers.

Kaz screamed, thrusting his sword point down just as the black-robed mage looked up in shock. The blade pierced the mage's throat, tearing into the mages body. An eruption of blood washed them all as the mage exploded with a concussive force of released power, flinging Kaz back into the air. He slammed into the side of the siege tower with a bone jarring crack and crumpled to the ground. The world around him went black.

* * *

"Forgive me, Kaz," a voice whispered. His eyes shot open in a panic, remembering the last time he had heard those words whispered to him. He saw Jonrell leaning over him and managed a hoarse croak. "What happened? Where am I?"

"The infirmary."

"What about Tomalt?" he asked starting to sit up.

Jonrell rested a hand on his shoulder and eased him back down. Kaz was amazed at how weak he felt. "His forces retreated after you killed the mage. We held the gatehouse."

Kaz looked down at his bandaged chest and arms. He raised a hand and felt that the left side of his head was also wrapped. "How bad?"

"The sorcery burned a portion of your upper torso and Wiqua said you cracked several bones when you fell. But don't worry, I told him not to heal you with sorcery."

Kaz sighed. "How long before I can rejoin the ranks?"

Jonrell laughed. "Not any time soon. You're hurt too badly."

"But I can still help…"

Jonrell cut him off. "You've helped enough. Without you, we wouldn't have held them off as long as we did, nor would we have been able to repel their last assault. Crusher even said as much and you know how he likes to take credit for doing everything."

So, I'm helpless.

Jonrell patted the part of his shoulder left unbandaged. "Rest up. We'll manage." He paused. "I need to get going. There's still a lot to do but I'll check in on you later."

Kaz nodded. "Go. Don't neglect your duties for me."

Jonrell stood and left.

Kaz laid there for several minutes pondering his situation. *I should be out there readying for the next attack.* He muttered a curse in his native tongue.

"Ah, Jonrell said you were up, and I see you're already back to your pleasant disposition."

Kaz tilted his head and saw Hag shuffling toward him amidst the press of beds filled with injured soldiers. "Leave me be, woman."

Hag pulled up a stool and sat down with a heavy sigh.

"Did you not hear me?" asked Kaz.

"Oh, I heard you, you cold-hearted snake," said Hag. "I just choose not to listen to someone who doesn't know what's best for them."

Kaz winced as she pulled away the bandages on his arm and began cleaning the blistered wound. "What are you rambling about?" Kaz muttered between shortened breaths.

"I'm talking about your pride. Why won't you let Wiqua work on you? He has enough power left to ready you by tomorrow."

Kaz gritted his teeth. "No sorcery."

"You're an idiot."

"You know how I…"

"I wasn't finished. Now shut up and listen." She paused. "As I was saying, you're an idiot. Jonrell needs you, and not just for your sword. He needs your will, your tenacity, and the strength you seem to impart to those around you. Would you throw away everything you've worked hard for over these past few months with the men because of your own pride?"

"Jonrell said I've helped enough and to get rest. If he needs me as you say, then why isn't he trying to convince me to see Wiqua."

"Because that's not who he is. He won't push his friends into doing something they aren't comfortable with. He cares too much about you to do that. That's why he sat at your bed the entire time you were out, and only left a few minutes ago when you woke up." Hag paused. "But I know he needs you and so do the other men."

She's right. Jonrell took me in and did his best to help me when no one else would. And now after all these months, most of the men seem to be treating me differently. All because of what I can do with a sword in my hand. When I'm truly alive.

Hag hadn't said another word. She washed the wounds on his arms, ready to apply a new bandage.

"Alright, woman. Go get your lover. But tell him that if he does me wrong, I'll kill him."

Hag laughed. "Don't worry, he only bites in bed," she said, cackling as she walked away.

CHAPTER 28

Standing in his stirrups, Tobin squinted across the parched land as the first rays of dawn bled into the leaden sky. The disciplined mount stood motionless beneath him. The Orange Desert Clan horses had been folded back into the bulk of the army once the Blue Island Clan forces landed on the mainland. The mounts would be pivotal to the Blue Island Clan's success.

Just as the scouts had reported, the Yellow Plain Clan fielded nearly forty-five thousand cavalry with another ten thousand on foot, more than doubling Tobin's army of twenty-six thousand.

His eyes drifted across the vast scope of their forces, surveying the long lines of horse warriors, ten rows deep, nearly a league long. Most carried short bows, others spears and javelins. Infantry was said to be stationed in their rear, just over the other side of the hilltop. He watched those mounted work themselves into a frenzy, riding back and forth across the distant ridge and kicking up clouds of dust as their war cries stretched out to him through the dead air. A sheen of sweat formed on his brow. The morning sun felt unusually warm.

"So many," said Walor, his voice barely a whisper.

"Aye. And that is why we cannot face them in the same manner we fought the others."

"I see that now."

Tobin nodded. The night before, when he had met with his most trusted men, Tobin had not only altered his father's plans, but he also changed how the Kifzo would be used in battle. As warleader, Kaz had always been the one to lead the Kifzo into battle from the front line while the rest of the army came in as support. Tobin knew such a strategy would not work today. Against these odds, he decided to spread the Kifzo among the main army, making them captains of smaller squads so that their ability would influence the others.

We need men to hold our lines against their charge, not just the center. If they encircle us, we are done.

Tobin had decided his role would be much different today as well. He would not lead the charge. Rather, he would survey the battle as it happened and send runners to issue his orders and changes in strategy as the battle developed. Some of the Kifzo had been uncomfortable with changing the role of a warleader. However, Tobin knew from the look in Walor's eyes that at least now someone understood his reasons. Tobin wanted the glory in battle that Kaz so often had hoarded for himself, but he had promised his father victory first, and he knew his philosophy bettered their chance at success.

Tobin assessed his troops. The strongest concentration of his forces, and the most heavily armored, waited at the center. Nearly seven thousand warriors, those most efficient with a spear and shield, stood ready to repel the Yellow Plain Clan's charge. The right wing consisted of another five thousand soldiers. Without a natural barrier to strengthen their position, Tobin held an additional three thousand light cavalry as a mobile reserve. The Orange Desert Clan warriors' strength in the saddle made them ideal for the role.

Ufer did not want to have such a large concentration of the desert warriors in one spot, so Tobin had ordered his strongest Kifzo to act as captains among them. Four thousand archers who could drop their bows and charge as swordsmen at a moment's notice supported the center. His entire heavy cavalry, some four thousand warriors, remained out of sight and he hoped in place.

"Are you sure of the positioning, Warleader? The left wing, with only three thousand?" asked Walor.

Tobin cast his gaze to the left, where he had placed his strongest fighters. "Yes. With the stream on one side, the Yellow Plain Clan will have difficulty flanking them. Besides, you will be there," said Tobin, grinned. "I know you will hold until reinforcements arrive."

Walor twisted his neck until it popped and grinned back. "I better join them then."

"We'll celebrate tonight when this is done," said Tobin.

As Walor left, Nachun, in his dark red robes, galloped up beside Tobin.

"All of the shamans are in place," said Nachun.

"I hope your plan works."

"It will. Trust me."

The clouds of golden dust began to settle as did the Yellow Plain Clan riders, though their horses continued to shuffle in disordered lines.

They are overconfident with their numbers. If we hold the initial charge, we can take them. It's the shamans I'm concerned with. But Nachun told me to let him worry about that. Tobin glanced over at the shaman whose face was expressionless. *How can he be so calm while I can't stop worrying over everything that can go wrong?*

* * *

The reverberation of cicadas hiding in the tall grass and meadowlarks chirping from trees bordering the stream filled the air. The neighing of impatient mounts and the clanking armor of fidgeting soldiers joined them.

In that uneasy calm, memories from the night before came to him. *I have so much to lose now. She actually said she loves me.* Such a revelation would obviously change their relationship. *She can no longer be considered a prisoner. No, not anymore. I will have to tell Father, when we speak of Mawkuk again.* He sighed. *What am I doing thinking about that now? I have to survive today first. How did Kaz do this, knowing Lucia was home waiting for him?* He shook his head. *Probably never even crossed his mind.*

"It begins," said Nachun, pointing.

Tobin followed Nachun's hand and saw a furious swaying in the tall grass, as if a sudden gust had come in. But the air remained still. "What is that?"

"Wolves. Hundreds of them. Perhaps more. They're meant to distract and cause disorder amongst our ranks. Their shamans are well attuned to the land."

"Archers then?"

The shaman shook his head. "I have a better idea. At least to start." Nachun raised his hands aloft, a ball of fire taking shape between them. On the ridge to Tobin's right, dozens of arms shot into the air following Nachun's lead, though each was absent of the growing flames now looming above Tobin. Time seemed to slow as the other shamans matched Nachun's pose and waited as the wolves sped closer to the Blue Island Clan's front lines.

Sweat soaked his hair and shirt under the immense heat of Nachun's fireball, but Tobin didn't flinch. His curiosity warred with his anxiety as he counted down the moments for Nachun to release the sorcery. Nachun had not been one to display his power, and Tobin was eager to see once again what his friend was capable of. The shaman trembled, his robes drenched as he maintained control over the ever growing ball of flames.

With a grunt, Nachun made a throwing motion and launched the sorcery forward. Tobin's eyes widened as they followed the streaking fire into the dry grass, less than two hundred yards away from his front lines. Within seconds, the fire had spread in all directions and engulfed most of the plain before them. Between heavy breaths and with a voice like broken glass, Nachun managed to speak. "The shamans I positioned to our right will ensure that the fire does not reach your lines, though they will allow the flames to burn most everything else."

Tobin could only manage a nod as he looked at the destruction. Sharp, high-pitched yelps joined a chorus of howls as the wolves tried to dash away from the flames. Screams and shrieks of pain sent a shiver down Tobin's spine.

How can anyone stop him when he is at his full strength? It takes dozens of shamans just to contain the power he unleashed. Tobin glanced over and saw Nachun weakened but not nearly as much as he expected. *I can still feel the power emanating from him.* He couldn't understand why any leader would ever let someone so powerful slip from their grasp. *The Red Mountain Clan, especially Charu, will rue the day they betrayed Nachun's family.*

Two giant wolves, far larger than any Tobin had ever seen, emerged from the inferno and raced toward the Blue Island Clan's formation.

"You may want to make use of your archers now," said Nachun.

Tobin signaled the archers to begin firing as others joined the two hulking shapes. "I've never seen wolves that large," marveled Tobin.

"Those are no wolves. Many of their shamans have the ability to change shape. A very dangerous practice, but once mastered, it is a very powerful tool. Before the fire, I would guess there were more than a hundred like those breaking free now. Those shrieks of terror you hear are not coming from the wolves. Those are the weaker shamans unable to protect themselves from the flames. The ones that approach are the strongest, though they will no longer be at full power. Your warriors should be able to handle them now without much difficulty."

"And the shamans who weren't part of the charge?"

"Busy keeping the flames from flowing across their lines just as ours are."

"So neither side is at their best."

Nachun nodded. "The battle is now mostly one of arms, I thought you would prefer that."

A cloud of arrows filled the sky and rained down on the charging shapeshifters, felling all but two of the creatures. Those stumbled into the front lines where waiting soldiers pounced on them with spear and sword, stabbing and slashing at the tortured bodies.

Tobin smiled. "You did well."

The conflagration of the plain dissipated within minutes and revealed hundreds of charred black lumps. Bits of gray ash lifted from the ground by a sudden breeze. The smell of burnt flesh reached Tobin and unsettled the horse beneath him. He saw the Yellow Plain Clan's mounts similarly affected and the warriors on them silenced, no longer so eager to advance.

"Will you attack now that they are shaken?" asked Nachun.

"No. We have a stronger position here," answered Tobin.

A lone rider emerged from their opponent's ranks with arms pumping twin sabers in a steady rhythm. Tobin couldn't make out his features but he knew the man was Sunul, their warleader. He had heard others speak of the man's fighting prowess.

He worked his horde back into a rage. Tobin gazed down at his own lines, where captains rechecked ranks. His men stood firm and ready, not shaken in the least by the display from across the field.

After an earsplitting chorus of war cries, Sunul led the charge of his army. Tobin sent half a dozen runners scrambling to issue his commands.

The pounding hooves from the charging cavalry kicked up dirt and ash to join the smoke in the air. The rolling cloud swallowed the horsemen.

Tobin issued the command for his archers to fire again. Arrows blotted out the sky before slamming into the enemy's ranks.

By the time the second volley reached them, the survivors had learned a lesson from their fallen comrades and raised round shields covered in hide to protect themselves. However, their shields were not large enough or thick enough to stop many of the shafts from reaching rider and horse.

As the third shower of arrows cascaded down, the first row of each of Tobin's line dropped to a knee while the row behind revealed loaded crossbows. Captains shouted the order to fire. Quarrels sped across the plain, striking the front line of riders. After each line fired, they dropped their weapons and took a knee, clearing a path for the next row.

The Yellow Plain Clan died in droves with the seemingly endless projectiles hounding them from every direction. Crossbow quarrels pierced their hide shields and leather armor, tumbling hundreds of men and horses to the ground, run over by those behind.

As the last row of infantry fired their crossbows, the Blue Island Clan lines rose to their feet and planted heavy spears into the dirt. The archers ceased fire as the Yellow Plain Clan closed. With the sudden reprieve, the enemy charge sprang to new life, the thousands remaining spurring their horses faster. Before impact, javelins and arrows were loosed into the Blue Island Clan's midst, but clanked off of the thick armor and steel shields Nachun had created. Only a few were able to pierce the tightly formed lines.

Some of the riders attempted to spin away from the front wall, but the push from behind and the sides was too great.

Tobin felt the concussive impact even from his position. Horses screamed as the infantry spears punched through their light barding, flinging riders from their saddles. The cavalry quickly recovered, slashing and stabbing with sabers. Death cries rose with the clouds of debris. Formations up and down Tobin's battle-line devolved into a maelstrom of bodies.

"They seem to be holding," said Nachun, as if he doubted.

Tobin's forces survived the initial clash but he saw weakening in the formation. The center line, which took the brunt of the charge, remained sturdy, benefiting from the concentration of his forces and heavy armor. The left flank, as he had suspected, gained an advantage from the stream and the bordering treeline.

However, the right wing started to get pushed back as many of the Yellow Plain Clan riders wheeled from the center in an attempt to flank the weaker side positions.

Tobin quickly sent out messengers to send Guwan and the light cavalry reserve against the exposed flank of those riders.

Tobin grew more anxious as the moments passed. He opened and closed his fists, itching to enter the fray. *Patience, Tobin. Not yet.*

The light cavalry swept in with arrow fire from the Orange Desert Clan's short bows while the Kifzo threw javelins and axes. The right flank quickly solidified.

A large number of the enemy at the rear of the charge had yet to engage. Tobin saw many shift their focus from the center, to Walor's forces at the river. Their surge forward coincided with the arrival of a swarm of bees. Distracted by the bees, Tobin saw his lines begin to lose ground. Tobin muttered a curse.

He shouted orders for half of his reserves to support the left flank, and sent the other half to add strength to his right where he was most concerned about his opponent out-maneuvering him.

He faced Nachun. "Can you negate the shamans?"

"Most of them, yes."

"Good. Grab any other shamans along the way to aid you. We have to hold the left," he said kicking his horse into a gallop and unsheathing his sword. He didn't bother to look to see if Nachun followed, for he trusted his friend would. He was right to command from a distance, at least for a time, but he had to act. The battle called to him. Time to prove himself worthy to be called warleader.

* * *

Tobin sped down the sloping landscape and raced past the reserves he had ordered to support Walor's forces. As he neared, he jumped from his horse and flung himself into the conflict where the line had started to buckle. He pulled a warrior from under the front hooves of a Yellow Plain Clan's mount then thrust his sword into the horse's chest which pitched its rider to the ground. Tobin finished the fallen warrior with a stab to the chest.

The Kifzo he had rescued called out for others to rally to Tobin's position. Tobin's sword moved in a blur through the foul air. Between strokes, he had managed to call out for spearmen to aid in holding back the pressing horsemen.

A shouted warning sent Tobin ducking as a spear-point impaled the warrior he fought. Walor took up position next to him, shaft in hand. Others similarly armed closed in. A long slash ran down the head scout's cheek but he managed a grin between heavy breaths. "Lead us, Warleader!" he yelled. Shouts of "Warleader" erupted.

Never have I heard anyone scream for Kaz in such a way. Thank you, Walor.

Tobin spun back into the press, into the tangled mass of bodies. The additional spears made all the difference as the Blue Island Clan warriors attacked the Yellow Plain Clan riders with greater reach, stabbing and thrusting at man and animal alike. Pressed so close together, the greatest advantage the enemy had over the Blue Island Clan had been taken away. The field turned into a frenzy of scattered blood and limbs. Lifeless forms accumulated beneath Tobin's feet.

Ducking, parrying, and countering his opponents' attacks, Tobin fought with a ferocity he could never match in the training circle. Covered in blood and smelling of death, he heard his name growled over the sound of ringing steel.

Tobin twisted around as a path opened between him and Sunul, the Yellow Plain Clan Warleader. Sunul held twin sabers.

Though shorter and thinner than Tobin, he struck an imposing figure. The hardness in the man's eyes spoke of the reputation he made for himself. Like the other warriors of the Yellow Clan, his armor consisted of leather, layered with yellowed animal bone in the most vital of areas. Sprayed with blood and ash, he could have easily been mistaken for a walking corpse.

A man Kaz had always wished to fight.

"I was hoping to face your brother," said Sunul.

"Kaz is dead."

"Pity, I wanted a challenge."

Sunul came at Tobin in a rush, spinning sabers in either hand. Tobin found himself immediately on the defensive as the two men clashed. He did his best to deflect the weaving cuts blurring before his eyes. He hoped some sort of pattern would develop but he failed to pick it out as the blades whirled in a calculated chaos.

With every slash, Tobin retreated. His single blade was not quick enough to match Sunul's speed and precision. Twice he chanced an attack and twice failed. Sunul's blades danced off the gauntlets covering Tobin's hands and forearms.

I owe Nachun yet again, or I'd be trying to continue with severed hands.

The armor he wore was superior, but Tobin knew it would not protect him forever. Mere moments into the fight, he found himself tiring, both mentally and physically as he tried to match the furious moves of his opponent. Doubt began to creep into his mind.

Tobin realized his best hope at winning lay in using his size and strength to overpower his smaller opponent. The thought struck him as he finally saw a pattern in Sunul's style. Barely noticeable, Tobin seized advantage of the next opportunity. Ducking below one blade and deflecting the other with his sword, he slammed his shoulder into Sunul's chest which sent the man sprawling. However, the first blade that Tobin had ducked under slashed back, downward across Tobin's chest. The pommel of Sunul's other saber twisted down and struck the hilt of Tobin's sword. The blade fell from his hand.

Sunul landed several paces back and rolled to his feet while Tobin dropped to a knee grabbing his chest.

"Pathetic. I have been setting you up for that since we began," said Sunul. "Most would have tried to counter it long before you did."

He is right. I'm not even the best swordsmen in my clan and yet I thought to challenge him. How can I be warleader? Tobin looked up as Sunul approached and saw his own blade was too far away for him to reach.

"I wish I could be there to deliver the news to your father that both of his sons are dead," said Sunul. "Though from what I've seen today, I'd say your brother was the greater loss."

Kaz, yet again. He seethed in anger. Rage replaced his earlier doubts and coursed through his veins, lending him strength. Twin axes whipped out to catch the blades of Sunul's sabers as they arced downward. "My brother was nothing," Tobin growled.

Tobin propelled himself up and forward, driving his head underneath Sunul's chin. Sunul staggered backward, blood dribbling from his mouth. He shook his head and spat while he moved in a ready position. Sunul started to issue a retort but Tobin was done listening and hurled himself toward the man.

Tobin's smaller battle axes spun in his hands and allowed him to press in close to his opponent. The hooked blades and metal shafts turned away each of Sunul's counterstrikes. Sunul's long sabers were at a disadvantage now as Tobin moved in closer. His opponent tried to regain a stronger position, but tripped over fallen weapons and contorted bodies. Tobin refused to let up his attack, even as one of those sabers sliced his ear. He was so focused on finishing off his opponent to prove himself worthy to be warleader and to be recognized as Kaz's better that he didn't even notice the cut.

Sunul's guard started to falter. The plainsmen's right arm dipped and Tobin's ax cut deep, causing one of the sabers to drop to the ground. Sunul's eyes widened in shock. He staggered and slashed wildly in panic with his other saber. Tobin caught the blade with one ax while coming down with the other, cleaving into the center of the plainsmen's skull.

Tobin's attention went to the battle around him and he readied himself for another opponent. However, there were none. Cries erupted from the Yellow Plain Clan that their warleader died and many on the left flank turned to flee. Others not in a position to do so simply yielded their weapons and bent a knee with head bowed.

His own clansmen watched in what appeared to be awe. For a battle that only moments before had been deafening, the left flank quieted. News of Sunul's death quickly flowed through the remainder of the battlefield and the enemy fled. The Blue Island Clan defeated the Yellow Plain Clan with Tobin as warleader.

A lone voice came from the right. Tobin faced the warrior who with sword held high, shouted Tobin's name in rhythm to the thrusting of his arm. It was the young Kifzo he had reprimanded in the village some days ago. Tobin saw the look in his eyes as he stared across the blood soaked ground and saw in them what he had always wanted.

Respect.

Loyalty.

Admiration.

Pride.

Others joined the chant until thousands of voices cried out his name in unison.

He knew then that they doubted him no longer.

CHAPTER 29

Jonrell stood atop the high keep and looked over the wasteland of Cathyrium.

The fires in the outlying city had burned out, but wisps of smoke still swam through the air. Broken siege equipment torn to splinters from heavy boulders stood in heaps. A temporary ceasefire had been agreed upon to allow Tomalt to gather his dead. Some of the Hell Patrol's old crew had not been fond of the gentleman's way of war, but Jonrell would not have it any other way.

Though they fight against me, they are my countrymen.

He rubbed away the sleep from his blurred vision. Like most, he had slept little. He spent most of his time along the walls or towers, encouraging men, checking over the state of the castle, and mentally collecting information.

"The next attack will be the last. He is running out of time and resources," said Kaz.

"Yes," said Jonrell.

Jonrell had asked his friend to join him on top of the castle's keep, hoping the warrior would provide a different perspective on events. Unfortunately, his perspective was a different sort of grim.

"What have you heard from your contacts in their camp?" asked Kaz.

He shrugged. "Either there is nothing to report or they've been discovered."

"Probably the latter," Kaz muttered.

Alone on the rooftop, Jonrell looked over Kaz. Wiqua assured him that Kaz could fight, completely healed, though the scarring on his face and arms would take time to fade.

"Why did you do it?"

Kaz turned. "Do what?"

"Allow yourself to be healed with sorcery."

Kaz worked his jaw and Jonrell saw him struggling to find the right words. "After all that you've done for me," he paused, looking down, "it is the least I could do. I'm afraid I have nothing else to offer."

Jonrell smiled and placed a hand on Kaz's hard shoulder. "It is more than enough." He paused and met the man's eyes. "Thank you." He sighed. "I see you struggling each day with the unknowns of your past. I can't imagine what that's like. Don't let the few memories rule you. You're a good man and an even better friend. One of the best friends I've had, for whatever that is worth. Don't forget that."

* * *

"Get those trebuchets loaded. One Above, Yanasi, pull your men back to the inner wall and take your marks from there. Arrows aren't going to be what brings them down," shouted Jonrell. *Hard headed girl. What's she going to do when I'm not around to look after her?*

Tomalt had grown tired of throwing men at the walls and wasting their lives. Only minutes ago, Jonrell had spotted eight robed figures strolling toward the castle through his spyglass. They approached confidently, as if they didn't have a care in the world. Behind them, Tomalt's ranks formed.

Two black mages, three green, and three yellow. And all I have are four to counter that, none of which are black. Caliva was right. I should have never let Krytien leave.

But it was too late for regrets. He had to make the best use of his assets. He pulled all resources back from the outer walls except the engineers and their siege equipment. He assigned his four mages to Raker and Drake, two in each corner drum tower.

Years of seeing mages in battle allowed him to guess their attack. The black robes, in the middle would use all their strength to bring down the castle's walls. The green robes would either add support to the black robes or aid the yellow robes in protecting them.

He knew his siege equipment would not be able to penetrate all of their defenses. However, with his own mages in each tower, he hoped they could weaken one target at a time and eliminate the yellow mages first and then maybe a green one or two. Those lesser mages would be concentrating on the protection of the black-robed mages more than their own.

They black robes will probably still breach the wall, but at least this way we'll be able to whittle down their numbers. It won't be pretty battling the black robes afterward, but at least they'll have to divert some of their power to protect themselves.

"Yanasi," he shouted up to the turret that sat atop the inner wall's gatehouse.

"Yes, Commander?"

"Where are they?"

"They just halted and are taking positions."

"Fire the trebuchets now. We need to distract them," Jonrell shouted. He looked at the runners who bounced up and down with a nervousness that bordered panic. "Get up to those towers and tell the engineers to let loose at their discretion."

The runners sped off, skirting around the soldiers falling back through the inner gatehouse. Satisfied, he walked through the inner gate and took a position out front where Glacar eyed Kaz with a menacing glare.

Crusher stood a few paces back, looming above everyone. He stood out even among the thousands still alive. "Now what, Jonrell?"

"Now we wait for the signal, and then rush his men as they come through the breach."

"What signal is that?"

"That all hell has broken loose."

* * *

"We got that sucker," hollered Raker, slapping the green robed mage on the back. After a few misses, one of the ballista missiles pierced a yellow-robed figure from across the field. *Ha. I wish I could see the look on the boy's face when he sees we drew blood first.*

A thought struck Raker. "Hey, I've always wondered why ya'll don't wear the same kind of robes, at least in battle. I mean, all those different colors sure makes it easier to prioritize targets."

The green robe mage wheeled. "Do you mind? This isn't as easy as you think it is, and I would rather not die if I can help it."

Raker spat over the side, "Don't get your skirt all bunched up. Just do what you gotta do and I'll keep out of your way." He turned and gave his men a look, pointing a thumb over his shoulder. "Mages."

* * *

Blood thumped in Drake's temple and he felt as though a stone block rested on his chest. He was both scared and excited as his men rushed to reload the mangonel.

"Raker got one," said one of his men.

A holler rose from his men as the first mage died.

One Above, he beat me to it. He's probably laughing over there and looking forward to rubbing it in my face. "What color were the robes?" he shouted.

The corporal answered back. "Yellow."

Drake grinned. *I know what will get Raker riled up.* "Turn all your attention to the closest green mage," he told the mages standing near the merlons.

"But Jonrell said take out the yellow-robed ones first," protested one.

"And I say we go for the green, and up here I'm in charge."

"But there is a chance we won't be able to pierce the shield completely."

"I want you to feign an attack at the top of his defenses first, but hold back some when you do so. I want him to think we're counting on the mangonel to penetrate his shields. When I say 'Now', shift your focus to the front of the mage's body and put everything you have into weakening his defenses there. The real attack is coming from the ballista. Can you do that?"

"I think so."

"Don't think, just do," said Drake, doing his best to sound tough. *Not bad. Maybe I'm getting the hang of this after all.*

Drake shouted over to one of the smaller towers further down the wall, where a ballista rested. "You fire that weapon when I give the command, not a second sooner or later."

"We're ready now," came a shout back.

"Alright, let's do this," Drake said, looking back to his men.

He gave the signal and the mangonel's arm slammed into the wooden crossbeam and rock flew into the air. As the rock reached its peak he shouted to the mages. "Now." At the same instant he dropped his arm, signaling the ballista to fire.

The green mage expected the attack to come from above and therefore could not recover to guard his front while maintaining the defenses over the black-robed mages. A missile hit the mage in the sternum, blasting him back and pinning him to the ground.

Drake jumped up. "We got him." He could have sworn he heard a curse from across the castle.

* * *

"…that cocky little…"

"Sir," said Senald cutting Raker off.

"Boy what's wrong with you? Don't ever interrupt a man while he's in the middle of a tirade."

"Uh, sorry Sir. It's just that it's happening," said Senald, pointing out across the field.

Raker felt the sudden thinning of air.

This is going to be bad. Really bad.

"Quick lads, get another round ready and aim for another yellow one. We ain't taking our chances with the others. We need another kill before they come at us full force."

* * *

The concussive force caused the outer gatehouse to burst apart. As Jonrell struggled to gain his breath, bits of debris fell from the sky and the granite wall glowed red.

A hand went to his shoulder and he faced Crusher. The giant's mouth moved, but the only sound Jonrell could hear was a high-pitched buzz. "What?" he yelled, shaking his head in attempt to clear out his ears.

"I said, that had better be the signal," said Crusher.

Through the gaping hole in the castle wall, Jonrell saw Tomalt's men rushing past the distant mages, racing toward the castle's breach. "Yanasi, open fire," he yelled and a volley of arrows flew into the closing masses.

He unsheathed his sword and held it aloft. This was the final stand. There was little left in the way of strategy now. There was only the will of one man against another, and for that, he needed to be here. He let out a cry and ran toward the gap. Pounding steps and echoing cries followed him.

Today the battle is decided.

* * *

Elyse pushed her mount through the low lying branches, Jeldor coming in beside her. His men had run the last several hundred yards after hearing the thunderous blast that shook her insides. They pulled up on their reins. "One Above, we're too late."

"No, Your Majesty. The wall has been breached, but the fighting continues. We still have time." He twisted about in the saddle and yelled out over his lines. "Captains, form ranks. I know you're tired, lads, but we're here now and ready for the payoff." He paused. "This is our chance to inflict a little payback on all those who've looked down upon us and our lands. Let's make all the effort we went through count."

A shout erupted and within moments, men began their march toward the castle at a double-time pace. The Duke turned in his saddle. "You'll be staying here, Your Majesty. I'll leave two squads for your protection."

"One is more than enough," said Kroke pulling in beside Elyse. "You need all the men you can spare. Besides, I'll be here with her."

Elyse turned in her saddle. "But don't you want to be in the mix to help your brethren?"

"Aye, but I've got my orders to see to your safety above all else and I've never been one to break command."

"Your Majesty?" asked Jeldor.

Elyse nodded. "Go. I'll be fine."

Jeldor managed a slight bow in his saddle and rode off as he shouted and pushed his men forward. Rygar rode with him, too worried about Yanasi to wait any longer.

Elyse looked over at Kroke who gripped the hilt of a dagger and twisted it in his hand as he watched the fighting from afar. "Thank you. I know this isn't easy."

Kroke's eyes seemed hollow, distant. "No, it's not."

She felt guilty. "I'm sorry. Perhaps, you should go after all. I'm sure a squad of Jeldor's men is enough to guard me."

"No," said Kroke. "I do not renege on my word, and if it's all the same, I don't trust anyone else to look after you after what we've been through."

Elyse looked up and smiled.

The two turned back to the scene in the distance, swarming bodies amidst a cacophony of screams.

* * *

His men had formed a barricade of sorts near the breach. They fought in packed surroundings, some climbing over fallen stone, as they dodged blows from the enemy. Their effort made Jonrell proud.

We will not be taken easily, Tomalt.

Jonrell did not want to lose ground, but the sheer number of Tomalt's forces caused them to slowly waver. As the two armies intertwined, arrow fire ceased, lest archers hit men from their own ranks. The mangonels and ballista had also been abandoned and Jonrell could see Raker now leading men with a wide grin while wreaking havoc with his mace.

However, nothing seemed to deter the sorcery that ravaged the presses. The entanglement of bodies, the coalescence of suffering and death, only grew worse with each attack from Tomalt's mages. The four mages Jonrell had at his disposal refused to give up, but they could not stop the tendrils of sorcery that crawled through the air toward his men.

Jonrell's forces fought with passion and ferocity but despite their effort they began a cautious retreat to the inner walls, lest the surging enemy surround them. Tomalt's men must have sensed the change. They pressed with even greater resolve, nearly climbing over each other to make it through the break in the wall.

One Above, help us.

A long, deep horn blast, echoed over the land and muted the chorus of battle. Its ominous call reached the ears of every man and caused heads to turn despite the immediate dangers around them.

Only a man from the mountains would blow such a thing. Elyse did it! She convinced Jeldor. Jonrell quickly relayed the message to his men and with renewed strength stood as firm as mighty oaks.

Jonrell dodged a blade meant for his head. Outside the castle walls he heard a separate clash of arms, distinct from the battle around him. The horn blasted again, further girding his men. Jonrell's opponent flinched at the noise and he made the man pay, slashing across his eyes, blade biting deep into the man's skull. He fell in a crumpled mass.

Jonrell scrambled up a pile of stone rubble to look out over the press of men.

Tomalt sat atop his white destrier, signaling a retreat before being pinned in the middle of two forces.

Jonrell hollered out to his men. "Let's send them to the One Below! We've got them on the run!"

Jonrell could not immediately climb down as soldiers rushed past him, anxious to make Tomalt pay with the battle turning in their favor. The last of the men trickled past him as he joined his men.

"You ain't going anywhere," came a voice from Jonrell's right.

He turned and saw Glacar lifting his giant ax over his head. Jonrell stumbled back and tripped over a corpse. He had never been so thankful for his clumsiness as the ax came down, narrowly missing his arm. "Glacar, what in the name of the One Above are you doing?"

"Something I should have done on Mytarcis when you followed Melchizan's every fool order for free. Something I should have done when you denied me those slave women. Something I should have done when you allowed that black devil to join us." He paused and revealed a yellow-toothed grin amid his mess of a beard. "I'm relieving you of your command."

Jonrell stared, dumbstruck. "Because of that, you're going to kill me? We've fought together for over a decade."

"Aye, too long to be taking orders from such a soft man. I'd much rather Ronav had never died. That man had more grit to him than you ever did."

Jonrell rolled away as the ax blade came down again. In his panic, he left his sword behind. Hurrying to his feet, he faced the hairy beast of a man, weaponless. "So, that's it? I'm soft and you no longer like the company I keep?"

"More or less. Though, I will say that one of those fine men you had me look into when in Lyrosene made me an offer I just couldn't pass up. The way I figured it is if I'm going to kill you anyway, why not make some money in the process. Besides, I ain't about to die for your cause. I've followed you long enough on your backward jobs."

Jonrell and Glacar circled each other. *So that's it. The weakness of every mercenary is money, though I thought my men were different. Who made the offer? I gave out more than a dozen names to him and Kroke. One Above, I sent Kroke with Elyse!* Jonrell shook his head. *No, Kroke may be a killer but he is a far better man than Glacar has ever been.*

"Enough," said Glacar coming to a stop. "After I kill you, I've got an army to catch up to. I'm sure Tomalt will need some good men, especially when he learns I eliminated you," he added with a grin.

Jonrell dodged to his left, reaching for a sword but was cut off by the burly man. The great ax swooped down toward his face again. He had overcommitted. He knew he would never make it out of the way in time.

A blur crashed into Glacar, causing the ax to fall off its mark. The two figures tumbled to the ground, grunting and screaming curses, in a tangled mass of limbs and steel.

Where did Kaz even come from?

Jonrell grabbed a nearby sword and took a step toward Glacar. A large hand swooped in and picked him up off his feet by his shoulder, dangling him in the air like a doll, before setting him back down. Crusher looked down, shaking his head. "This is their fight."

"Are you crazy? I'm the one Glacar tried to kill."

"Today, yes. But Glacar has been looking for ways to either kill or maim Kaz for months. Kaz probably hasn't said much to you because he didn't want to cause any more problems. But now he has cause to fight back. And there is no stopping someone like Kaz once his blood boils."

The commander looked around and saw that the four men were somehow alone in the shadows of what remained of the castle's outer walls. Outside of the walls, the fighting carried on and he heard Jeldor's horn booming, signaling an inevitable victory. He was glad to have such reassurance because he could not take his eyes off the two men circling each other, one as heavily built as a bear, the other as agile as a panther. They faced each other, ax against sword.

Seeing the hate in their eyes, Jonrell replied. "I understand."

Kaz wiped away spit from his cheek.

"That's right you black devil, you're nothing to me," said Glacar, grinning. "Killing you will be one of my favorite tales to tell."

"Then you've lived a pathetic existence," said Kaz.

Glacar roared. Their pacing ceased amidst an eerie silence in a space that had only moments before been riddled with sounds of death and disorder.

They collided in a maelstrom of slashes, and thrusts, weaving in a blur that left Jonrell dizzy as he tried to follow their movements. He had seen Glacar in battle many times over the years, but never had he witnessed anyone match the man's ferocity and combat instinct. But with every swing of Glacar's ax or stab of the spear-headed pommel, Kaz's sword deflected the blow and countered with startling speed. The rumors of Kaz's deeds in battle no longer seemed so farfetched to Jonrell.

Within moments after their initial clash, Kaz had taken the upper hand and forced Glacar to step around and over the mangled bodies and melted granite that littered the ground.

A faint voice from above startled Jonrell, whispering, "I've never seen any man fight like him. He should have been born a Ghal."

Jonrell shook his head. Never had he heard a Ghal make such a claim, as the race lived in a constant state of war. But unlike Crusher, he found little joy in the duel. Glacar had tried to kill him. They had always had a bit of a shaky relationship, but he was still a member of the Hell Patrol. To see two of its members fight in such a way made him nauseous.

The man who put him up to this will die. I will see to that myself.

He seethed in anger, not only at the betrayal, but because he felt helpless watching Kaz fight a man Jonrell knew he could never defeat.

I would already be dead if not for him. I've made many bad decisions in my life, but Kaz was not one of them.

Kaz pushed Glacar to the ground. He hit hard with an expulsion of breath, but managed to throw a fistful of dirt as Kaz closed. Kaz stumbled back, wiping his eyes, curses tumbling from him in his native language. Glacar pushed himself up, chest heaving.

In a panic, Jonrell attempted to intercede but Crusher reached out and grabbed him once again. "Where are you going? I told you this fight is between them," said the giant.

"Glacar is going to kill him."

"This is the way Kaz would want it to be. No interference."

Jonrell saw the finality in the giant's eyes. Crusher didn't remove his hand from Jonrell's shoulder.

Jonrell turned back to the fight as Glacar flashed a savage smile, hefting his mighty ax with both hands. Kaz shook his head rapidly. Even blind, he tried to ready himself.

Jonrell cried out. He ripped his shoulder painfully free of Crusher's grip as the wide blade descended. But it never found its mark. Kaz's arm shot forward, his sword penetrating through Glacar's mail until it protruded from the mercenary's back. Glacar's mouth hung agape and blood dribbled from it. Kaz jerked his blade free. Glacar clutched at the mortal wound, trying to stem the flow of blood. He locked eyes with Kaz. "You're still a black devil." He crashed into a heap of stone and his body relaxed.

Kaz stood over the body with his massive shoulders rising with each intake of breath. Kaz rubbed at his eyes with the palms of his hands.

How did he do that?

The horn sounded again, long and low, three successive blasts announcing victory.

We won. Jonrell looked at the bodies of his men and those of Tomalt's strewn about, enemies who months before had been countrymen. His gaze kept returning to Glacar.

But at what cost?

CHAPTER 30

Light headed, Elyse sat on the splintered remains of an old siege tower. She had ridden through the charred ruins of Cathyrium with Kroke shortly after the battle. But in her haste to see her brother, she avoided the carnage around her. Now as she surveyed the battlefield and looked over the thousands of corpses, the blood and gore assaulted her senses. She found her legs weak and her mind in a whirl.

It reminds me of that day in the courtyard when Nareash killed without prejudice. The day everything changed. Only this is worse.

"Are you alright?" asked Jonrell sitting down next to her. "You don't have to do this."

"I'm fine. I need to do this. Some of these men gave their lives to preserve my rule. The others to end it. The least I can do is walk among them where they've fallen and pay my respects by saying a prayer to the One Above for their souls."

Jonrell nodded. "You've changed a lot in the weeks since you've been gone. You're stronger."

Elyse shrugged. "Circumstances forced my hand."

"The assassination attempt?"

She nodded. "Yes. The whole process was a turning point of sorts I guess."

"You kept your head in the end. And because of that we won here today."

Elyse cast her gaze upon the destruction before her, watching soldiers strip the dead before throwing the naked bodies into massive piles where they would later be burned. "Victory is an awful thing."

Silence stretched as neither said a word. They sat there for some time together and Elyse realized she clutched her brother's hand like she so often did as a child. She smiled at him. "It's so good to have you home. I missed you."

He squeezed her hand tight. "I missed you too." He let out a sigh, barely audible.

"You don't sound completely convinced."

"No, it's not that. I was thinking about the attempt on your life and then Glacar's attempt on mine. Both would have succeeded had Kroke not been watching over you and Kaz over me."

She nodded. "They are both good men. You are lucky to have found them."

"Aye. But the death of your guards and that of Glacar puts me no closer to discovering who was behind the deception. I'm almost inclined to believe that the same person had a hand in both attempts."

"Was Kroke unable to help? I saw you questioning him."

"He doesn't know his letters and Glacar had carried the names I had them look into while in Lyrosene. Kroke was only following Glacar's lead."

"So that person is still out there," said Elyse, a bit of fear in her voice.

"Yes. And given that they were able to sway your guards and a member of my crew, even a disgruntled one, tells me that the person has a great deal of power." He turned to his sister. "You need to be extra cautious going forward."

"As do you," she added.

He smiled. "Of course."

"So what's next?"

"I've sent messengers for Jeldor to return here so we can regroup. I know he wanted to keep pushing Tomalt, but with his supplies so far behind his main force, he's going to find himself in a less favorable position than Tomalt in two or three days. Besides, our forces need as much time to mend as Tomalt's does. I expect Jeldor to arrive in a few hours."

"But won't Tomalt just retreat back to Namaris and wait for us there?"

"He'll try, but when he gets there he'll be quite upset with what awaits him."

Elyse noticed the slightest of grins. She cocked her head to one side. "What are you hiding?"

"Oh nothing. I gambled a bit while you were gone and only moments ago discovered it paid off." He pulled out a smooth, polished, light green stone from his boot. He handed it to her.

"What is it?"

"A little something I had Krytien make for me before I sent him away. I sent him to Floroson shortly after you left for Ithanthul and commissioned Lady Jaendora to release several thousand troops under his command."

"But he's not a soldier."

"Maybe not in the traditional sense but he understands strategy better than most. Anyway, I knew Tomalt would leave only a small garrison behind to defend Namaris when he decided to finally march against Cathyrium. So I tasked Krytien with retaking the city. Tomalt will think twice about attempting another siege on Namaris with Lady Jaendora's troops garrisoned there and after his losses here." He gestured to the stone. "That green color is telling me that Krytien succeeded."

"But if I hadn't been able to convince Jeldor of an alliance, or if we hadn't arrived on time, you may have lost and Namaris would hardly matter then."

Jonrell shrugged. "Perhaps, but you did convince Jeldor so that's a moot point."

Elyse nodded. *He is so sure of himself, even with a gamble. A good commander has to trust their gut and go with it, never looking back.* "What else is there to do?"

"Plenty," said Jonrell, pushing himself to his feet. "But first, I need to help my men. There are still a lot of pyres to build. Then a solid meal and a good night's rest. Everything else can wait until tomorrow."

* * *

The door closed with a click and Jonrell turned to face his room. He found himself staring down the sight of a cocked crossbow aimed at his unprotected chest. He had just given his armor to Cisod for repairs.

And what did I tell Elyse earlier today about being careful?

At the other end of the loaded weapon was a boy shaking, tears forming in his red eyes.

"Mal, what're you doing?"

"What does it look like I'm doing?" the boy answered in a quavering voice.

"It looks like you are about to make a big mistake," said Jonrell while taking a step forward.

Mal stiffened. "Stop right there. Don't you dare move or I'll kill you."

Jonrell froze. "Alright son, I'm not going anywhere."

"I'm not your son so quit calling me that."

"Alright, I'm sorry. I…"

"You're not sorry," said Mal cutting in. "You're not sorry for anything. You ruined my life. I was happy in the Hideaway. I was somebody. I was in charge of my own men and one day Denneth may have placed me in charge of his army. But here? Here I'm nothing. You've found something useful for everyone to do. Even Drake who's two years younger than me is commanding men in battle. You had *me* shoveling coal in a forge."

"Look, you're right. I know I've been a real heel to you, but you have to understand, I've had an army to command and a battle to win."

"Don't give me that. You've made time for others. Raker, Yanasi, Kaz, even that idiot Crusher. But you haven't once talked to me like you said you would when we were back on Slum Isle. And there were more than enough opportunities to do so on the ship, on the ride into Cathyrium and even at the dinner table. But you never did anything for me."

Jonrell gave a sigh. He knew Mal was right, he just assumed the boy understood the stress he was under. *I haven't been fair to him though. He does deserve better. One Above, it seems I always miss something regardless of how much else I get right.*

"Well, aren't you going to say something?"

Jonrell saw the hurt in Mal's eyes and let out a heavy sigh. "I can only promise you that I won't let it happen again and swear to you that it was never my intention to cast you aside."

The boy's hurt faded and his eyes narrowed into an intense hatred. "I'm tired of your promises. And I won't let you break them to me anymore."

Jonrell started to speak but found himself suddenly out of breath and staggering backward. He slammed into the door behind him and looked down. A quarrel stuck out from his chest, only the fletching visible. He gasped for air as blood seeped out of the wound and turned his shirt a crimson red.

* * *

Elyse wept. Kneeling in prayer, tears poured from her eyes and fell to the cobble floor beneath her, pooling into a puddle. She had been crying for hours and was surprised she still had tears left to fall.

Jonrell was dead.

His body had been found in his room, killed by one of his own. The reasons would never be known as the boy took his own life after firing the crossbow that ended her brother's.

Elyse knew little about Mal but remembered the longing in his face at a dinner months ago, and how he had looked up to her brother.

What could have caused him to change? Why would he take Jonrell from me?

She hated Mal, though she knew the One Above would frown upon her for it. Her head tilted upward toward the small altar where she had been praying. It was a contrast from the majestic cathedral of Lyrosene, or some of the more fantastical structures built in honor to the One Above spread throughout Cadonia. After the burning of the city by Tomalt, the small, unadorned chapel nestled in a secluded cove of the castle was the only place left for her to worship the One Above.

Elyse cast her eyes down in shame, not for her hate of Mal, but for how her brother's death had shaken her faith at the worst of times. She tried to remember her discussions with High Priest Burgeone but they helped little. The same questions kept repeating themselves in her head over and over. *One Above, why did you allow this to happen? How could you take him from me now?*

She shook her head. *This is my fault. If my rule had been stronger, war and all its destruction would have been avoided.* She paused, fearing she knew the answer to her previous questions. *You took him from me so I would lose the throne, didn't you?*

Why else? Someone else must be a better leader for your people. Without Jonrell, our forces will surely fall. She didn't want to believe such things, but she also recognized the hopelessness in her situation. Jonrell's death devastated her army. Jeldor had refrained from saying anything just yet, but Elyse caught the brief glimpse in his face, the horror that he had made a mistake aligning with her.

How long will he wait before aligning with someone else?

She heaved into another fit of sobbing. A firm but gentle hand touched her shoulder and she frantically wiped away the tears and sniffled. "I'm sorry for my behavior, it is not befitting of a queen," she said, apologizing under the assumption that Lord Caliva had enough of her hiding.

"Your brother died. Your grief is nothing to be ashamed of."

Elyse whipped her head about and saw Kaz standing over her, face drawn in hard lines. She didn't know why his presence made her more self-conscious, but she stood up anyway and straightened her skirt. She winced at the stiffness in her legs from hours of kneeling. "I had not expected to see you here."

"Things are getting unruly in your absence."

"They are angry?"

"Frightened. There are too many questions. They need someone to stand behind, someone to lead them. You must come out and speak to your people."

"I can't. I am not the kind of person that inspires."

"Jonrell thought you were."

"And now he is dead..." she said, her words trailing off.

"That does not change his opinion of you. Your soldiers and lords both need to see that their queen is resolved in finishing what she has started."

"I'm not so sure that I am," Elyse said, looking away. "Perhaps the best thing to do is relinquish my crown and hand it over to someone more fitting."

Kaz spat and Elyse jumped, aghast. "This is a place of worship and honor. You must not treat it with such disrespect."

Kaz shook his head. "This place is neither to me. In a few short hours you entered a strong woman and have now turned into a feeble girl. There is no honor here right now."

"My brother died!" she yelled at him. "What do you expect me to be?"

"I expect you to be the person Jonrell thought you were. Would you allow his efforts to go to waste?" He paused, staring into her eyes. "Honor him in death as he honored you while he was alive."

"And what will you do to honor him now that he is gone?" she asked.

He looked down, his voice low. "I said I would aid him in securing your kingdom, and in return he would help me uncover my past and my home. He was a great man and without him I might be dead or lost. His death does not change the promise I made to him." He took a knee and withdrew his sword, holding it out before Elyse. He bowed his head.

"What are you doing?" she asked in shock.

"I swear to you my sword. I will do all that I can to see your brother's wishes come to pass. You are of his blood and I see in your eyes just as I saw in his, something good. Something better than what I see in others."

Elyse fought back tears once again at the gesture. To have someone from another land be so sincere moved her in an odd way. But then a sudden realization came. "Stand up, Kaz, for you are only one man."

He stood up at her command. "Others will do the same."

"Out of love and respect for Jonrell? Out of guilt? They will not fight for me."

"Perhaps not at first," said Kaz, his blunt honesty wounding her fragile heart. "But in time, that will change."

"And who will lead my army?" she asked. "I am barely a queen. I know nothing of warfare."

"General Grayer or perhaps this Jeldor...."

"No," said Elyse, cutting him off. "Grayer is a smart and good man, but he does not have the skills to command and rally men as my brother did. Jeldor is a better man than many credit him for, but he is still looking out for his own interests, at least for now. Neither will do."

Kaz shrugged. "Then you have an army without a commander it would seem."

"No, I do not. I have a great warrior who has just sworn his sword to me and promised he would honor my brother's name."

Kaz's eyes widened. "I cannot. I am too different. The men..."

"Jonrell told me that many of the men who fought next to you have changed their prejudices. Others are likely to do the same over time."

"But they are soldiers, not nobles. Jeldor might..."

"Jeldor will do as I say," said Elyse, her voice hardening as a queen's might. Her voice softened again as she realized she was taking out her anger on the one person who had sought to help her. "The question is, will you? Will you lead my army?"

There was a long pause as Kaz weighed her words, stroking his goatee. "Yes."

She looked into his eyes and saw his passion and honesty and believed him. "And I will continue the promise my brother made to you. I will try to help you find a way back to your people."

He nodded.

She turned back to the altar and caught the eyes of the One Above's likeness. They seemed softer than before after this stranger to her land had calmed her. *You took Jonrell but gave me someone in his place.* Her hand went up to her neck where a necklace once hung, the green stone her brother had given her. *And you gave me someone as well, Jonrell. As you promised, when I need you most, you continue to watch over me.*

"Your Majesty?" said Kaz.

Elyse faced Kaz and smiled. "Please, in private call me Elyse." She stepped forward and found herself wrapping her arms around him, sobbing once again under a mix of emotions. The sadness of Jonrell's death swirled in her mind but now she was overwhelmed with joy knowing that someone would stand beside her in the times ahead.

Kaz's body stiffened at her touch. She briefly questioned her gesture. But after a moment, his thick arms enveloped her. Elyse knew it was unfitting for a queen to be caught in such an embrace with anyone, let alone someone such as Kaz. Yet she didn't care.

CHAPTER 31

The aftermath of any battle brought as much work as the fighting. Tobin first saw to the well-being of the wounded and then afterward handled the containment of the prisoners. Others already began the process of stripping bodies of their weapons, armor, and valuables. Tomorrow they would complete the process and then bury or burn the bodies, depending on what time allowed for.

Tobin wanted to oversee the entire process personally, but Walor convinced him to see a healer for the gash across his chest first after giving orders. Stripped of his armor, the healer hurried to tend to the wound, shocked that Tobin had not lost more blood. Once bandaged, he returned to the work at hand.

Late that night, he finally allowed himself to return to camp, the last to arrive. A decision he made, unlike the countless times when Kaz ensured Tobin could not enjoy spoils of victory.

Throughout the encampment, bison roasted over bonfires while warriors circled around, celebrating the day's victory. Exhausted, they found renewed energy by filling their bellies with food and drink and enjoying the entertainment Bazraki's advisors had brought in anticipation of victory. Dancers and singers, both male and female, acted out ancient scenes from their history.

Tobin made his way through camp. Bone tired, he forced himself to stand up straight and avoid shuffling his feet. Though all he wanted to do was sleep in Odala's arms, he knew it would be some time before he would have a chance to rest. As warleader, his presence during the celebration would be expected. And he still had to speak with his father.

I'm surprised he didn't send someone to take me away from the battlefield. He did call for Nachun though. Perhaps whatever he told father was enough to satiate his curiosity of today's events.

The shaman made his way toward Tobin just then. Tobin called out. "I was just thinking about you. I'm on my way to see father."

Nachun ducked his head and shook it, coming up close to whisper in Tobin's ear. "Your father can wait. You need to see Odala."

"What do you mean? I'm sure someone else can check in on her," said Tobin, trying not to stutter.

"Don't play coy with me. Your relationship with her is not a secret. Most of the camp has known for some time."

Tobin tensed.

"Relax," said Nachun. "You are warleader. Not one of your men has an issue with your decision. And as your friend, I am happy that you've found someone."

"I see."

Nachun smiled. "Good. But you must go to her now. One of her guards came to me while searching for you. Something must have happened for she was crying hysterically."

Tobin was ready to race toward her tent but Nachun gripped his arm, much tighter than he thought the thin shaman was capable of. "Remember who you are Tobin, and more importantly where you are," said Nachun, casting his eyes about.

Tobin looked around and nodded. Nachun eased his hand away.

It would not be fitting for a warleader to run after a crying woman under any circumstances. Compose yourself, Tobin.

* * *

Not bothering to announce himself, Tobin pushed his way through the tent flap. *If everyone knows of our relationship, then what sense does it make for me to continue the charade?*

Odala lay curled up in her bed hugging a pillow. She looked up sobbing with blood-shot eyes. "What are you doing here?" she asked, ice in her voice.

Tobin saw a look of disdain in her eyes that he hadn't seen in some time. He brushed the look off, and strode to her side, sitting on the edge of her bed. "One of the guards told Nachun you were upset. I came right away," he said, draping his arms around her.

"Don't touch me," she said, sitting upright and pushing him away.

Tobin leaned back in surprise, eyes widening. "What's wrong, my love?"

"Liar. You don't love me. It was just something you said to get what you wanted, to use me."

"Will you tell me what is going on?"

"Bazraki has sent someone to kill my father."

"Impossible. Where did you hear that?"

"Soyjid told me."

"And how would your skinny little brother know such a thing?" asked Tobin through narrowed eyes.

"I don't know, but I believe him. He is never wrong about these things. He said Bazraki sent messengers to my father this morning before the battle even started, one of whom was an assassin. When my father's camp went to bed, he was going to sneak in and kill him for his failure in drawing away more of the Yellow Plain Clan's army."

"That's ridiculous. There is no way Soyjid would know such a thing."

"Go ask Bazraki and see for yourself."

"He and I talked briefly about your father this morning and he gave me his word he would not do anything."

"Then he is a liar. Just as you were when you promised me that you would save my father's life."

"Odala, listen to me."

"No. Get out. I never want to see you again. Who do you think I am? Some common whore you can make empty promises to?"

Tobin started to speak again but saw that it was pointless. Odala rolled away from him and threw the covers over her head, sobbing once again.

* * *

Scowling, Tobin pushed his way past the guards as he exited Odala's tent, nearly knocking one of the men over. He thought about talking to Soyjid about how he knew of Mawkuk's fate, but decided it could wait. He needed to hear the truth from his father first. He set off toward Bazraki's tent. Tobin's mind was a maze of confusion as he tried to piece together the conflicting information. His father had told him that morning that they would discuss Mawkuk's fate after the battle, and he would not act until then.

And what reason does Soyjid have to lie? But for that matter, what reason did Father have to lie to me?

"Warleader," said Ufer, pulling in beside Tobin.

"Not now."

"But it is something you should know…."

"Can it wait? I am on my way to see Bazraki," said Tobin.

"It concerns Odala."

Tobin stopped.

"She is upset, isn't she?"

Tobin said nothing.

"She believes your father sent someone to kill Mawkuk?"

Still, Tobin remained silent.

"Her father lives Tobin, at least for now."

Tobin worked his jaw, unsure how to respond. "How do you know all of this? Did my father send someone to kill Mawkuk?"

"Yes. A group of messengers was leaving this morning before the battle. They intended to sneak through the Yellow Clan's ambushes and deliver a message to the Gray Clan. Among them was a young Kifzo that I trained myself. He was in disguise, which is why I grew suspicious. Bazraki was sending him to assassinate Mawkuk."

Odala was telling the truth. How did Soyjid find this out? And why would Father lie to me? "Then it is only a matter of time until Mawkuk dies."

Ufer shook his head. "No, Warleader. I removed him from the group and replaced him with someone else I instructed to protect Mawkuk."

Tobin was taken aback. "You defied my father? Why?"

"Few have ever followed Bazraki. Surely you must know that," said Ufer, pausing for a moment. "We learned long ago to let him believe what he must, but we know he is not the reason for the Blue Clan's success. Your uncle was responsible for our training and so we followed him, then we followed Kaz, who led us. After today Tobin, there is not one among us who would follow anyone but you. We won today based upon your battle plans. You were the one to defeat Sunul in combat, not your father." He paused again. "I know you have a relationship with Odala and therefore I assumed that you would frown upon her father being killed without your knowledge."

"If Bazraki were to find out about this, he would kill you."

Ufer shrugged. "The decision is yours. The Blue Clan is yours. We will do as you tell us." Ufer turned and left Tobin standing in disbelief.

* * *

"I see that you decide to grace me with your presence only at the end of the day, when everyone else has been tended to first." Bazraki began to speak before Tobin even had a chance to close the tent flap. The sound of his voice came as a surprise. Seeing his father at the back of the tent, standing ominously between the red coals of two braziers, caused him to forget his own fury for a moment.

"There is much to do after a battle Father…"

"El Olam," said his father in a hard tone.

Tobin clenched his jaw. Tobin chose not to acknowledge the comment and continued on. "I was tending to the wounded and prisoners, sending out scouts…"

"You were allowing the enemy to escape," Bazraki shouted. "You should have pursued them."

Tobin shook his head. "They were mounted. We would have had to give up superior position to do so and they would have run us down. We will finish them on better terms. They are weakened. We took over ten thousand captive and I estimate they lost almost twenty thousand more by our hands."

"And how many did we lose?"

"Seven thousand."

"That is too many of our own and not enough of theirs."

"I did what you commanded of me. I brought you victory."

"A hollow victory. You should have crushed them. And you would have, if you had not defied me once again. Yes, I was told that my plans were changed. The heavy cavalry were completely removed from battle."

"Not removed, we had them approach from the opposite side of the stream to our left to take out their infantry before they joined the fray. They ensured the Yellow Clan could not rally their rearguard and mount a flanking attack."

"You should have used them as a wedge, striking against their center, breaking them in half. Kaz would have listened to me. He wouldn't have allowed them to escape. Now I will have to clean up your mess."

Kaz would have been wrong. He was about ready to tell Bazraki as much when his father started to speak again.

"But that is not what I spoke of earlier when I meant I was the last to be attended to. My guards told me you first met with Nachun and then Odala. No doubt the shaman told you how distraught your little swamp whore was knowing her father's death was imminent."

Tobin barred his teeth. "She is not a whore. And regarding Mawkuk, you said you would not act until I spoke with you tonight."

"And since when does a ruler answer to his warleader. You answer to me," he yelled again before bringing his voice back down. "After you left my tent, I knew right away that Mawkuk must die, as a lesson to you. I never had to teach such lessons to Kaz. He would have never presumed as much as you do."

"I am not Kaz, Father."

"El Olam! Even now you defy me. This little whore of yours is clouding your mind."

"You will refer to her by name," said Tobin, tightening his fists.

Bazraki grunted. "So, you take her side over mine. Already, she handles you almost as deftly as Nachun does."

"What?"

"He is the root cause of all of this. In Nubinya, I asked you to watch him, and to keep me informed of his doings. Yet, all I have gotten from you is pieces of useless information and nothing of value. And then I hear stories such as the one today, in which he set an entire battlefield aflame and it took dozens of our own shamans just to contain it."

"He keeps the extent of his powers secret. As do most shamans."

"No. Nachun is an enigma. He shows just enough for others to be wary, but never enough to gauge what he is capable of."

"What are you saying?"

"I'm saying he has outlived his usefulness. He has given us enough and I dare not keep him around any longer. He is too dangerous and too arrogant, a deadly combination. And perhaps, after he is gone, you will realize how much he influences you." He paused. "Of course, you will be the one who needs to dispose of him. He would never expect it from you."

Tobin's head spun. He had strode into camp with the intentions of giving his father an account of the day's battle and garner his praise. But he had just learned how vile a man his father truly was.

He has lied to me, abused me, and belittled me at every turn, all the while praising Kaz for his monstrosities. And now he wants me to kill the person who has done everything in his power to help me. I will not allow it.

"No."

His father laughed, taking Tobin off guard once again. "No? I expected as much from you," said Bazraki, his smile turning into a look of disdain. "Still I thought to give you one last chance to prove yourself to me."

"Prove myself? I have spent my entire life proving myself to you, *Father*. But it was never good enough for you. Nothing ever was." Tobin spat.

Bazraki took two quick strides forward and raised a hand to strike his son. Tobin caught it and threw his father's arm back down. "I told you that you would never strike me again," said Tobin seething.

"Your brother would never dare such a thing. When he returns, he will be warleader once more. Until then, *I* will lead the armies."

Now it was Tobin's turn to laugh. "You don't understand, do you? You are nothing to them. The army is mine and mine alone. The assassination on Mawkuk has already been stopped. That's right. You think you lead. They would rather kill you first then to be led into slaughter. They know you are nothing on the field. Your plans for today were pathetic. We would have all died had I been stupid enough to follow them. I am done begging for your recognition. I don't need it. I have my men. I have my woman. And I have a friend in Nachun. All of them have done more for me than you ever have."

"Kaz would…

Tobin grabbed his father's throat, pulled him close and whispered. "Kaz is dead, *Father*." Tobin's blade slid into Bazraki's side as he drew him tighter. "I know because I watched Nachun do it." His father tried to struggle then and Tobin twisted the blade. "And I helped him hide it from you."

Tobin held Bazraki close until he felt the life leave him. Then his father's body slid to the floor with a soft thud. He stood over his father for some time, staring at his blood-soaked torso. He blinked away his daze as the celebratory music reached his ears once again. He looked at the knife still in his hands and expected to feel depressed or perhaps even overjoyed. But he felt nothing.

For that is what he was to me in the end.

Tobin wiped the blade on the front of his father's vest but kept the dagger in hand as he walked outside, unsure what he might find.

Ufer said that they were mine but it is one thing to say those words, another to mean it.

His mind relaxed upon exiting the tent. No one stood watch. In the place of Bazraki's personal guards, Tobin noticed spots of blood, and marks in the dirt from bodies being dragged away. Tobin looked up. At a nearby fire, his officers stared back at him. They greeted him with a simple nod or inclination of the head.

They know. They understand. And they approve.

A small space cleared near the flame, a place where his father would have sat. He sheathed his dagger and moved to the place of honor. Sitting, he looked across the dancing flames and met Nachun's gaze, dark eyes peeking through a hooded silhouette. His friend gave him a smile. The shaman bowed his head and Tobin nodded in return.

He saw Ufer as well, which reminded him that he had yet to bring news to Odala that her father would live. He thought about getting up, but he dismissed the idea.

No. This is my place tonight. With my people. My clan. And tonight nothing else matters.

* * *

He watched Tobin emerge from Bazraki's tent, face lined with a hardness he hadn't seen before, bloody hand clenched tight around a clean dagger.

He did it.

Tobin met the eyes of the men who acknowledged their warleader with a sign of respect.

The warleader walked around his men and took the seat where Bazraki would have been positioned. Only after settling down did it seem that things clicked into place inside Tobin's mind. Tobin looked across the blazing fire and met his eyes. Victory.

Victory for us both, my friend. Sacrynon's Sceptor will be mine again.

From beneath the red hood of the High Mage's robes, Nareash smiled.

Steel and Sorrow: Book Two of the Blood and Tears Trilogy is available now in paperback and for your ereader!

Thank you for reading my story. If you enjoyed it, please consider leaving a rating or review at the site of purchase as well as other places such as Goodreads and Librarything. Like many other indie authors, I do not have a marketing team working for me and a positive review (even if only a couple of sentences long) can go a long way in enticing others to give my works a try.

Thanks again for your support.
Joshua P. Simon

ABOUT THE AUTHOR

Unlike most authors, Joshua did not immerse himself into the world of books as a child. After finishing graduate school, he quickly made up for lost time by buying and devouring countless graphic novels. Remembering his love of the original Conan movies, he moved on to the fantasy genre with the compilations of Robert E. Howard. He was hooked.

Since then, he has moved on to other authors such as Glen Cook, Joe Abercrombie, George R.R. Martin, Steven Erikson, Paul Kearney, Steven Brust, Peter V. Brett, Patrick Rothfuss and many more.

Joshua was inspired to write and create his own fantasy world after reading Glen Cook's Black Company series. Thanks to a vivid imagination, he soon found himself with more ideas than he knew what to do with. After some prompting by his wife, he took the plunge.

When not writing, Joshua lives a life devoted to God and spends time with his beautiful family. He is employed as an accountant.

Contact Joshua through any of the following:
BLOG: www.joshuapsimon.blogspot.com
EMAIL: joshuapsimon.author@gmail.com
FACEBOOK: www.facebook.com/JoshuaPSimon
TWITTER: www.twitter.com/JoshuaPSimon

Sign up for Joshua's newsletter to be the first to hear about new releases and receive exclusive content.
http://joshuapsimon.blogspot.com/p/newsletter.html

www.ingramcontent.com/pod-product-compliance
Lightning Source LLC
Chambersburg PA
CBHW050902250626
47155CB00001B/69